NEW YORK REVIEW BOOKS
CLASSICS

T0286646

NAKED EARTH

EILEEN CHANG (1920–1995) was born into an aristocratic
family in Shanghai. Her father, deeply traditional in his ways, was
an opium addict; her mother, partly educated in England, was a
sophisticated woman of cosmopolitan tastes. Their unhappy marriage
ended in divorce, and Chang eventually ran away from her father—
who had beaten her for defying her stepmother, then locked her in
her room for nearly half a year. Chang studied literature at the
University of Hong Kong, but the Japanese attack on the city in
1941 forced her to return to occupied Shanghai, where she was able
to publish the stories and essays (collected in two volumes, *Romances*,
1944, and *Written on Water*, 1945) that soon made her a literary star.
In 1944 Chang married Hu Lan-ch'eng, a Japanese sympathizer
whose sexual infidelities led to their divorce three years later. The
rise of Communist influence made it increasingly difficult for
Chang to continue living in Shanghai; she moved to Hong Kong
in 1952, then immigrated to the United States three years later. She
remarried (an American, Ferdinand Reyher, who died in 1967) and
held various posts as writer-in-residence; in 1969 she obtained a
more permanent position as a researcher at Berkeley. Two novels,
both commissioned in the 1950s by the United States Information
Service as anti-Communist propaganda, *The Rice-Sprout Song* (1955)
and *Naked Earth* (1956), were followed by a third, *The Rouge of the
North* (1967), which expanded on her celebrated early novella, "The
Golden Cangue." Chang continued writing essays and stories in
Chinese and scripts for Hong Kong films, and began work on an
English translation of the famous Ch'ing novel *The Sing-Song Girls
of Shanghai*. In spite of the tremendous revival of interest in her
work that began in Taiwan and Hong Kong in the 1970s, and that

later spread to mainland China, Chang became ever more reclusive as she grew older. She was found dead in her Los Angeles apartment in September 1995. In 2006 NYRB Classics published a collection of Chang's stories, *Love in a Fallen City*, and in 2007, a film adaptation of her novella *Lust, Caution*, directed by Ang Lee, was released.

PERRY LINK is Chancellorial Chair for Teaching Across Disciplines at the University of California at Riverside. He translated China's Charter 08 manifesto into English and recently co-edited *No Enemies, No Hatred*, a collection of essays and poems by Liu Xiaobo. His latest book is *An Anatomy of Chinese: Rhythm, Metaphor, Politics* and his translation of the autobiography of the Chinese dissident astrophysicist Fang Lizhi, *The Most Wanted Man in China: My Journey from Science to Exile*, will be published in early 2016.

NAKED EARTH

EILEEN CHANG

Introduction by
PERRY LINK

NEW YORK REVIEW BOOKS

New York

THIS IS A NEW YORK REVIEW BOOK
PUBLISHED BY THE NEW YORK REVIEW OF BOOKS
435 Hudson Street, New York, NY 10014
www.nyrb.com

Library of Congress Cataloging-in-Publication Data
Zhang, Ailing.
 [Chi di zhi lian. English]
 Naked earth / by Eileen Chang ; introduction by Perry Link.
    pages cm — (NYRB Classics)
 ISBN 978-1-59017-834-8 (paperback)
 I. Title.
 PL2837.E35C35513 2015
 895.13'5—dc23

                    2014039705

ISBN: 978-1-59017-834-8
Available as an electronic book; ISBN 978-1-59017-835-5

Printed in the United States of America on acid-free paper.
10 9 8 7 6 5 4 3

INTRODUCTION

It can be embarrassing for a China scholar like me to read Eileen Chang's pellucid prose, written more than sixty years ago, on the early years of the People's Republic of China. How many cudgels to the head did I need before arriving at comparable clarity? My disillusioning first trip to China in 1973? My reading of the devastating journalism of Liu Binyan in 1980? Observation of bald lies in action at the Tiananmen massacre in 1989 and in the imprisonment of a Nobel Peace laureate in more recent times? Did I need all of this, and more, before catching up with where Chang was in 1953 in her understanding of the language and politics in Communist China—how things worked in daily life, beneath the blankets of jargon? In graduate school I did not take *Naked Earth* and its sister novel, *The Rice-Sprout Song* (also published in 1954), very seriously. People said the works had a "KMT [Nationalist government] bias." How silly.

Readers of NYRB Classics will know Chang as the author of *Love in a Fallen City*, a collection of her best-known stories from the 1940s, finely translated by Karen Kingsbury and delightful for their evocative language, psychological insight, moral acuity, and close observation of Chang's social milieu, the Chinese urban elite. In *Naked Earth* and *The Rice-Sprout Song*, Chang turns her attention to the years 1949 to 1953, and she writes about parts of China—agricultural villages, a Communist newspaper office, soldiers in the Korean War—that were new to her. Given her background, one might ask how she could make this transition as smoothly as she did. Certainly her skill in imagining the private thoughts of people as they interact, so expertly honed in her earlier fiction, continues to serve her well; in addition she seems, like George Orwell, to have almost a sixth sense for immediate comprehension of what an authoritarian political system will do to human beings in daily life. She looks past the grand political system itself, showing little care to rebut it on its own terms; she focuses instead on the lives of people—how they feel and behave as they adapt to what the system forces upon them.

Still, a question remains of how Chang could know about land reform in the Chinese countryside or about the Korean War without firsthand experience of these events. Perhaps sensing a need to address this question, Chang writes in prefaces to both *The Rice-Sprout Song* and *Naked Earth* that the novels are based on true stories. (She had never offered similar assurances about her earlier stories.) Chang did travel to rural China, at least briefly, in the years immediately before and after 1949, but most of the material for her novels seems to have come from secondhand accounts or from published sources. "Self-criticisms" by officials and descriptions of famines had appeared, after combing for political correctness, in the state-run press. Chang could read past the propaganda overlay and infer what had happened. She also appears to have learned from *The Sun Shines over the Sanggan River*, Ting Ling's Party-approved long novel (published in 1948 and winner of the Stalin Prize in 1951) about land reform in Communist-held areas in the 1940s. Chang Ch'ien-fen has noted a broad range of "intertextuality" between *Sanggan River* and *Naked Earth* on questions that range from how farmers wash their hands to what public "struggle sessions" look like. The main difference is only that Ting Ling feels a continual need to invent "model behavior," while Chang does not.

Chang shows how the linguistic grid of a Communist land-reform campaign descends on a village like a giant cookie cutter. There are Poor Farmers, Middling Farmers, Landlords, Bad Elements, and more. (Formal terms are capitalized in this translation.) When actual life doesn't fit the prescriptions, so much the worse for actual life. Make it fit. A "cadre" (a technical term for a functionary in the Communist system) complains that the farmers have "always been backward.... All they ever see is the bit of material advantage right in front of them." This leaves them "afraid to be active." Perhaps they don't want to be active? No, answers the organization, they are reticent only because they fear "the revenge of the Remnant Feudal Forces." When finally coaxed to complain, they sometimes—oops! —complain about the cadres, not the Landlords.

Eventually the farmers, like everyone else, figure out that their personal interests depend on correct verbal performance. There are certain things you are supposed to say and certain ways you are supposed to say them. "Tell the truth!" is a command that you recite your lies *correctly*. An unimpeachable exterior becomes everyone's goal. One young woman suffers a torrid criticism session, ends it with a self-denunciation, and then steals away to weep in solitude. Someone discovers her and accuses her of "only pretending to accept criticism." Thinking quickly, she explains that, no, hers are tears of gratitude: "Everybody was so concerned about me, so enthusiastic in helping me to make Progress." Does her explanation pass muster? Yes, but less because it is credible than because it reinforces the exterior mask that says "I submit to the organization." To the powers that be, that demonstration is more important than what she actually thinks.

Over time, the need to maintain a correct exterior turns public political language into a kind of chess game. You make moves in order to get what you want, and you avoid bad moves that would bring punishment. During the Three-Anti campaign in 1951, when nearly all Communist cadres are scrutinized for corruption, waste, or bureaucratism, Ko Shan, a Party member and newspaper manager in public but a "tubercular nymphomaniac" (in C. T. Hsia's apt phrase) in private, is forced onto a stage for self-criticism:

> I have nothing to say in my own defense. I feel very much ashamed that even now—after so many years spent in the very nucleus of the struggle—even now there still exist in my consciousness certain bad traits of the petit-bourgeois. I have this Tendency toward Freedom and Looseness. And then when I fought in the guerillas I got into the Guerilla Style of behavior.

Ever since then I've found it hard to Regularize my life. Now the matter of man-woman relations. My starting point was comradely love. But, it has gone out of bounds and has led to Obscure Behavior.

The crowd who is listening to her is aware that her oration is only a series of chess moves aimed at minimizing punishment. There is prurient interest, though, in the question of the illicit lovers. People heckle her to name them. Trapped before the Masses, Ko Shan needs to betray at least one lover, but which one? Liu Ch'üan, the young protagonist of *Naked Earth*, whom Ko Shan has recently seduced (despite their difference in age), is in the crowd listening and is terrified that he will be named.

"It's Chang Li," Ko Shan finally says, choosing not to name Liu. Chang is a slick official whom the reader already knows to be contemptible. We feel relief that Ko Shan, however cynical, retains at least enough humanity to protect the naïve Liu.

But no, it turns out. When Liu later visits Ko Shan's house to thank her, she explains that "I mentioned Chang instead of you because I could trust him not to get me into a bigger mess than what I am in already. Which is more than I can say for you." She had named Chang because he was better at manipulating the language game, that's all. It had been another self-interested chess move on her part. Liu then asks her why Chang, who was also present at the meeting, had not shouted out "Liu Ch'üan too!" in order to split the blame. Could it be that Chang, for his part, had a bit of humanity somewhere inside him?

"What good would that do him?" Ko Shan responds. He would "just make an enemy without making things any easier for himself." Chang, too, had made a cold chess move, and nothing more.

Eileen Chang's acute observation of political language in China in the early 1950s is useful in understanding patterns that have persisted ever since. Maoist extremism has passed, but it remains true that an incorrect word-performance in public can be costly to a person's interests, and it is still the case that one person can earn credit by reporting the misstatements of another. When Liu volunteers to fight in Korea (escaping the political cauldron of Shanghai), he notices that he feels watched even after moving abroad. He "wondered if anybody who had lived under Communist rule could ever feel unwatched again." And indeed, in 2015 Chinese graduate students in California still keep nonstandard political views under wraps when speaking in the company of other Chinese students. Only among well-trusted friends does one venture to "live in truth," in Václav Havel's phrase. In the early 1950s Liu and his girlfriend Su Nan inhabit "the cozy little igloo of their love, made of ice but warm and homey within." Today, the igloos are not so frozen to the ground, but are still there.

And the people on top, the system's beneficiaries? Perhaps they, at least, are free of worry? Here, too, Chang is clairvoyant. Near the end of *Naked Earth*, Liu reflects that "As long as one man like him remained alive and out of jail, the men who ruled China would never be safe. They're afraid, too, he thought, afraid of the people they rule by fear." Had Liu foreseen that in 2015 those "men who ruled China" would still be spending hundreds of billions of yuan annually on "stability maintenance"? Chang seems even to foresee the paradoxical connection between communism and luxury that has emerged recently in China. After normal human values have shriveled, where does a human being turn to measure success? Only material scales remain, and in *Naked Earth*, we see already how officials in the regime have begun to take this route: villas, banquets, concubines. Chang died in 1995; how surprised would she be to see the stupendous wealth of the Communist super-elite today?

The distinguished journalist Tai Ch'ing has suggested that the Communist Party failed to buy off Chang, even with lures like "member of the Political Consultative Conference or Vice Chair of the National People's Congress." I cannot vouch that such offers to Chang were made, but Tai Ch'ing, who grew up in the family of Marshal Yeh Chien-ying, who was a confederate of Mao Tse-tung, has considerable credibility on such topics. What we do know is that Chang accepted a grant from the United States Information Service

(USIS) to write *The Rice-Sprout Song* and *Naked Earth* after she left China in 1952. This fact has been widely noted, and its significance sometimes exaggerated. It is far-fetched to imagine that the USIS distorted Chang's writing. She is too powerful a writer for that—too "immune from being tricked," in Tai Ch'ing's phrase. Indeed there is irony in the fact that the U.S. government still has not collected what it paid for: Its understanding of the language and politics of Chinese communism still lags far behind what Chang offered it sixty years ago.

If nothing else, the beauty of Chang's writing makes it hard to view as anyone's propaganda. After a rain squall on a dusty loess plateau, trees "were still sniffling and shedding big tears." At a nearby river, "Long wisps of yellow mud trailed sluggishly in the current, like half-beaten egg-yolk ..." On the whole, *Naked Earth* has less of this than Chang's 1940s novellas do, but it would be a mistake to view this change as a compromise with USIS style. Chang has matured in this novel to a sparser naturalism, to a plane where "the shimmer of the unsaid," in Marianne Moore's phrase, can say even more than brilliant metaphor does.

—PERRY LINK

AUTHOR'S NOTE

IT SOMETIMES happens that when I describe one of my stories, I'm met with a puzzled look. "This really happened!" I'll say (maybe a touch defensively), as if that automatically increases the story's worth. Of course whether a story is good or not really has nothing to do with whether it's true or not. Even so I've become almost compulsively fixated on reality, believing that real experience, no matter whose, will never become stale, but will remain always fresh and evocative.

Naked Earth is based on real people and their true stories. Fiction is, at heart, not reportage, however, and in this novel I've changed the names of characters and some places; I've drawn from many stories and compressed, trimmed, and reorganized them into the story you read here. As large as my canvas is, I can't help but fall short of showing everything going on in China today. The recent Five-Anti Campaign, for example, appears nowhere in my book but has affected the lives of ordinary people even more profoundly than did the Three-Anti Campaign.* I was limited as well by the limits of my characters' perspectives. Not that my aim was ever to cover absolutely everything, it was instead to capture the atmosphere of the time, as best I could. The book is not intended to be a comprehensive report; my hope is that readers, in turning its pages, get a whiff of what real life was like for the people living through those days.

—EILEEN CHANG

---

*This note appeared in the original Chinese-language edition of *Love in Redland*, published in 1954 in Hong Kong. In 1965, Chang translated and adapted the novel for an English-speaking audience under the title *Naked Earth*. The revised edition does in fact include reference to the Five-Anti Campaign.

NAKED EARTH

I

THE YELLOW dust rolled on, across what was once called the Central Plain because it was considered the center of the world, surrounded by barbarians. Two trucks sped along the highway one after the other, in two balls of yellow fog.

A plump middle-aged man in the standard civilian Liberation Suit of bluish gray cloth stood on the running board of the second truck. He was the driver's assistant. His eyes popped out in his choleric red face as he shouted supplications to the slow, lumbering coal truck just ahead of them. He had shouted himself hoarse but either his words were drowned in the roar of the engines or the coal-truck driver pretended not to hear him.

When they had reached a bend in the road the other truck finally, in a burst of conscience, swung out of the way and let them move up front.

"Let's slow down a bit," the assistant said to the driver, "so they'll also eat some dust."

The driver nodded.

Hanging on to the window frame with one arm, the assistant twisted around to look back, grinning happily. Now and then his plump face would suddenly go all red and blotchy again with rage and he would yell back, "*T'a ma ti!* Your turn to eat some dust!"

The truckful of young people started to laugh. One of them said half seriously, "This driver's *tso-feng*, style, is no good. He should go under discussion. Maybe we should call a meeting tonight." He winked at his comrades.

They were all students from various universities in Peking. When the People's Government mobilized university students to take part in the Land Reform, all the Active Elements in the student body vied with each other in signing up. Some of them had just graduated this summer.

Liu Ch'üan, one of the new graduates, sat at the back of the truck where it jolted the worst. He had his arms crossed loosely, elbows resting on his knees. The sun was still broiling hot though it was already autumn. His bluish gray summer uniform, soaked through with perspiration, clung in ripple-marks on his back. Warm puffs of wind blasted the dust against his face like a flapping, stinging, coarse veil. He frowned and could hardly open his eyes, but he was smiling. He was tall with a thin, dark gold face dimpled on one cheek, and keen narrow eyes.

"The east is red;
The sun has risen;
China's produced a Mao Tse-tung…"

They had started singing in a corner up front. With a sudden lurch towards the side of the road the truck just managed to miss a mule-cart coming from the other direction. Half a tree and a big clump of green reeds swept into the open truck and switched against the faces of the riders. The girls shrieked and squealed with laughter, piling on top of one another as they ducked. One of them pulled off a leafy branch from the tree and started to beat time with it on her friend's back as they sang.

They sang a Land Reform song they had just learned, "Unite, hey!—Tillers of the land!…" But they liked the old favorites best, like that one beginning with "Our China, so big and wide." The tune was probably adapted from some Russian song. It had the gray, windy sadness that vast spaces bring.

The road gradually sank and the bare smooth banks on either side kept rising until they stood up sheer, like yellow mud walls. The earth was loose and sandy in this part of the country. Every time a mule-cart passed with its iron-bound wheels it dug deep ridges in the road. Centuries of traffic had worn the road into a ditch from ten to twenty feet deep. Sitting high up on the truck the students could just see the yellowish green tree tops on the plain.

Some of the riders began to complain that their legs had gone to sleep, so they shifted position as best they could. A pretty girl now sat facing this side, framed in a hole in the crowd. Her skin had the bluish pale translucency of fresh-peeled lichee flesh and her eyes were wide splits in the ripe fruit showing the moistened lacquered surface of the purplish black seed within. Liu Ch'üan looked at her. The fold of her eyelid made a long deep line fading out at the end with an upward sweep. The wind had plastered a small green leaf on her hair. She had short hair curling outward a little at the ends. Set against the dully throbbing, changeless yellow countryside, her head and shoulders made a startling little picture, distinct and yet infinitely far away, like a patch of sky reflected in a wayside puddle.

Just glancing in her direction once or twice made Liu Ch'üan feel that everybody was watching him. She was too pretty. Before they got on the truck they had each announced their own name and the university they came from. And they usually mumbled it half laughing, feeling that self-introduction is a ridiculous thing if you perform it seriously. But somehow all the male members of the group had managed to catch Su Nan's name and knew that she was a graduate of Yenching University.

Liu Ch'üan turned and looked the other way, fanning himself with his cap. Then it occurred to him that this was really superfluous with a roaring wind blowing straight at him, so he put the cap back on his head. The wind immediately snatched at it. He caught it just in time.

He could not remember hearing Su Nan talking to anybody. But she looked happy. She was carrying an oil-paper umbrella and she often stuck it out, brushing it against the trees so that it kept bouncing back jerkily with a sharp noise like ripping silk. The sleeves of her bluish gray uniform were rolled up above the elbow, showing thin young arms.

The singing died down when throats went dry. The girl who had been beating time with a tree branch was Yü Ling, a classmate of Liu's. She leaned over and tapped him on the shoulder with her long whip of a bough.

"Hey, Liu Ch'üan, Liu Ch'üan," she called out. "How much longer to go?"

Because he did not answer at once the tree branch knocked him on the head. "Hey, Liu Ch'üan! We've covered half the distance, haven't we?"

He didn't like it much when he saw Su Nan looking at him. "No use asking me. Ask the driver!" he said smiling. Maybe this was nothing between classmates, but other people might misunderstand. They were all cadres now, he told himself. And for a low-ranking cadre, one of the worst offenses was to *nao nan-nü kuan-hsi*, get up man-woman relations. Besides, they were setting out to do a very serious and important job. This kind of *tso-feng* would give the leaders the wrong idea.

The man who represented the leaders in this group was Comrade Chang Li, a party member, an organizer sent down by the Cultural Bureau. In his middle thirties, Chang was of medium height, with full, long blue-green cheeks and rather full mauvish pink lips. He sat quietly smiling among these effervescent youngsters, trying to get all their names straight. Liu had introduced everyone he knew to Chang. Liu had been active in the Students' Association of Peita, the University of Peking, so he had been in constant contact with similar groups in all the other universities. He was also a member of the Youth Corps and was being considered for admittance into the Party. Chang obviously regarded him as a leader among the students and relied on him to maintain order in the group.

The dusty, creamy glare of the sun gave them a headache. They all dozed off sitting back to back, until they were wakened by the soreness at the end of the spine where the jolting hurt them. Thus they alternated between sleeping and waking, headache and rump-ache.

Towards mid-afternoon it looked like rain. The sun became a

furry, soft white spot in the oppressive uniform gray of the sky. The truck was now bumping along at breakneck speed. Rain would turn the dust into mud as slippery as rice gruel. Wheels wouldn't be able to move an inch in the mire and it would be disastrous to be stranded in these parts, miles away from anywhere. The driver stepped on the gas.

Liu Ch'üan's last nap was cut short by a burst of song. He looked out the back and saw rain. The drenched young people at the back were singing, defiantly cheerful. The truck had already turned out of the ditch and was running along a narrow lane with broad fields stretching away flatly to the sky on both sides. They passed a *kao-liang* patch, the stalks taller than a man. It was the season of the "green gauze curtain," the affectionate name the farmers give to late summer *kao-liang*. Then came cabbage patches and the small humps of burial mounds and an occasional thatched hut. In the greenish twilight of the shower, everything looked dark and clear like preserves swimming in a green glass jar.

The driver looked over his shoulder and said something to Comrade Chang. He nodded "We're there!" Everybody cheered.

The vegetable patches gave way to an endless stretch of yellow mud wall about ten feet high. In this part of north China all villages had been walled in as protection against brigands.

With sudden shouts and clanging cymbals and thumping drums a crowd of peasants surged forth from a rectangular entrance dug in the wall. White towels tied around the militiamen's heads bobbed behind the soaked and tattered paper flags they were waving. A double file of youths and children moved forward wriggling the Rice-sprout Song. The girls had trouble with their sticky wet silk sashes which clung to their bodies and legs instead of whirling gracefully around them.

The people on the truck, a bit nervous at this noise, could not hear the slogans being shouted. But of course these were the villagers out to welcome them in spite of the rain. They waved back shouting "Thank you, kinsmen!" and broke out into the deafening chorus of "Unite, hey!—Tillers of the land!" Meanwhile the truck had splashed its way through the crowd, pushing them into the field or against walls, their little bamboo flag-poles tilting *en masse* like windblown reeds.

When the truck finally pulled to a stop, the crowd had been left behind. But two men who were presumably *kan-pu* (cadres), puffing along behind the tail-gate, caught up with the truck as it slowed down. They were all ready to help everybody down but seemed a bit put out upon noting the youth and good looks of the girls in the group, fearing criticism if they should appear too eager to hold the young women by the hand. They decided instead to lead the way to the temple where their guests were to be quartered. Sitting on top of a small wooded mound, the vermilion-walled temple had two large white vertical signboards on either side of the gate, both saying "Primary School of Han Chia T'o, 3rd District."

The fast walkers in the welcoming party were catching up now too, gongs and cymbals clanging thinly in the damp. The Land Reform Workers, their knapsacks on their backs, jumped down from the truck into the mud and hurried after the *kan-pu* up the steep winding steps of crumbling brick. Liu Ch'üan lingered behind to herd them along. Then he ran up alone, shielding his head with an arm. Midway up the steps an umbrella tilted over him.

"Comrade Liu," Su Nan said.

"No, it's all right," Liu said smiling in perfunctory polite refusal. Then he took the umbrella from her. "Let me hold it." After a few steps he realized that he was holding it away from himself, almost at the length of his arm. He hadn't been so old-fashioned with other girls he had known at college. But he was not at ease with Su Nan. Water slid off the edge of the umbrella in silvery sheets, dripping on his head. He was considerably worse off than before. And then he also had to slow down his pace. Two could not run as fast as one. Su Nan probably noticed his plight. She said nothing, but as they neared the end of the climb she was walking quite close to him, forcing him to come under the umbrella.

Those who had arrived before them were crowded on the porch

of the temple, busy shaking their caps and wringing out their trouser legs. Everybody looked up when they came in together. When Liu Ch'üan went up to talk to the men he thought he could sense quiet disapproval, then had an uncomfortable feeling that he was becoming supersensitive.

Chang Li was surrounded by several village *kan-pu*. He turned to introduce them to the students. The secretary of the Party branch office, Pao Hsiang-ch'ien, Go Forward Pao—a name obviously adopted after the Liberation—was a youngish farmer with thin, birdlike good looks, rather high-shouldered in a high-collared white Chinese shirt.

"Comrades, I wish I could find the words to tell you how happy we are at your coming," Pao said smiling. "All of you have Culture. We have a lot to learn from you."

"Not at all, not at all," Chang said. "It's we who ought to learn from you. You *kan-pu* are closest to the people."

"The comrades must be hungry." Pao said to Sun Fu-kuei, who had been introduced as the Farmers' Association Organizer. "Tell them to hurry up with the dinner." He turned with an apologetic smile to the Land Reform Workers, "Nothing to eat here. We've got thirty catties of white flour ready and a hundred eggs. Didn't dare kill a pig—we weren't sure whether you comrades would be able to get here today. You know, meat won't keep in this weather."

Chang protested, "Please don't bother. We'll eat whatever there is."

"We don't have to eat white flour," Liu joined in. "Fact is, you don't have to cook separately for us. We'll board with the farmers."

Pao scratched his head and laughed uncertainly, blowing through his teeth. "Raining like this—" he said after a moment, "Better eat here and go to bed early. You comrades must be tired out."

"Besides, there's no trouble at all. Everything's at hand. Everything's at hand," added Sun.

"It seems to me we better not start by Taking the Opposite Stand from the group," Chang said to Liu with a smile. "Whatever question comes up, it's got to be United with Actual Circumstances. We can't be Dead Brained, set on having our own way. That's also a form of dogmatism." He laughed.

Liu was taken aback by the reprimand, which he felt was quite uncalled for. Maybe Chang had resented his speaking up with what might be misconstrued as a tone of authority and thought it was a good idea to snub him before the other students in order to build up his own prestige within the group. Liu noticed Su Nan looking at him. She must be thinking that he had been trying to show off. And instead of gaining face, he had lost it. He flushed and it took all his will power to stay smiling. Above all he must not have it said of him that he could not take criticism.

They all went inside the temple and sat down in a dark, deserted schoolroom. Chang asked Pao how many Party members they had in the locality. He informed Pao that all the different organizations should hold separate meetings the next day in order to Communicate the Policy. All the *kan-pu* had turned up in the temple, the chairman of the Farmers' Association, the chairman of the Women's Association, the captain of the local militia, the head of the village and his assistant, the Party Organizer and Party Propagandizer. Most of them still retained some of their peasant shyness. They squatted quietly at the door listening to the talk. Some squatted outside under the eaves, staring into the rain as they listened.

Militiamen scurried in and out, hugging sacks of flour and baskets of eggs. A man brought noodles piled in a high mound in a scarlet-painted wooden basin. The noodles, neatly tied on top with a bit of rose-red paper ribbon, cascaded downwards like thick limp strands of beige-colored hair. Liu could tell from the man's round-eyed, self-effacing look that this was not their ordinary fare at the village. He suddenly felt like a wealthy patron of the temple staying for the night, feasting on butchered meat, desecrating the god worshipped there.

Soon he smelled the fragrance of large flat cakes baking in dry pans. Reminding himself that he must not sulk, he said brightly,

"Where are the drivers?" Nobody had seen them around. "I'll go and find them. Dinner's about ready," Liu said.

He thought it was still raining when he walked down the steps under the trees which were still sniffling and shedding big tears. But the sky had cleared and there was in the air a touch of the golden haze of setting sun. The cicadas had just started singing, a bit wheezily. The long syrupy threads of sound ran on unbroken from tree to tree.

A knot of people had gathered around the truck parked on the wayside. The rain had washed off the dust from the cab of the truck. Children were peering at their own reflections in the dark green metal doors, aglow with the last rays of the slanting sun. They doubled up, slapping their knees, helpless with laughter, as if they were the funniest-looking objects in the world. Men and women, both wearing odd little sleeveless blouses of white cloth, also bent down peering and giggling but barking prohibitive phrases at the children. Somehow it came as a shock to Liu that he could understand the few words that floated up to where he stood, halfway down the steps. Perhaps there had been a moment when he had felt, with a guilty twinge, that these people were as foreign to him as Malays or Ethiopians.

A short girl with greasy shoulder-length hair and a broad savage face, not unattractive, had been squatting beside the truck holding up her baby, trying to make it look at its own mirrored image without much success. A beardless old man with a basket slung on one arm came up from the rear and stood staring, his brows arched high in surprise on his vacuously handsome, smiling face.

The old man had been standing there for some moments before a man turned to ask him, "Your son back from the market yet?"

The old man hemmed and hawed absentmindedly as he continued to gape at the truck.

"Sold anything?" the other man asked.

The old man looked away vaguely as if he had forgotten some important errand and at once started across the field. He treaded carefully on the narrow winding footpath, crossing his bare feet daintily with every step, his blue tatters flapping in the breeze. After he had gone some distance he glanced back over his shoulder at the truck. He was still smiling, with brows arched high in the same pleased and astonished expression. About twenty yards from there he looked back again with the same smile and raised brows.

The crowd appeared to take no notice of his departure. But presently the man who had spoken to him sniggered. "Scared him off."

"Bet you they didn't sell any of it," a woman said. "Who buys pork this time of year? It's neither the New Year nor a festival."

"Must be all spoiled, in this heat. Over twenty miles to the market and back," said the man.

"Spoiled! Must be cooked!" she said. "Crazy to kill pigs at this time of year."

Another man sighed. "Ai! He might as well kill them while the killing is good."

Liu instinctively drew behind a tree as if he did not want to risk being seen, so he could hear more of it. He must have pushed against the tree trunk, making it shake, because the cicadas stopped singing.

The people down below stopped talking. They just stood looking at the truck.

"Did these people come down from the District Headquarters or the *hsien*—the county?" a man finally said.

Nobody answered. But another man said, "They'll never be able to get up anything around here. Now, over there in Seven Mile Fort where there's a big landlord they sure had fun," he said giggling. "Before they even struggled against the landlord, his red silk, padded blankets were already piled on the beds of the *kan-pu*."

The crowd tittered. While nobody told him to stop babbling, some of the more prudent people started to move away.

"Think I'll go and see if they've sold any of the pork," a man said. "I don't know but that I'll get some and have crescent dumplings for dinner. Might as well."

It looked as if soon everybody would be gone except perhaps the children. Liu came down the steps shouting from far off, "Hey, kinsmen! Anybody seen the drivers?"

They turned startled faces towards this shape coming out of the dark.

"I'm looking for the drivers. Anybody know where they've gone?"

They began to wander off nonchalantly as if they had not heard him and the children started to run. Again Liu had a baffling sense of racial and language barriers between them.

But then one of the men turned and pointed down the road. "They're at the co-operative," he said.

The girl with the baby said worriedly, as if he had uttered some indiscretion, "Let's go home, *hai-tzu te tieh*, child's dad." She stood watchfully with the baby in her arms, waiting for the man to get safely in front of her. The frightened baby burrowed into the dark nest of hair piled on her shoulders.

Liu turned quickly away from them and strode down the road between darkening fields. Here and there a hut with walls of *kao-liang* stalks tied together stood by the wayside. But the co-operative store was built of bricks. He could see the little one-roomed building from afar. The lamp had already been lit inside. He wondered what the drivers were doing there. What could they buy in a poky little place like this? Besides, they would be going back with the truck to Peking tomorrow.

He walked up to the little folding door and pushed it open. Two red-eared men with their backs to him stood drinking at the counter that cut across the cozy, yellow-lit room. Inside the counter there was a chimney-stove used to bake sesame cakes and a kneading board and a board for chopping meat, each perched on its own tall stand. Bolts of cloth and bars of soap lined the wall. The clerk was dipping wine out of an earthen jar with half of a dry gourd. He poured it into the men's blue-rimmed, pea-green bowls.

Liu went up and slid an arm about the shoulders of both the driver and his assistant. "Come along. Dinner's ready," he said. "You people certainly know your way about around here."

"Have a drink with us, comrade," said the flushed driver. "You need something to drive out the cold, after getting soaked to the skin the way you have."

"No, no danger of catching cold in this weather," Liu said laughing "You about finished? Dinner's ready."

They paid and drifted out after him.

Right after dinner they made ready to sleep, the men and girls in two separate schoolrooms. Floor space had been cleared for little heaps of *kao-liang* stalks arranged in orderly rows. Liu was grateful for his soft pallet though the *kao-liang* stalks weren't too fresh and smelled a bit moldy and ratty. The darkness was loud with the long-drawn squeaks of night insects in the courtyard and the squawks of frogs after rain. Moonlight coming in through the carved latticed window fell on the stone-paved floor in little patterns like old coins of white jade, round with a square hole in the middle.

Liu was kept awake by his thoughts and the veteran mosquitoes of autumn. The stone floor under him was pressing harder and harder against his back and as the night wore on, the moist cold breath of stone seeped through the straw. Rats scuttled along the beams and chased each other over the floor like a brood of puppies, scattering the men's shoes.

He heard the first faint cockcrow. The loud snoring around him seemed to have died down as if the sleeping men were now far away from him. Their rafts were well over to the other shore of the night while he still had endless darkness ahead of him. He was filled with impatience with himself. The *kao-liang* stalks under him rustled incessantly with his turning. But what woke up Chang Li was probably his clapping his hands to kill mosquitoes.

He saw Chang sit up and then walk out of the room, dragging his shoes, probably to relieve himself in the courtyard. After a while Chang returned to his pallet and sat yawning audibly. The shadowy white of his undershirt stood out against the moist darkness.

"You aren't asleep, Comrade Liu?" he asked. "Not used to this kind of accommodations, eh?"

Liu was going to say that he couldn't sleep because of the mosquitoes. But the hint of mockery in Chang's voice put his back up. After a slight pause he said smiling, "No. I was thinking: conditions aren't so simple in this village."

"Conditions are never simple anywhere.—Why, have you heard anything or noticed anything?" Chang seemed interested. Liu heard the *kao-liang* stalks rustle as the other man groped around his pallet for cigarettes. A match rasped and Liu watched Chang light his cigarette. Chang held the match up. "You smoke?"

Coming over to get a cigarette Liu sat down beside Chang and told him about the villagers gathered around the truck, what they said about the Land Reform.

Chang laughed when he heard that at the Seven Mile Fort, the *kan-pu* had availed themselves of the landlord's padded blankets before he was even struggled against. "Some of the *kan-pu* have gone corrupt—there's no doubt of that. All they're after is luxury, enjoyment of life. But we can't carry out this work all by ourselves. Got to rely on the *kan-pu*. We must use this work to educate the *kan-pu*."

His voice was firm and yet light-hearted. It did Liu good to listen to him in the dark.

"And the farmers. Ai!" Chang sighed, half laughing. "They've always been backward. You can't imagine how foolish they are at heart. They don't know good from bad. Often take the enemy of the people for a good man. All they ever see is the bit of material advantage right in front of them. Short sighted. They swing with the wind and it makes them unreliable. Full of Change-of-Weatherism, thinking that no government can last, everything passes away like a spell of good or bad weather. So they're afraid to be active, afraid even to take things given to them free, in case the old government will come back and take revenge on them. They're such cowards, when a leaf falls they're scared it'll crack their heads open."

Liu was very much surprised at his low opinion of the farmers. "But if they're like this, how are we going to work out this Land Reform? We can't settle things arbitrarily. We're supposed to Follow the Route of the Masses."

"Follow the Route of the Masses means relying on them and stimulating them, helping them, starting Thought Mobilization. That's our real job, to lead."

Liu smoked silently. "Yes," he finally said, and after a while he went back to his pallet and lay down, watching the red tip of his cigarette. The moonlight had crept close to his head. He reached out to it and looked at the dim, ancient milk-white coin in the flat of his palm. He closed his fist gently and then opened it again to look at what he had in his hand. He thought of Su Nan sleeping in the next room, perhaps with a jade coin of moonlight balanced on her forehead. She was the most beautiful girl he had ever seen.

Chang spat and lay down, squeezing out his cigarette on the stone floor. "Now be careful you don't set the *kao-liang* stalks on fire," he said smiling.

2

EARLY in the morning when the cicadas just started to sing, they sounded young, high-pitched and frail. Egg-yellow sunlight slanted down the yellow mud walls that lined the straight narrow lane. Heaps of human excrement dotted the ground near the walls. A group of uniformed men trudged down the lane—Land Reform Workers with knapsacks on their backs, still half asleep, with the local Party man, Go Forward Pao, leading the way. The dust under foot was dead silent, wet with dew.

They passed a small folding-door, its black paint whitened with age, that opened out of the smooth dirt wall. Pao beat on the door with the flat of his palm, shouting "T'ang Yü-hai" twice. Without waiting for an answer he pushed the door open and walked in. The others trailed in behind him into a square courtyard with a trellis climbed over by cucumber plants.

"Ai! T'ang! T'ang Yü-hai!" Pao shouted.

A worn-looking woman emerged from the house and stood smiling embarrassedly on the low stoop of beaten earth. She rolled down her sleeves and kept pulling at them and smoothing them.

"*T'a tieh* has gone down to the field, Comrade Pao," she said, referring to her husband loosely as "his dad."

Pao pointed out Liu Ch'üan to her. "This is Comrade Liu. He'll stay with you as your guest. Remember that these comrades are here to help us. The least we can do is to look after them well."

"That's right. That's as it should be," the woman said smiling. "We know. The Farmers' Association sent word last night."

"Go in and look around, Comrade Liu. No need to stand on

ceremony. You're among your own people." Pao hurried off with his other charges.

"Come in and sit down, comrade," the woman said a bit uncertainly, adding "Have you eaten?" which was the usual phrase of greeting, any time of day.

"Not yet."

"Yo!" She gave a small cry, expressing concern. "Then I'll go and light the fire. Shall I steam some *mo* for you?"

"Don't bother to steam them. I'll just have them cold."

"Come in and sit down," she kept saying. As she led the way into the house she lifted her chin and yelled into space, "Erh Niu! Fetch some steamed bread—Better warm them, maybe?" she said to him.

"No, really. Don't trouble."

He followed her into a room almost entirely taken up by the *k'ang*, the bed of beaten earth with a stove built in underneath to keep it warm in winter. One or two empty baskets and earthen jars stood amidst a bedraggled heap of straw in the farthest corner of the vast bare *k'ang*. But the family seemed to be faring better than average. The uneven wall surface had been halfheartedly whitewashed. But Liu could see that the roof leaked; broad tearstains of dismal yellow ran all the way down the big white patches. The woman made Liu sit on the *k'ang* while she stood leaning against the doorway.

"How many children have you got?" Liu tried to make her talk. He must learn to get close to the Masses.

"Ai," she sighed. "We had two boys but we've lost them early. There's only a girl now. The older boy lived to eleven," she said, wiping her eyes.

He asked her other questions about their family.

"The Tangs are not from this village, not in the beginning," she said. Though she had been married for almost twenty years she still referred to her husband's family as "the Tangs," with a kind of maidenly reserve. "When Erh Niu's father was in his teens he came here with his parents. They'd been refugees in a famine. They had a hard time getting on their feet. Now at least they have their own land to till." With his prompting she prattled on some more about the old days but he noticed that she did not say much about present conditions.

A girl about sixteen or seventeen came in, wearing a faded purple blouse and pants and a black apron. Holding up the corners of her apron she walked up to the table and flung it up. A number of dark cup-loaves rolled clattering over the table. They sounded as hard as iron.

"Nothing nice to eat, comrade," the mother said, pulling out a stool for Liu from under the table. "Really shameful. And the bread not even steamed." Then she fussed, "Erh Niu, sweep the *k'ang*—look how messy it is."

Erh Niu climbed on to the *k'ang* and swept it with a little broom made of *kao-liang* stalks bunched together. She moved about on her knees, sweeping with long dry rustles. Her pigtail had fallen forward, dragging along the hard smooth earth. She would snatch at it and toss it back over her shoulder. But in a moment it would slip over her shoulder again and sweep the *k'ang* ahead of the broom. Patiently she kept thrusting it back.

The woman had been looking at the girl's slender back and her plump naked golden feet showing above low-cut blue cloth shoes. "Erh Niu," she suddenly said, "go and get some salted turnips for the comrade. I'll sweep the *k'ang*."

The mother kept glancing back over her shoulder while she was kneeling and sweeping and did not relax until the girl had come back, put down the bowl of salted turnips and was finally gone.

Then she turned her worried eyes to Liu, watching him eat. "Can you get used to this kind of food?" she said smiling. "I heard you're all students that came down this time."

Liu smiled. "What if we're students? Does that mean we can't stand hardships?"

She also smiled. "I'll get you something hot for lunch," she said.

"Don't trouble about lunch, Aunt T'ang. I'll be going out in a minute."

"I heard there's going to be a meeting today. Are we in it?" She squinted at him with knitted brows.

"Are you members of the Farmers' Association? Or the Women's Association?"

"We weren't in the Farmers' Association because they said we're Middling Farmers. But this spring there's been all this talk of *chiu p'ien*, Correcting Deviation, and they tell us that Middling Farmers are also members." She turned and shouted toward the door, "Erh Niu! Go and find your dad. Tell him to go to the meeting. You hear me, Niu? And you go and listen at the women's meeting, see what they say. You hear?"

The bread tasted like it was full of sand. It crunched under Liu's teeth and was hard to swallow. He asked for some water. The woman went to boil water but it wasn't ready yet by the time Liu finished his breakfast.

"I'm going out now, Aunt T'ang!" he shouted on his way out. He passed Erh Niu hoeing the cucumber patch under the trellis. She wiped at her flushed perspiring face with the back of her hand but did not look up.

He was going back to the school. They were all supposed to meet there. But he was not sure he knew the way. He turned back at the gate after a moment's hesitation. Seeing that the girl was so shy, he pulled a long face before he addressed her. "To get to the school, do I go straight towards the east?"

"Towards the east, but..." She gestured inanely with her hoe, then she leaned on it, thinking. "Walk eastward, and turn when you come to that date tree. Then you walk on until you see that *lü* (green) bean patch. You go through that door in the village wall and there you are." She came up to the gate and pointed as she talked. The wind had split her bangs, pushing them to the sides of her forehead, emphasizing the oval of her face. Her profile was classic, with straight long eyelashes shading the liquid black glow of her eyes.

"Erh Niu! Aren't you gone yet?" Her mother called out from within when she heard her voice. "I told you to go and call your dad to the meeting."

"What's the hurry? They haven't sounded the gong yet," Erh Niu answered. Still, she leaned her hoe against the wall, took off her apron and dusted her clothes.

Liu was going to ask for more details about the landmarks but he thought better of it. Anyhow, he was sure to come across other students or villagers on the way. So he just thanked the girl and walked off. He wondered if Aunt T'ang always got so jittery whenever a comrade came near her daughter.

The village seemed deserted in the quiet of the forenoon. The cicadas' loud eternal singing had become a ringing silence in his ears. The exact sameness of the dirt walls made it difficult to remember the way the little lanes went. He was pausing at a corner studying a tree leaning out of the wall when a voice spoke behind him.

"That's not a date tree."

He turned round, startled. It was Erh Niu. "Lucky that you're going in the same direction," he said smiling. "Otherwise I might really get lost."

Erh Niu smiled and gave a small pull to the skirt of her blouse, straightening it, and as if checking it, turned away to look at her pale shadow on the sunlit mud wall.

The ground was extremely uneven, sloping upwards on both sides, and in the middle of the lane where it was lowest there was only room for one. So Liu continued to walk on a step ahead of her. If he turned to speak to her he wouldn't be able to see where he was going. And besides, there really wasn't anything to say. For a long while the only sound was the scuffing of loose earth under their feet.

"Have you joined the *hsüeh tzu pan*, the learn-to-read class?" He finally thought of something appropriate to say.

"Yes."

"You must have learned quite a lot of characters, then."

"Don't know any."

"No! You're being modest, aren't you?"

"Next turn is to the north." Though she did not answer his question, there was laughter in her voice. She must be keeping it back with difficulty.

Vegetation flashed green through a rectangular opening in the high pale mud wall around the village.

"That's a *lü* bean patch," she pointed out.

"Oh. Those are *lü* beans," he said.

"I knew you wouldn't know," she said with a half suppressed giggle. He had to laugh too.

Coming out of the doorway they stood under a big tree on a little hump by the wayside. The first thing he saw was the temple—a glimmer of red wall among the green trees on the rise of ground across the road. All around stretched the dark crimson swaying sea of ripening *kao-liang* and the bright green squares of wheat with chalky little ochre-yellow paths in between zig-zagging up to the horizon.

"Is your land dry land or watery land?" Liu asked. They called rice paddies "watery land" in this part of the country.

"That's our land over there," she pointed.

"Ai-yah, then we've passed it long ago," he exclaimed.

"And this here is the school." She pointed to the temple.

If he still couldn't find the school at this point he must be an utter idiot, he thought. He thanked her and added, "I'm really sorry to make you go out of your way and come this far."

"We're used to walking," she said carelessly, her eyes already straying to the busy scene across the road. Many students were climbing up the temple steps, uniformed boys and girls waving to one another and shouting messages. She seemed much interested in the goings-on.

Liu walked down the hump alone. He looked back from the road. She was still standing up there, pulling a tree branch down to her with one hand and swinging it idly. The sun was on her, turning her sun-bleached hair into the same shade of golden brown as her face and arms so that she was all one color like a figurine of polished wood. But the instant he turned to look, she swung round and disappeared through the doorway. The tree branch had been released so abruptly that it bounced up and down for a long time, green and leafy against the blue sky.

Liu was still staring up at the swinging bough when Su Nan

stepped out of the doorway. He looked again. It was Su Nan all right, shielding her face with a notebook, her cap pushed to the back of her head because of the heat. The way he stood there looking up, it was just as if he was waiting for her.

He nodded and smiled. "Very hard to find your way about in this place," he said. "I was lucky I met somebody from the village who took me here. You're marvellous, you got here all by yourself."

Su Nan started to laugh. "You think I know the way? If I didn't follow you people, I'd never have made it."

"Oh, you saw me walking in front of you?" He had wanted to ask, "Why didn't you call me?" but somehow he didn't say it.

"Who's that girl? Very lively."

"She's from the family I'm staying with. Their name is T'ang. She's going down to the field to call her father to the meeting. Happens to be on her way."

Perhaps this explanation was superfluous. Anyhow Su Nan didn't seem much interested. He had hardly finished, when two other girls passed by and she ran up to greet them, catching them by the arms with more chummery than she usually displayed and went up the steps chattering with them, leaving him behind. If it was some other girl he would have thought it was nothing unusual. But he felt baffled because it was Su Nan and wondered what he had said or done to offend her. If he thought she was displeased because of Erh Niu, he ought to be pleased. But not being so conceited, at least where she was concerned, he was in a bad mood all day.

After the Land Reform Workers' Corps had mustered at the temple they split up into two teams to attend the meeting of the Farmers' Association and the Women's Association separately. The meeting was just routine. Chang Li and some of the students gave talks on the principles of the Land Reform, starting from the Origin of Private Property. It was like a lesson in social history from the Marxian standpoint and easy enough for the students. The speakers' subjects overlapped so that the meeting lasted almost six hours.

It was dark when they returned to the village. Liu was met at the door of the Tangs' house by a slight man with a foot-long pipe in one hand and red-bronzed arms and shoulders coming out of a sleeveless white blouse. He guessed it was T'ang Yü-hai, his host.

T'ang nodded and smiled. "Come and sit in this room here, sir." He led Liu to the same room that had been shown him in the morning. Apparently he didn't even know enough to say "comrade." His wife had been more glib in using the word. The men were usually slower and more reserved, Liu thought.

Erh Niu came in after them, bringing the oil lamp. But the table tilted to one side and wouldn't hold the lamp. The dirty floor was uneven. She left the lamp on the *k'ang* and went out and got a brick which she tucked under a table leg. Still kneeling, she looked up to see if the table was now level, bent down to adjust the brick, peered up again and then gave the table a little push to see if it wobbled. The lamplight was feeble and flickering, but Liu suspected that she had reddened her lips and cheeks and she had a small pink flower in her hair which he did not remember seeing in the morning.

T'ang sat on the *k'ang* sucking his pipe. His long face was deeply seamed.

"Today's meeting was too long, wasn't it?" Liu said conversationally. "A little too long?"

T'ang laughed politely. "Not so long. No so long." Again he fell silent.

Liu thought he looked worried, so he explained to him all over again the general picture of the Land Reform. In answer to Liu's questions he said he had eleven acres of land, reaped less than ten *tan* of grain every year, which just left the family enough to eat after paying the taxes in kind. A Middling Farmer like him had absolutely nothing to worry about, Liu told him. His property was under government protection. The Land Reform was based on the principle of Level both Ends without Touching the Middle.

But T'ang still brooded. "There's this talk of pooling all the land and redividing," he finally said. "Is there anything to it?"

"No, there's no such thing. Where did you hear such a rumor? Nobody's going to touch the land of Middling Farmers."

"Then that's all right. That's fine." T'ang sighed with relief. "Ever since I heard that talk of redividing, it's been troubling me. There's nothing special about my land, but I'm used to handling it, I know its nature. Take that piece near the creek. I bought it the year before last from Yang Lao-erh, Yang Number Two. Nice land, but the Yang brothers were a bunch of no-goods; they'd let it go to waste. The earth was hard like anything. Ever since I got it I've turned it twice a year and I'm always carrying baskets of ripe earth to it on a pole, padding it all over with ripe earth. Now it's not bad at all—best land I've got. I'd sure feel bad if I had to exchange it."

All his land had been bought piecemeal, acre by acre. According to him every acre had a past, either unfortunate or with lots of ups and downs, and it always had its own special quirks, fears, likings and susceptibilities. T'ang was unexpectedly long-winded about it, like all silent men once they had got started on a favorite subject. Liu did not mind listening. He was pleased at having made him open up.

Erh Niu had been out of the room and back again, leaning against the doorway listening. T'ang's wife called them to dinner. She had made flat barley cakes baked in a dry pan. When everybody had sat down around the table she told Erh Niu to put a pot of water on the stove. The fire was still going strong.

Erh Niu removed the wooden lid from the huge brown water jar that stood next to the stove. She took the half gourd off the wall to dip for water, but first she took a hurried look at her own reflection in the shadowy brown depth. She pushed her flower back a little and looked again but did not seem to be reassured. Then she took it off and tucked it into her hair, stem upwards. The pink flower fell softly in absolute silence onto the glassy brown surface of the water and floated motionlessly over one eye on her mirrored face. She too was motionless as she leaned over looking in, one hand resting on the green glazed rim of the jar.

"Why are you taking all this time to get a bit of water? Takes as long as embroidering," her mother grumbled, calling out to her from the table. "What are you looking at?"

"I was wondering what's the matter with today's water. Such a lot of mud at the bottom," Erh Niu said.

She fished the flower out, shook it dry and put it back in her hair. Hastily filling the pot with water, she set it on the stove and joined the others at the table. Liu avoided looking in her direction because he did not want to embarrass her. But he had seen her looking anxiously at herself in the water. His vague uneasiness was perhaps tinged with a sense of pleasure just as vague and remote.

3

FOR THE last few days the Land Reform Workers' Corps had been busy with *Fang P'in, Wen K'u*, Visiting the Poor and Asking about their Pains. In small units of two or three they paid visits from door to door. To catch the men at home they had to work until late in the evening, trying to engage the farmers in conversation and pumping them to make them *T'u K'u Shui*, Disgorge Bitter Fluid. Once every day the Reform Corps met in the village school for Collective Reporting, sorting out the material gathered that day and discussing it.

"The People still have scruples. They dare not speak out," Chang Li said. "They're scared of the revenge of the Remnant Feudal Forces."

The Corps tried to find out whether it was the landlords that they were afraid of or the village despots. The few landlords in Han Chia T'o had very little land for rent and could not live on their income from the land. They generally had some member of the family who was in business or who taught school in town, sending money home regularly to help things out. There were a few local *hun-hun*, gangsters, but none of them was powerful enough to be called a despot. Go Forward Pao had been a ne'er-do-well before. But since he had mended his ways after he became Progressive and had, furthermore, been made the Party Secretary of the Branch Office, nobody was inclined to speak ill of him. The two men who had been *chia chang*—block leaders—during the Japanese occupation had been appointed against their will. Their job had been mostly to take up collections to provide for food and supplies for the Japanese army or the army of the puppet government, whichever happened to be passing through the district. They had to make up the deficit out of their own pockets and had to sell their land to do it, later even their houses. One of them had been appointed after his predecessor had gone half crazy with grief. If anything, the villagers were sorry for them.

It would seem that the people in the village had no real complaints against anybody. But the members of the Corps tackled the job with youthful zeal. They went at it as if was artificial respiration, throwing themselves on the peasants, pressing hard on their stomachs to force out the water. And slowly, in one case after another, the Bitter Fluid was Disgorged.

The most common grievance the students heard was that after the harvest last year when the whole country-side competed in paying tax ahead of the final date, the village *kan-pu* had been too keen on winning the Red Flag. They had kept after everybody, threatening that those who delayed the payment would have to help build roads. When that didn't work too well, there had been arrests and beatings. Han Teh-lu, classified as a Poor Farmer, had been so badgered that he had broken down and cried four times. Many of the farmers had been forced to sell their seeds before their crops were ready for harvesting.

Some accused the *kan-pu* of discrimination in *tso fu-tan*, calculating the Individual Share of the Burden. Then there were several people who claimed that they had lost over half of their crops last year through floods and bugs. They had already reported themselves as famine cases, which according to government proclamations were entitled to a tax reduction. But the *kan-pu* had talked and talked to them, refusing to let them alone until they had agreed to "voluntarily ask for exemption from tax reduction."

The members of the Corps had been excited and enthusiastic during the Extraction of Bitter Fluid. But when it came to Collective Reporting, they were somewhat at a loss. All they had collected here were complaints against the *kan-pu*. Nothing really serious. But no mention at all was made of the landlords.

"The hatred of the farmers here for the landlord is not deep," Liu concluded.

"If their hatred for the landlord is not deep, it's because their Political Awareness is not high," Chang Li said. "That's why they don't resent the fact that they've been exploited. And you people just look at it from the surface and decide arbitrarily that their hatred for the landlord is not deep. That just reflects on the extent of your understanding of The Policy."

So the entire Corps went under the most thorough discussion and self-examination.

Go Forward Pao made a suggestion to the Corps that they might dine on Struggle Rice cooked in big pots every day at lunchtime. The members of the Corps would eat together with the *kan-pu* and militiamen so they could all keep in touch. "As it is now, we have to look all over the place whenever we want to get hold of anybody," Pao said. "The rice is there, ready at hand. It's the Fruit of the Struggle that we collected this spring during the Extermination of Bandits and Gangsters. It's been in the safekeeping of the Farmers' Association."

"That's the People's property," Liu Ch'üan said at once. "We shouldn't be the ones to enjoy it."

Su Nan, who seldom spoke, also said, "We're supposed to Share in Three Things when we come to the country." She meant "share the food, the living quarters and the labor of the farmers." "We aren't helping in the fields because there isn't time. If on top of this we are eating better than other people, it would be a bit too much. The family I'm boarding with belongs to the Destitute Farmer class. They're living on bean husks and rice husks."

She was not the only one boarding with Destitute Farmers. Some of them were naturally anxious for a change of diet. "To save time we are not helping in farmwork. It saves time too to eat Struggle Rice together, with everybody at hand," they argued. "There is a time limit to this Land Reform, you know. It's most important to complete it as soon as possible."

Opinions differed. They broke into a hubbub.

"You comrades are here to help The People to get up a Struggle," Go Forward Pao said. "What if you eat a few meals off The People— it's as it should be."

"Then does that mean that if we don't eat, we won't help, and there'll be no Struggle?" said Su Nan.

Chang Li gave her his support. "It's true that it won't look good if we eat too well. Got to Consider the Effect."

The talk of Struggle Rice was shelved. But then it turned out that nobody had paid attention to the ventilation in the storeroom of the Farmers' Association, so the grain had turned warm and was beginning to redden after a particularly hot summer. Part of it had begun to sprout. So there was really no reason why some of it shouldn't be taken out and disposed of.

Big mud stoves were built in the courtyard of the school to cook lunch for everybody connected with the Land Reform. It was whispered among the members of the Corps that Go Forward Pao and the chairman of the Farmers' Association were smuggling large quantities of rice and flour out of the granary, secretly selling them in town and charging it all to the daily consumption of Struggle Rice. Other *kan-pu* had talked because they were kept out of it. Chang Li must have also heard of this. But Pao had already worked himself into Chang's good graces. So the matter went no further.

With the work of *Fang P'in, Wen K'u* coming to an end, the Corps was busy writing a Collective Report to the district government. Everybody helped with the copying. The part assigned to Su Nan seemed specially long. She hadn't finished copying yet when everybody left the school office. A red candle stood on a tall pale yellow mud candlestick. A lithograph portrait of Sun Yat-sen faced a colored print of Mao's portrait on the peeling whitewashed walls. Slogans written on two strips of white paper flanked each of the portraits like the traditional antithetical scrolls. The brass nails on a scarlet waist-drum strung high on one wall gleamed in the candlelight. Pasted in tidy rows under the drum were the schoolchildren's essays written on flimsy green-checked paper. The faint stench of sticky Chinese ink filled the room.

Chang Li came, saying, "Let's give it a Shock Attack. I'll help you copy, we'll get it done tonight so we can send this off early in the morning. Let's see how far you've got."

He bent down to look, standing behind her, fanning himself with his cap, half for her benefit. The flame of the candle jumped in the breeze. It jumped again and again with each stroke of his cap. Su Nan kept her eyes fixed on the sheet of paper in front of her but the shifting of light and shadow across it made her feel a bit dizzy. Trying not to show her annoyance, she put down her pen, gave him half of the rough draft and pushed the candle-stick a little toward the other side of the table. But instead of going over to sit on the other side, Chang remained leaning against a corner of the table. He stood the sheets of manuscript on the table and tapped them to make them a tidy stack.

"I've been watching you, Comrade Su. You're doing fine. And at today's meeting what you said shows a high degree of Thought Element. You carry on," he said smiling, patting her on the shoulder. "When we go back to Peking I'll Reflect it Upward. It ought to pave the way to your admittance into the Party."

His hand rested on her shoulder. Su Nan went on copying as if not noticing it, but she swivelled around a little as she was turning over a sheet of paper and his hand came off. "I'm willing to learn," she said smiling, "But I don't think I have in any way given an outstanding demonstration."

"To ask to be outstanding is still a petit-bourgeois way of looking at it." As he spoke he had already taken her left hand which was resting on the paper. But she wriggled out of his grasp. The shadows of her lowered eyelashes fell in long thin spidery lines over the deepening crimson of her cheeks.

"You've grown thin, hey? How is it that you happen to be quartered in a Destitute Farmer's house?" Chang bent down to look into her half averted face. His mouth was close to the candle so that the flame was now trembling with every word he breathed. "How about moving you to a Midding Farmer's house? You need a change."

"There's really no need for that. When we volunteered to come down here, we didn't expect to have a good time."

"Youth is always stubborn." He laughed, blowing the thin orange flame away from him. "Never mind. The Organization will take care of this. The Organization always feels concerned about workers who show promise."

"But really, Comrade Chang, what we've gone through is nothing, as hardships go."

"You should go step by step when learning to stand hardships. No sense in ruining your health. After all, 'Your body is your capital in the Revolution,'" he quoted. His hand was again on hers, fondling her wrist, sliding up her forearm. "You have gone thin," he said.

This time she pulled away abruptly and stood up. "I'll go and get some people to help copy this. It'll be much faster," she said to the door as she hurried toward it, flushed and unsmiling.

"Tell the school janitor to go and get them." He came after her, shouting on the dark porch, "Lao Han! Lao Han!"

There was no answer. Empty rooms reverberated with the echoing "Han!...Han!" She got really frightened at the sound.

"No, I'll go myself. I've got to go anyhow—haven't had my supper yet." She almost ran out of the pitch-dark courtyard.

At the village she rounded up several co-workers and sent them to the temple while she stayed for supper. The others had almost finished copying by the time she came back to the temple with another girl she had recruited. Chang was as affable and jovial as ever. When the work was done they lit lanterns and returned to the village together.

But the next day at noon when they were having Struggle Rice, Chang strolled toward Su Nan, his ricebowl in hand. "Comrade Su, this kind of *tso-feng* is not so good. Mind the effect on people."

Su Nan was speechless with surprise, thinking that he was referring to what happened between them the evening before. Surely he wouldn't have the guts—or the face—to tell everybody about it?

"Fish the fly out and be done with it. But no, you're throwing away the whole bowl of rice gruel." Chang pointed with his chopsticks at the rice bowl she had abandoned on the table. "Wasting the People's Blood and Sweat. I seem to remember you were the first to object to eating Struggle Rice, on the ground that it's a waste. Now that's a very good example of the most typical fault of the intelligentsia—*Hao kao, wu yüan*, Fond of the Lofty, Aim at the Remote."

"Comrade Chang, you're being too Unscientific," Su Nan said furiously. "Flies carry germs—even primary school students ought to know that."

"The fly has been cooked; it's dead; the germs are all killed. This is not hygiene you're talking of—just the petit-bourgeois obsession with cleanliness."

"But I saw it fall into the gruel. Look, its legs are still moving." She snatched up her bowl and held the fly up with her chopsticks to show him.

"So what? The farmers would have eaten up everything just the same. What makes you think your life is more valuable than a farmer's?"

All the kan-pu and militiamen stood around watching curiously. Chang began to feel that it was unwise as well as unseemly to prolong the argument. He was not used to dealing with women and must have been more hurt and upset than he had realized.

"We're all comrades together," he dropped his voice and said smiling. "If anybody gives you his opinion, he means well, he's helping you to make Progress. Your way of taking criticism is not so good, Comrade Su. We ought to bring it up for discussion in the unit meeting."

Liu was very angry at the injustice, but he was just the least bit surprised at the way Su Nan had quickly lost her temper and had immediately started to shout back at Chang.

She also regretted it. She ought to have known better. Even if she had exposed him, telling about his attitude toward her the previous evening, she wouldn't get any support from the Organization. All she'd have done would be to ruin her own future.

During the unit meeting that day, everybody had to take turns commenting on her behavior. A few co-workers, Liu among them, tried to shield her with mild criticism. But they were cried down and accused of Small Circle-ism. The young men and girls of the Corps had learned a lot since they came down to the country. They had their own futures to think of and could not afford to pass by this opportunity to win distinction and get a good fitness report out of

Chang. They attacked Su Nan with gusto, calling her "feudal," "capitalistic," "*hsiao-chieh*, young lady," "poisoned by Western Imperialistic Thought." The onslaught ended only when Su Nan had finally castigated herself to everybody's satisfaction, outdoing all of them in name-calling. But the subject was brought up again the next day when somebody pointed out at a meeting, "Comrade Su Nan has been seen going out alone into the fields, where she cried for half an hour. So it would seem that she's only pretending to accept criticism. At heart she still resents it."

After some pause Su Nan said in a halting voice, "Yes, I did cry. Because I felt so moved. Everybody was so concerned about me, so enthusiastic in helping me to make Progress." Tears stood in her eyes.

The matter was finally dropped.

The members of the Corps sat in at the daily meeting of the *kan-pu* at the co-operative store. The purpose of these "secret" meetings was Brewing Objects for the Struggle. One day there was a sudden shout during the meeting. "Spies! There're spies!"

"It's Han T'ing-pang, the landlord!"

"Sure, it's him! I saw him peeking at the door!" Several *kan-pu* rushed out and came back with Han T'ing-pang, his arms pinned behind him. The militiaman posted outside the co-operative was scolded for allowing him to snoop around.

Han was sallow and lanky. His slightly grizzled hair was parted in the middle and hung over his steel-rimmed glasses. He wore blue canvas shoes under his long gown of wrinkled white glass cloth.

"What are you doing here, Han T'ing-pang?" Pao thundered at him.

"I came to see the department heads. But when I saw that you comrades were having a meeting, I didn't dare come in. Didn't dare come in." Han kept nodding and smiling, making innumerable little bows as he spoke.

"What have you got to say?" Chang Li asked.

"I want to give land to the government." Han tried to reach for his pocket. A *kan-pu* took a small cloth package from him and presented it to Chang Li.

Chang chuckled as he opened the package. "It's been said that the landlords have three tricks when they give away land: 'Give what's bad; give what's farthest from the village; give very little.'"

Go Forward Pao leaned over to look at the land deeds. "Sure, he's trying to cheat with that rocky patch he has way over on the other side of the woods. And this piece of 'watery land' has been absolutely useless ever since the creek changed its course."

"Anyhow, it's against our principles to take it. This land will have to be returned to his tenants. He has no right to give away what doesn't belong to him." Chang wrapped the papers in the piece of white cloth and tossed it to the ground at Han's feet.

"Now get out! Get out!" Pao said. "He's just here to eavesdrop. I know these people—they'd give anything to find out what's going on."

Still protesting with little bows and smiles, Han was hustled out of the room and the meeting continued. Chang wanted to know Han's background and past history. It seemed that he had inherited about forty acres of land and had gone to high school in town. Relatives had helped him to find clerical jobs in Peking and Chinan but he never could keep them because he didn't know how to get on with people. Every now and then he would go up to Peking for a short visit with his father-in-law. After one or two months of fruitless job-hunting he would be back again in the country. He had been scared by the talk of Land Reform and had made an attempt to escape to Peking, leaving his wife and children behind. That was half a month ago, when the village gate was already being watched. He had been stopped by the sentry and brought to the Village Public Office. After some questioning he had been released but from then on several watchmen were assigned to guard his front and back doors.

Go Forward Pao asked at the meeting if it would be against the rules to arrest him at once. Further delay might give him another opportunity to escape. There was also the danger that he might hide or destroy his land deeds. The decision was made that his tenants should go and settle their accounts with him and ask him for the land deeds that ought to be theirs.

Han had five tenants altogether. The Farmers' Association summoned them and taught them a fiery little speech which they were to deliver when they demanded the deeds. They were all ready to go, but by that time one of them had disappeared. Another went to find him. One by one they all slipped away. The *kan-pu* waited and waited. Finally Chang, Pao and Sun had to go themselves to look for them. The men were all working in the fields.

"What you doing here? What's happened to all of you?" Sun yelled at one of the men, jumping high with exasperation. "You're to go to Han T'ing-pang! Denounce him and get the land deeds back!"

The man felt the top and back of his shaved skull and smiled at him conciliatorily. "Yes, Comrade Sun—but it's very embarrassing. After all, old tenant, old landlord. My family has been renting land from his family for generations back."

Pao and Sun swore, "These blockheads! *Ssu lo-hou*, dead set on being backward. You can't do a thing with them. 'You can't help slush to climb walls.'"

"Don't be so impatient," Chang said. "In this work there're bound to be times when you bump your head against a nail."

The tenants were again summoned to the co-operative. After a lot more explanations and coaching, they finally went to Han T'ing-pang's house. They obtained the land deeds from him with the greatest ease, without having to go through the process of dramatic accusations and settling of accounts, tracing Exploitations three generations back. The Farmers' Association was highly dissatisfied with the performance. In the next *kan-pu* meeting Sun Fu-kuei spoke up with his customary bluntness. "I've always said it's no use. Never will get them to kick up a row. We don't even have one Big Landlord, while the Poor Farmers and hired men come up to a hundred and sixty-odd families. How much land can each expect to get? What have they got to fight for?"

Go Forward Pao also said, "Each family won't get as much as one acre of land. And right in front of their eyes they see the Rich Farmers and Middling Farmers with their ten or twenty acres, absolutely untouched. If we're going to divide the land, let's take it all and divide it—if you ask me. Guess nobody will mind getting two acres of land to play around with. See if The People don't rise at that. You just watch!"

After an uneasy silence there were some whisperings among the Land Reform Workers. Then Liu said aloud, "This is against The Policy."

Somebody added in a more moderate tone, "Perhaps it's not advisable to have too many Objects for the Struggle."

"We ought to limit the Area of Attack," Su Nan said.

Chang made a quick decision. It appeared to Liu that this might not be the first time that he had heard of the proposal. "We can't just hug the regulations tight and close our eyes to all other factors," he said. "In different localities there's a great deal of difference in the proportion of population to the amount of arable land. So it's impossible to go by set rules in classifying people according to the amount of land they own. The classifications made in the past could have been incorrect. If there are any such cases, let's bring them up for rediscussion."

Most of the *kan-pu* didn't quite get it but after he had it explained to them, they grew lively, with everybody talking at once, naming many people who could be classified as landlords.

Even Hsia Feng-ch'un, the shy and inarticulate Propaganda Officer of the Party Branch Office, spoke up excitedly, "There's Han Ch'ang-so. As the old saying goes, 'One able-bodied young man; three acres of good watery land'—amounts to a lot, you know. He even got himself a wife last year." Hsia himself could not afford to get married though it was more than a year since he became a *kan-pu*. He never got much out of it. Being rather slow-witted he was always kept out of things by Pao and Sun.

The Chairman of the Women's Association also opened her mouth for the first time. "The wife's got a new padded jacket too. Some real fancy cotton print."

Amid eager chatter, a list of names was drawn up. T'ang Yü-hai's name was among the first three. Although T'ang had no tenants and could not afford a regular hired man, there were several day laborers who had worked for him during the busy seasons. The Farmers' Association summoned these men and mobilized them to Struggle against T'ang.

The men were all timid and quite speechless before the authorities. Except for Feng T'ien-you, who was one of the best stiltwalkers for miles around and had a commanding presence, his ruddy long face theatrically black-browed. He alone spoke up, with considerable hesitation, "I dare not lie in front of you comrades. I don't know about T'ang, but when I worked for him, I ate what he ate. And there's never been any trouble when it comes to getting paid."

"Ai-yah, wake up, old Feng! Are you too dumb to know when you're being exploited?" Pao said. "Just think, if he doesn't exploit poor people, where did he get all his land from?

"That's because his whole family has been working hard all these years. Men, women or children, they all go down to the fields to work. When his dad was alive he worked in the fields when he was well past seventy."

"Don't be so silly, old Feng. You're defending those who ride on poor people's necks and turning against your own brothers in poverty. Your elbows turn outward, eh?"

"It isn't that, Comrade Pao. A man can't do without a conscience. Old T'ang hasn't treated me badly, considering. That year when my dad died, even my own granduncles and grandaunts refused to help, and it was he who lent me money to buy the coffin."

"So that's it!" Chang Li broke in. "He's bought your heart with this bit of *hsiao en, hsiao hui*, petty favor, petty boon."

"Don't be so foolish," Pao said. "What's this petty favor, compared to what you're really entitled to, if you settle your accounts with him? I won't be surprised if he has to give you half of his land."

Pao was quick to notice a slight nervous movement in Feng's face that might mean a flicker of interest. "Now think it over, Feng T'ien-you," he said heartily, slapping him on the shoulder. "Don't be so dead-brained. It would seem that you'd rather die than be well off."

Chang slapped him on the other shoulder. "Today is the day that your luck changes."

"The world nowadays is the poor man's world. The man who's poor always has the last word, just as if he's three generations older than everybody else," Pao said. "You just go and make a row, and ask for the back wages that he must owe you. Don't worry, the Government is right behind you."

Feng hung his head and said nothing. But the other men with him started to mumble something about T'ang having given them less wages than was their due.

"You hear? You hear?" Pao said to Feng. "They're talking. You're the only one who still defends him, content to be his *kou t'ui-tzu*, dog's leg."

"Must have been bribed," Chang said. "What did he give you?"

Feng cried out, "No, nothing! Whoever took anything from him, may his right hand rot if he took it with his right hand, may his left hand rot if he took it with his left hand!"

"Then why don't you speak the truth?"

They pressed him further and Feng finally admitted haltingly that the money T'ang lent him was "*yen-wang ts'ai*, a loan from the king of hell." A high rate of compound interest had been charged. So in recent years he had never got paid when he carried water for T'ang, padded loose earth over his land, repaired ditches and ground wheat and wheat-stalks for him.

Liu had been watching with smouldering indignation. Twice he had written a short note on a slip of paper, passing it to Chang. Each time Chang had crumpled it into a ball after glancing at it and stuffed it into his pocket, and had gone on with the questioning and prompting. Liu reminded himself that he could not speak out strongly for T'ang since he was staying in T'ang's house and could very well be accused of having been bought or softened up. But in the end he could not stand it any more. "Comrade Chang," he said, "I don't hold with mobilizing the Masses in this manner. It doesn't encourage them to tell the truth."

"What do you mean?" Chang looked at him coldly. "We're always talking of mobilizing The People, but when The People have really Risen, you don't think we're going to get frightened and try to gag them, are we? I tell you, nowadays nobody can gag The People when they choose to speak."

Liu was about to speak again but Chang cut him short. "Comrade Liu, it seems that you have taken the wrong Class Route. You're due for some Self-Examination. Think it over by yourself first. We'll discuss your problem some other day."

His last words were clearly a threat. Liu fell silent, and after that nobody else dared say anything.

When the meeting had ended and they were on their way back to the village, Su Nan caught up with Liu and whispered, "Really, it's too undemocratic."

At first Liu did not speak. Then he suddenly burst out furiously, "You saw what happened today. Anybody who so much as opened his mouth must be the landlord's *kou t'ui-tzu*."

"All right, all right, that's enough," another young man in the Corps whispered as he brushed past them. "If anybody should hear, they'll say we're Holding a Small Meeting."

Su Nan hurried away without another word.

Liu lagged behind the others. He dreaded going back to the Tangs. If he should behave as if nothing had happened, he'd feel too hypocritical. But of course it was out of the question to tell them anything. On top of breaking the discipline of the Corps he would be committing the most serious crime of Sabotaging the Land Reform, punishable by death. Besides, what good would it do to warn them? The Tangs could not get away from the village and even if they could, they had nowhere to go.

Liu walked slowly, taking the long way home past the ditch to the west of the village. The tall old willow by the ditch stood golden in the setting sun. The days were quiet now without the cicadas.

Somebody was squatting on the stone slab across the narrow ditch, washing clothes. Liu took no notice of the flowered purple blouse and pants and did not realize that it was Erh Niu until he had come quite close. And then he was too stunned to turn round, but went on walking toward her.

He stood on the bank, only a few steps away from her, but he did not look at her. Instead he looked down into the thickly flowing water, specked with pale bits of straw. Long wisps of yellow mud trailed sluggishly in the current, like half-beaten egg-yolk floating in the egg-white.

Erh Niu had seen his reflection in the water. She pretended not to notice, waiting for him to address her. But for what seemed to be a long time, he just stood a little way from her looking downward, saying nothing. At first she felt surprised, then she started to blush. With the passing of each mute second she got redder and redder. The short rod she was pounding clothes with continued to rise and fall with mechanical rhythm. Then she gave a little scream. The rod had slipped out of her hand and was bobbing and pivoting very fast in the water, a slim cylindrical fish that was both stupid and incredibly agile as it swam swiftly downstream.

She made no movement to retrieve it but her cry had wakened Liu. He stepped off the bank, wading after it. Though the water was shallow, there was a strong current and his movements were too abrupt. He almost lost his balance but he managed to get hold of the rod.

When he staggered back and climbed up to shore, Erh Niu was standing sheepishly on the stone slab, at a loss for words. Seeing the water trickle down from his trouser legs in a hundred shining threads, she just exclaimed, "Ai-yah, look at that! Look at that!" by way of apology. She didn't seem to notice that the water in the lumped up wet clothes she held in her arms was also dripping onto her feet.

"It doesn't matter." Liu handed the rod back to her and bent down to wring out his trouser legs. The wet cloth had turned a deep gray.

"Look at that!" Like all northern country people Erh Niu had a horror of getting wet, probably through a very limited acquaintance with rain or any other kind of water. "And there's nothing to change into. I just washed your other suit."

"It doesn't matter. It'll get dry soon." He nodded and turned to go. "I'll go home first, then."

This time he walked fast because the wet trousers clung icily to his legs and the wind was a bit cold after sundown. The mud at the bottom of the ditch had stuck to his rubber soles, making a thick padding through which he felt the ground giving way softly under his feet at every step. It gave him an uncomfortably befogged feeling.

Inside the village wall he came across two other members of the Corps in the lane.

"What's the matter with you?" they asked in astonishment. "Fallen into the creek?"

He nodded vaguely. If he told them that he had been helping a girl to get back her rod for pounding clothes, they would be sure to make fun of him.

"How did you fall into the creek?"

"My feet slipped," he said briefly. "Lucky the water isn't deep."

"Such a joke!" One of the young men giggled and whispered, "If anybody around here should go jumping into the river, it ought to be the landlords instead of you, the land-reformer."

Liu had to join in the laughter.

When he came back to the T'angs' house, T'ang's wife also exclaimed as soon as she saw him, "What happened?"

He was going to tell her, but then he thought of her habitual dread of any man in uniform paying special attention to her daughter. There was no point in getting her into a state. "I slipped and fell into the ditch," he said.

"Ai-yah, you didn't get hurt anywhere, did you?" she said. "Quick, go and dry yourself before the stove. You'll catch cold."

T'ang Yü-hai came back from work. He put down his hoe, went and lifted the cover off the water jar and drank from the half-gourd dipper. He dipped again and this time he held the water in his mouth and spat it on his grimy hands, rubbing them together.

He didn't seem to be paying much attention when his wife told him about Liu falling into the ditch. He took his time washing his hands with a few mouthfuls of water, then wiped them across his sleeveless white blouse, leaving long yellow mud streaks.

His wife in turn grew silent. Liu shuffled his feet uneasily, standing before the stove. The water in one of his rubber shoes gave an embarrassing little squeak.

T'ang took his long pipe from a niche-like recess in the mud wall. He stuck his pipe into the stove to light it, then he dragged a bench over and sat down to smoke, hunched forward and staring vacantly before him.

He'd had an argument with his wife today. There were a lot of rumors in the village these few days and many Rich Farmers and Middling Farmers were feeling jittery and trying to give their land to the government. T'ang's wife had tried to persuade him to offer half of his land to the government. He had said nothing.

"What else can we do?" she had said. "You feel pained—don't I feel pained? Bought it acre by acre, and now, handing it out in a huge big piece."

At this she had started to cry and said, "Ai! Not that I'm blaming you, but really—it's not worth it. All your life you've stinted on food and stinted on clothes. All you want is to buy land. And last spring, to buy that piece of land from the Kengs, you had to borrow all that grain—two hundred catties. You haven't paid that back yet and look what's happened now!"

Sighing and nagging in an even strain, she had brought out the little wooden box where they kept the land deeds and again the tears had streamed down her face. "In the old days we just wrapped them up with a piece of rag. Then later when we'd got more of them we wrapped them with mulberry-bark paper and then made a little cloth parcel. Then you made this box and I said even then, 'What for? We're not like those rich people with their special blackwood box for land deeds.' I wouldn't be surprised if it's this box that's brought us bad luck—not that I'm blaming you."

He had just sat there without speaking. When she had sorted out the land deeds and had again put pressure on him to go to the co-operative store and offer them to the government, he had simply stood up, taken his hoe and carrying it on one shoulder had gone down to the field to work.

Now it was evening and everybody was home. His wife was thinking that as long as Liu was here, they might as well try to worm some information out of him. So she said to her husband after a longish silence, "Ai! Such a lot of things are being said in the village these days. Really, you don't know who to believe. But what I say is: 'Don't you worry, Erh Niu *t'a tieh*. It's got nothing to do with us. We've slaved hard all our lives and have nothing to show for it except those few acres of land. It's scarcely been three days since we started to eat full meals. Whoever they're going to Struggle with, it won't be us, I tell you. Who do you think you are?'"

Though she was addressing her husband, her eyes rested on Liu. Liu remained standing before the stove with his back turned to her.

"Didn't Comrade Liu tell you not to worry?" the woman said to her husband. "He said it's got nothing to do with us."

She meant to engage her husband in conversation and maybe start an argument, forcing Liu to comment on the subject. However, such subtleties were well over T'ang's head. Even when she coughed and winked at him he failed to take notice. He just sat smoking in silence. When she had gone on talking alone for some time, she had to stop.

Erh Niu brought her washing home. T'ang's wife was kneading flour. Affecting an air of solicitude but obviously regarding it as a diverting piece of news, she told her daughter about Liu falling into the ditch. Erh Niu could not help letting out a giggle as she turned to glance at Liu. He was in no mood for secret jokes but he had to return her smile as their eyes met. It was probably the consciousness of having a secret between them that made her quickly turn her head the other direction and give way to half smothered giggles.

"What are you laughing at?" T'ang, who had been sitting hunched up smoking all this time, suddenly raised his head and demanded loudly.

"Nothing." Now she was spluttering with laughter. Liu began to feel worried.

"Silly child!" T'ang glared at her. He was afraid that Liu would feel offended at being made such a figure of fun. Frowning deeply, he lifted his long pipe and knocked her on the head with the little brass bowl at the end of it.

Erh Niu cuddled up to him, rubbing her head hard against his shoulder. She seemed to be specially fond of her father today, so full of affection for him that she did not know what to do about it.

"The bigger you grow, the sillier you get," T'ang grumbled as he caressed her hair. Then he sighed for no reason.

It pained Liu to see them so happy together. Soon it was supper-time. After supper T'ang's wife washed the bowls and chopsticks in a wooden bucket. After wiping the table Erh Niu went out to the courtyard and took Liu's uniform off the washline—the suit she had washed today. It was already half dry. She spread it on the table and smoothed her palm slowly across it, pressing down hard so that the blue-gray cloth looked almost like it had been ironed.

Liu went and got a spare lamp and lit it by tilting it against the oil lamp hung above the stove. He went back to his own room, taking the lamp with him. He thought he would sleep early to avoid talking with the Tangs. He was just going to lie down on the *k'ang* when T'ang's wife shouted, "Somebody to see you, Comrade Liu!"

"Who is it?" He came out buttoning his jacket.

He never expected to see Su Nan standing in the middle of the room. She had her hands in her coat pockets and was slapping her-self idly, puffing out and deflating the pockets in turn. The dim lamplight lengthened the shadowy deep cut of her eyelids and ac-centuated the porcelain thin rim of her pink lips.

"Have you people finished supper?" she asked.

"We've just eaten," Liu said smiling. "Please sit down."

"This comrade here—what's your honorable name?" T'ang's wife said conversationally.

"My name is Su. Is this your young miss?" Su Nan asked T'ang's wife, putting her hand on Erh Niu's shoulder.

"Yes, this is our slavegirl," T'ang's wife answered.

Erh Niu bowed her head still lower as she continued to smooth Liu's uniform with her palms, working with greater concentration than ever.

"What's your name?" Su Nan stopped to look at her.

Erh Niu smiled faintly but she kept her eyes riveted on the clothes spread flat over the table. A flushed, stubborn look had come on her face.

"Name of Erh Niu," her mother answered for her. "Already seventeen this year, and still an absolute idiot," she said smiling.

"You're just saying that out of modesty," Su Nan said. "I've seen her around. Liveliest girl in the village." She suddenly noticed Liu's shoes, covered with yellow mud. "Why, where have you been today?" she said in surprise. "You've waded in water?"

"Just now on my way back I was walking along the ditch and I slipped and fell inside and got all wet," Liu explained. As he spoke, somehow his eyes strayed toward Erh Niu as if in guilt. This was the second time that Erh Niu had heard the story. This time she was far from amused. From what could be seen of her lowered face, her cheeks were puffed out with pique and her eyes were dark and unhappy.

Liu thought it was so unreasonable of her. What made her think that he was afraid of telling Su Nan the truth? He had just told her mother the same thing. He couldn't very well go back on his story in front of everybody. But though he reasoned thus to himself, he felt unaccountably ashamed and apologetic.

Su Nan went to the door that led to the inner room and peeped in. "Is this your room?" she said smiling.

"Yes, come in and have a look."

As soon as she entered she took a folded sheet of letter paper out of her pocket and handed it to him after unfolding it. "I wrote a letter," she whispered. "If you agree to what I say there, sign your name at the bottom. I hope to get as many signatures as possible."

Liu needled the lampwick into giving more light and ran his eyes hurriedly over the letter. Then he read it a second time just to gain time. His only comforting thought was that hers was the only signature at the bottom. Perhaps she hadn't shown it to anybody else yet.

"Of course I agree," he said. "But I don't think you should send this letter."

Su Nan smiled. "Sure, I know you can't write letters to Chairman Mao just like that. It's an Unorganized and Undisciplined Action."

"And furthermore, nothing will ever come of it," Liu said. "We are not Party members, we have no connection with the Organization. What we say just won't be taken seriously."

Leaning against the table she drew her forefinger back and forth across the tiny flame of the lamp, quickly so that the finger never got burned. She kept at it with childish absorption. But finally she raised her head and looked at him. "But the way they're running things around here! I don't think Chairman Mao knows."

Liu did not speak. After a while he said, "Chairman Mao himself has said, 'To correct a wrong, you must go further than what is just.'"

"Still, you can't just struggle against anybody, with no standard, no principle!" Sudden anger made her raise her voice a little.

Liu stopped her with a slight shake of his head. He glanced back at the door over his shoulder and whispered, "Let's go out for a walk. We can talk outside."

She took her letter back, folded it and stuffed it into her pocket. As they came out of the room Erh Niu was squatting in front of the stove, poking at the ashes. T'ang and his wife sat across the table, smoking and sewing respectively, both looking tense. Obviously they thought Su Nan's coming had something to do with them, it being too late for ordinary social visits. And she had pointedly got Liu to go into the other room where they had held a whispered consultation. And now she was going away with him.

The smooth yellow mud walls looked clean and dismal in the frosty blue moonlight. They walked along the dirt path between earthen houses which had not changed much for the last two thousand years. The moon was so bright that cocks mistook it for dawn and crowed, cracked and quavering, all over the countryside. Some houses they passed were too run-down to have doors. Across the deep blackness of the courtyard, a faint glimmer of unearthly dark yellow light showed through the rounded, humped mud house, exactly like a burial mound peopled with ghosts. Sometimes there was the sound of children crying feebly. It was like those old stories of post-mortem child-bearing which told of live babies dug out of graves.

It was impossible to talk stumbling along the uneven ground, one after the other. They finally stood still and turned toward each other.

"I want you to promise me not to mail that letter," he said. When she did not answer, he said, "Did you show it to anybody else?"

"No."

"I'm glad you didn't." His relief was mingled with and all but drowned by a delirious flush of happiness at the thought that she had come to him first, out of all the people. It was difficult to keep talking in a worried tone. "Really, right now we have no status whatever. Within the Corps we're regarded as the Masses. We can't save anybody even if we ruin ourselves doing it."

"I know," she said after a pause.

"For instance, that day—picking on you for no reason—it was really too ridiculous. I was furious, but I thought it's no use getting into direct conflict with him. There's nothing we can do at present except to be patient."

Su Nan sighed shortly. "Let's go back. If somebody should see us there'll be more talk of Small Circle-ism."

"I'll walk you home."

On the way back the dogs suddenly started barking and there was a regular stomping of feet marching in step. The house lights went out quickly one by one. Liu and the girl stopped under the eaves of a house and peered out at the small band of militiamen moving past the lane ahead, with lanterns lighting their way. The ones that walked in front held rifles and wore cartridge belts. After them came some men with their arms tied behind them. At the rear, they could see the white towels on the militiamen's heads bobbing in the moonlight.

"Looks as if they're making arrests," Su Nan whispered.

"We better wait here for a while," Liu whispered.

The barking of dogs had spread to the east end of the village. Liu and the girl tried to guess which house the militiamen were entering.

The dark blue vault of northern sky dimmed into a powdery misty pallor toward the center where the moon was. The full white moon looked down coldly as it had done during all the past dynasties. Like a mirror it never remembered faces.

Liu wished that he and Su Nan had met in some other age. It couldn't have been worse than now, when he never even dared to speak to her. A few years earlier would have made all the difference.

"Is your home in Peking?" he asked.

"Yes, I've always lived there."

"It's funny we've never met. I've lived there all my life just like you."

A long, low chair-like stone structure for pounding grain stood under the eaves of the house. Su Nan sat on it, leaning forward against the handbar. Liu wanted very much to touch her hair. But he was afraid that she might think that he was taking advantage of the situation. He would be abusing her trust and friendship and it would spoil everything.

Not much could be seen of her in the dark. He stood at her back, the toe of one of his canvas shoes kicking soundlessly at the low stone slab. He was still painfully hovering on the brink of the irrevocable gesture when she turned her head very slightly so that her backward glance barely brushed past him. But she must have known. Abruptly she hunched forward, pressing her cheek against her hands on the handbar as if overcome by sudden shyness.

Then Liu put his hand on her hair and when she twisted away from him, he held her hand over the hand-bar. After a moment he said, "I wonder where we'll be sent to when we Obey The Distribution."

"I don't know. What did you put down, when you filled in the forms?"

"I said I'd prefer to work in north China or eastern China. But that doesn't mean anything."

"Yes, they might still send you anywhere. They say it's best not to emphasize personal preferences."

"Maybe we'll meet again in Hsinchiang."

"Yes, who knows?"

"There're worse places than Hsinchiang."

Su Nan said half laughing, "I heard that in Kansu there's so little water, you have to cook rice with the water you've washed your face with."

They both talked fast, lightly and nervously, laughing a little, well aware that whatever they said was just camouflage over the fact that he was holding her hand.

But she suddenly turned rigid and pointed wordlessly at a large ball-like black shadow under the wall at the next corner, some distance away. It could be a squatting man.

Startled, Liu called out loudly, "Who's that there?"

No answer.

"Who is it?" he shouted again, striding toward it.

"Sentry," the militiaman said curtly and spat on the ground.

"Let's go back. It's getting late," Su Nan said.

In silence he walked after her past the squatting sentry. When they had turned the corner they happened to look up and saw another black shadow squatting on the roof of a house. That must be another sentry. They said nothing for the rest of the way to the house Su Nan was quartered in.

She went in. He was walking home alone when he again heard the regular footsteps, coming from behind and getting nearer, it seemed. The dogs in the neighborhood were again barking loudly. The barking sounded cold and desolate, with a curious feeling of distance derived from the vast empty silence of the night. The village was so dead quiet, Liu could hear from far off the desultory talk among the militiamen. The rhythmic thumps of the footfalls, the faint sound of the voices and the short, scattered barks of the dogs rose and fell, humming in his ears, so that he began to suspect that he had heard nothing, it was just the blood pounding in his ears.

The yellow dirt path, drained colorless in the moon-light, stretched straight ahead. He stumbled on and on between the pale thick walls, as if in a dream, half lost in heavy sleep.

The marching steps were always behind him. He even had a crazy idea that if he should make the wrong turn they would follow him blindly and would never find their way to the Tangs' house.

4

THE BEAN oil in his lamp was nearly all burned up. A small green oval pearl of a light still stood erect in the dregs at the bottom of the soot-stained metal dish. Instead of lighting up the cave-like mud room it merely filled it with crowding, hulking blue-black shadows.

There was no light in the other rooms, and not a sound. The Tangs seemed to have gone to bed. Perhaps they were also under the illusion that if they kept quiet they would be overlooked.

Liu stuffed all his things into his knapsack—toothbrush, socks, underwear. He had to move out at once, back to the school. It was against the regulations for a Land Reform Worker to stay in a land-lord's house. You had to Draw the Line Clear. Of course he knew that he did not have to leave in this much of a hurry. It wasn't his fault, after all, that he had been quartered with the Tangs. It was just that he had no wish to see what was about to happen.

When he rushed out again into the moonlit courtyard, the door-way was blocked by the militiamen swarming in with their lanterns.

"Who is it?" one of them barked at him in a military manner.

"It's me. Member of the Land Reform Workers' Corps."

A lantern was lifted and thrust close to his face. After that they just pushed past him into the courtyard, shouting, "Where's T'ang Yü-hai? He's to come out at once! He's wanted for questioning!"

Liu jostled his way out of the door and went half running down the dirt lane. In a moment he had left the hubbub behind him.

Then he suddenly remembered he hadn't brought along his other suit, the one that Erh Niu had just washed. He felt disgusted with himself for remembering such a trivial thing at a time like this. Still, he had better go back and get it, since it was his only change of clothes. And he'd better go right now, taking advantage of the confusion. If he were to go there alone tomorrow, T'ang's wife and Erh Niu were sure to cry and beg him to help them. The scene was just what he dreaded. Besides, it might take a lot of explanation if someone saw him going into their house after tonight.

So he forced himself to turn back. Long before he came to the Tangs' door he could hear the wife's shrill whine penetrating the hubbub. "I beg you, *t'a yeh-men*, masters, do a good deed—let him off! All you masters are do-gooders, and we're all neighbors here—"

"Don't waste our time with all this silly chatter. Tell T'ang Yü-hai to come out quick!"

"Where is he? No use hiding—it'll be adding crime upon crime. Tell him to come out quick!"

"Let's search the house."

The woman talked fast through her sobs. "Why do you want to arrest him? In the first place we're not landlords. And in the second place we've always been law-abiding. The child's dad has never done anything against his conscience in all his life. Ask around if you don't believe me. All neighbors here—don't you know about us?"

"Shout once more—" a man threatened her, "Shout once more and you'll be tied up and taken along with us, too."

"Comrade Liu!" Erh Niu's voice cried out desperately. "Where's Comrade Liu? Where's Comrade Liu? Where's Comrade Liu gone to?"

The first thing Liu saw when he came into the courtyard was Erh Niu. He also saw his uniform—after it had been smoothed out it had again been hung out to dry. Erh Niu had been frantically pulling at the sleeve of the uniform as if it were his arm.

Liu felt that he was the most despicable person in the world as he went up and took his pants off the washline, then reached for his tunic. As soon as Erh Niu saw him she dropped his sleeve guiltily. "Comrade Liu, save my dad!" she cried out. "You save my dad!"

"*T'a ma ti!* He's gone up on the roof!" a militiaman was shouting. "*Tso t'a ma ti*, hit the son-of-a-bitch!" A gunshot banged.

"Help! Somebody'll get killed!" Erh Niu forgot herself and grabbed Liu by the arm, shaking him hard, "Beg you! Beg you! Save my dad!"

Liu managed to wrench himself free. He tried to take his tunic off the washline but his hands were shaking and somehow it wouldn't come off no matter how he pulled at it. He could not understand. It was the kind of thing that only happened in nightmares.

Then he realized that the tunic was all buttoned up in front so that it was strung securely along the line. He had to unbutton the whole row of buttons, with fingers that were clumsy from exasperation and anger with himself. He never looked at Erh Niu but he was aware of her bright stare, her face a pale blue mask in the moonlight, her eyes glittering stupidly like large silver beads hung suspended in the black peepholes of the mask.

"Roll down the roof to us while you can," somebody yelled upward. "If you don't come down at once we'll shoot to kill! Send you home to your granny!"

Bang! Bang! Another two shots. A crouching black shadow on the roof swayed into sight against the sky for the briefest instant before it came tumbling down. The crowd broke into a tumult and Erh Niu shrieked, "Dad! Dad!" as she pushed into their midst.

Liu made off with his uniform.

He identified himself for the sentry at the village gate and got out without much difficulty. Soon he was climbing the steps up the hill toward the school. It gave him a slight jar, even in his stunned state, to see that a pair of lanterns hung over the temple gate, lighting up the vertical white signboards. The vermillion doors silently ajar in the stillness of the night had a strange, expectant air. Nobody was at the gate, but when he went in he found the rooms brightly lit. Chang Li was still up and all the important *kan-pu* were there. They put him up in Chang's room. Liu heard from them that all the arrested landlords would be locked up in the two dark rooms where the firewood was stacked, in the back courtyard of the temple. A few minutes later someone came along with the news that T'ang had only been hit in the arm by a bullet. Liu supposed that he felt more or less relieved to hear that. Altogether he did not quite know what he felt about playing the part of a clown in a tragedy. The next morning when he changed into his other uniform he found a button missing. He must have torn it off when he was trying to pull the tunic off the washline.

After breakfast T'ang's wife came with a basket, bringing food for her husband. She insisted on seeing him, saying that she was worried about his wounds. When the militiamen refused to let her take the food in to him, she sat down on the ground and cried. Liu could hear her from across the courtyard. She was loudly blowing her nose, sobbing and bawling out, "People came and sealed everything up. Came early in the morning. Pasted a slip of paper on the cupboard, another slip on the rice jar...Two rooms sealed up out of three. No matter how you kowtowed, begging them to paste a slip or two less, they stuck another one on the grindstone—even the salt jar and oil jar were sealed up!"

The day of the Great Struggle Meeting she was there early at the meeting-ground, weeping and kowtowing to every *kan-pu* in sight. "All neighbors. All neighbors for over twenty years," she said. "You just have to lift your hand a little, and he'll pass through. Do a good deed—*k'uan-ta, k'uan-ta t'a pa!* 'Magnanimous' him! 'Magnanimous' him!" She had learned to use the new term.

"Get out, get out!—No place for you to make a row," Sun Fu-kwei snapped at her as he hurried by.

One of the Land Reform Workers was more patient and stood talking to her. "You better be Firm in your Standpoint," he cautioned her. "You've been oppressed and enslaved by this man who's your husband. About time that you should wake up. If you keep on waiting to join your fate with his, you will be on trial before The People too!"

When she saw that the young man was good-tempered, she wouldn't let go of him. "Do a good deed, comrade! Take pity on him, he's slaved hard all his life. All he got for it is those few acres of land. Even if all the land is taken, so long as you leave him his life, for the rest of his years he'll work like a buffalo and a horse together to repay you *yeh-men*, masters."

"*Ch'ü, ch'ü, ch'ü!* Go away, go away, go away!" Go Forward Pao walked over and said.

But they did not throw her out. The rules did not say that land-lords' families could be barred from the meeting. T'ang's wife re-mained standing in front of the platform peering around through her tears, looking for people to plead with. Her running eyes and nostrils glistened, glassy and bubbly. More people were coming in. The hum of voices rose in waves and she was beginning to feel more dazed and lost. Only the rough splintery boards of the platform hard against her back felt real.

This time the Mass Meeting was held in the vacant lot in front of the ancestral temple of the Hans, the largest clan in the village. There was a stage there under the big elm trees, facing the temple. Travelling troupes used to play there during the New Year and the festivals in more prosperous times. To shelter the stage four wooden pillars painted red held up over the stage a small black-tiled roof with upsweeping corners. The two front pillars had slogans pasted on them, handwritten on two strips on white paper in the style of antithetical scrolls, "Farmers of the nation—unite!" "Smash to bits the Feudal Forces." A huge white banner specifying the nature of the meeting and the locality ran across the front under the eaves. Grimy old blue cloth curtains were hung at the back. A yellow haze of sunlight came slanting down to the empty stage through the half-bare branches of the trees.

Headed by their teacher, the school-children filed into the meet-ing ground holding paper flags, singing shrilly. They were stationed up front in the eastern corner. Then came the local militia, all carry-ing rifles, wearing leather belts over their white Chinese blouses, their cartridge belts and hand grenades slung crosswise over their chests. They lined up impressively before the platform and some made a half circle behind it.

Sun Fu-kuei, the Farmers' Association Organizer, pushed his way through the crowd, booming through a big cardboard trumpet in a thick, rumbling, faraway voice like a god from the sky with a bad cold. "All the women stand on the west side! On the west side! The

Youth Vanguard Corps stand over here, next to the schoolchildren! Over here! The Youth Vanguard Corps over here! Don't move, anybody, once you've found your proper place! Children who have to go to the toilet, take them out right now! Later nobody is to go out. Hey, you people huddling at the foot of the wall, come nearer, you can't hear over there!"

Most of the *kan-pu* and the Land Reform Workers were distributed evenly throughout the Masses to spur them on and to keep an eye on them. Chang Li stood at the very back with a small knot of unassigned Land Reform Workers as if they were merely interested observers. But Chang wore his pistol for the first time since he came to the village to enhance the display of The People's might and as a precaution against the possibility of any Bad Elements creating a disturbance during the meeting. He looked calm and smiling, his hands locked behind his back, but he was nervous and tense like all stage directors on the opening night.

The Chairman of the Farmers' Association went on the platform and rang a bell to announce the commencement of the meeting. He gave a short speech. Then the various injured parties came up the platform from among the crowd and made their accusations in turn. While they talked, the *kan-pu* and the Positive Elements in the audience kept interrupting their speech by shouting slogans, duly echoed in thunderous tones by the crowd.

"Should have planted more speakers," Chang mumbled worriedly, half to himself. "Not enough speakers. They jump in and they jump out, but always the same faces."

Then he turned and whispered to Go Forward Pao, who had quietly come over to stand beside him. "Go and speak to the Chairman of the Women's Association. Tell her to push harder. Why don't I see those women sticking up their fists?"

Pao hurried off. After some time he again wandered back to Chang, saying, "I got two men to bring buckets of water. I guess everybody needs a drink. The Masses have shouted themselves hoarse."

"The water better wait," Chang said.

"You're afraid it might slow things up?"

Chang half nodded. "And it won't do either to have everybody moving about, leaving their posts. With nobody standing watch over them, they might not roar out when they should or stick up their fists."

For a while there was nobody on the platform. All heads were turned back, straining to look at the entrance to the meeting-ground.

"*Lai-la! Lai-la! Tui-hsiang lai-la!* Coming! Coming! The Objects are coming!" everybody was whispering.

More militiamen trooped in, bringing the Objects for the Struggle. The prisoners were not tied up; they looked tidy and well-scrubbed as they walked in with bowed heads between the guards. In the hush that had fallen, the militiamen lined up around the platform, raising their hands in unison and snapping off the safety catches on their rifles. The metallic clicks rang out flatly in the deepening silence.

The guards and the men circled slowly around the crowd, heading for their appointed place at the righthand side of the stage, under the trees.

An arm suddenly shot up in the people's midst, and Sun Fu-kuei trumpeted skyward through his cardboard loudspeaker, "Beat down the Big Feudal Exploiting Landlords!"

"Beat down the Big Feudal Exploiting Landlords!" shouted the crowd. Sun's arm was instantly lost in the thicket of arms that shot up around him.

From where Liu stood, he could hear the Chairman of the Women's Association stamping her feet in exasperation, exhorting her charges, pointing them out by name, "Put some pep into it, Third Aunt Hsia! Louder, louder! And hold your fist tight, my good aunt, aunt of my very own! Hold your hand up like this—you think you're waving to a lover, for heaven's sake?"

"Always follow in the footsteps of Chairman Mao!" Sun boomed.

"Always follow in the footsteps of Chairman Mao!" the crowd thundered back.

The Objects for the Struggle were led up the platform, one by one, and the injured parties went up to accuse them of the wrongs they had done them. When it was T'ang Yü-hai's turn he walked up with a limp. Liu saw that one arm was bandaged.

Watching Feng T'ien-you taking T'ang to task, demanding his back wages, Chang murmured, "This Feng T'ien-you is no good. Got a bad case of stage-fright." He looked disappointed. He had thought Feng was his brightest discovery.

"Well, he's a good stilt-walker," Hsia, the Party Branch Office Propagandizer, commented with a farmer's maddening complacency. "Best stilt-walker in these parts, for as far up as Paotingfu."

For a moment Chang thought he would slap the man's mindlessly calm face staring straight ahead toward the stage.

Go Forward Pao was also watching with them. Pao said with a slight shake of his head, "You can't help slush climb walls. All slush—all of them."

"As I've always said, you shouldn't rehearse them too often," Chang said irritably. "Rehearse too many times and they become like a gramophone record. No feeling."

"But they've got to rehearse! Otherwise they can't remember all those words," Pao said smiling.

Chang said, "Instead of having them memorize a set piece, you should have emphasized more on the *su k'u ch'uan lien*, Complaint Link-up. Get them to visit each other and Air their Grievances, practice their speeches on each other. There wasn't nearly enough of that done."

Pao knew better than to argue with Chang, who seemed to have forgotten that it was he himself who said that too much of the Complaint Link-up might prove to be unwise. The more talk, the more chances of leakage, he had said. It was best to keep the landlords in the dark about the charges brought against them until the day of the Struggle.

"You and your Petty Favors! You expect you can buy my heart that easy?" Feng struck a pose, standing with one hand on his hips, the other outstretched hand jabbing at T'ang's nose. But his delivery was poor. His voice, almost a whisper, would rise in sharp jerks and fall off again uncertainly. Sun Fu-kuei did his best to help him out with the slogans, like the chorus in a Szechuan opera, joining in at the end of a singer's line to help prolong the last note.

"Smash up Feudal Landlords!" everybody yelled after Sun.

"Farmers all over the world are one family!"

"We support Chairman Mao!"

"Follow Chairman Mao all the way!"

After a rousing round of slogans, when it was quiet again, Feng seemed to have forgotten what he had to say. For an awful moment he and T'ang just stood awkwardly side by side on the platform.

Then somebody below shouted, "Why isn't T'ang Yü-hai kneeling? He's got no right to stand on this platform!"

A man fetched two mud bricks. The two militiamen holding T'ang by the back of his blouse, pushed him to make him kneel on the bricks.

Feng pulled himself together and rushed forward, seizing T'ang by his collar. "Don't think you can get by just by kowtowing, T'ang Yü-hai! We've got to settle our accounts today. Five years ago when my dad died, you pretended to be so kind and helpful, didn't you? Said you'd lend me money to buy the coffin. Once I get into this *yen-wang ts'ai* I can never pay it back. Not to the end of my days! Isn't that true? Speak out!"

T'ang kept still, facing the audience with bowed head. Kneeling, he looked taller than when he was standing up. He was so close to the edge of the stage that Feng could not get in front of him and could only direct his attacks at his profile. The golden smoke of slanting sun drifted across the tableau they made. Pale blue dust floated in slow waves down the broad beam of sunlight which had lit up the stage as it had always done in the past whenever there was a show on. The villagers watched with a vague sense of surprise and unreality. Some of the troupes coming to play here were pretty down-and-out but the costumes had never been so ragged.

Feng repeated his charges about the *yen-wang ts'ai*. From where he stood, Liu thought he detected a faint flicker of expression cross T'ang's half hidden face. He fancied it was meant to show scorn or cynicism but such expressions were foreign to T'ang; he succeeded only in looking bitter. Feng must have seen it too. He again stopped short.

"Don't be afraid of him, Feng T'ien-you!" Sun shouted from below, not using his loudspeaker so as to be more distinct. "Just say whatever you have to say. You have the backing of the Masses!"

Flushed and angry, Feng gave T'ang a violent push, knocking him off the bricks so that he sprawled in a heap on the platform. The Positive Elements in the audience started to yell, "That's right! Hit him! Hit that bastard son of a dog! Hit that mistress of a dog! Pull him down here—give everybody a chance at him!"

The two militiamen helped T'ang get back to a kneeling position. This time Feng slapped him and spat in his face.

"Let's all spit on him!" Several men clambered onto the platform.

T'ang bent forward as much as he could, tucking his head under him to shield it from the rain of spittle, mixed with blows. His face was set in a mulish calm, at once guarded and remote, as if thinking that all they could do was wet his feathers, while the real him was wrapped into a small package tucked in the bosom of his blouse.

The struggle against the prisoner had reached its climax. A high conical white paper cap was slapped on his head. Written on it was the slogan "Exterminate the Feudal Forces." Then he was led down the platform to give way to another landlord. When all the landlords had been Felled in the Struggle, the big white banner across the stage was taken down and hauled off by two men holding it stretched out between them by bamboo poles. The banner headed a parade out of the lot and through the village. The militia marched behind it, taking with them the landlords wearing their conical caps. The villagers, each in his own group, followed in their wake, shouting slogans. After the parade the landlords were sent back to the school to be locked up again.

5

AFTER the Great Struggle Meeting the work entered its tensest phase. In another mass meeting called on the next day, a Committee for the Survey of Land was elected to judge the quality of all the land around the village. The Land Reform Workers helped calculate the number of acres. The abacus rattled and clicked from morning till night at the co-operative and those students who did not know how to use the abacus had to do long sums in arithmetic. They also had to calculate all the back wages and the amounts owed by the landlords through generations of exploitation.

Chang Li left all this routine work to the Corps members while he assisted the *kan-pu* in the other half of the work of getting the landlords to pay their debts—the part called *Wa Ti Ts'ai*, Dig for Bottom Wealth.

Quite a number of Corps members were now living in the school. All of them had moved out of the village in a hurry like Liu Ch'üan, their former hosts having been promoted from Rich Farmer or Middling Farmer to the rank of Landlord. They slept in the school office far from the back courtyard, but they often heard the shrieks at night. Nobody dared ask questions though they all knew it was the *kan-pu* working at the Digging for Bottom Wealth.

Chang Li looked very pleased when he told Liu, "T'ang Yü-hai has admitted that he has fifty silver dollars buried underground. There's probably more than that. Don't make the mistake of looking down on those people. They may not look like much, but as they say, 'Better to be fat inside than fat outside.' That's why the intellectuals like you are easily taken in by them." He chuckled.

Liu forced a smile. "I suppose you can't tell from the way they live. The Tangs certainly live very frugally."

"Sure. That's what I'm telling you—looks don't count. Besides, when you think they live poorly you're still judging from your city standard of living."

Sun Fu-kuei came into the room. "Shall I take him there right now, Comrade Chang? His family might dig it up before we do and change the hiding place."

"Didn't he say he's the only one who knows? And anyway, if they were to dig it up they would have done so before now. Okay—you might as well go and see."

"Comrade Liu," Sun turned to Liu and said, smiling, "You've stayed with them, you probably know the house well, every nook and cranny. How about coming along?"

Liu felt Chang looking at him with a slightly amused air, probably thinking that he would again commit Tender Emotionalism and try to get out of it. So he answered at once, "All right, let's go."

Sun brought four militiamen with rifles. Liu also got a battered old musket to carry. They took T'ang out of the dark room in the back courtyard. One of the militiamen held the rope looped around his right arm and leg. T'ang's clothes were spotted by dust and blood-stains and he hobbled much worse than when Liu last saw him at the Struggle Meeting. His eyes were almost closed in his swollen face. Liu doubted if he had enough wits left to know his former lodger was among the guards taking him to the village.

As they came into T'ang's courtyard Liu could hear T'ang's wife hissing breathlessly inside the window, "Erh Niu! Dad is back!" She came running out of the house. Nobody paid her any attention as they marched T'ang in and the woman seemed afraid to speak to them lest she should say something to make them change their minds and take T'ang back.

To Liu's surprise the room seemed much the same as before. Two bundles of fuel-straw lay on the ground before the mud stove. There was T'ang's long pipe in the little recess in the bumpy wall. Only the room had a flashy and dishevelled look with all the glaring white slips of paper pasted slanting every which way like price labels over the furniture, the kitchen utensils, the doors. Erh Niu stood a little way off, looking at them with her hands wrapped tight in her worn black apron. She made no sign of recognition when she saw Liu.

"Go get a hoe," Sun said to T'ang's wife.

The woman exchanged a nervous look with her daughter, then turned to Sun with an uncertain smile. She had thought of that time when somebody in the village had done wrong and a *kan-pu* had hit him on the head with a hoe, killing him with one stroke.

"Ma, aren't the hoes and ploughs all sealed up?" Erh Niu said.

"That's right," her mother said quickly. "They're all sealed up in the shed, Comrade Sun. We dare not touch them."

"Nonsense! When I tell you to get it, of course it's all right. Now go get it! Quick!"

T'ang's wife still hesitated. But after one look at their rifles Erh Niu decided that they wouldn't need a hoe if they had wanted to kill T'ang. She ran to the shed where they kept the grindstone and all the farming implements, broke open the sealed door and fetched a hoe. A militiaman took it from her.

"Close the door," Sun said.

Erh Niu and her mother watched them thrust the hoe into T'ang's hands.

"Now dig, and be quick about it." A militiamen gave him a kick from the back.

"Take that broom away," Sun said, and they took the broom from where it stood at the back of the door and threw it across the room.

"Dig for what—*t'ien na*, heavens!" T'ang's wife quavered.

T'ang lifted his hoe and as it swung down heavily, he tottered forward after it and nearly fell.

Liu felt he had to do something. "Here, let me have the hoe." Leaning his rifle against the door he grabbed impatiently at the hoe. "And tell him to get out of the way. It'll take all day, the way he is digging!"

Erh Niu must have realized that he was doing T'ang a good turn. Her face became more set in its closed, resentful look.

T'ang seemed afraid to let go of the hoe. Raising it high overhead he brought it down again blindly, tottering forward with the stroke. Liu would have got hit if he had not ducked and stepped aside. However, T'ang had not been a farmer all his life for nothing. He was handy with a hoe even when he was unsteady on his feet. It did not take him long to dig a shallow hole in the dirt floor behind the door.

With the door closed the room was darker than ever and the smell of turned earth was strong. T'ang's wife suddenly went cold with a new fear. Could it be that they were making him dig a grave for himself?

The loose earth piled in a half ring around the hole rose higher and higher. The militiamen stood around leaning on their rifles, kicking idly at the small lumps of earth. Sun went and sat down on a bench by the table. Lifting an earthenware teapot with both hands, he drank gurgling from its mouth. Then he loosened his belt and walked over to the hole, watching with the others. Presently he demanded, "How come there's still nothing at three feet deep? Is this the spot or no?"

T'ang leaned forward panting, resting on his hoe.

"Speak!" Sun said. "Speak the truth! Where is it buried?"

When the question had been repeated many times T'ang finally mumbled, "Don't know."

"'Don't know!' Didn't you say distinctly you have fifty silver dollars in a jar buried behind the door?"

"Fifty silver dollars!" his wife exclaimed. "Where have we got any silver dollars, my old Lord Heaven? Where did all this talk come from?"

"Enough, enough! None of your acting!" Sun told her. "It's plain that you've dug it out and buried it somewhere else. Now get it out quick."

She started to weep and bawl. "Get what out? Never even heard of this much money in all my life! Whenever he had any money he bought land with it. And last spring we went into debt buying that piece of land from the Kengs. Now whoever heard of anybody paying interest for borrowed money when he has big handfuls of silver buried underground?"

"How should I know how you people figure things out? Anyhow, whatever you don't know, you always know how to act poor. That's one thing you people are good at."

T'ang seemed to be frightened by all this bawling and had started to dig again.

"*T'a ma ti*—he sure can play the fool!" Sun happened to turn round and saw what he was doing. "What you digging for, when you know it's not here? What kind of an act is this? *Ma teh pi!*"

The more Sun yelled at him, the more industrious T'ang became. Stroke by stroke he patiently widened the hole.

"*Ma ti!*" Livid with rage, Sun kicked at him, sending him staggering back, nearly knocking over a militiaman and finally falling half in and half out of the cavity, with the pile of loose earth slithering in after him.

Sun turned again to the woman but she swore there wasn't a single silver dollar in the house that she knew of. After a fruitless search of the house Sun said, "Let's go. No use talking to them. These people—they're the kind that 'won't weep till they see the coffin.'—Now you be careful, T'ang Yü-hai. This time when you go back there, you're not going to be let off that easy. You and your tricks! Who's got time to fool around with you, digging at your dunghill?"

T'ang's wife and Erh Niu followed them into the courtyard. On their way out Erh Niu suddenly caught hold of T'ang and pressed her face against him, weeping loudly. "Dad, why did you lie?" she cried. "My dad is a tough man, he never lies. What have you done to him? Dad, what's happened to you, dad?"

T'ang said nothing. Half of his face gave a little twitch when his salty tears soaked into the open cut across his cheek.

The militiamen pushed Erh Niu off with curses, but she butted her head against one of them, yelling, "I'm going to have it out with you people! Today I don't feel like living!"

"This slavegirl!" her mother cried out desperately, trying to hold her back. "This slavegirl!"

The butts of several rifles were hitting at the girl's head and body. "Ai-ya, help! Help! Please, the child is an idiot—don't mind her, just this once—" shrieked her mother, and when Erh Niu was knocked down she fell over her, shielding her with her body. "Let her off this time—I kowtow to you! I kowtow to you!"

Liu stood staring from the door of the house. Without quite knowing what he was doing he had cocked his rifle, aiming it at the group. Then he lowered it when he saw Erh Niu raising herself on her elbow. She spat on the ground, making a dark red stain dotted with several white things which must be teeth.

"You're looking for death!" a militiaman panted as he continued to kick at her. "Looking for death!"

"Let's go," Sun said impatiently. They took T'ang back to the school.

6

THE NEXT day Liu was among the Corps members sent out to measure the fields and look into the matter of Black Land, hidden, unreported land. When they came back in the evening he heard that all the landlords had been sent to the *hsien* prison. There wasn't much hope for them once they got sent up to the *hsien*, village. The only ones left were Han T'ing-pang and his wife, who were still detained in the back courtyard of the school. Liu was surprised to learn this because Han was definitely a genuine landlord. How was it that he alone got special treatment? Then he learned that it was because they had forced Han to write to his relatives for money to pay back what he owed his tenants for exploitation going back for generations. Han had written urgent letters to his father-in-law in Peking and the old man had sent some money but nothing like what was expected. So they were still making him write letters. They had high hopes for him.

After the events of the past three days Liu wanted nothing more than a moment alone with Su Nan, if only to talk over all those things that shocked him so deeply. But there were always so many eyes and ears around. That was a part of living the Collective Life.

The *hsien* government sent them a message saying that the landlords of Han Chia T'o had been tried and sentenced and were going to be shot the next day. The village militia and the Land Reform Workers' Corps were invited to send representatives to witness the execution.

Chang and Liu were among those chosen to represent the Corps. The next day they started out before dawn, walking all the way to town. The mass execution was to take place outside the city wall, but as they hadn't been in town for a long time they took the opportunity to go shopping on the main street for toothpaste, soap and sweets.

The morning sun shone down the empty yellow dirt street, spotted here and there with mule and horse droppings and bits of straw. All the little shops had mud counters. When they finished shopping they came across a street barber who carried all his implements on a flat-pole. Liu took off his cap and felt his hair. He needed a haircut, so he stopped the barber and sat down on a stool by the wayside. The pharmacy he sat in front of had a mulecart hitched near its door. The mule chose to urinate just then, splashing noisily right into the barber's brass basin placed on a low washstand.

The barber cursed richly. The pharmacy was built around a big tree. Half of its scaly black trunk bulged out of a side wall. The huge forked branches stuck out of the roof and the sun had lit up the treetop. When Liu looked up he saw two golden green leaves drifting down against the blue sky, scratching the rows of black tiles on the roof and then floating slowly down until they finally landed among the little black heaps of short hair at his feet. It was early in the day and nobody was in a hurry. And yet for T'ang Yü-hai this was the last hour. When Liu thought of this he felt the edge of the barber's razor cold against the back of his neck.

After he had his haircut he went with two other Corps members to find Chang Li at the *hsien* Public Security Bureau. But Chang had already sent somebody out to find Liu. When Chang saw them he came up to them calling excitedly, "Where's Comrade Liu Ch'üan? Hey, Comrade Liu, there's a new task for us! Here's a letter from Peking. The two of us are to go back right now. We're assigned to a new task."

Chang was evidently as surprised as Liu was by the order. The Organization had mentioned him and Liu in the same breath. Either he was slipping or Liu had considerable backing. In which case he had made a mistake in continually reminding Liu of his place, putting on the airs of an old *kan-pu* in front of him. Now he tried to make it up by suddenly getting very chummy. Sending away the other two Corps members on some excuse, he showed Liu the letter from Peking. It said they were to wind up the task at hand as soon as possible, come back to Peking for instructions and start south immediately to report to the East China Branch of the Resist-America Aid-Korea Association in Shanghai.

"Haven't seen the papers for a week," Chang said. "Just now I borrowed some newspapers from the people here. There's this new Resist-America Aid-Korea movement going on. Everybody's in it."

He showed Liu the week-old newspaper. It carried the Joint Declaration of the various Democratic Parties. "The American imperialists have started a war of aggression against Korea on June 25th of this year," the statement said. "Their dark schemes absolutely do not end with the destruction of the Democratic Republic of Korea—they want to take possession of Korea, they want to invade China, they want to rule Asia, they want to conquer the whole world ... As everybody knows, Korea is a comparatively small country, but its strategic position is very important. In invading Korea the purpose of the American imperialists lies principally not in Korea itself but in the invasion of China, as the Japanese imperialists have done in the past ... The people of the entire nation are now extensively and enthusiastically asking to be allowed to struggle, through voluntary activities for the holy task of Resist-America Aid-Korea, Protect the Home and Defend the Country."

While Liu was reading the newspaper, Chang put an arm around him and whispered, "We better go back early today—there're so many things that haven't been settled. It's best to see to the more important points before we leave. Let a thing drag on unattended, and it might become a real problem, don't you think so? Those village *kan-pu* are no use. *T'u pao-tzu*, mud pies, all of them. Nothing inside them but earth."

Liu made affirmative noises absentmindedly. He supposed that a *kan-pu* of the Revolution had to be psychologically ready all the time to be whisked off to another post a thousand miles away on short notice. But being new at it, he scarcely knew what to think except that he would be leaving Peking. He had thought that after they got back to Peking he would be able to see more of Su Nan. He hadn't realized how much he had counted on it.

"It's time now!" The other two Corps members bustled in. "Come on, let's go."

The *hsien* militia had taken the prisoners out of jail. The throng of invited spectators trailed behind them through the streets and out of the town gate—representatives of the *kan-pu* and militia of the surrounding villages and country towns.

The prisoners walked in single file, the ends of the thick ropes looped around their ankles tied together to make one long rope dragging in the dust across their pale shadows on the sunlit ground. Each one of the condemned wore a white placard giving the name and the nature of his crime. It stood on a little stick of split bamboo stuck into the back of his collar. Liu's eyes found the placard marked "T'ang Yü-hai, Feudal Landlord." T'ang was still wearing his dirty white blouse though the weather had turned cold. The placard stood high and erect out of his collar, above his drooping head. The thin white paper on its frame of split bamboo rattled in the cold wind.

Some of the townspeople also trailed along to see the execution. There was a clearing just outside the city wall. The captain of the town militia shouted "Halt!" to the guards and then, "Right turn!" From a marching column the prisoners had turned into a horizontal row facing the fields.

The militia ranged themselves in a row immediately behind them, aiming the rifles at their backs in case anyone should try to break away and run.

"Kneel down!" shouted the captain.

Some of the prisoners were dazed and slow in obeying. But one after the other, they all knelt.

The row of militiamen behind them started to walk backward to the bark of "One, two, three, four, five..." Ten paces away they stood still, then knelt on one knee and took aim.

Bang! the noise of all the rifles going off at once was not very loud in the open fields. Still, it sent all the birds flying up from the trees, and the purplish gray watch-towers on the city wall.

Then there was an unexpected sound, high and quivering. Several of the prisoners lying face downward on the ground were shrieking and twisting about on the stained grass and tearing it out by the roots.

"Again! And aim carefully this time!" the captain shouted, red with anger, feeling that he had lost face in front of all the village *kan-pu*.

But his men did even worse the second time. Owing to the scarcity of cartridges they never did have much chance to practice shooting. And they were too nervous now. Their targets were no longer a row of tame, obedient backs. Instead they faced a line-up of unruly, crazily wriggling corpses, still startlingly alive after the volley.

Chang Li came forth from the crowd, drew his gun out of its holster, went up close to the bodies on the ground and walked down the row.

He looked at the captain. The captain nodded approval and stood blank-faced as Chang pointed the gun at the head of the first man on the ground, hesitated a second, and then fired. He moved quickly to the next body. It was motionless now, but Chang aimed again and fired another shot. Holding the pistol still pointed at the earth, he turned around and began to walk back toward Liu. He looked pale, but he walked steadily, almost with military precision. Thrusting the gun with its twist of red ribbon hanging from the ring on the butt into Liu's hand he said, "Come on, it's your turn. It's a hard thing to do. But they're enemies of the Revolution. There's another one over there. Let's see you dispose of him.'

Liu walked toward his victim mechanically, gun in hand. Lucky the man is lying face downward, he thought. And T'ang Yü-hai was not the only one wearing a white blouse. The placard also faced downward and he could not puzzle out the writing through the back of the thin paper. There wasn't time. He heard the bang of his shot and then, a long moment later it seemed, he felt the gun jump warmly in his hand.

The narrow body on the ground shuddered and all ten fingers dug deeper into the earth. Liu did not wait to see the man grow still.

He shot at him again, two or three times, and stopped only when the pistol gave an empty click. He had been afraid that the man would twist around in his agony and show his face.

He walked back and returned the gun to Chang.

"Not bad! You've certainly got it in you!" Chang put an arm around him and patted him.

Liu walked off to watch the men from the Public Security Bureau making arrangement for putting the bodies on exhibition before the townspeople. He wiped the sweat from his face while nobody was looking. Even if it had been T'ang Yü-hai, all he had done was to put him out of his misery, since he was as good as dead anyway. There was no call to feel as he did.

Chang wrangled a lift for all of them aboard a truck going to Paotingfu. They got back to Han Chia T'o village in mid-afternoon. The execution had made Liu forget that this was the day for *Fen Fu Ts'ai*, the Distribution of Floating Riches. All the landlords' clothes, furniture and household goods had been concentrated in Han T'ing-pang's courtyard because it was the most spacious. "Better have a look—these mud-pies have probably made a botch of it," Chang said. They hurried over to see.

The courtyard was like a bazaar. Chairs and tables were piled together, and earthenware jars of all sizes, wooden buckets, wooden basins, padded blankets, brooms, wooden boards for chopping meat and vegetables, tiered baskets for steaming bread, mats for the *k'ang* trimmed with blue or black cloth. All the articles were soaked through with a deep dark indoor odor from years and even centuries of usage, so that they smelled strange under the blue sky and sun. The jostling, sweating crowd milled around, breathing garlic. "Ai," Liu thought. "Even when they have nothing else to eat, these bumpkins always stink of the stuff."

Amid the great din and confusion the Land Reform Workers were busy examining papers, affixing seals, handing out articles. The original idea had been that the People should draw lots for everything. But Go Forward Pao said, "The thing a person draws may not be what he needs. Our motto should be: *ch'üeh sha, pu sha*; Supply

Whatever is Lacking." So they asked every family to fill out a form listing in order of urgency the things that they needed most. Every case came up for discussion at the unit meeting. The unit then decided what to give in each case and issued a paper to be exchanged for the piece of goods. Thus the situation remained open to the manipulation of a few *kan-pu*. Some of the People complained behind their backs, "If we'd known it's going to be like this, we'd have voted for drawing lots, then trade around. That's the fairest way, after all." But there weren't many saying that. The majority were philosophical about it. "It's not so bad, considering that you're getting something for nothing," they said.

Liu saw Su Nan standing in a mat booth distributing padded blankets. Hsia Feng-ch'un, the Party Branch Office Propagandizer, got one of green cloth printed with small, starry white blossoms. He was distressed to find it quite old and worn and insisted on giving it back and getting one of his own choice. Su Nan refused to take it back. He argued endlessly and was getting crimson in the face and neck. Liu waited by the booth for a long time. He was anxious to tell her that he would be leaving in a day or two. But she wasn't free to talk to him and finally he had to walk away.

A farmer pushed by him holding a clock of imitation black marble with the minute hand missing. Some of his neighbors were admiring it but the man kept shaking his head helplessly, with a tinge of sarcasm in his smile. The farmers always had been contemptuous of this kind of gimcrack. Maybe it was partly out of self defense because they could not afford such luxuries. What they really coveted were the good strong plows, the spades and kitchen knives, the pots and pans and big jars.

Liu saw Sun Fu-kuei coming with a bamboo pole and ropes, happily stringing up a huge brown jar and carrying it away on his flatpole. The jar looked familiar to Liu. A bit of the blue-green glaze on the rim had been chipped off. It must be the Tangs' water jar. When he saw Sun squatting before it on the ground, tying the thick ropes crisscross around it, he could not help remembering that time Erh Niu had looked into the water at her own reflection and the pink flower in her hair had fallen into the water. Then he thought of T'ang Yü-hai coming back from the fields, dipping water out of the jar, drinking from the gourd dipper and spitting it out to wash his hands. Where is T'ang Yü-hai now, he thought. Here somebody is going off with his jar.

He was tired out by the long hike in the morning and by the rough ride home. His body ached all over as if he had taken a beating. He felt dazed and numb, holding off events he did not want to think about. He pushed his way out of the crowded courtyard, thinking that he would go back to the school and lie down for a while.

Han T'ing-pang's house was the only brick house along the lane. He could see T'ang's house as he turned the corner. He understood that two other families had moved in there but Erh Niu and her mother had been allowed to stay on in the shed. He wondered if Erh Niu was badly hurt from being beaten by the militia the other day. As he passed by the house he saw that the worn black-painted folding doors were wide open and two new mud stoves had risen from the levelled earth of the courtyard. The afternoon sun lay warm and still on the two mud steps that led into the blackness within the house. Nobody was around. Of course, everybody must have gone to see the Distribution of Floating Riches, except Erh Niu and her mother. If he should slip in and see them now, maybe nobody would know.

A yellow hen emerged into view, lifting its feet high to step across the cucumber creepers trailing on the ground. Poking its head suspiciously left and right to make sure that it was alone, it finally mounted the steps and with infinite caution, walked into the house.

He must go in and ask about Erh Niu. For all he knew she might be dead. "You should care," he told himself. "You've just killed her father." Because he knew the man he killed had been T'ang Yü-hai, though he hadn't admitted it to himself.

He turned abruptly from the door and quickly walked away, nervous at the thought that he might run into Erh Niu or her mother if they should be coming out or going home just now.

The school office was littered with makeshift beds, just boards set on benches. He lay down on his bed. Nobody was in. They were all helping at the distribution.

The room darkened long before dusk, so that the paper windows seemed to grow steadily brighter. He watched the dirty yellowed paper gradually turn pale. He felt as if he had been ill all day as he lay without moving in the unlit room, with the whole courtyard to himself. Darkness descended on him in downy black flakes.

Then he saw a shadow pass across the whiteness of the paper window. A moment later somebody was standing at the door. Though the person had her back to the light he could tell it was Su Nan. He sat up.

"You're back," she said with a small smile.

He stood up. "Do come in. Sit down."

"I heard them say you'll be going back to Peking in a day or two. I want to ask you to mail a letter for me."

He took the sealed envelope from her. It was addressed to a Mrs. Su in Peking. "Is that your home address?" Liu said.

"Yes."

He went on studying the envelope. "May I write to you?"

"Of course. And come and see us when you have time."

"I won't be staying in Peking. Chang and I are going to Shanghai."

She seemed startled. "You're going to Shanghai?"

"To do Resist-America Aid-Korea work. I don't know yet just what we'll be doing."

After a moment of silence he stepped across another bed to get to the table. He poured out a cup of tea from the pot in a tea cozy woven of greasy yellow split rattan. "Better have some tea."

Su Nan stood leaning on a corner of the decrepit table. She pulled out an empty drawer, closed it and rattled it open again, looking into it.

Liu said, "I wanted to tell you as soon as I came back this afternoon." Then he said, "I've wanted to talk to you all this time. There're so many things that I feel I have to talk about."

"Me too. I'm so bottled up. The way things are done—I, I just can't get used to them," she said bitterly.

She did not see the shadow of a man that had appeared on the window behind her. Liu tugged at her sleeve to stop her from speaking. In his haste his own sleeve tipped over the teacup. He caught hold of the cup but the tea ran all over the table.

The shadow moved slowly past the window, carrying with it a misty yellow fuzz of light. It turned out to be Old Han, the school janitor, bringing a candle on a clay candlestick.

Liu snatched up Su Nan's letter from the wet table and looked at it in the candlelight. The ink had run, blurring the characters on the envelope.

"That's all right," Su Nan said. "Just change the envelope."

"I've got one here." He found an envelope and a pen for her. "You better take the letter out first and see if it's wet."

She tore open the soaked envelope, took the piece of folded paper out and read it. Liu was surprised to notice that the paper was almost blank, with only one or two lines of writing on it, and that a sprawling scribble, obviously written in a great hurry. For a moment he suspected that her purpose in writing this letter was just to let him know her home address.

She wrote on the other envelope and wetted her finger tip in the spilled tea to seal it up. Then she carefully peeled the stamp off the old envelope and stuck it on the carved window frame to dry.

"I wonder where you'll be working. Maybe not in Peking either," Liu said. "But if I write to your home, you'll always get the letter, won't you?"

"Yes, they'll forward it to me." Crumpling the spoiled envelope into a ball she used it to wipe the table. But first she moved his cake of soap and packet of toothpowder to a dry place. "Did you buy these in town today? I forgot to ask you to get me a piece of soap."

"The fact is, I won't need any of those things, since I won't be here. I wish you'd make use of them."

She took the toothpowder and rolled over the top of the paper packet, crimping it up until the paper became too thick and stiff a wad to be turned over. Printed on the packet was the trademark, the full view of a large multi-colored butterfly crudely painted but warm with color in the candlelight.

There were voices and footsteps out in the courtyard. "Where's Old Han? Hurry up with supper, Old Han. We have a meeting after supper." Several Land Reform Workers came into the room.

"What meeting?" Liu asked.

"The Farmers' Association meets tonight," one of them told him. "Probably because Comrade Chang is leaving and some things will have to be settled ahead of schedule."

"Hey, Liu Ch'üan, exactly when do you expect to leave? And where are you being sent to?" The others crowded around him, full of envy and a new respect.

"I better go and get my supper," Su Nan said and hurried off, taking the toothpowder and soap with her.

7

THE MEETING that night mainly concerned reporting to the District Government about the Fruits of Struggle. Most of the Land Reform Workers, without quite knowing what it was all about, had caught on to the idea that the report would be a delicate matter, hedged about by the hidden strife and tension among their leaders.

It all started with the grain discovered in the hollow wall of Han T'ing-pang's house. The Hans had a hired man, Miao Yung-so, who went to the Land Reform Workers' Corps with the information that one of the walls in Han's bedroom was hollow, with bags of rice, wheat, and *kao-liang* flour and maize stored inside. A search proved him to be right and the foodstuffs were confiscated.

This find was made just as the Land Reform Workers and the *kan-pu* were in the midst of reclassifying the village population as part of the preparatory work before the division of land. Miao, the hired man, belonged to the Destitute Class, one grade below a Poor Farmer, and therefore entitled to get more land. As an informer he should have been promoted another grade, which would make him Special Class, equivalent to the Soldiers' Families, even better than a Destitute. But Go Forward Pao bore Miao a grudge because once they had quarrelled while gambling during the New Year. Now he said Miao had never been Positive and seldom came to meetings. So although he was Destitute, he was not a Respectable Destitute. So in the end Miao barely made the grade as a Poor Farmer.

Chang naturally considered this confiscated grain as Fruits of the Struggle, to be entered in the Fruits Account and reported to the District Government. But Go Forward Pao kept putting it off, saying the villagers insisted that, instead of handing it all over to the government, it should be split up among them. He persuaded several Positive Elements in the village to go around stirring people up, clamoring for their share. If the grain was divided among the villagers, the amount everybody received would of course remain under Pao's control. He needed something too, just then, to sweeten up the Positive Elements. They were the only ones who ever made any noise. Once their mouths were stuffed with food, there would be no danger of anybody complaining of unfairness when the land was divided among them in another week or two—the great event everybody was waiting for.

Chang didn't let on he had guessed all along this was what Pao had in mind. But now when he came back from the *hsien*, knowing he would be leaving, he called a meeting of the *kan-pu* at once. At the meeting he told them, "For us who work among the Masses, the first requirement is that we must have the power of discrimination. Without judgment, Comrades, we cannot fulfill the tasks Chairman Mao Tse-tung has entrusted to us. We ought to listen carefully to all the kinds of voices that come from the Masses and be able to tell the difference. This time, for instance, there's a lot of talk about concealing the grain, not reporting it. Now it seems to me this chatter is not the real opinion of the Masses. It's just one or two Bad Elements trying to make trouble, taking advantage of the Backward Thought of the Masses. Comrades, we'll have to find out the real source of this opinion and expose the Bad Elements before the Masses, show them up for what they really are."

Pao rightly took this as a threat directed at him. He felt a bit nervous and decided to sacrifice the two Positive Elements who had made the most noise, to identify them as Bad Elements.

During the meeting of the Farmers' Association that night, Chang pointed out to the villagers that it would be wrong not to report the confiscation. At the same time he cleared the Masses of all blame, insisting it was not their idea but the conspiracy of a few Bad Elements among them.

Pao took an active part in tracing the talk back to the Bad

Elements who had supposedly started everything. The two men dared not mention Pao, fearing his revenge. The Land Reform Workers' Corps would soon be gone, but Pao would be here the rest of their lives. There was nothing they could do except bow their heads and admit their guilt. The Masses of course said nothing. In fact some of them were quite pleased to see these Positive Elements get their comeuppance. A resolution was passed by unanimous vote that the Bad Elements were to be tied up and beaten with sticks.

Chang was set on having this business attended to before he left. Pao also was anxious to dispose of another matter while Chang was still here. It concerned the landlord, Han T'ing-pang, and his wife, who were still detained in the school. The *kan-pu* had patiently waited for Han's father-in-law to ransom him. But aside from the small sum of money in response to his first letter, further entreaties had produced no results. Sooner or later the couple had to be disposed of.

Pao had scruples, however. Being an extremely clever and observant man, even if uneducated, he knew the way the Government usually did things. At the beginning of a new movement they always encouraged the *kan-pu* to go at it with abandon, giving them a free hand. But as soon as there were enough signs of discontent among the Masses, the Government took measures to *Chiu P'ien*, Correct the Deviation. The slogan would be: "A cook can reboil half raw rice; a horse can turn round and eat the grass behind it." But in making redresses they could not resurrect any of the men they had shot, nor would they give back any of the confiscated property. The only remedy left was to punish the "over-leftist" *kan-pu*. The imprisonment or demotion of a few low-ranking *kan-pu* was a small price to pay for bolstering the Government's support. Pao did not worry much about the promotion of the Rich Farmers and Middling Farmers to the rank of Landlords, and their subsequent execution. Chang had been in charge here when this took place. If Han T'ing-pang and his wife were to die, it had better happen while Chang was still around. Then it could be blamed on Chang if there should be any trouble later on.

So Go Forward Pao secretly approached Han's tenants and told them to go and make a row outside the jail. They were to complain that all the other landlords had been executed while Han alone had been spared and they remained unavenged. Everybody in the village knew about Pao turning against his own accomplices, and Han's tenants were afraid of falling into the same trap. But they dared not try hedging or bargaining. Their spirits were broken when they saw with their own eyes T'ang Yü-hai and the others being taken to town to be shot.

The next afternoon while Chang was in the school office checking over the accounts of the Fruits of the Struggle, he heard people shouting in the back courtyard.

"*Ma ti*, that bastard son of a dog is certainly getting off light!"

"So unfair! Everybody's had their revenge except us! We—want—our—revenge!"

"Drag the turtle's egg out of there and do him in right now!"

"Kinsmen, kinsmen!" It was Go Forward Pao's voice pleading with them, smooth as silk. "You go home first and wait a few days. Wait till I Reflect your Opinion Upward. Anyhow, you can rest assured that the Government's opinion will be the same as yours, because yours is the opinion of the Masses. Don't you worry!"

The more he pleaded, the louder they yelled.

"*Pu hsing!* Won't do! The Government is too generous! The dog's bastard has been having an easy time!"

"We've waited long enough! When is he going to pay back the money he owes us?"

"Get him out of there and let us do the questioning! If we aren't paid at once, we'll string the turtle's egg up!"

Pao rushed to the front courtyard to get help from Chang. "What shall we do? Han T'ing-pang's tenants are kicking up a row. They want to take the two of them out and *ta li kan t'a-men*, do them in with great force."

Chang looked up from the accounts and scratched his head with an inverted pen. He was alert enough to notice how the disturbance died down as soon as Pao came over to the front courtyard.

"Han's tenants—aren't they the same people who refused to go and get the land deeds from him that time? They've certainly made progress very fast." He smiled at Pao. "What made them so Positive all of a sudden?"

Pao smiled back at him. "Well, however dead-brained they may have been, I should say they have awakened by now. Seeing with their own eyes the Great Struggle Meeting going off with a bang and all those landlords shot, they know that the world has really changed—it's a poor man's world now."

"Hmm, yes." Chang had to nod, smiling. Turning to the other Corps members in the room he said, "You see, the Masses have really risen! Now that the Masses have risen, we mustn't be frightened and shrink back and become the Masses' Tail."

"Right!" Pao said quickly. "I'll go and get all the other comrades; we'll all go and look on. We'll pump gas into them, all right."

All the Corps members were summoned to the school. Chang met them below the stone steps in the front courtyard and gave a little speech to prepare them psychologically before they went in to watch what was going to happen.

"We are not one-sided humanitarians. As it has been so well-put by Chairman Mao, 'The Revolution is not a dinner party; it's not writing, or painting, or embroidery. It can't be so refined, so unhurried, so elegant, so gentle, polite and modest. The Revolution is an act of violence by which one class overthrows another. A short reign of terror has to be created in every village in the country. Without this, the activities of anti-revolutionary forces in the country can never be suppressed, and the power of the gentry can never be overthrown.' We should also remember another of Chairman Mao's sayings, 'To correct a wrong we must go further than what is just; without excesses we can never correct a wrong!'"

After his explanation everybody looked at his neighbor, a bit jittery and at the same time childishly curious and excited. As they trooped into the temple, heading for the back courtyard, they passed the schoolroom where the children were having their lesson. The teacher read one sentence from the book and all the students repeated after him in a tuneful chant, swaying their bodies sidewise on the benches. The afternoon sun was on them and the voices were drowsy. As the Corps members walked past and the shrill monotonous chorus gradually receded behind them, they had a strange feeling that they had left behind the world they knew.

All of them tried to find the right expression upon entering the back courtyard—just the right shade of gravity, dignified without being funereal. As they approached the low flight of stone steps they saw that a thick rope hung down from the eaves. It hung loose, swaying a little in the breeze. Several tenant farmers were standing around, looking nervous. The atmosphere was thick, as if somebody had hanged himself here and the body had just been taken down and removed.

All the Corps members stood waiting under the eaves. Go Forward Pao and Sun Fu-kuei also came. Then several militiamen dragged a middle-aged woman out of the windowless room at the back where they kept the firewood. It was Han T'ing-pang's wife, heavy with child, wearing a striped gray blouse and pants, streaks of her bobbed hair plastered by sweat to her bruised, sallow face.

"You Big Feudal Exploiting Landlord! Facing death right now, and you don't know enough to be afraid!" a Positive Element shouted. "We've been too polite to you all this time. You don't seem to appreciate it. You want to be Reactionary to the very end. Today, if you still won't *t'an pai*, confess, we're going to take your dog's life!"

Though the woman hung her head, it was impossible for a pregnant woman to look humble. She looked infuriatingly proud and overbearing with her belly thrust far out.

"Tie her up! We'll 'string up half a pig' for her!"

"Look at the slut," the Positive Element shouted. "Old enough to be a granny. And she's still breeding brats for old Bloodsucker Han."

Several Positive Elements directed the tenants to push her down on the ground. Quickly they tied her left arm and left leg together with the rope that hung down from the eaves. When they pulled at the other end of the rope, she went up in the air, left side up. Then they tied her right arm and right leg together and hung two heavy wooden buckets on the leg.

The woman began to moan and mumble indistinguishably, begging for mercy. The sun coming in under the eaves lit up the top half of her body, hanging head down. A fly flew through the sunlight, turning gold all over. It circled and settled on her nose, which had been beaten into a blob.

They had a tubful of water ready. Two tenants lifted it between them and started to pour water a little at a time into the buckets hanging from her leg.

"Ai-yo! Ai-yo!" Her groans rose higher and her face gradually came alive with pain as more water splashed into the heavy buckets. The fly slowly flew away.

"Quick, *t'an-pai*, confess! Where's the rest of your money? And your jewelry? Where did you hide them?" a Positive Element shouted at her.

"Ai-yo! Ai-yo!" She kept changing the tone and pitch of her groans as if trying to find in certain sounds a momentary relief, however slight.

"Quick—speak! Speak and you'll be let down. You can go home right now if you *t'an-pai*. Where's the money? And the gold? The gold rings?"

"There isn't any!" she panted. "Ai-yo, there really isn't! Ai-yo, my ma! Ma-a ya! I die of pain! Can't bear it any more!" With her head hanging upside down, the skin on her face was drawn up so that she looked much younger. Her eyes were bright and she seemed to be grinning.

The Corps members consciously avoided standing too close to one another; it might appear they huddled together in fear. They were not so much afraid as ashamed and repulsed at the sight of the pregnant woman strung up in mid-air like a lumpy, triangular rice cake. They tried not to shuffle their feet or stir uneasily.

"Well? Are you going to *t'an-pai* or aren't you?"

"Ai-yo, I'm wronged, I'm innocent! Ai-yo, what sins I must have committed in my last life, to deserve such a death!"

"Think you're going to die now? That easy?" Pao could not help laughing out loud.

"Come on, hurry it up!" Sun said. "We've got to break through this fort of bigotry today."

"Ah…" A sudden long shriek sailed high in the air. The sound was so coolly clear and shrill, for a moment it was difficult to tell where it came from.

There was not much water left in the tub, but the tenant who had lifted it suddenly found it too heavy for him. It half slipped out of his hand as he set it down with a thump, splashing water on his feet.

"Speak! Speak quick! Any gold?" asked a Positive Element.

"*Yu, yu*; there is, there is! Ai-yo, spare me! There's a gold ring!"

"Where's the gold ring?"

"There's a gold ring! Ai-yo, ai-yo! Spare me, *t'a yeh*, master!"

"Where is it? Speak, quick."

"Can't remember—Ai-yo! Let me down so I can think—"

"You'll be let down as soon you've said where it is."

"In the hollow wall! In the hollow wall!"

"Nonsense! The wall has been searched. Even if it were a needle we'd have found it."

"Then there isn't any left," she said, panting.

"All right, so you won't talk—you're asking for it! Reactionary to the very end!"

The rope with pig's bristles woven into it was biting deep into the swollen flesh of her wrist and ankle, tied together. The groans had stopped.

"*Ts'ao t'a nai-nai*," Sun swore. "Fainted!"

"Splash water on her face," Pao said.

A tenant reached down for the tub and emptied it over her face, flooding the stone floor. Water dripped down from the tips of the greasy strands of hair.

"Ai-yo! Ai-yo!" The groans resumed, only they were more like sighs or just the sound of outgoing breath. Her eyes, now dull and half open, were the only lusterless things on the glistening wet face.

"*T'an-pai*, quick! Otherwise I, your father, will be at you again!—*Ma-ti*, no more water!"

The man looked around and happened to spot in the crowd a little boy he knew, who had apparently sneaked out of the schoolroom to watch the free show in the courtyard. "Hey, Keng Hsiao-san, Little Number Three Keng," the man called out. "Go get a bucket of water!"

But the child was frightened. He turned and ran, dropping his head between his shoulders.

"*Hsiao kou t'ui*, little dog's leg! Landlord's spawn!" the man cursed.

"I'll go." Another man picked up the bucket and walked down the steps.

"Ai-yo! Ai-yo!" With eyes closed, the woman seemed lulled by her rhythmic groans.

Liu stood rooted with his hands in his pocket. He had held his fists tight all this time and his arms had gone to sleep. When he tried to change his stance he found he could not take his hands out of his pockets and had to slowly unfold his fingers first.

"Why does he take so long?" the Positive Element grunted. "I'll go and see." He pattered down the steps. The little boy was still hanging around the courtyard, reluctant to go back to his classroom. He was squatting at the foot of the wall in front of a large rock, trying to tilt it back with one hand to look for crickets underneath. Seeing him, the Positive Element suddenly changed his mind and strode over, bending over him to lift the stone. The boy again scurried away, frightened.

"*Ma-ti*, since we're at it, might as well have our fill," the man said. Holding the boulder with both hands he walked up the steps and threw it with a loud thud into one of the buckets hanging beneath the woman. The crowd gave a shocked cry as the water splashed over them. If the woman screamed, it was drowned in the din. But after the general tumult there was silence, in which a kind of lapping sound could be heard, curiously gentle and yet heavy, like ducks' feet paddling in shallow water. The body still hung there, but blood was flowing down the trouser leg to the foot and wrist bound together, then dripping to the ground below, the crimson wisps slowly fanning out in the water on the floor.

The bucket was still swinging from the impact of the boulder. The woman's body swayed with it, head down, turning now this way, now that way, but aloofly, with a disinterested, far-off air. The wind fingered the greasy strands of her hair.

Pao was the only one who spoke after the pause. "*Ma-ti*, so quick!. Certainly had an easy time! Come on, let her down and carry her out."

All the Positive Elements and tenants crowded forward to help untie the rope. Liu saw Su Nan looking around dazedly. He walked up to her quickly and propelled her down the steps, holding her by her elbow. "Let's get away from here," he heard himself saying.

He took her out of the school. It would only take a few minutes for them to get back their self-control, but right now he felt they had better go where nobody was watching. Walking down the mound, they crossed the road and went into the fields. Somehow it was surprising to find it was still daytime and the sun was still out. The brownish yellow fields extended all the way to the far horizon. The warmth of the sun on their backs, interlaced with cold whiffs of autumn wind, began to make things feel more real.

He was walking after Su Nan on a footpath when she half turned around and, without taking her eyes off where she was looking, whispered to him, "What's that?"

A mule was pulling a cart around a field in circles, occasionally shifting course abruptly. City-bred, with no knowledge of farming, they could not tell what function it served. There were some people standing on a foot-path shouting, but at this distance they could not hear what they were saying. The cart seemed to prefer to run over the stumps of chopped off trees in the waste field. Otherwise it seemed quite aimless in its erratic circling, unless that was a plough attached behind it. But, it was not a plough; it was a long grayish black bundle dragging on the ground. A moment later Liu realized that it was a man. He had heard of a form of punishment called *nien ti kuntzu*, grinding the earth-roller. This must be it. The man was Han T'ing-pang then.

It seemed to Liu and Su Nan as they stood watching that the

mule cart was whirling around like a truck out of control and might rush at them crazily any moment. Su Nan suddenly turned and walked away, dragging him after her. She knew what was going on. Her fingers felt cold against his and hard as sticks.

They walked swiftly to the village wall, turned with it and kept walking. After they had gone some distance they stopped, flattening their backs against the wall. They felt all hollowed out as if all their insides had been taken out. The setting sun had turned the great stretch of mud wall behind into a bleak pale orange.

They settled back against the wall without moving. Then Liu found that they were still holding hands. He drew her hand toward him but she seemed hardly to notice it, though finally she did turn round to look at him.

Liu suddenly put his arms around her, pressing her face hard against him as if to squeeze out all the sights and sounds of the world outside.

"Su Nan," he whispered. Then he said, "Su Nan, I'll never forget you."

She neither moved nor answered. But after a while she abruptly lifted her head to glance at him and then looked quickly away as if displeased. "You sound as if we're never going to see each other again."

"All right, then I'll forget you," Liu said smiling. "I'll forget you as soon as my back is turned."

Though her face was turned away from him he could see her cheek sticking out roundly, so he knew she was smiling.

He kissed her. For a moment he shut out the things he had just seen.

"When are you leaving? You're lucky to leave!" Su Nan said.

Instead of answering, he just held her tighter.

With her cheek pressed against the top pocket on his tunic she could hear paper crackling in his pocket. She rubbed her face against it a second time to hear the crackle.

"That's your letter," he told her. "I really don't feel like posting it. Once it's sent off there won't be any."

"Then take it with you to Shanghai and mail it from there."

"Won't your family think it's queer if they get a letter from you and it's postmarked Shanghai?"

She smiled. "Well, you're going to get some mail yourself. Don't worry."

"But you can't write me until I've written to tell you my new address, after I've got there. Figure out how long that will take. At least three weeks."

It was impossible to kiss and have a good look at each other at the same time. With an effort he drew back to look at her, holding her at arm's length. "The first time I saw you, we were all singing on the truck, remember? I listened hard, trying to tell your voice from the others!"

"My voice is no good."

"Your singing voice is higher than your ordinary voice, but it's beautiful, too."

Su Nan looked down and started to laugh, leaning her forehead against his chest.

"Why do you laugh?"

When he had asked for the third or fourth time she said, "I never sang that day. I just opened my mouth and pretended."

They both laughed a long time, unable to stop.

"I guess we're both a bit hysterical right now," Liu said.

Abruptly they stopped laughing and leaned their heads back against the wall. They turned to look at each other. Liu could not help thinking that if the smooth mud wall were to tilt back to become the *k'ang*, and he were to see her face like this every night and every morning, his days would be safely locked in happiness at both ends and it would not matter what happened in between.

So he made a resolution which was so simple he felt it was ridiculous. He must do a good job from now on in the hope of getting promoted step by step in the hierarchy of *kan-pu*. When he had attained a rank equivalent to that of a regiment commander he would be allowed to marry. What he had seen in the village had been brutal. But there had to be excesses during a Revolution.

"I may come back from the south very soon," he said to Su Nan. "And then of course, it may take a long time. But in any case, within a few years I think I can manage to arrange for both of us to work in the same place, then we'll always be together." He tried to turn her face toward him. "Say something. Say it's all right."

At his insistence he felt her nod slightly against his shoulder. After that she seemed unable to face him. He had to force his mouth on hers. There was nothing left except the small sound of the wind in the grass, stirring uneasily on the edge of their consciousness. Someone might come any moment. The long withered grass made a chill rustle like a crusty old centipede crawling, dragging its rows of legs along the ground.

"You had a haircut," Su Nan said. "I was wondering what made you look different."

"Yes, I had it cut in town yesterday."

"No wonder you look like a country bumpkin." She reached up to stroke his hair. The next moment they were apart, walking side by side along the wall at a respectable distance from each other. Footsteps and voices had turned the corner behind them. It sounded like Sun Fu-kuei and one of the Positive Elements.

Liu and Su Nan thought they might go somewhere else and talk. When they reached the end of the wall and hesitated before turning into the main road, they saw that the lamp had been lit at the co-operative store. They had not realized until then it was getting dark.

Somebody waved at them from the window of the co-operative. "Liu Ch'üan! Comrade Liu! Comrade Chang is looking for you! Something about the Fruits Accounts."

Liu had to go inside. And once there he could not get away. That evening he was entitled to retire early, since he and Chang would be leaving early next morning. But he displayed what Chang extolled before the others as "matchless passion for work" and sat up half the night in the co-operative with Su Nan and the others, clicking an abacus.

Returning to the school he packed up and then went to sleep with his clothes on. He had scarcely fallen asleep when he was awakened by Chang. It was still pitch dark. The school janitor brought in a lamp and their breakfasts. Go Forward Pao, Sun Fu-kuei, Hsia Feng-ch'un and several other *kan-pu* came to see them off, fighting for the right to carry their packs.

"We feel so bad that you have to leave in such a hurry," Pao said with all the wistfulness he could muster. "Just when we've really got acquainted."

"We hate to leave too," Chang said, wringing his hand. "Everybody has been so affectionate. Real comrades!"

"It's too bad you can't stay to see the finish of the Reform," Sun said. "We were planning a big celebration. A lion dance and a show and stilt walking."

"We have Feng T'ien-you," Hsia pointed out. "Best stilt walker in these parts."

Again Chang experienced the urge to slap the man's stupid face. Ignoring Hsia, he clapped Pao and Sun on the shoulders. "Better turn back now, all of you. You still have lots of important work to do."

"No, don't send us back," Pao begged. "Give us a few more pointers. We'll feel so lost without you."

"No! Don't be so modest," Chang said. "It's we who have learned a lot from you."

"We feel like walking you to the *hsien*." Sun said.

"Well, 'Even if you walk with us a thousand miles, in the end we still have to say goodbye,'" Chang quoted sentimentally.

After more such exchanges, they finally parted outside the village.

"Hope you come back. Drop in on us any time!" Pao shouted, waving.

The sun had not yet risen. Pink and orange clouds striped the sky. The dark earth beneath the high heavens looked even flatter than usual. The thin, wavering sounds of distant cockcrows rose like smoke all along the horizon.

As he walked Liu kept peering into the fields in the half light. The sight of the short stumps of felled trees made him feel jumpy. The birds were chirping loudly with the coming of dawn. If there had been anything like what he'd seen yesterday sticking to the stumps, it would be picked clean by the birds.

Looking away from Chang's back ahead of him, he noticed a shadow squatting in a waste field. It looked vaguely like a woman digging for sweet potatoes. Something made him look back when he had gone on for a short distance. In the increasing light he was almost sure now that it was Erh Niu.

As they went on walking and the cart track gradually sank, the rising dirt banks on either side blocked off the view. The earth smelled wet with dew. Liu found himself walking along a passage filled with the faint dull fragrance of soil, slightly suffocating. The terrifying countryside was at last shut out. Maybe he was never to see it again.

He suddenly said to Chang, "You go on ahead. I have to stop and relieve myself."

Walking in the ditch Chang wouldn't be able to see him unless he specially spied on him.

Liu ran back onto the plain and went behind a tree. From there he peered down the road to make sure nobody was looking.

Erh Niu seemed frightened when she saw a man in uniform racing toward her. Pulling her tattered blouse across her breast she half stood up as if getting ready to run.

"Erh Niu! It's me!" Liu called her name for the first time. "How are you? You all right? I've been wondering how you were."

Erh Niu squatted down again indifferently, digging into the ground with her bare fingers.

He stopped in front of her under a tree waiting to get his breath back. Then he said to her. "I'm going away right now. I won't be coming back."

While she still said nothing, she raised a hand and poking her fingers into her matted hair, gray with dust, tried to comb it with her fingers. Much of her hair had come loose from her pigtail, falling about her face and onto her shoulders. Combing it, she suddenly seemed to realize that all the mud and dirt on her fingers had got into her hair. She dropped her hand quickly.

"I'm worried about you," Liu said.

She seemed to have forgotten again and started to comb her hair with all ten fingers.

"Erh Niu—" He was going to say how sorry he was and now he hoped she did not think too badly of him. "Tell your mother that I've left," he went on to say. "Tell her I'm sorry I wasn't able to help you. I feel very bad about it."

The sun had risen. On the yellow-lit tree top and all over the branches, hard little green dates stood out against the light amidst the sparse foliage. The dates were pointed at both ends and the green was just beginning to be flushed with an orange tint. She had laughed at him before for not knowing what date trees looked like. He still wouldn't have if it hadn't been for the dates.

He stood under the tree not knowing what else to say. "Erh Niu. You're still very young," he finally said. "Young people should never give up."

She shook her head slightly. It could mean that she would not give up. But then two lines of tears coursed down her cheeks and she rubbed at her face with the back of her grimy hand.

For a long time he did not speak. Then he said without moving, "I've got to go now. Take care of yourself."

She lifted her head, looking at him for the first time and, with a smile, nodded slightly in quick dismissal. With her front teeth knocked out her grin was at once childlike and shocking.

He turned round and walked off at a brisk pace, overtaking the leaves of the date tree that fell off and skidded rustling ahead of him.

8

IT WAS like being shut inside a gramophone cabinet, cooped up with the pounding, grinding rhythm. Loudspeakers on the train blared out Liberation songs and Soviet music from morning till night without intermission. No matter how fast the train hurtled on, it could not shake off the envelope of music, could not throw off the strong sweet gummy strands of sound. Loose ends of melodies flapped outside the windows and over the top of the cars. The train sped across the dreary sallow flatness of north and central China in a flash of strident song.

When it was getting dark and the lights were turned on, a girl's high silvery voice called through the loudspeaker, punctuating her speech with rhetorical pauses, "Supper—is now—beginning—to be served.—Supper—is now—beginning—to be served."

Next she rattled off a series of seat numbers. Passengers in *juan hsi*, soft seats—a new term to substitute for the bourgeois-sounding "first class"—were to go to the dining car in shifts according to their seat numbers. Passengers in *ying hsi*, hard seats—equivalent to the second or third class of the old days—would eat later.

Chang Li and Liu Ch'üan were in hard seats. They had not had dinner yet when the train stopped at one of the smaller stations and the peddlers walked past the carriage windows, tempting them with cold donkey meat, mutton jelly, hard-boiled eggs and cartwheels of inch-thick flat-cakes. Not many peddlers were allowed in the stations nowadays and they were made to wear special aprons, for fear there might be enemy agents among them.

"Look," Chang said to Liu, pointing at a "blackboard newspaper" that stood on its wooden stand in the dimly lit station, facing the train. They could barely make out the chalked bulletins, windblown and faint, on the shiny black-painted board. "It's praising the railway workers." Chang said. Leaning forward he read out with relish, " 'In the past few days workers on this line have been clamoring for Patriotic Overtime in addition to the old Shock Attack Overtime and Competitive Overtime which have, in themselves, already achieved spectacular results. Our Passenger-Affairs Officers think nothing of working 27 hours at a stretch. Since the beginning of this month there have been three cases who worked over 30 hours at a stretch, and two cases more than 35 hours. There have even been cases of over 39 hours.' Isn't it great?"

"I don't think it's right just to go after efficiency alone. The workers' health should also be taken into consideration," Liu said.

"I dare say the leaders don't approve either. But what can they do about it?" Chang said. "This is just the workers' voluntary, spontaneous passion for work, I tell you. I understand it's like that now in factories all over the country. Isn't it great? You can't imagine what a difference it makes to the worker's morale, to know that he's Liberated now and his own master."

Liu murmured agreement. He wondered how much of this Chang believed. The train started to pull out of the lighted station. The stationmaster and all the porters and peddlers, white-aproned men and women with baskets on their arms, were lined up in a row, standing at attention to salute the departing train. This was another new custom, probably adopted from the Russians. Chang thought it was a rather touching little ceremony. "See how devoted they look," he said. "It's right that all workers should learn to respect the machines under their care."

When they returned from their dinner, the other passengers were either napping or trying to read newspapers under the weak yellow overhead lights. The music was more deafening than ever. Fortunately, Chinese are not too susceptible to noise.

The girl on the loudspeaker suddenly screamed. "The great— Huang Ho—Iron Bridge—is ahead!—is ahead!—The great—Huang

Ho—Iron Bridge—is ahead!—Let's heighten—our watchfulness!
—Let's close—all the windows!—Let's defend—the Express!—Defend—the Huang Ho—Iron Bridge!"

Everybody stood up and all the windows were banged shut. But Liu's window stuck. Chang, who sat near the aisle, leaned over to help him and when it was no use, shouted for the porter. "Passenger-Affairs Officer! Comrade Passenger-Affairs Officer!"

The porter was not in sight. But a soldier of the Liberation Army had appeared, shouldering his rifle, pacing slowly down the aisle and back again.

Liu continued to wrestle with the window. The wind was very strong because of the train's speed. The man in the seat ahead spat out into space while attending to the window next to his, and the spittle was blown right back, drops of it sprinkling on Liu's face. He frowned and felt for the handkerchief in his pocket.

His hand froze inside his pocket. He had noticed that the soldier had stopped by his seat, holding his rifle tensely. He dared not take his hand out. The soldier was obviously afraid he was reaching for a hand grenade which he was going to hurl at the bridge.

The thundering and clattering of the wheels were amplified, now that the solid ground had given way to the bridge. In the blackness outside the window, big diagonal crosses flashed jerkily past in succession—the silhouetted bridge rails. In a moment the last cross had disappeared and the thundering rattle of the wheels subsided back to normal. The soldier, though still watchful, lowered his gun. Liu forgot what he had wanted the handkerchief for. When he pulled it out of his pocket he just wiped the sweat off his forehead.

"Comrades!" the loudspeaker was again screeching girlishly. "The Express—has now—triumphantly—passed across—the Huang Ho—Iron Bridge!—Triumphantly—passed across—the Huang Ho—Iron Bridge!"

She sounded as if they had just won a battle. Liu began to wonder if there were very many accidents along this line. If the rails were blown up by guerillas or special agents and then repaired again, the newspapers would naturally neglect to mention it. The bridge must be a particularly crucial point.

But Liu did not really believe there was much of this kind of thing going on. More likely, the authorities were jittery because they believe in being perpetually on guard against everyone.

The Passenger-Affairs Officer had turned up with a soot-encrusted kettle, adding hot water to everybody's tea, as if in celebration of their safe crossing of the bridge. The man wore a wrinkled dark blue Liberation Suit like everyone else, but with a white armband. He was lanky, young and dull, yawning in people's faces as he leaned over their tables. Working his way down the aisle he weaved a little with the motion of the train, holding on to the back of seats.

In time he stood sleepily before Liu's table, lifted the cover off Chang's glass with one hand, his other hand holding the big kettle high, to shoot a foot-long arc of water into the glass. But he missed it and watered Chang's leg instead.

"Ai-ya—ai-yo, ai-yo! *T'ung ssu le!* I die of pain!" Chang jumped up shouting, bumping the kettle out of the man's hand, splashing the scalding water all over the feet and ankles of both of them. He yelled louder. The Passenger-Affairs Officer was also howling now.

"He's done it on purpose!" Chang's eyes were red with fury and tears. "*Hao chia-huo!* Boiling water—and he looks you in the eye and just pours it over you! I'll be darned if he hasn't done it on purpose! I'm going to speak to the comrade responsible for the train. There are saboteurs around!"

The Passenger-Affairs Officer just squatted on the floor moaning and wailing, unable to speak.

"*Ma-ti!* Must be a spy!" Chang shouted. "*Ma-ti!* Have you any idea who I am—who my father is? Why, you almost killed me! The Revolution still needs me—you know that?"

"Let it go, Comrade Chang, let it go!" Liu stood to help hold him up. "Better go to the medical room right now. Get the Hygiene Officer to put on some medicine and bandage it for you. The sooner the better. Delay might be dangerous—really. Let me handle this creature. Just leave him to me. Don't worry, he can't run away. If he jumps off the train it's his funeral."

Still shouting abuse, Chang hobbled toward the medical cubicle at the other end of the train. The two Hygiene Officers were women and not bad looking. After they had applied the medicine and bandaged his leg and both his feet, he stayed to chat and they asked him to be sure to come around again tomorrow to change the bandages. With another cozy chat in the clean-smelling little cubicle to look forward to, he was more or less pacified when he returned to the carriage.

Everybody was already in bed. The backs of the seats had been turned up to make upper berths. Liu had taken the upper to save Chang the trouble of climbing.

Unbuttoning his tunic, Chang sat down on the lower berth, crouching because there wasn't room. The floor under his feet was glistening wet; it had probably been wiped with a mop. The air smelled of the dirty mop.

The railway authorities no longer took pains to segregate the sexes in the arrangement of sleeping berths. There weren't any curtains over the berths either. This was one of the very few changes that had been made quietly, without any publicity. While it had occasioned some whispered complaints, it was perhaps not altogether unpopular. Chang glanced at the girl on the opposite berth. She had her face to the wall and her long hair fanned out over the pillow. She was muffled up to the neck in a woolen blanket. Spread out over the blanket, her padded, dark blue Liberation jacket looked enormous. Gray flannel trousers were spread next to it, in the right order. Still, she was not in her jacket and trousers but underneath them. It made a difference.

It would be still better after he had lain down, when the three-foot gap between their pillows could easily be bridged by his imagination. But part of his anger returned when he remembered that, by going away to have his leg attended to, he had missed seeing her undress.

"*Ma ti*, see if I don't give the Railway Bureau a piece of my mind," he said loudly to Liu, partly for the benefit of the other passengers. After what had happened to him, it would really be face-losing if he were to keep quiet about it. "All this Patriotic Overtime, Competitive Overtime and what not, extending the working hours on and on and on. Who's to be responsible when there are accidents? The leaders—all they know is to ask for '*hsiao mieh shih-ku*, the extermination of accidents.' How can they avoid accidents when they go at this rate? The passenger's life and limbs have no protection at all, I tell you!"

Liu did not answer, pretending to be asleep.

The loudspeaker was silent at last. The monotonous click of the wheels was soothing in the unaccustomed quiet. Travelling light now without the music, the train rushed on, smooth, heavybodied and indifferent, occasionally with one of its segments pushed up a little as if shrugging. There were miles and miles of the same black night ahead.

9

LIU COULD not remember who it was—some old Chinese writer—who had said about the unhappiness of leaving someone you cared for, "Even if I go to the ends of the earth, I will be sleep-walking." There was an unseeing, unfeeling grayness in going among strangers. And in his case they would have to remain strangers because he dared not really talk to any one. The things he was experiencing in Shanghai now only became real to him when he pictured himself telling them to Su Nan. Not in his letters, of course, but some day, when he saw her again. It got so that sometimes right in the middle of an event, while it was still happening, he could hear his own voice telling her about it.

There was that time he had gone to the office of the *Liberation Daily News*, the biggest newspaper in Shanghai. His own office, the Resist-America Aid-Korea Association, had sent him there to ask for some photos of American atrocities in Korea. They had wanted the pictures for the *China Pictorial*. Comrade Ko Shan, the head of the Reference Department at the *Liberation Daily News*, had told him to wait while she went to look for them in the reference room.

A Chinese typewriter tapped slowly and hesitantly in the next room. Desk phones kept ringing. Employees rushed around, light on their feet, bending over to whisper to colleagues at other desks. The room was dark because it was so big. All the desk-lamps had already been turned on. On Comrade Ko's desk the lamp under its green glass shade shone full on a bright pink blotter, a large pink rectangle as spotlessly clean as a woolen sample, only much larger.

"Looks like the Reference Department hasn't got much work to do," Liu told himself while waiting.

From what he had heard, there wasn't much to do at any of the newspapers, though it was hard to believe that, when witnessing the scene of hushed activity around him. All the news was supplied by the Hsin Hua News Agency. It was easy for the editors; even the headlines were supplied. Reporters had become obsolete. They could not interview important personages and were not wanted at law courts and scenes of murders, rapes and robberies because the papers no longer carried such stories on the assumption that these things were just not done any more.

Liu supposed that it was the same in all the big organizations. He could not say he was exactly overworked even if the hours were long. Much of the time was spent in meetings and waiting around for meetings and in Self-Improvement. He had to start out for the office at six o'clock in the morning to attend the Newspaper-reading Class at seven, one hour before going to the office.

Liu had been sitting by the desk for a long time. He looked across the vast room. The green desk lamps seemed to float in the semi-darkness like lotus lanterns set drifting over water on the fifteenth night of the seventh moon, All Souls' Eve. Then he saw Ko Shan coming in, walking among the green lamps. He was surprised that she reminded him strongly of some stage or film actress he had seen, though he could not place the actress at the moment. Perhaps it was just her carriage, the combination of self-possession and self-consciousness peculiar to actresses.

She had one of those pretty moon-faces hollowed out at the cheeks. Her eyes under half-closed lids had what was traditionally known as the smoky look—as if veiled by smoke or distance. Her hair had been permed but she had allowed it to grow long and straight and merely pushed it behind her ears. It fell over her shoulders in rumpled half curls. A green-striped shirt collar showed above her dark blue double-breasted Lenin Suit, slim and belted, with trousers.

She did not fit in with his idea of an old *kan-pu*. But she was certainly holding too responsible a position for a new recruit. Of course you could not tell. Sophistication in appearance could also be a mark of rank. Some of the men *kan-pu* above a certain rank had dropped their uniforms for foreign suits and the women had blossomed out with new perms and colorful Russian shawls. But he doubted that Ko Shan was that important.

After she sat down at the desk he realized why he had not thought she looked anything extraordinary when he first saw her. In the bright light of the table-lamp she looked rather faded and drawn and was only pretty on and off, in flashes, with a toss of her head, a smile or glance.

She sat looking over the photographs before she passed them to him. They were good clear snapshots, dark in tone, with an air of authenticity. The first picture showed a soldier standing with hands on hips beside a tree. He was visibly blond. A half-naked woman was tied to the tree. Another soldier was bending over, picking up twigs to pile at her feet, apparently to build a fire.

Liu turned the picture this way and that in the lamplight, examining it closely. If there were signs of faking he could not see them. "How in the world did they manage to get this picture? It's very valuable—just what we need" he said.

"German soldiers. That's all we've got here," she said carelessly, without smiling.

"German soldiers?" He was slightly bewildered.

"During the War against Fascism— Yes. You'll have to make the woman's hair darker," she pointed at it with her pencil. "It doesn't look very black."

The woman in the picture looked distinctly Caucasian. "Where was this? In Europe?" Liu asked, and at once realized the superfluity of his question when she just ignored it.

"The hair will have to be darkened. And you'll have to make some small changes in the soldiers' uniforms," she said. "Here's a picture from a foreign magazine of American soldiers drilling. The uniform is shown quite clearly. You can refer to it."

"But—" He did not know what to say. "We haven't got anybody who can retouch photos," he finally said.

"It doesn't take an expert," Ko Shan said, smiling. "Even the professional retouch man at the photographer's can only draw eyelashes on women's eyes, one by one, like rays of the sun in children's drawings. Not much use in this case."

Liu was silent as he flipped through the half dozen pictures.

"Let's see the first one again," Ko Shan said. "Oh, yes—" she tapped on the woman's breasts with her pencil eraser. "You can blacken this part to show that these have been cut off."

"Blacken it—entirely?" Liu said uncertainly. He imagined it would look like a black brassiere he'd seen the lacquered girls wear in the ads in the second-hand American picture magazines he used to look at once in a while when he was a student. But he was too embarrassed to tell this to the woman officer he stood beside. He looked down at the part in her hair and saw the white skin underneath.

"Well, perhaps not entirely. In big blotches, maybe, so it will look like bleeding wounds. Use a bit of imagination."

Seeing that he still looked troubled, she added reassuringly, "It really doesn't matter how you do it. You know how our printing is at its present stage, making great strides but still room for improvement. The picture will probably come out blurred enough so that you won't be able to tell what it's all about. You'll have to rely mainly on the caption. The caption has got to be arresting and to the point."

"Yes, of course," Liu murmured as he wrapped up the photos.

Ko Shan tilted her head back and looked at him with a half smile, her eyes pale and distant. "Maybe you think: what's the difference between this and the lies and distortions of the imperialists?"

"Of course there's a difference," Liu said blushing.

"Well, what's the difference?"

"A difference in the essential nature of the act." Sometimes it was best to be brief with an air of finality.

She continued to look at him with a faint smile. He was beginning to think that he would have to do better than that. But then she dropped her eyes to the rubber tip of her pencil with which she was tapping the table. "Yes," she said, adopting that flat casual tone which Liu found seasoned Communists often employed when they did not wish to sound preachy. "First of all, we definitely know that the atrocities of American soldiers in Korea are absolutely a fact. And when we publicize that fact, it's not enough just to rely on verbal reports. The Masses demand that reports should be—you know—Concretized. Therefore photos are necessary."

"Right. I agree with you completely." Putting the pictures away quickly, Liu stood up to go.

She remained seated, eyeing him in a half-smiling appraisal. Liu again wondered how she stood in the Party, whether she was in a position to comment on him to his superiors, adding some damaging remark to his record.

Quite abruptly she held out a hand across her desk, half rising, flashing at him a Party-mannered smile, wide, bright and warm, clean to the point of being sterilized "We'll keep in touch," she said.

10

"COMRADE Liu! You're wanted in the meeting-room!"

Liu turned from his desk and saw Comrade Ho, the Culinary Officer, standing at the door of the front office holding a baby in his arms, the two-year old boy of Ts'ui P'ing, Liu's superior. Ho had been an army cook and had been with Ts'ui for years. Because his Revolutionary History was long, although he still did a cook's work after the Victory on All Fronts, he now enjoyed the living allowance of a battalion commander, eating well and drawing more pocket money.

"Warm day, isn't it?" Chang Li looked up from the papers he was working on. He always made a point of being friendly with Ho.

"Sticky as hell. Nothing like this up north," he grunted. Summer uniforms had not yet been issued. Ho had unbuttoned his lumpy padded uniform of soiled light yellow cloth all the way down the front, showing his bare chest. Jolting the baby up and down, he walked up to the tall window. They were high up in one of the few skyscrapers in Shanghai. The city below was a sea of gray and red bricks, mostly gray, in a tumbled-down, widespread heap. Chimneys and boxy little Western-style buildings pushed up darkly here and there.

"Living so high up," Ho muttered. "Bad for a person. No wonder my feet get all swollen. They're hanging in mid-air all the time."

"Must be awful for you to be cooped up here all day," Chang said sympathetically. "But when you go to the market you can stretch your legs a bit, huh?"

He snorted. "That's only a few steps away. Not enough to get the smell of earth back on your shoes."

Liu put away the blurry snapshots he had been retouching with a Chinese brush. Taking a writing pad he hurried off to the meeting-room at the other end of the corridor. He had heard that some Democratic Personages were coming down for a meeting this afternoon. He would be acting as recorder.

Ts'ui P'ing's wife was already there to play hostess. She was talking to the only woman among the Democratic Personages, and probably the only woman lawyer in Shanghai. Ts'ui's wife headed the secretarial department and was known by her maiden name Chu Ya-mei. It was no secret around the office that Ya-mei had been a peasant girl in the old Communist area in Shantung while Ts'ui had been a college student when he joined the Revolution. She was a blooming young woman, a little thickset but otherwise attractive, with bobbed hair that swept forward from behind her ears making a thin black crescent on each of her wide pink cheeks.

The guests were drinking tea. Nobody was looking when a small door opened on the far side of the sofa and Ts'ui and two of his aides trooped into the room. All the guests stood up in some confusion. After a round of hand shaking the three newcomers sat down by themselves on the sofa, rather stiffly and evenly spaced, with Ts'ui in the center. Ts'ui was young looking in his immaculate black woolen uniform. According to the unwritten rules his position did not as yet warrant his wearing foreign suits, although he was already expected to wrap himself in a certain amount of mystery and drama, like making surprise entrances.

After chatting for a while, everybody went over to the long table and the meeting got down to business. Liu took the humblest corner seat at the far end of the table.

The guests did all the speaking. It was understood that Ts'ui and his wife were only sitting in on the meeting, and were not to speak unless the situation called for a little steering. Ts'ui took a little brocade box out of his pocket and got out a seal of chicken-blood stone, which looked something like soapstone but had deep crimson blotches. He looked it over and then fumbled for a toothpick to clean the engraved lines, which were clotted with the dry vermillion ink. He was not being inattentive. Attending meetings was something like breathing; Ts'ui had learned to take it easy. His face was pale and oblong, with three-cornered long black eyebrows. He was irritable, even querulous at times, but Liu thought, looking at him from across the table, that there were worse bosses.

Seals were the newest craze among the *kan-pu*. When Liu had first come to Shanghai last winter, Ts'ui had used wooden chops on documents subjected to his approval. Now he had a collection of seals of good stone or ivory to choose from. The fad was started by a Shanghai businessman who hit on the idea of giving his *kan-pu* friends something other than Parker pens and wrist-watches— something really distinguished and personal. No matter how jittery about taking bribes a person might be he need have no qualms in accepting a seal with his own name beautifully carved on it.

The speakers droned on. Once when Liu looked up from his notes he saw that Ts'ui had put away his seal and was blowing his nose with what appeared to be a striped handkerchief. He must have stared, because Ts'ui hurriedly thrust it back into his pocket, and Liu realized that it had been a sock. Lately, as the weather warmed up, Ts'ui was in the habit of removing his shoes and stockings as soon as he sat down anywhere, and scratching between his toes. Long ago he had contracted athlete's foot from long marches and life in the country. Most of the old *kan-pu* suffered from the same thing, and when they sat down they invariably drew up one of their legs, to scratch their toes.

Ts'ui's drawn-up knee showed above the edge of the table. His face, leaning against the black-trousered knee, looked absorbed. But it seemed to Liu that somewhere about him there was a mocking swagger that showed he was not totally unconscious of offending petit-bourgeois fastidiousness. Liu felt he ought be ashamed of himself. After all, athlete's foot was as much an occupational disease of the Revolutionist as tuberculosis was.

Ts'ui's hand appeared above the table, reaching for the glass of tea in front of him. Liu was also drinking his tea. At the sight of Ts'ui's pale fingers curled around the glass, somehow the tinny smell of the weak tepid tea revolted him. He put down his glass hastily and never touched it again.

At the end of the meeting Ts'ui and his wife and his aides stayed behind to talk to the Democratic Personages while Liu left the room with his notes.

There was nobody in the front office. His mind still on the meeting, he returned to his desk. But this was not his desk. His desk was a big dark one designed for two people to sit face to face across it. Now a small orange-tan one stood in its place. A wide crack ran all the way across the top and there were grains of sesame in the dusty split.

The desk-lamp, paste jar and ink-stand and some of his things and Chang's had been moved to the windowsill. He pulled open all the desk drawers a little wildly. Where were the photographs he had been working on? Those were probably the only copies in the whole country. He did not like the idea of having to tell Comrade Ko Shan at the *Liberation Daily News* that he had lost them.

He dashed out into the hall. He knew where to find Chang. He would be in Comrade Ho's cubicle down the hall, sitting on the Culinary Officer's bunk smoking and chatting away. Ho liked to talk about the old days and gossip about his superiors. And Chang, probably believing that knowledge is power, was always interested in Tsui's doings, his wife, his favorite dishes and general likes and dislikes.

"Found a bit of ink from his new carved seal on his shirt. Thought it was lip-rouge," Ho was saying when Liu came to his door. "*Haugh!* Such a big row! Talked about divorce. Such a row! The Organization had to send a Big Old Sister to talk her out of it—"

He stopped when he saw Liu. He had no use for a non-Party member. He did not ask Liu to come in—not that there was enough room for three persons. He had a cheerful little place. An office boy had slept here when it had been the office of a foreign firm. The lower half of the peeling whitewashed wall had been pasted over with foreign Sunday comic sheets—*Donald Duck, Bringing Up Father* and *Terry and the Pirates*. He had put his padded military coat on a hanger, hooked on a nail above his bunk. Then he had hung his spare cap on the nail. The coat and cap blocked off part of the gaily colored horizontal strips of comics. The clothes looked like a giant lumbering across fairyland, his head dipping forward between his shoulders.

"Comrade Chang, what's happened to our desk?" Liu asked.

"What do you mean—something happen to our desk?" Chang asked fuzzily.

It seemed to take a lot of explanation for Chang to understand what had happened. Liu could tell from his vagueness that Chang sensed trouble and was trying to keep out of it.

"No, I have no idea," he said. "That's funny. Better ask Comrade Ts'ui or Comrade Chu—I suppose they want it somewhere else. Did you see them anywhere?"

Of course he knew very well they had been at the meeting. Otherwise he wouldn't be playing truant. Chang had been sort of letting himself go lately. Liu knew that it was because their job here was as much a disappointment to Chang as it was to him. In the beginning they couldn't help but let it go to their heads a little, to be singled out in the country and sent down to Shanghai to work at Resist-America Aid-Korea, when there was already a vast organization there doing just that—but evidently not to Peking's satisfaction. True, they had not been charged with any secret mission. But the summons had spoken for itself. It had looked as if they both had bright careers in front of them.

When they first came, the Shanghai office must have wondered whether they were *kan-pu* low in rank but in direct contact with High Places and had been planted here as spies. Liu felt ashamed recalling he had been surreptitiously pleased at their attitude, half suspecting they were right—after all, they ought to know more about such things than he did. But the staff had obviously changed their minds and now did not hesitate to show the two of them exactly where they stood. Liu had read that "The ranks of our propaganda workers are one and a half million strong." A very depressing statement. How on earth could he ever hope to win distinction and get ahead?

Liu went to look for the coolies. Some of them must have helped to move the desk. He hoped that nobody had cleaned out the drawers yet.

He passed the office of Comrade Ma, whose husband was in charge of personnel. The door was open and he thought he saw his desk inside.

"Excuse me, Comrade Ma," he looked in and said to the woman, who was walking up and down nursing a baby through a pocket that could be conveniently opened by unbuttoning a button. She was one of those women *kan-pu* who look like little Eskimos. Even a light uniform looked thickly padded on her. "Is this the desk we had in the front office?" Liu asked.

"Yes, I had it moved to this room," she snapped at him, tossing back a strand of short bobbed hair from her oily dish face.

"Excuse me, I've left some important documents in the drawer."

She asked loudly, as Liu hurried toward the desk, "If they're so important why didn't you lock them up? Who's going to be responsible if they're lost?"

"Well, I always lock up before I leave, but just now I was only out of the room for a while, "Liu explained, "I didn't know the desk would—"

"You'd better be more careful next time," she said severely. "Working in an Organization, the most important thing is *pao mi*, Security Measures."

She continued to pace around as if unruffled, feeding her baby. But when he left the room with his photos he could sense her stopping by the desk for a moment, watching him. She probably thought he would have tried to get the desk back if she hadn't scared him off.

Comrade Ho was hovering at the door of the front office. Chu Ya-mei was in the room talking loudly when Liu came in. "All this talk of regularizing, regularizing. And here they're getting more guerilla-style everyday! It's grab and run all the time. And in broad daylight!—Look at this!"

She looked at the little desk. She was gnawing the tips of her bobbed hair as a man might chew the ends of his moustache. "How can we put this here with people visiting all the time! And there might be international friends dropping in any moment!" She had been talking a lot about international friends lately, ever since it had been known that her husband was to help entertain the World Youth Delegates who were on their way from Peking.

Chang was over at the window sorting out their belongings on the windowsill.

"Seems we only have dead people here—all dead!" Ya-mei went on to say. "What have you been doing, old Ho? What are you here for, anyway? One day the roof will be lifted from above your head and you won't even notice. All you ever do is to sit there and *la, la; la, la*." She always said "pull" instead of "chat," meaning pulling the thread of conversation to lengthen it.

She was very good at "pointing at the mulberry tree while scolding the *huai* tree," a folk-art practiced mainly among women, especially country women. The *huai* tree was Chang in this case. Liu was certainly glad he had been over in the meeting room when this had happened, or he would have been blamed for it too.

Just then a Communications Officer, or messenger boy, came in and said to her, "All sold out, Comrade Chu. *Haugh!* Never saw such a crowd! Such a long queue, it had to make three turns on the curb."

"I knew it—I knew there was going to be a big crush." Ya-mei was furious. "That's why I sent Old Ho there early yesterday afternoon. And the fool couldn't find the place."

"I waited for three hours," the Communications Officer said. "I was moving up to the door when the man came out and said there were no more. All sold out."

"Been here over a year now and can't even find his way about," Ya-mei turned and said to Liu. "I heard yesterday the government has put a batch of pickled pigs' feet out on sale, so I sent him to get some. Comrade Ts'ui has always liked pickled things.—Couldn't find the China Products Company! You don't know how many times I've told him: 'Old Ho, the city is the basic point of study now. At least get to know the roads. Learn to read the signs.'"

Liu wished she wouldn't address these remarks to him. Comrade

Ho was standing there smiling awkwardly, pulling the brim of his cap down hard, as if to make it sit more firmly on his head. He was probably used to Ya-mei's nagging but Liu knew he would resent strongly anything Liu might say and would also resent it if he should smile and say nothing.

"I didn't know the people around here are so fond of pigs' feet," Liu said carefully.

"Well, they know these are good pigs, that's why," Ya-mei said. "Pigs killed and sent north across the border. Of course people up there don't eat the feet like we do. That's why there are all those feet left. The very best pigs. Thin-skinned, really paper-thin, I hear."

"I wonder how everybody got to know about it, that they're the feet of export pigs," Liu said.

"There's no keeping things from these people when it has to do with something tasty. They always smell it out."

Comrade Ho had turned to go, thinking Ya-mei had finished with him.

"You better start in right now to learn to read and write, Old Ho," she said. "Instead of sitting around all day and just *la, la; la, la*, like an old woman."

"Oh, in the army everybody was supposed to learn Culture," Ho said lightly, to show it was nothing new to him. "But I never got round to it. No joke, marching sixty, seventy miles a day carrying three big pots on your back. The Comrade Instructor always said to me, 'Now you're the Culinary Officer. Take care of those pots as you would your own eyes—'"

"That's enough! Don't try this on me," Ya-mei said. "All this self-glorification! You've got a bad case of Deserving Official-ism, Old Ho. No longer willing to learn. And when you've made a mistake you won't even accept criticism."

He smiled, holding on to the brim of his cap. He had pulled the cap far down in front in order to leave plenty of exposed space at the back of his head for him to scratch.

For a while the bristly noise of scratching was his only way of answering.

"You teach him to read and write, Comrade Liu," Ya-mei said. "Go at him whenever you have a moment to spare. Your Standard of Culture is high. You ought to help him."

Liu wished she would stop. The smile had left Comrade Ho's face. Looking blank and unconcerned, he had half turned toward the door, shoving his opened jacket back with both hands to get a little breeze.

"He's getting on in years, so his memory is no good. You'll have to be patient with him. But you help him to make Progress, and I'll help you to make Progress—all right?" She gave Liu a big, warm Party smile.

"Certainly," Liu answered rather formally. "Whenever there's a chance I'll avail myself of your instructions."

"How are you getting on?" she asked. "How do you find the work? Not homesick, are you?" She always said the same things but she had a heartwarming way of saying them. In a moment she would be saying that they were all one big family. As a matter of fact it was true, Liu thought as he watched Comrade Ho go out the door. They were like a typical big family where it was difficult to avoid stepping on people's toes, whichever way you turned; where you often get caught between two persons and get yourself bruised for nothing.

"We really ought to have a nice long talk some time, so I can get to understand your State of Thought," Ya-mei said. "Only Comrade Ts'ui and I have been so rushed lately. But don't hesitate to come to us any time if you have any problems or anything. Don't stand on ceremony!" she said reproachfully, smiling with a light frown, giving him several impatient little slaps on the shoulder. "You're in the *ko-ming ta chia t'ing*, Big Family of the Revolution!"

She was pointedly fussing over him and ignoring Chang. It was a bad day for Chang. Again Liu thought how lucky he was to have been in the meeting room during the exchange of the desks.

Going into the adjoining office she turned round at the door. "Oh, have you got that speech ready? I don't want anything long. Just a little talk."

"I thought you wouldn't want it till Thursday," Liu answered.

"I'd like to go over it first, just to see that the Standpoint is correct."

"All right, It'll be ready in a minute. I've got most of it down."

While he was putting finishing touches to the speech Ya-mei was to give to the Women's Association of Hsüchiahui, Chang whispered jokingly, "Can't do without you for a minute. Be careful. The boss might get jealous."

"My colleagues might—before my boss does," Liu thought. He was going to say something deprecatory about his being just an errand boy, but any such remark was almost certain to get repeated to Ya-mei. He just smiled bleakly in answer and let Chang think that he was well-pleased with himself.

11

LIU WENT into the next room with the script of the speech. The Ts'uis' combination bedroom and office was a large, confusing place, with a jumble of worn red leather armchairs, dark oak desks, swivel chairs and filing cabinets. A washline stretched slanting down from the steam pipes to the handle of the unused ice-box, a Westinghouse, that stood beside the double bed.

Ya-mei was over at her desk telephoning. Ts'ui was lying on the sofa reading the evening newspaper with one leg swung up, stepping barefoot on the cool plastered wall. A woman Service Officer, an amah in her Liberation Suit, was holding the two-year old boy, poising his little bottom in the air, above the white enamel chamber pot. Another woman Service Officer squatted before a little charcoal stove, fanning the tiny fire with a newspaper. Something was cooking in a red-flowered enamel basin covered with another wash basin turned upside down over it. This family had an air of camping out and making the best of things with veteran resourcefulness. There was also a kettle of water sitting on a hot plate, its wire trailing across an expanse of empty floor. The dusk was growing outside the window and the light was on. The scene looked quite unreal in the golden gloom of the lamplight.

After Ya-mei finished telephoning she took the paper from Liu and pored over the speech, her forehead knotted in an automatic frown. She tended to be difficult on such occasions.

"Can't you put in some figures?" she asked. "I thought the papers are full of them. We want more facts here and less theory."

The last time he had put in statistics she had had difficulty in translating the number of digits into ten thousands, hundred thousands and millions and had resented being straightened out. Now she would cut him short by suddenly discovering some "serious political error" somewhere.

"Not so many difficult words," she said. "You must remember these women I'm addressing are mostly factory girls and housewives. Their Standard of Culture is very low. Very low."

Liu rather suspected that she could not pronounce such words herself. He had tried once before to put it all down in plain colloquial language. But she had pointed out that over-simplification could be a form of distortion and might cause misunderstanding among the simple-minded. Still, she had delivered that speech just as it was.

Fortunately for Liu, she now started to talk about the women who would be in the audience. The suburbs being more backward than Shanghai proper, the women there were extremely ignorant and oppressed, she said. But the Association was doing great work among them.

"I've been telling A Ching here to go to the Women's Association in her alley," she said, pointing to the young amah fanning the stove. "Her husband ill-treats her and takes away every cent she earns. And her mother-in-law is always trying to get them to quarrel." She launched on the woman's life story. She spent interminable hours talking to each new amah, cross-questioning them about their birth place, their father's occupation, how many people in the family, how they got married, and all about their husbands and in-laws. All the amahs were screened before they were taken on. Ya-mei was merely idly probing around as a matter of interest—just *la, la*.

"A Ching, don't be afraid to expose your husband," she paused to admonish the woman. "Nowadays the poor have Turned Over and the women have Stood Up! Don't be afraid, the Masses are right behind you! The Women's Association will give him a good talking-to. They'll win him over, don't worry. And if he's going to be a Fort of Bigotry you can always get a divorce."

A Ching listened politely, her mouth hanging open in what was meant to be a smile. Her pale, heavy face seemed impregnable. But then they always looked dubious, Liu thought, even if they were quite ready to act on your advice. You never could tell. The thing was just to ignore them and say your say, loudly and over and over again, as Ya-mei was doing. He supposed it would never do for a propagandist to be too sensitive.

"Her husband keeps telling her she's sold to his family," Ya-mei told Liu. "Just because her family got thirty dollars from them as a betrothal gift.—It won't do now to have such feudal ideas! Not after the Liberation! The women have Stood Up now!"

She went over the story several times, returning to every forgotten detail, and interrupting it with endless exhortations and explanation, partly for Liu's benefit, it seemed. He had the feeling that she thought she was helping him to make Progress as she had promised. She was holding a little glass with her back to the tall window. All the lights of the city had blinked on in the diluted purple-gray twilight, the color of grape juice stain. Traffic noises floated up softly. The small clear jangle of a tram bell came through the partly open window. Liu wondered how he had ever got up here, in this gray disordered room in a skyscraper. The hum and stir of the city down below filled him with an impatience close to fear. Time seemed to go faster in the world below and would not wait for him.

Ts'ui had not said a word or paid the least attention to him all the time he was in the room. He had just lain there reading the evening paper. Could it be, as Chang had said a while back, Ts'ui was getting jealous? It was ridiculous, but it was just possible Ts'ui did not like to have him around so much. Liu was determined to get away at the first lull in Ya-mei's story-telling, and he did.

There was to be a meeting after office hours. Liu's unit was supposed to get together with another unit for the Cross-Flow of Experience. But as usual nobody was on time. After waiting around for a while in the meeting room, watching the clock, Liu slipped back to his office to work on the photos. The next day was the deadline for the *China Pictorial* to go to press.

He was alone in the front office. It was so quiet it gave him a slight turn when he heard Ya-mei speaking in the next room. The doors were never shut tight. She was speaking to Ts'ui and there was a quietness in her voice which showed that they were alone.

"You're worried again," she said. "I can see you're worried."

When he did not answer she said, "Well, don't mope. Let's practice again."

"All right," Ts'ui said gloomily.

Liu was astounded to hear rapid kissing noises. He supposed that they must have taken for granted that there was nobody in the room outside, as it was after hours. He ought to get away at once before he was discovered. But for a moment the shock pinned him to his seat. As they do to all romantic young men, most married people looked humdrum to him and not the least bit in love with each other. Certainly the Ts'uis had never struck him as a particularly amorous couple.

"Let's begin at the beginning," Ya-mei said, giggling a little.

There was the sound of footsteps, which broke into a run as they approached each other. Promptly the staccato kissing sounds began again, in pairs. Then Ya-mei gave a half-playful little shriek of pain.

"If you'd been wearing glasses they would have been knocked off," Ts'ui said dispiritedly.

"You always think of the most awful things."

"A lot of them do wear glasses," Ts'ui said. "I've seen pictures of them taken in Peking."

It dawned on Liu that Ts'ui was practicing for the party to be given for the World Youth Delegates. Liu had heard that all the delegates had been greeting everybody with spontaneous bear-hugs and lightening kisses on both cheeks, Russian style.

"The important thing is to smile," Ya-mei said. "Don't look so grim. Smile!"

"And get my teeth knocked off? And somebody'll get bitten on the face."

"Ai, those foreigners!" Ya-mei sighed. "Must be worse for them than for us. So much more nose to bump into. It's just that they're used to it, I suppose."

"What gets me is this swinging your head right and left, right and left, you get so dizzy," Ts'ui said. "A few times is all right, but with fifty people grabbing at you, one after the other—I guess I'm too old for this sort of thing."

"If you were old the Organization wouldn't have you at a meeting of World Youths," she answered. "The Organization ought to know."

Her reasoning must have reassured Ts'ui, though he still sounded gruff when he said, "Well, let's have another go at it."

But this time the hurried smacks had scarcely begun when Ya-mei screamed. For a while neither of them spoke.

Then she said, "I'm never going to practice with you again." She seemed to be crying.

"All right. Never mind," Ts'ui said.

"And you're not going to practice with anybody else either."

"But—with men," Ts'ui said patiently. "With men."

Liu did not stay to hear the rest of it. As it was he was very lucky that nobody had seen him in the front office. If the Ts'uis got word of it, they would think he was eavesdropping.

The meeting had been scheduled for half past six. It was past seven now. Only two people turned up from the other unit. Chang was napping, bending over the table. To avoid talking, Liu also pretended to doze off in his chair.

He knew it was no laughing matter, Ts'ui's practicing. If he was clumsy or seemed lukewarm in the mob kissing scene he would have lost face for his country and his Party in front of international friends. His career would suffer for it in spite of his long Revolutionary History. Liu felt a little sorry for him.

After ten or twenty years of roughing it and deliberately dropping all his manners, he was now required to turn suave overnight. Then Liu could not help thinking: since it was so difficult for men like Ts'ui to adapt themselves, why not skip the intermediate phase of rustication and let young men like himself come out front and face the world?

As a matter of fact it had been done. He had heard of some high school boys and girls just out of school who had been given a year's training and sent to the friendly countries as embassy staff members. All of them were under twenty. Perhaps a college graduate like Liu was already considered too old. He had been exposed to all kinds of poisonous influences in the old society and was not to be trusted until he had been thoroughly tested. The shortcuts in officialdom were not for him. Liu had to wrench his mind away from the subject. Always thinking in terms of promotion—he felt it was all the more despicable because it was so futile.

Everyone had finally arrived. Liu roused himself and sat up straight. In these informal meetings where everybody was required to say something, the trick was to speak up as soon as possible and say the expected thing before it got too repetitious. The meeting did not take long, once it got started.

At quarter past eight Liu and Chang were on the crowded tram, going back to their hostel. The rush hour on trams and busses came much later since most office workers did not go home until seven or eight. The harassed-looking, skinny little conductor expertly plowed a path through the passengers, singing out hoarsely, "Move farther in! Still plenty of room inside! Come right in! Come right in! Come sit in the parlor! Why is everybody hanging round the doorway? You think there's a tiger inside there to eat you up?"

Liu kept his money in the envelope from one of Su Nan's letters. As he took it out of his pocket he felt, as always, a twinge of tenderness. But tonight she seemed farther away from him than ever. He drew out a limp, discolored JMP bill and put away the creased envelope. There was a good supply of these envelopes so he always changed them when they got torn. She wrote fairly often. The letters themselves were nothing much, though. She was now working in the Chinan branch office of the New Democratic Youth Corps. It was a hard life but she was happy there. She was confident and optimistic about the future of their country and hoped he was well and happy and making fast progress.

The letters made him feel that he did not know her any more. Of course his own letters to her were just as unsatisfactory. The Organization might open their letters at any time. Writing too often and writing obvious love-letters were frowned upon. Still, her over-cautiousness maddened him sometimes. What's the use, he would think. Their case was hopeless anyway.

He had heard stories of girl *kan-pu* cajoled into marrying old *kan-pu* who had given up much for the Revolution and ought to get their rewards now. Sometimes the girl was engaged already. The Organization would send some Big Old Sister to talk to her, talk and talk and talk, night and day, for days on end. Eventually she had to agree.

Having given the matter considerable thought lately, Liu decided to take such stories with a pinch of salt. The girls had simply decided in the end to marry for position and comfort—or anyhow, relative comfort. Lots of women had been doing that from the dawn of history. There was no reason why they should not go on doing it even if they had, on becoming *kan-pu*, joined the Revolution, technically speaking.

He believed that Su Nan was not that kind of person. In spite of their brief acquaintance he felt he knew a lot about her. But, knowing her, he felt sure that if anybody had been making marital overtures to her or putting pressure on her, she would not give the slightest hint of it in her letters, not wanting to upset him. And the knowledge of that kept him worried all the time.

How many years could she wait for him? What was there to hold her to him, except those few stolen moments that grew less and less real as time went on? It had been as unbelievable as those secret betrothals in "The Gilded Phoenix," "The Twin Pearl Phoenixes" and "It Rained Flowers." In these stories the boy and girl always "secretly booked up their whole lives in the back garden." In the old days she would have considered herself "booked" once he had touched her skin, even if it was just her face and hands. That was no bond at all nowadays.

Liu hung on to the strap, looking at the row of faces reflected in the dark window glass. There was a woman who looked a little like Su Nan. It was easy for him to think so, with all the lights along the street passing through her face and hair, and neon signs like jewelled brooches sailing through her.

The man standing next to Liu had his eyes closed. He held his ticket in his mouth. The pink strip of paper hanging from between his lips looked exactly like a long tongue and was frightening against the grayish yellow of his face with its sunken cheeks. He swayed a little, hanging on to the strap.

12

THE PAPERS said half a million people were going to take part in the Labor Day parade. A dealer in sheep waiting for a chance to cross the route of march had apparently given up and had tied his small flock to a tree on the close-packed sidewalk. The wool on the sheep was dark and ragged with the dampness of early summer. Five or six of them nosed around on the tiny square of earth under the plane tree. From the look in their apathetic faces they did not really expect to find anything edible and were grazing just for the lack of anything better to do. They paid no attention whatsoever to the people crowded around them. Now and then one of them would turn and glance indifferently at another sheep.

The procession had stopped to allow a dancing dragon to go through its little routine. The dragon's body was just a big white cloth tube with scales drawn on it, and the shop assistants who had been designated to manipulate it for the occasion did it clumsily. The cyclindrical white length of cloth was in motion above the head of the crowd, going up and down in even waves to the furious banging of cymbals. Presently it was pulled straight and poised level and motionless in the air. While it rested, another light blue cloth tube had started to ripple up and down a little distance away, half submerged by the crowd.

Liu Ch'üan stood in line, resting on one leg. He looked at the sheep by the wayside. They were probably on their way to the slaughter house. Still, he thought he would like to scratch them under the chin.

Then a little boy among the spectators went and squatted before a sheep and chucked it under the muzzle. Liu felt a sudden tie of kinship with the boy. So he was not the only one who wanted to do that.

Up ahead of the front rank of Liu's group were the employees of the Shanghai Optical Company. A man and woman leaned on a little cart bearing a huge pair of cardboard spectacles, they had been pushing. The man turned around and said to the man carrying the company banner behind him, "I'm all dragged out, Ch'en. You better come and help Miss Hsu push the cart."

"What's the matter?" asked the man named Ch'en.

"My piles!" the man groaned. "And you know I walked through half the city before the parade even started! Left home when it was pitch-dark—trams not out yet. Had to walk all the way to the shop to assemble. And I live so far off!"

"I used to dread parades too," the woman said. She was scrawny and tall. A small bespectacled face peered out from under her cap. Her Liberation Suit, belted, made long vertical creases like box pleats down her flat chest. Stringy bobbed hair fringed the back of her cap, still a sign of unusual progressive zeal among the women of Shanghai. To cut off the curly ends of permed hair was for them as momentous a gesture as a Buddhist nun shaving her skull at her initiation.

"I used to complain too," Miss Hsu said. "But it sort of grows on you. It can develop into a habit—parading. Now I don't mind it at all, walking down the street with everybody looking at you," she said, her face aglow for a moment.

"You don't have piles, I guess," Ch'en said. "I don't mind the walking so much. It's the waiting, standing around all the time." Ch'en appealed to his listeners. "Why do we have to assemble at six when we don't start out till nine?"

"Next time you remember to bring a little stool," she said. "Sling it on your back, like some of the people from Wing On's store did. Such a good idea!" She sighed wearily. "Ai! It'd been perfect if I'd thought of bringing a stool."

"Well, why don't you sit down on your cart for a while?" Ch'en said.

"I was afraid all this cardboard would collapse on me," she giggled. But she lowered herself on to one side of the cart and settled back gingerly against the handbar. "Ai-ya! Better than any sofa!" she exclaimed with half-closed eyes.

The procession started to move again. Liu helped a Communications Officer push a small prisoner's van with Comrade Ho huddled inside it, masked and dressed as President Truman. Chang Li as Chiang Kai-shek crouched inside another van, bandaged and plaster-crossed to show the People had defeated him. At the sound of a gong they both crashed up against the bars and pranced around, posturing like Tibetan devil dancers, now threatening, now leaping away frightened. Their bodies dwarfed by their enormous hook-nosed, shiny pink masks that reached down to their chests, they were as jerky and unreal as colored paper cutouts appliqued on to the drab, crowded scene.

Peddlers carrying baskets threaded in and out of the column, whispering the names of their wares in a low chant—long fritters, fritter-twists, sesame rice-flour balls, buns, red bean cakes. When they could not filter through the column they marched by its side.

To save money most of the paraders had brought their own food —sandwiches, steamed loaves, hardboiled eggs, thousand-layered flat cakes, Shantung style. It was hours before lunchtime, but the sight and smell of all the peddlers weaving in and out of their ranks reminded people that they were hungry. Soon throughout the crowd paraders were taking paper parcels out of their pockets, unwrapping food, offering samples to each other. Ch'en playfully snatched a sandwich from another clerk who worked for Shanghai Optical. In revenge the man bit off a good third of Ch'en's bun. There was a lot of laughter and comments on the quality of the food.

"Whatever we Chinese do, it always includes eating a meal together," Liu thought. "Start out in the morning when it's still dark and you think it's worse than a labor detail—all day on your feet. Bring out a steamed bun and it turns out to be quite a picnic after all."

He hadn't been feeling very well this morning and had thought briefly about staying in bed. But it was wiser to march in the parade since everybody knew it was much worse to be absent from celebrations like this than to be absent from work. Now, when he started to eat what he had brought, thinking that he must be getting weak from hunger, he knew he was really ill after one mouthful of the cotton wool bread. He supposed he had a fever. The scattered talk around him seemed to jump at him, loud and sudden.

"It's drizzling," said the man with piles, looking upward and making a disgusted, phlegmy noise in his throat. "*Ts'ao na*," he swore. "And I didn't bring my raincoat."

"I didn't either," Ch'en said. "If you have it on all the time, it's too hot. This weather can get awfully hot when the sun comes out. And it's such a bother to carry anything when you're tired. After ten miles one *catty* gets to be ten."

"Might have known it was going to rain," the other man grunted. "Ever had a parade when it didn't rain?"

Ch'en did not answer. It was a standing joke that it always rained on parade days ever since the Communists came. The Study Unit had already pointed out to them that this was an acute form of Change-of-Weatherism as it obviously implied that Old Heaven was not on the side of the Communists, so they could not possibly last long.

An apprentice carrying a dancing lion on his back walked with bowed head and hunched shoulders, holding the paper lion by its front paws. Its rotund pale green body looked ridiculously long, the way it hung down straight from the boy's back, its round rump dangling close to the ground. The paper-tasseled tail dragged on the wet, dark brown asphalt. But the boy was tired and he no longer cared.

Everybody was past caring now. Paper flags were carried tilted back, resting on shoulders. Men spat on the ground and sauntered lazily with dragging steps like beggars hired to carry wreaths and mourning banners in a funeral procession. A young boy noticed it too, whispered it to the man beside him and there were snickers as they turned to look at the large, fern-bordered portraits of Stalin and Mao being carried like portraits of the dead.

It rained harder when they reached the crossroad where there was a Comfort Station. At the sight of the company banner the workers in the station started to shout, "Our respects to the comrades of the Shanghai Optical Company! Come on, straighten up, comrades! Comrades of the Shanghai Optical Company, we salute you!"

"Really does something to you, doesn't it?" Miss Hsu burbled. "A real pick-me-up."

The drenched paper flags had become pink and green tatters but all the flag poles now stood erect. The people at the Comfort Station, who were shop assistants and shop-girls themselves, dipped enamel mugs into huge earthen jars and handed out cold tea in the rain.

The column proceeded. A woman among the spectators suddenly stepped forward under a big black umbrella. "Hey," she said, and thrust a raincoat into Ch'en's hand.

"Yieh!" somebody exclaimed in surprise. "If it isn't Mrs. Ch'en bringing him his raincoat!"

"Hey, Ch'en! Your missus really takes good care of you, eh? Just dotes on you, it looks like. Been standing here waiting in this rain, scared that you'd get wet." There was a babel of laughing voices.

"As faithful as Meng Chiang Nu going all the way to the Great Wall to bring her husband winter clothes."

Ch'en said, blushing, "Cut it out! No point to it, all this leg pulling—an old married couple like us!"

He held his bamboo stick under one arm while he struggled into the raincoat and buttoned it as he walked. The black umbrella had moved away swiftly, disappearing down the street. The column had gone another block and all his colleagues had stopped teasing him. But Ch'en was still protesting, "There's nothing between us, no feelings at all. Never have anything to say to each other when I get home."

Nobody answered. They were cold and wet and very tired. The man with piles was the only one who muttered, "Hadn't been giving me any trouble for some time now. Couldn't even feel them—almost forgot them. I just knew something like this would happen!"

"Ah, cut it out! What's the point—pulling my leg, and no end to it!" Ch'en said happily, obliviously. Nobody else's wife had waylaid them with a raincoat. It had given him much face.

Liu looked at him. Liu could never get over the way life around him went on as usual, after what he had seen out in the country. These people here were hardly touched yet by the change of government. Maybe life was a bit harder with longer working hours and all the added chores, like meetings and parades; still they were able to carry on much as before and find comfort in the texture of life itself. Nothing as big and sweeping as Land Reform had swept over them yet. But how long would it be before it was their turn? Then Liu wondered if he wasn't feeling sorry for them because he was envious. Even if their time was borrowed and running out, that did not make their lives any less real.

This was the season for sunny showers. The sun came out and the rain flashed silvery white against the blue sky for an incredibly long glorious moment. Then it stopped and the pavements quickly dried. Liu's clothes dried on him. The sleepy pressure of the warm sun on his back was vaguely disagreeable and made him shiver. He knew he'd had this coming for a long time. Like all men who are seldom sick, he had just ignored it at first, then, when it didn't go away, he suddenly grew panicky. He felt as heavy as a corpse as he dragged himself along, doubled up over the handbar of the cart. Hot needles of sweat pricked through the thick swollen numbness that coated him.

The long golden day seemed as endless as the road. In moving westward the procession had come to the residential districts. People began to sidle off and desert when they came near their homes. With typical Chinese logic they reasoned that it was not such a serious offense to desert now, since it was already late afternoon. And curiously enough, their unit leaders apparently shared this view and "kept one eye open and one eye closed," as the saying went. The ranks gradually thinned out and the ground was strewn with discarded paper flags.

Liu said to the Communications Officer next to him, "I'm sick. I'm going back to the hostel. Tell the unit leader I'm sick."

It was very quiet as soon as he turned down the side street. The noise of the gongs and cymbals and brass bands, already growing faint, emphasized the sunny silence. The only vehicle on the empty street was a big pushcart manned by soldiers of the Liberation Army, parked in the middle of the road. The chubby troopers looked more Japanese than Chinese except for their black cloth peasant shoes. They waited, leaning on the pile of sacks on the cart, their faces turned toward the main road. Liu had heard that they had been told to keep their distance with the local people in order to maintain their dignity. They never once glanced in his direction though he was the only moving object on the street.

He passed a steamed bread stand with no keeper in sight. The pyramid of cup-loaves was covered by a piece of grayish cloth. He was feeling better now. But somewhere inside himself he was holding still, waiting for the wave of sickness which he knew would soon return.

All the shops had hung flags out over the main road. Here on the side street only one shop, a cigarette-and-candy store, had two flags hung out above the signboard in the approved fashion. But between the crossed flags where the twin portraits of Stalin and Mao ought to be, they had hung—probably for reasons of economy—two identical portraits of the same girl, Lü Mei-yü, a one-time Peking Opera actress whose picture had been used as a trademark on Beauty cigarettes for the last thirty years. The familiar pink-and-white face smiled down from the large color prints, the kind that were given free to retailers. She wore a band around her head in the pre-war western style, and her hair made dipping waves in the center of her forehead.

The little shops huddled between gray brick houses and alleys which had fanciful names written in large faded gilt characters on the gray cement arched entrances. An occasional hanging room bridged the mouth of an alley. All the houses looked so secure in their protective dinginess and commonplaceness. Their air of permanence exasperated Liu.

The pushcart of a cloth vendor was parked by the roadside, making a more or less stationary stall. Nobody was around. A baby lay sleeping on the cart between two tall stacks of cotton prints. It was a lovely day. As he walked along a familiar feeling came over him, the sadness of youth swinging free, having nothing and nobody, and with nowhere to go.

.

13

WHEN HIS temperature did not go down for three days Liu went to see the doctor. The Organization had a standing arrangement with one of the government hospitals for the medical care of its *kan-pu*. Liu stood in a long queue that filled the large hall-like waiting room with its coils and trailed into the corridor. When he finally got to see the doctor he was told to come again the next day to have his lungs fluoroscoped.

So it was his turn at last to get tuberculosis after seeing it happen to so many college students and young *kan-pu*.

After standing in the queue all day he could not get out of bed the next morning. Paradoxically, he thought he would not be able to go to the doctor until he got better. He was not too keen either to learn his fate. What if he had TB? Imported medicine was so expensive the Organization certainly hadn't any to waste on the likes of him. The most he could expect was that they might try the new Soviet "cure by sleep" and "cure by exercise" on him.

He would be expected to carry on just as before. They were always telling people not to be overscrupulous about their health. The Organization would be willing to overlook his handicap if he himself would. His chances for getting ahead would be neither better nor worse than before. Unless of course, he had an acute breakdown. Then he would probably be sent back to Peking to his widowed stepmother, who could hardly make both ends meet as it was.

He remembered seeing in a newsreel a handsome new sanatorium they had up north—was it in Harbin?—but it was for model factory workers only. The film showed several patients, Stakhanovite heroes whose health had been broken by the new speed-up programs. They looked spruce and correct in their dark Liberation Suits walking up the flight of light-colored, broad cement steps, coming back to sleep at the sanatorium after a day's work at the factory. They went upstairs to their ward and hung up their caps carefully on the wall above the row of white iron beds.

"The only thing cheap in this country is human lives," Liu thought and then felt a quick start of guilt for letting the thought break through. And it does seem as if cheap things don't last. Look at himself—hardly been put to use for a year and already heading for the rubbish heap.

He closed his fingers around one of the black iron rails on the bedstead. It cooled his palm deliciously. But almost immediately he became aware of a dim churning in the void that had floated up inside him, working up into a fit of nausea. He let go of the rail and abandoned himself to the burn of fever.

The strain of overwork and undernourishment had started from his last year at college, after the Liberation, when the students' days suddenly become crammed full to bursting with heavy extracurricular activities while every month the food grew a little bit worse. He had not minded then, bolstered up as he was by faith and optimism. And perhaps he would not have broken down now if not for the change in his outlook.

But when your faith is your fortune, somehow you don't lose it so easily. There is always something in you which takes good care of it and sees that you get your faith lifted. Liu was just beginning to get acquainted with that part of himself which was unbelievably resilient and persuasive and always had his best interests at heart.

Much as it pained him, now that the Land Reform had receded into a proper distance he felt he could understand it better. It was like stepping back from an oil painting. The rough savage daubs of color began to take on meaning and he could see what the picture represented. Has anything ever been accomplished on this vast scale without coercion and the destruction of blameless lives caught in the movement? Take the building of the Great Wall, which we are so proud of, he thought. No, perhaps that is not a good example. The tyrant Ch'in Shih Huang Ti had been in charge. But history must be full of such instances.

No, the Land Reform was a thing quite unprecedented in Chinese history. Good or bad, the fact remained that the landless farmers been given land. And land talks to them as money talks to other people. Then this was the first time anything had ever been done that affected the great stone heart of the peasantry. Before, no matter how many roads and railways had been built, they had always had to circumvent this gigantic boulder in the path of progress. The farmers might smile and nod and kowtow but from long experience they knew better than to believe a word you said.

Even now they were no different, he thought, but they would change. He had seen Li Hsiu-chung, a woman labor model from the old Communist areas, in a newsreel. She had come to Peking to be presented to Chairman Mao and attend a meeting. She was a lanky woman with bound feet. Her long, thin, careworn face looked over fifty though she might be younger. In her floppy jacket and baggy pants tied tight at the ankles she staggered briskly and efficiently on her tiny feet up the aisle of the meeting hall. They threw confetti on her. A close-up showed her startled, shyly laughing face. Liu could never forget the happiness on that face. Who had ever made a fuss over her in all her life? What if this sort of thing was just an empty gesture, as Liu knew it to be, the pat on the back which had proved to be so effective when it went with the whip hand, and was extracting superhuman efforts from an exhausted people? The thing was: who had ever bothered before? He found himself asking the question angrily, helplessly furious with the people who had been here before the Communists for landing his generation in the present fix. And once again he was back miserably at where he had started.

The hostel was deserted in the daytime. The room he shared with Chang smelled of sweaty canvas shoes, like a school dormitory. The window was open, its dirty glass panes misty white in the setting sun. Flies buzzed around the bowl of rice gruel on the table. The coolie had brought it in the morning and left it standing there all day. Liu turned over in bed to face the whitewashed wall dotted with crimson tadpole-shaped stains of bedbug blood.

He heard footsteps and voices on the creaky stairs. Turning around he was amazed to see Ts'ui P'ing, well-groomed as usual in black gabardine, entering the room, followed by Ho, his Culinary Officer, carrying a flour sack.

"No, lie down, lie down, Comrade Liu," Ts'ui said when he tried to sit up. "How are you feeling? Better today?" Ts'ui drew up a chair and sat leaning forward, away from the wet face-towel hung on the chair back. He beamed at Liu with hands joined and arms resting on widely parted legs. The bedside manner did not come naturally to him but as an old Party campaigner and officer in the Communist Army, visiting the wounded and sick must be all in the day's work and he had apparently developed a kind of competence in it. Liu knew he did not mean to stay long because he did not slip off a shoe or sock.

"Everybody misses you at the office," Ts'ui said grinning. "They all want to come and see you. I said no, I'll forward the message. Better get well quick. Here, I brought you half a sack of flour. Tell the cook to make something for you. Got to eat to get well."

Liu knew it was customary for a superior to visit a sick staff member, bringing him Face and some flour instead of flowers. But he resented the man's presence in the room, coming, as it were, as a part-owner of the world, breezily intruding upon the squalor and sickness of his own making. And yet all the same Liu felt his eyes smarting at Ts'ui's comforting words. He had to swallow his tears angrily, wondering if it was his present frame of mind that made him so forlorn and abject, or if there was not a certain snobbishness in the most genuine feelings.

The next week he was well enough to go to the hospital. Consultations did not start until two in the afternoon but the queues were formed early in the morning. The women brought their knitting and carried on polite conversations about their ailments. There was the usual preoccupation with food. Almost every patient had a relation who would come and relieve him in the line at lunchtime. And when he came back from lunch he would tell the other person, a little reluctantly and mostly in grunts, but with an air of suppressed excitement, about what he'd had in one of the small restaurants he had found nearby—a minor adventure since he was not familiar with the locality.

Toward mid-afternoon when the line was moving up sluggishly, everybody was outraged to see a woman pushing her way briskly through the crowd, cutting across the queues. Liu saw that it was Ko Shan of the *Liberation Daily News*.

"Does she have priority?" he thought. "So undemocratic."

"Ai-ya, you're so late!" exclaimed a uniformed young man standing near the head of the queue. "Look, it's almost your turn already!"

"My timing is perfect, isn't it?" Ko Shan said smiling, fanning herself with a big brown envelope which looked as if it contained X-ray pictures. Probably she was also a TB case, Liu thought.

"Look what time it is!" the young man cried, baby-faced and plaintive, thrusting his wristwatch under her nose. "I'm really going to get it when I go back there."

"Who told you to come?" she said. "Could have sent somebody."

"Not those Service Officers. They can't read—might get into the wrong queue," the young man said, self-consciously jocular, aware of all the people listening. "Might get into the surgical queue or the Tissue Cure queue or the maternity queue."

"Well, one thing about you, there's no danger of your getting into the maternity queue," she said lightly. "They'd kick you out."

The young man colored slightly when he heard people giggle. He forced a laugh and was about to speak when she cut him short.

"Why aren't you going if you're in such a hurry? Get out, get out!" She swung her big envelope at him once or twice as if driving away flies.

Then she saw Liu. The long queue made several turns in the hall so that he stood quite close to her though he was far behind. She came over immediately and shook hands. "Haven't seen you for some time, Comrade Liu," she said. "I've been looking for you. I telephoned your office."

"Oh, I'm sorry," Liu said. "I haven't been in for days. I've been ill."

"Not serious, is it?"

"No, I'm much better now."

When she came over the young man again had to stand in her place in the queue. "Hey, I really have to be going!" he shouted.

"We're thinking of putting out some pamphlets," she lowered her voice slightly and spoke fast so that not everybody could hear. "The people over in your place are interested too, so it's going to be a joint project. Can you come over to our office, say tomorrow?—Ought to be a Shock Attack job really."

"Yes, sure, I'll come over—if I'm back on the job tomorrow, that is," Liu said. "But if they want to Shock Attack, maybe we can send you somebody else—"

"Ko Shan, I've got to go now!" the young man yelled lividly.

"All right, go!" she flung at him, then turned to Liu. "Yes, they want it done as soon as possible. But the fact is, we're still behind on the research part of the work," she said with a sudden confidential smile. "You come when you can. I'm always there after six in the evening."

She strode back to her place in the queue. The young man was already gone, having stomped out in a huff when she told him to go. But the others had got the idea by now that she was somebody. The gap had not closed up when she stepped in.

She must be married to the boy, Liu thought, the way she treated him. At least they were living together. Liu supposed he was also a *kan-pu*. It was difficult to tell with everybody wearing the same Liberation suits and Lenin suits. But if he was a *kan-pu* he must be a new one on the bottom rung of the ladder, otherwise he wouldn't be so scared of being late for work. But she must be pretty important, Liu thought, to have this kind of a semi-dependent "little lover."

From where he stood he could see the fanning movements of her big yellowish brown envelope jutting out into view. She did not look around. Soon the door to the consultation room opened and she went in while another patient pushed his way out into the crowd, ducking his head like a cabinet minister avoiding cameras, secretive and important looking.

After a few minutes the door opened again. Ko Shan came out, buttoning her tunic. For a brief instant she stood darkened against the whiteness of the frosted glass pane on the door. She was the kind of woman who looked best in silhouette, like some flowers, plum blossoms for instance, with their posturing, leaning branches. She twisted around and lifted her big brown envelope at him in an abbreviated wave. Then she disappeared into the crowd, creating a slight stir which he could feel washing pleasantly over him for long moments later. The sense of pleasure—or amusement as he preferred to call it—frothed thinly over the stone that weighed on his heart as he waited to see the doctor.

14

THE NEXT evening he sat waiting for Ko Shan by her desk, staring down at her unstained bright pink blotter. In this work you learn to appreciate waiting, he thought. It's the only rest you ever get during the day.

He looked at the copy of the *Liberation Daily News* on her desk. The X-ray had found nothing wrong with his lungs, so he was very happy and easily amused. He read through the news story of some Italian priest who had just been arrested for espionage. There were two photos, one showing the lethal weapon in the priest's possession, a long bread-knife, and the other showing his "planned means of escape," a swimming suit and a life belt. Was he going to jump into the Whampoo River when things got too hot for him, swim out to sea and follow the Chechiang Fuchien coast down south to Hong Kong? Liu's own unit could have made a better job of it.

Ko Shan was a long time in the reference room. She had told him when he first came that they were planning a pamphlet tentatively titled "A History of the Aggression Against China by the American Imperialists," the first in a series.

"It'll be a sort of summary of all the national disasters of the last century," she had explained. "And you trace them to the one country that's been at the back of it all the time. The facts are all there, but it'll take some analysis to dig them out. The American imperialists always have their clams tucked out of sight. Not like Japanese and Germans."

Together they ploughed through the material she had finally brought out, sheafs of yellowed newspapers and thin, old, virginal copies of gray-covered pamphlets no one had ever opened. It was a lot of work but it appeared to Liu that they were not really pertinent to the subject and would not be much use to him. "Maybe we ought to do a little more research on the subject," he suggested.

"This is the best we can do for you," she said smiling. "As I said, it's all a matter of having the right viewpoint and keeping to it. The facts are all there."

"I guess I'll take some of this home and go over it again," he said without enthusiasm.

"Sure, take it along. There's another book; I've got it at home. You might find it useful. It's about Chiang's betrayal of the Revolution. You know how the Anglo-American group had a hand in it all. We better go and get it right now. This has been held up long enough."

On their way out she looked at her watch and said, "It's almost nine. You haven't had supper yet, have you?"

"That's all right. I'm not hungry," Liu said smiling.

"Let's go and get something to eat. I didn't have supper either."

Liu hesitated, doing a swift calculation of the amount of money he had in his pocket. It was an embarrassing business to be a *kan-pu* in a backward city, living under the Communist system while the world around him was still operating on a capitalistic basis.

"It's on me this time," she said smiling. "I want to try the Park Hotel grill room. Haven't been there since they started to serve *ta ping, yu t'iao* and bean milk." (*Ta ping*, big cakes, and *yu t'iao*, long fritters, are the classic combination that makes up a coolie's breakfast. And bean milk is the cheapest drink.)

"Yes, I've also heard that they've Turned to Face the Masses," Liu said with a laugh.

They walked the few blocks to the towering Park Hotel with its ground floor of black glass. The grill room was practically deserted. It looked like a mausoleum under the few remote fluorescent light tubes on the high ceiling supported by huge square pillars. There were dusty potted palms.

"Sorry, we only have *ta ping, yu t'iao* in the morning. You'll have to order from the supper menu tonight," the waiter told them.

So they both ordered noodles. Liu said, looking around, "I'm sure they do better business than this in the mornings. Lots of people must come just for the novelty."

"Oh, I don't know—when they can get the same *ta ping, yu t'iao* at the corner stall," Ko Shan said.

"But it's more comfortable here, you can sit and talk."

"Not many people have time to talk over breakfast. And if they come for the atmosphere, it seems to me rather oppressive. Too many ghosts."

"Yes, this is really the tomb chamber of an era," Liu said, rather pleased with his neat turn of phrase even if it probably was not original.

They had a table by the window. The limp white tablecloth was stained brown by soya sauce. A warm strong breeze blew in from the black space of the Race Course across the road. A chattering movie-going crowd streamed past the window against a background of flitting, blinking lights made by passing pedicabs.

"How do you like Shanghai?" She offered him a cigarette.

"Most backward part of the country," Liu said smiling.

From the way she smiled he knew it was not quite the right thing to say. She made him feel that it was bad form to protest too much. Besides, he shouldn't talk as if he thought she was trying to Comprehend his State of Thought, gauging the degree of his Progressiveness or Backwardness, as the case might be. He felt reasonably sure that was not why she was having supper with him—although that would not prevent her from having a quick look at his State of Thought, as long as they were here.

"Nice picture they're showing here," she said, indicating the Grand Theatre next door with a slight movement of her head. "The color is very good."

"Yes, I like Soviet colored films," Liu said. Reddish brown tints predominated as in the paintings of old masters. "They're very artistic," he said. "Not loud or cheap." He refrained from adding "like American technicolor."

"You didn't see this one?"

"No, I didn't get to see it."

"Is Old Ts'ui driving you too hard?" she said smiling. But she did not pursue the subject. It was a rare experience for Liu to be talking to someone who was not pumping him about his superior and his superior's wife, nor interested in what he really thought of them, in order to tell on him. Still, Liu felt less at ease here than in the newspaper office where there were lots of people around. Even their new privacy was only assumed, with the idly watching waiters as invisible as the ever-present stagehands on the stage of a Peking Opera.

He told himself that it was ridiculous to think that she was after him. Did he fancy himself the beautiful maiden in melodramas who invited rape and seduction at every turn, he jeered. He had snuffed out his flicker of suspicion hastily, though he had also suspected—and had dismissed the thought just as hastily—that he had done so in order to be able to go on with a clear conscience. Then again he would argue that if he had wanted to go on, it was just to see what all this was leading to—if anywhere. Perhaps it's wise to "rein in your horse at the edge of a cliff." But to do that, he told himself, you have to get to the cliff first.

She was talking about the Native Products Exhibition that was going to open next month in the Race Course but she stopped and was smiling at him. The smile was out of context. Did she think that it was he who had put his knee against hers on purpose? Or was she smiling because he had not been encouraged by her gesture to put his hand on her leg? He told himself that she was probably unaware of it, but would notice if he was to move away from her, and would then think that he was a young man of enormous conceit and tainted imagination.

He carefully took a deep puff on his cigarette and flicked off the ashes before he shifted his knee away, so that enough time had elapsed to show that he thought nothing of it.

The noodles came. When she called the waiter after they had finished eating and told him "*Chung tan*, close the account," the waiter seemed unsure of to whom to bring the bill. Liu did not like to see Ko Shan do the paying. He knew he ought not be affected by the conventions of the old society which always expected a man to pay, but he had a bad moment wondering if the waiter might think he was a kept man, especially as she was older than he.

He had thought she might be a little angry with him. But when they came out into the street and passed a billboard advertising a coming Korean film, she had turned and said, half-laughing, "You must see it and give it a nice write-up. I'll let you know when they show it in the projection room. They're getting the subtitles translated."

She called a pedicab and he climbed in after her. The open cab slid with a silent flowing motion down the grayly lit flat broad road, facing the night wind. The back of the pedicab driver's blouse bellied out like a full sail.

"It gets quiet very early now," Liu said. There were few lights on and practically no neon signs.

"You should see what it's like after midnight. That's when I usually get home," she said. "Quite eerie."

"That's the trouble with newspaper work. You keep such late hours," Liu said, conscious of the slight contact of her slim hips. He caught himself half wishing that she were fatter so that there would be less room.

With a slight bump over the rise, the pedicab sailed into a dark lane lined with old foreign-style brick houses with high stoops. Ko Shan used a flashlight going up the steps. She pushed open the door and they stepped into the dimly lit hallway.

"It's an apartment house," she told him as they went up the stairs together. It seemed to be one of those old houses sublet as furnished rooms. That must be the caretaker speaking on the telephone somewhere along the corridor and calling raucously, "Number five, Miss Tung!" Then there was the high-pitched loud slap-slap of leather slippers, Miss Tung coming to the phone and the caretaker going away from it. After a shrill, enquiring "Wei-ei?" the talk over the phone quickly degenerated into cabaret girl baby talk.

Ko Shan had a large room on the second floor. The walls were painted a medium shade of bluish green that somehow suggested a hospital ward. The few pieces of dark furniture were ill-assorted and nondescript. Clothes and towels and stockings were hung carelessly over the brown-painted bed-ends. A stack of folded blankets ran along the side of the bed against the wall in Chinese fashion. There were covers; the stale white sheet was bared, somewhat disconcertingly, to the light of the hanging bulb. Used glasses stood everywhere, on the floor too, several in saucers with cigarette ashes in them. Liu saw something rather touching in the sloppy anonymity of the room. It spoke of the experienced Party member who was psychologically conditioned to the hazards of the underground days, when she and her comrades never used to stay long anywhere and had to clear out at a moment's notice, leaving nothing of themselves behind. They were the ones who had really discarded all their luggage, whether material or sentimental, he thought with envy.

Ko Shan asked him to sit down and poured him a cup of tea. Then she found him the book. "You might as well look through it right now, so if there's any question we can have it out now, instead of waiting another day."

She went to open the window and draw the curtains of plain light green cloth. A strong breeze washed into the stale stillness of the room and the curtain passed softly over Liu's head and face, coming from behind his chair, muffling him for an instant in its fusty, ample folds, cool and limp from the dampness.

"Your hair is all mussed," Ko Shan said. She straightened it for him, sitting perched on the arm of his chair.

"It doesn't matter," Liu said absently, his eyes on the book. He half-raised his hand toward his head, then dropped it because hers was still there, smoothing back his hair. He felt her eyes on him, as tangible as the hand. Then she also looked down at the book, bending to see how far he'd read.

The curtains again licked toward them with the wind. In warding them off she had to steady herself with her other arm stretched along the chair back. Liu could feel through his clothes the veiled glow of two half globes of light, warm against his back where her tunic touched him. The book began to talk nonsense. He saw his hand on her bare arm and heard her laugh. Her low laugh was so close it was no more than a warm breath brushing against his face and yet it seemed to tinkle far away in a mist.

He half turned as if he wanted to look at her. But instead he just watched his own hand slowly stroking her arm, moving upward. In spite of everything, he would not have been surprised to meet some kind of opposition. He was a bit startled though, by the vigor of her giggling resistance. But the more she struggled, the more points of contact.

Liu gave her arm a tug, not hard, but it seemed enough to dislodge her from her perch and she slid onto his lap. Even then his cursedly stubborn sense of incredulity hung heavy over him, blunting and befogging all his sensations. She sat in his lap laughing, with her head bowed, one arm around his neck. She apparently wore nothing under her Lenin suit. He found himself looking down into the deep V collar, where the skin turned markedly from pale tan to white where he could see her breasts start.

"It's late. It's too late." He found it necessary to speak in short sentences.

"Why must you go?"

"It's late. And I live in a hostel," he said. She could not have helped noticing him swelling and his pulse throbbing against her. It was so embarrassing that he felt quite angry with himself and with her. He pushed her off him, stood up and went over to the table, gathering his notes and newspapers and pamphlets. She came over and picked up his cap from the table and watched him smiling, whirling the cap round and round on fingers held erect and close together.

"Why must you go?" she asked again.

Liu reached for his cap but she hid it behind her. He was smiling tensely, angrily, feeling ridiculous as he snatched at it again, reaching around her. She had passed it to her other hand. Then they heard somebody knocking at the door.

She went swiftly toward it. Pulling himself together with an effort, he half turned from where he stood to see who it was. But instead of opening the door she turned the key softly in its lock, leaving it there. The click of the lock must have been audible on the other side of the door. After a pause the knocking was resumed with louder, more insistent raps.

She tiptoed back, whispering to him, probably feeling the need for an explanation, "You better wait till the person is gone, whoever it is, if you don't want to be seen."

She spoke conversationally, with a pleasantly conspiratorial air. But it became clear to him in a flash how far he would be implicated merely to be seen in her room at this hour of night. The conventions of the old society still held good, it seemed. Sickeningly, the rule against "getting up man-woman relations" came to his mind.

He remained standing by the table, stacking up his books and papers. The knocking stopped and the room filled with a strained, listening silence.

She came close to him to whisper "Don't talk unnecessarily."

Liu suddenly grinned at her and asked in a low voice, "Who is it?"

"How should I know? I'm inside the room as much as you are."

"Is it the man at the hospital?—who stood in line for you?"

"What?" she said vaguely. Then she laughed. "Could be. You open the door and look, if you want to know so much. I can't tell you. I can't see through wood."

"Well, I can see from the window when he goes out the front door," Liu said, going to the window. Suddenly it became very important to him to know whether there were many or just one.

"Don't be silly," she said. "You want to be seen?"

"It's all right, he can't see me," Liu said half laughing. He leaned out the window, pulling the curtains taut behind him to block off the light in the room.

"Stand back, you devil! What is there to see?" Ko Shan kept laughing and tugging at him.

Looking down he saw a dark figure step out on to the faintly il-lumined high stoop. He could just make out that is was a man in uniform, and probably a young man. The figure paused going down the steps. Liu thought he was about to turn and look up, and show his face. Then Liu blinked and shied away from a beam of light that hit him across his eyes. For a confused second he had the idea that the man down there had trained a searchlight on him. But it was Ko Shan's flashlight. She was turning it straight on his face, almost pressing it to his cheek.

"Well, don't move!" she said laughing. "You want to be seen, don't you? Don't you?"

In his keyed-up state the probing warm white light in his face, intimate and physical, was more than he could bear. He tussled with her for the flashlight, first bending it back to avert the beam from his face. The next moment he was holding her in his arms and kissing her. He did not realize he was holding her too tight. It seemed to him she was a beautiful and horrible nightmare, sitting heavy on his chest so he could not breathe.

The curtains flew high into the room behind them and returning, were sucked tight for a long moment against the window frame and against the bodies of the two of them at the window, hemming them in a private one dimensional blackout. Then with a deliberate sweep the hood of darkness was lifted off them. The curtains were up and Liu was aware of the two of them standing framed in the lighted window. He looked down into the lane, then he quickly took a step back, still holding her against him. "He's still there," he whispered. "He can see us."

"Turn out the light then, if you're really afraid of being seen. But I thought you didn't mind," she taunted.

Liu went immediately to the light switch. It did not occur to him that after the light went out she would not be anywhere near and he had to grope through the unfamiliar room, tripping over things. In his unreasoning, tearing impatience, mingled with a lingering disbelief, he thought it not impossible that she had slipped out of the room at the last minute. When he had caught her, he ran his hand hastily up and down over her clothes, scarcely pausing at the satisfying round weights of her breasts, to make sure that all of her was there. She kept writhing and making little protesting noises. Stupidly, he tried to thrust a rough hand through her belt and trouser band. It was fortunate that she wore exactly the same clothes as he did, so that in spite of the fumbling and tussling he did not have much trouble with the hooks and buttons. He had never been very enthusiastic about putting women in uniforms, whenever he gave the matter any thought at all, but now he could see a point to it.

Putting out the light seemed to have been a signal that immediately summoned the watcher in the lane. There was now a furious banging on the door.

"Ai, is the house on fire?" Liu whispered. They both broke out laughing.

"Maybe," she said.

Feeling childishly, innocently united with her in their laughter and the ridiculous but no less real sense of danger, Liu asked again in a new confidential tone, "Who is it anyway?"

"Why do you keep asking? You scared?"

"Why should I be scared," he answered, briefly considering the possibility of the old door giving way or being cut open by an axe.

"Maybe just now when you were turning off the light you pressed the wrong button and rang the bell for the servants," she joked.

"I'm not that dumb," he said, slightly indignant.

"No, you're not dumb. You're smart. You know everything. Everything," she teased, because by now it was evident that he did not know everything, as she had already guessed. She liked that. It was always a good feeling to be the first woman in the world to somebody. It was to be re-made once again in all her mysteries and perfections.

The hammerings and kicks on the door sounded especially loud and close in the dark. In the besieged blackness of the room, which had grown small and thin-shelled under the thundering blows, it was like being shut in a trunk adrift over the booming heaving sea. But for Liu, once he had muddled through his first moments of confusion into some workable arrangement, the din had faded away and he alone was the sea, as he was the trunk riding on its waves and as he was also the man squeezed inside the velvet-lined case, luxuriously and deliciously stifled, tortuously titillated by the soft fleshy suffocating narrowness that was the only world he had ever known, in which he had ever lived and moved.

Very soon he was at the end of his endurance and went helplessly frenzied with the joy of total abandonment as all his feeling and urgency drained out of him quickly in a warm flood. He was dying and in dying was flying away a Taoist spirit, rising lightly so that the grave could not hold him and fell away, sucking the last flesh off him and he saw with a helpless detachment his soaring self dwindling in the sky.

Then there was nothing left but his nakedness perspiring against hers, and against the folds of his pushed-up tunic. But he did not want to move off her. He slid his hand with incurious unquestioning content along the side of her body, past the delicate hip-bone and roundness of thigh. Then her body moved restlessly and hunched under him; she turned her face away and seemed to be fumbling under the pillow for something. There was the rustle of tinsel. Then the sound of a striking match grated on his drowsiness. The frustrated scraping was repeated several times on a matchbox slightly damp from the weather. A small yellow flame rimmed with blue mist leaped into being, lighting up her half-averted face with a cigarette between her lips. In its brief moment of materialization, her face with its fragile shallow curves of cheek and profile looked so untouched, it shamed and outraged him. And when it was dark again, after the match had been thrown away, he could see the faint gleam of her wakeful eyes, as steady as the glow of the cigarette tip.

He put childishly demanding lips on hers to keep her from smoking. When she kissed him back he could feel her mouth smiling. She stroked him soothingly, not wanting to get him all excited again just yet, not when they had all night before them. She knew it was early yet because she could still hear the trams and busses going. The knocking had stopped now.

Night passed slowly outside the window, tram bells tingling on her ankles, her pale full skirt the curtains billowing into the darkness of the room.

15

HE DROPPED in on her whenever he could, usually in the mornings or early in the afternoon. She got up late because of her late working hours, so when he came she was invariably sleeping, and was usually asleep too when he left. He began to feel that he was an erotic figure that existed only in her dreams. And it was true too that the time he spent away from her became shadowy and unreal and he only came to life between her legs.

Parts of her loomed constantly in his mind. It seemed that he could only think of her anatomically. He had never known he could be like this and was quite unnerved by the discovery of this new side to his character. Perhaps this disgust with himself had something to do with that other passionate need he felt to read something else into their relationship. And perhaps it had been there all along—the feeling that he was sleeping with a doctrine, a way of life, and was in communion at last with what had always been unattainable to him through faults in his background and character—an exacting god, a perversely tormenting destiny whose significance eluded him.

Seeing Ko Shan in that light, sometimes he wished that her *tang hsing*, Party characteristic, was stronger, that she would spout Marx-Leninism even in bed. It was ridiculous to expect that of her since old Party members almost never talked "theory" on the Ma-Eng-Le-Ssu (short for Marx, Engels, Lenin, Stalin) level, to avoid making mistakes. She never talked about her work to him, either, when they were alone together. Not that there was ever time for anything but making love on these occasions, or that Liu would have it otherwise at the time. But when he was away from her and got to brooding, he rather resented being shut off from that part of her life, as if his rightful place was only in bed.

He had no way of knowing just how much she believed, how much she retained of the first young ideals which had prompted her to join up. He wondered whether doubts and disillusionments were things that were beyond her, and she was just a very ordinary woman committed to a hazardous and unrewarding career by her girlish enthusiasms, using the Communist vocabulary slickly as she would any other kind of fashionable jargon.

While she told him very little about herself, she did say how she came to join the Revolution when he asked her one day. "I chucked college and went into the interior with one of those amateur theatrical companies. We circulated from village to village, doing Anti-Japanese Propaganda plays. That was during the war. The company was flat broke half the time. The hardships we went through just to keep things going! But it finally broke up, after two years. We were all college students, but there were one or two who had connections with the Organization. That's how some of us got absorbed into the Party."

Liu could imagine her as she had been then, with long curls bunched into two short thick braids swinging stiffly over her shoulders. She must have been the prettiest girl in the company, and therefore would always be playing the screaming, heaven-invoking heroines who got raped and had their families butchered by the Japanese and their houses burned down. Liu knew something about those wandering amateur theatrical groups though they had been before his time. Some were just patriotic student organizations. Others were secretly sponsored by Communist plants in the universities, often without the knowledge of the other members. The city-bred young people, as stagestruck as they were patriotic, faced up heroically to the hard life, though of course, in time, there were gripes and bickerings, a great deal of grasping selfishness and random love-making, with the sick gray feeling of rootlessness setting in.

Liu could picture the years Ko Shan spent touring the provinces and after that, when she had passed under the Party's direct control.

A lot of men must have fought over her. As if on a dare, she would have taken pride in giving herself away with no strings attached. The Party had tolerated, if not openly encouraged, this sort of thing, perhaps on the theory that the pleasure of love greatly mitigated the hardships which might be otherwise unendurable to middle-class recruits. And at no cost to the Party, it might be added. Those were the heydays of Cup of Water-ism. Now that the Party had gone respectable with success, the cup of water had become a glass of bootleg whiskey, outlawed but still easily obtainable, as Liu had just found out.

Ko Shan was a real product of the times, he felt, whatever else she was. He gloried in her hardness and never ceased to wonder how a figure of steel forged in the furnace of the Revolution could turn all soft and vulnerable when exposed to his potency. Because once he had got over his first awkwardness, she told him that she had never known anybody like him. She often gave him the feeling of being trapped in her own machinations and, after leading him on, ended up being brutally ravished every time. While knocking around the towns and country of the hinterland she had picked up the trick of *Chiao ch'uang*, bed calls—lilting groans and protests and appeasing endearments in thick, creamy, nasal tones and tremulous little cries, begging to be let off or begging to be hurt more. It always drove him wild and he could never quite get rid of the feeling that here was a stray bit of the Party, cornered and at his mercy and he was getting his own back. He knew it was silly but he could not help it. Often when he was elsewhere with other people, the warm flush of his secret satisfaction would steal all over him and he would have a sense of immense wealth and power, going about incognito, a modest or overcautious millionaire wearing a plain blue cloth gown lined with rare fur.

He felt ashamed whenever he thought of Su Nan. But there were so many contradictions in his mind, so many things he would rather not think about. As people say, "*Shih to, pu yang, chai to, pu ch'ou.* A lot of lice—no longer itchy; a lot of debts—no longer worried."

One day he went into Ts'ui's office with some papers for him to sign when he came back. He was surprised to find Comrade Ma there, the woman who had appropriated his desk. She had scarcely been on speaking terms with Ya-mei ever since the desk incident. But now she seemed to be visiting with Ya-mei and the two were talking and giggling like bosom friends.

"Never saw the likes," Comrade Ma was saying. "And the way she went up there to recite Pushkin, wiggling her bottom—"

"That torn shoe!" Ya-mei said with conscious superiority. In the Old Area where she came from they called loose women "torn shoes." Liu guessed that they must be talking about some woman they met at the "evening meeting" they had attended yesterday. Everybody at the office had heard a lot about the party.

On his way out the chatter started up again and he heard Comrade Ma say, "Really, she doesn't want any face at all! You saw the way she was making a play for the Soviet specialist? Always after him to *kan-pei*!"

"The amount of vodka she put away!" Ya-Mei giggled.

"And you heard what Old Lin was going around telling everybody?—What if our Comrade Ko can't speak Russian? Her eyes can speak Esperanto!"

"*T'a ma ti*!—sounds as if he's quite proud of it!" Ya-mei swore, laughing.

Liu realized with a shock that Old Lin must be Lin I-ch'ün, the head of the *Liberation Daily News*. So it was Ko Shan they were talking about.

It was not as if he did not know what Ko Shan was like, though he did have reason to believe that there had not been anybody else ever since he went with her. He was very angry with the gossiping women, and with Ko Shan too, for giving them cause to talk like this about her, even if there was nothing in it. He could not get it off his mind all day. He managed to get off earlier than usual and went to her place.

The table-light was on beside her bed in the darkening room. She was sitting propped up in bed reading the papers.

"I was afraid you'd have left for the office," Liu said.

"Maybe I won't go today." Then she added, "Since you're here."

Ignoring her last sentence which was clearly an afterthought, he sat down on a chair near the head of the bed and said carelessly, his hands rammed deep in his pockets, "Having a hangover?"

"No, but I shouldn't have had anything to drink at all, with my cough," she answered. "Why, how did you get to be so well-informed all of a sudden? Who told you?"

"Oh, I heard it from that what's-his-name—can't pronounce it— you know, that Soviet specialist."

She looked at him and started to laugh. "Don't talk nonsense!"

"Why?" he asked. "Is it so impossible that I might also know a Soviet specialist or two? So many of them around."

Ko Shan glared at him from the corner of her eyes.

"But I don't understand Esperanto, you know," Liu said half laughing.

"What's that?" she said.

"I've never learned Esperanto. So it's no use your speaking to me with your eyes."

She leaned over to hit him, over-reaching herself and pitching sideways over his lap. "You evil thing," she giggled. "You're getting worse and worse all the time."

"Am I? I'm learning fast, eh?" he teased.

She spluttered with laughter. "Sure. You're getting to be a real bad influence on me." Lying with her head in his lap she looked up at him, stroking his cheek. When he took her fingers off his face she knew things were still worrying him, so she said pouting, "No, you've got to tell me where you heard such rubbish."

"Didn't I tell you? That Soviet specialist has been talking to me about you."

"What Soviet specialist? I know—it must be those two women over at your place who've been making up things! Those two are genuine, authentic mud-pies. Scared to death when they see foreigners but jealous all the same when somebody else gets all the attention. And they make up all sorts of awful stories behind your back; they'll stop at nothing."

Liu had to admit to himself that there was something in that. It was quite likely that Ya-mei and Comrade Ma had felt that way about it, possibly without realizing it themselves.

He did not say anything but Ko Shan could see he was wavering. "I don't blame them—women are like that," she said indifferently. "Jealousy is about the strongest emotion they ever feel."

"Really! Is that so?" Liu said politely.

"You needn't be afraid to agree with me, thinking that I might take offense. Because I'm not like other women. I'm never jealous."

"Is that so?" Liu said politely.

"Is that so? Is that so?—what's the matter with you?" Again she put up her hand to feel his cheek and he returned her caresses. She was ticklish and wriggled till she slid her head off his knees. Seen upside down, her face looked unfamiliar and glowingly exciting. Looking at her he thought, perhaps inappropriately, of long ago when he had sat on the school lawn, leaning back, dropping his head over the back of the bench to see the golden sunset upside down. All the colors were so much brighter, fresher, it seemed like a different world.

He bent down to kiss her throat and she said, "Really, I'm never jealous. You can have all the girl friends you want. I'll never interfere."

"That's fine," he said absently. His kisses had strayed.

"You never tell me anything about your other girls."

"There aren't any, you know that."

"Well, before you met me!" She harped on the same theme all the rest of the time he was there that day.

"I told you there's nothing to tell. You want me to make up some conquest and then boast about it?" he said.

"*K'o-ch'i, k'o-ch'i!* Modest, modest!" she said smiling.

"And you never tell me anything yourself, when you could have told me a lot if you'd felt like it," he said.

"If I tell you, you'll be jealous. If you tell me I won't be jealous."

"That's very good of you," he said smiling. "As you said, it's a rare virtue in a woman—not to be jealous. But I'm afraid I'm not the kind of man to bring out the best in you. I'm just not popular with girls."

"Still won't own up! I'm going to kill you—kill you—" Her arms snaked around his neck in a strangle hold. "Don't think you can wriggle out of it this time! I want a full report about that girl friend of yours."

Liu sighed. "What girl friend?"

"Hfm!" she snorted, half laughing. "You think I don't know? I've got all the facts here. I'm just giving you a chance to confess, and you better not miss it if you know what's good for you."

"I happen to know this way to extort confessions," Liu said laughing. "Can't you think of some other way?"

She glared at him and poked a finger forcibly at his forehead, tilting his head back. "Don't want you any more!" she said in the tone people use toward children. "I'm going to stick a stamp on your forehead and mail you to Chinan. See if I don't."

Liu paused perceptibly before he asked, smiling, "Why Chinan?"

She smiled at him. "You'll be addressed to Comrade Su Nan, New Democracy Youth Corps, Chinan Branch, Chinan."

He winced inside to hear the name and address mentioned under these circumstances. "How do you know there's such a person?" he said, still smiling.

"I tell you, my intelligence net is more far-reaching than yours and what's more, my information is always reliable, not like yours. Huh! I'll never get over this—coming here to make a row just because of some malicious gossip, absolutely groundless."

"I didn't come here to make a row," he said.

"No?" she said. "You should have seen the way you looked when you first came. Weren't even going to look at me!"

He was content to let her have the last word, busy savoring the experience which all this painfully disturbing talk had only succeeded in localizing instead of spoiling.

Triumphantly she flicked her cigarette ashes over the edge of the bed without looking, right into one of his shoes. That night, back in his hostel, when he took off his shoes before going to bed, he saw the ashes smeared on the sole of his sock. He smiled, a mixture of tenderness and annoyance flooding over him.

Now how on earth did she find out about Su Nan? He thought of all the possibilities. He had never told a single soul about Su Nan. Although Chang had been with them during the Land Reform, he did not suspect anything. And there was nothing in their letters, even if they did correspond regularly. Had Ts'ui or Ya-mei been opening his letters and gossiping about him? His mind leaped to the old envelopes he used to carry about on him to keep small change in. Nowadays everybody was told to economize, to turn a used envelope inside out and use it again. So when Su Nan wrote to him she always made use of the envelopes of his letters to her. Her full name and address were plainly visible on the inside. And of course Ko Shan had had plenty of chances to search his pockets. That must be it. Probably her only clue too. But he knew that if he were to ask her next time he saw her, she would never admit it.

He had felt guilty every time he took money out of the envelope when he had first started going with Ko Shan. But somehow he had not stopped using it until some time later, shrinking from making the change because, he told himself, there was something theatrical in the gesture.

Her letters kept coming. It pained him to see each one. He was writing less often, always telling her he was busy, and she seemed to take him at his word. Anyhow, theirs were the most ordinary kind of friendly letters, so that he felt it involved no deception on his part to keep certain things from her. Besides, how did he know she hadn't anything to hide from him? He would not be surprised if she had formed similar attachments, now that he knew that sex was not such a tabu as it was made out to be and need only be managed with discretion. Maybe with girls it was even more inevitable, whether they liked it or not. How long could an attractive girl hold out under the pressures from outside? He had noticed that she had spoken of her superior several times and then stopped mentioning him. It could be that something had happened. There might be others too. But he could not stand the thought and preferred to feel guilty himself.

He really ought to write and tell her the truth, tell her not to wait for him any more. This was no time for waiting and thinking and planning. He was through with all that. A girl is light and a woman is warmth. He was grateful to Ko Shan just for being close by and being a woman, though he had never thought of it like that. But he was grateful and he had come to think that she was good at heart and would be still better if she had someone who really cared for her.

He went to see her one steaming rainy afternoon. It was miserable weather. He knocked and tried her door but it was locked. She must have gone out. He took his pen and notebook out of his pocket, tore off a page and wrote her a note. "You were not in when I called. I might be able to come again tomorrow afternoon." He did not sign his name because she would know. He folded the sheet of paper over and bending down, slid it under the door into the room.

It was pouring when he came downstairs. He stood on the stoop and waited in the hope that the worst would soon be over, and that if he waited a little longer she might come back. The stinging, idle slap-slap of slippers ran up and down the dim old corridor behind him. There was a forbidden game of mahjong going on; he could hear the stealthy pit-a-pat of the tiles through an open window. A baby was bawling and a voice was teaching Russian loudly over the radio.

He had to go now. Opening his umbrella on his way down the steps, he turned to look up at her window. The light green curtains had flown out and were waving at him when they were suddenly sucked back into the room, fleeing from big, hard raindrops pelting the half open window pane like dry beans. Liu wondered if the proofs of the pamphlet were still on the table by the window where she had left them yesterday. They were the latest in the series they had been working on. He remembered that she had brought back the proofs the other day. The thin flimsy paper would melt into paste if it got wet and they'd have to start on another set.

He had returned to the bottom step when a bang overhead made him look up again. The window was closed, with sheets of water running over it. The green curtain hung straight and narrow and still, imprisoned behind the glass.

Liu stood in the downpour staring up, then he walked away quickly in great anger.

There never was anybody up there but she. The servant or care-taker of the house did her room for her, but if it had been the servant he would have answered the door.

The next day when Liu came to see her, there was a dark ruddy-faced young man there named Chou, who worked in the Vigilance Section of the Cultural Bureau. Ko Shan introduced them and did most of the talking. The two men were polite but had very little to say to each other. Liu could see that Chou was grimly determined to out-stay him. He finally had to look at his watch. It was earlier than what he imagined it to be, but he had slipped out of the office on a fake errand and really ought to be getting back.

"Have patience," Ko Shan said. "You know what those people are like—can't expect them to be punctual, they're so rushed."

"Who's coming? You waiting for somebody?" the young man asked.

She seemed reluctant to talk, but she tilted her chin slightly to-ward Liu and murmured vacantly, looking at neither of them, "Comrade Liu here wants to see Old Pai on some business, so I asked them to meet here. We're going out to tea."

"Which Old Pai?" the young man said, visibly startled. "You mean our Old Pai?"

She smiled at him. "Now don't go and tell everybody in your of-fice, though it's nothing special."

"Old Pai is coming *here*? I thought he's having a meeting."

"Did he say that?" she said smiling. "Well, maybe I shouldn't have told you."

The young man laughed. He still seemed a little dubious but he soon remembered an appointment and excused himself hastily.

Ko Shan stretched and yawned as soon as he was gone. "Isn't it sickening? If I didn't scare him off with his boss, the bench would rot under him before he got up!"

Liu smiled. "You can't blame him, Maybe he thought you want him to stay. How was a man to know?"

She gave him a withering look. "None of your lip! If you're so smart, why couldn't you have thought of some way to get rid of him?—Left everything to me."

He didn't answer.

She flopped into his lap and gave a little jerk that set her swinging slightly on his legs. "Now you've got to make it up to me."

"Make up for what—the loss of his company?" Liu joked.

"Now if you're going to get nasty on top of all this—" She dropped her head wearily on his shoulder. "Here I was waiting for you; I knew you were coming today. And that little grub popped up and just sat and sat and sat. Might have wasted the whole afternoon." She rubbed her cheek against his. "Were you caught in the rain yesterday?"

"Oh, it was raining all afternoon."

"I got soaking wet downtown."

"I thought you were home," he said. "Saw you close the window."

She opened her eyes wide. "You're seeing things! If I was home, why didn't I let you in?"

"How should I know?"

She hit him on the back with a playful fist. "What do you mean?" she asked incredulously. "You saw *me* here closing the window?"

"What difference does it make," Liu said listlessly, "whether it's you or whoever you have with you."

So he had not seen distinctly who it was and did not even know whether it was a man or a woman. She immediately became aggressively indignant, slid off his knees onto the sofa and tried to drive him off it with wild pushes and pummelling. "All right, you go! Go away! I'm fed up! Picking on me, spying on me all the time! Let me tell you: Yes, there was somebody here yesterday! Old Li. You haven't met him. He's married and his wife works in the News Publication Department. He lives in a men's hostel and she lives in a women's hostel, so what can they do? He talked me into lending them the room. Just for the afternoon. That's very common nowadays, with everybody living in hostels."

"Sure, there's nothing wrong in that," Liu said smiling. "Perfectly legal too, since they are married. I don't see why you had to keep it secret for them."

"I wasn't keeping it secret! Only I didn't feel like telling you because I didn't like the idea too much myself—sort of turning my place into a cheap hotel. Besides, I didn't know you were going to be so silly."

He knew she was lying, though it was a good smooth lie, something he could pretend to accept without losing face.

Then it was bedtime. It always was, with her. Feeling bitter and greedy for compensation, Liu submitted himself to the influence of *Ch'uang Kung, Ch'uang Mu*, Old Father and Mother Bed, the traditional peacemakers in conjugal quarrels. The bed too has its pair of guardian gods like the door and the kitchen stove. And these domesticated gods are usually married couples, like cook-and-butler teams.

Liu looked down on the face he knew so well from this angle, framed on the straw pillow mat with its chalky red-and-green border of woven patterns. He looked searchingly into her curved, smiling eyes. All he saw was his own face reflected in her pupils, mildly distorted, convex and chinless, the nose magnified and elongated, the small eyes anxious and peering. He was furious at the sight of it. If only he could bruise her some way she did not like.

Her eyes had dissolved into bright moonlit water and they were narrowed in her flushed smile as though to keep from running over. She suddenly bent her head forward and drew him down to her, pressing her lips against him between his neck and shoulder and sucking hard.

"What for?" he asked.

Her movement had seemed intent but unemotional, with an animal purposefulness. The blunt softness of puckered lips pulled steadily on him. It ached a little and he began to feel queer, as if she was drawing in some spirit or air or energy from him in a small quiet stream. A thrill ran through him that was almost like fear. "What are you doing?" he said, smiling.

She took her mouth away for a moment to inspect the spot under his shoulder. "*Hu Sha*, sucking the sunstroke out of you."

"I'm not ill," he said.

"Just to make a mark on you, so you'll think of me whenever you see it." When she had removed her lips the second time there was a small purplish red bruise on his skin, like the *sha* marks that people make by pinching or scraping the flesh with a copper coin.

He looked curiously down on his shoulder. "Won't it ever come off?"

"Not for two or three weeks."

He lowered his lips to her shoulder with sudden urgency. He would have her branded as his, if only for two or three weeks, if only so that her other lovers would know that someone had left this on her and feel pained. But he didn't have the knack of it. All he did was to wet her with saliva. It was as hopeless as trying to dent or scratch the warm smooth surface of river water. A man could only drink his fill and go away.

"Hey, no biting!" she screeched, laughing, pushing his face away.

He gave up. A sadness overwhelmed him as he fingered her hair on the pillow. A curly strand had got caught in the coarse weave of the pillow mat. He disentangled it without thinking, fanning it out with a slight rustle, passing his fingers over it and looking at it. Abstractedly, he listened to the measured crunch-crunch of the bed mat.

"I know it's too much to ask—to think that you'll ever think of me when you're not here." She gave him one of her lingering, plaintive glances.

He buried his face in her hair, which smelled slightly of oil and cigarette smoke. Then his muffled voice said, "Say something nice to me. For a change."

"Say what?" she said laughing.

"Something nice."

"No, you'll just go plumb crazy. Frankly I'm afraid of you when you go crazy," she said in her low musical, injured tone.

She was probably afraid that he would be through too soon, he thought. "You'll get mat burns," he said smiling.

"A lot you care," she said in that same hurt tone which could be so fetching.

Then Liu lifted his head, listening to the knocking on the door.

"That must be Comrade Pai," he said wryly.

"Who?"

"Old Pai—Small Chou's superior. Didn't you say he's coming?"

She broke out laughing. "Yes, it might be him. Talk of the devil."

The knocking became louder and the door-knob turned once or twice. Then all sounds stopped.

"Remember the first time you were here?" she said softly. But of course she knew he would not be thinking of the first time, but of the day before, when he had come and gone away.

"What's the matter?" she said laughing, giving him a little slap on his buttocks. "It's all right, you can't hear from outside."

"No, you can't hear a thing from outside," he assured her with a slight smile, his head still turned toward the door.

She looked at him sharply.

He thought the man must have left already. But then a tiny white triangle appeared on the floor just under the door, swiftly growing larger and larger. It became a rectangle, a folded sheet of paper pushed in through the slit under the door.

It was suddenly too much for him. He sat up and reached for his clothes.

"What's the matter? Don't be crazy!" She also sat up and put her arms around his waist from behind, half laughing. He just went on tying his shoelaces.

She saw from his full, unhurried movements that he was not going after the man, but just leaving. And she got very angry. "All right, go! Nobody's going to stop you!" she said. "Really—getting crazier and crazier! Seems I can't even have a letter sent to me without you throwing a fit! It's getting to be a disease with you, this awful dirty-minded suspicion. I've had enough of you, you Fort of Bigotry, retrograding eighteenth-century brain! Now you go—roll out of here! But don't you ever come back again! From now on we don't know each other!"

Liu did not say anything. He was still dressing. She suddenly grabbed his bare arm and stubbed out her cigarette on it. He threw her off hard and she fell back across the bed, hitting her head against the wall with a sharp, wooden thud. Something in him whimpered with rage against himself for making it even more ridiculous than it was. He stalked out of the room, not wanting to slam the door. It slammed anyway.

16

THE NEWSPAPERS had stepped up the campaign for the "extermination of imperialist elements wearing the cloak of religion." The
latest figure in the limelight was a Father Riberi, a native of Monaco
who had just been arrested. Ko Shan was sent to the reference room
to search for all available material about him, proof of his Anti-
People Crimes. Where exactly was Monaco, she wondered.

As Riberi was not a well-known figure, it was like looking for a
needle in a haystack. The only time Ko Shan could find that his
name had appeared in the newspapers was when he had been sent to
China as Minister from Monaco. A blurred photo showed him presenting his papers to Chiang Kai-shek. The entire letter of state was
quoted. Monaco hoped that the friendship between the two nations
would be ever on the increase, expressed admiration for Chiang, the
head of the Chinese national government, and felt confident that
China was marching toward a brilliant future under his leadership.
It was a routine letter, worded in the usual diplomatic phrasing. But
since that was all there was, she brought it to the chief's room. He
had told her that it was very urgent, that "the top level is placing
great importance on the Riberi case."

She knocked on the door. "Come in," Lin I-ch'ün's voice said.

When she pushed the door open, she found that he had a guest,
Shen K'ai-fu, the head of the Hsin Hua News Agency. Shen nodded
at her without rising from his seat.

"How are you, Comrade Ko?" he said smiling, looking at her a
little curiously. He must have heard that one about her linguist eyes,

she thought. His brief appraising glance cut sharply through the pale dough of his good-natured plump face, which closed up again smoothly after it. He was tall and stout, wearing a summer suit and fashionable rimmed glasses. His hair was balding at the back and worn long at the sides, probably from a sense of compensation.

"Have you been to see Chao Yen-hsia, Comrade Ko?" he said lightly, graciously including her in the conversation but not really expecting an answer. They had apparently been discussing the Peking Opera actress who was the latest hit in town. With Chairman Mao a Peking Opera fan, going to the opera was the thing to do among persons of rank.

"You've seen her in *Yu T'ang Ch'un*, haven't you? That's the limit," Lin said chortling to Shen. "When she's singing about her husband being poisoned by his other wife—you know that line: 'All seven holes bleeding, he went to Hades'—she points quickly to her two eyes, two ears, two nostrils and one mouth, one after the other, quick as lightning. Then when she comes to 'he went to Hades' she sticks out her tongue quickly, between notes, as if he'd been strangled and his tongue left hanging out. Never a single line without hamming it up with gestures. When she sings 'I' she must point to her nose."

Shen smiled. "Well, don't you think this is also one of her good points?" he said mildly, but with an unmistakable gentle firmness in his tone which showed that he was applying some principle of Marx-Leninism to the subject at hand. A short, marked silence followed, the hush that always came with the invocation of the dogma. Shen seemed to be nodding his head inwardly over his line of reasoning, which he did not care to go into just now, perhaps because the occasion did not call for such sententiousness.

Lin said quickly, collecting himself, "Of course those gestures do help to make things clear." He wondered if Shen was having an affair with the girl. Or had she become the favorite of somebody still higher up? "The gallery likes it," he said half laughing, though his eyes were watchful. "And the gallery represents the Labor Masses of the city, even if it contains many impure elements, not quite up to the *kung-nung-ping*, worker, farmer, soldier standard. Anyhow, this Chao Yen-hsia is on the right road."

Shen nodded slightly. "Chao Yen-hsia is not bad," he said abstractedly. He still seemed to be teetering on the edge of some profound ideological truth which was to remain unvoiced.

Lin decided that it was not Shen himself, or he would not be defending her so openly. Besides, Shen's preference for young girls was well-known. Chao Yen-hsia was young for an opera singer of repute but perhaps too full-blown and earthy for his taste. Then her patron must be somebody higher up. He never got to hear about anything these days, he thought irritably, feeling as if his paper had been scooped. There was a lot of rivalry between the Party newspaper and the Hsin Hua News Agency since many of their functions overlapped.

Ko Shan was just about to slip away inobtrusively, but Shen stopped her with a gesture. "I'm going," he said, heaving himself up from his seat. "I've wasted enough of your time, Old Lin. Now you can attend to Comrade Ko."

"No, I can come in later. Nothing important," she said.

"What is this?" Shen asked, reaching for the old newspaper she had in her hand. "Let's have a look."

"It's about Riberi," she said.

Lin came over at once and peered at it over Shen's shoulder.

Shen ran his eyes hurriedly through the item and read the letter of state twice. He gave his glasses a little upward thrust. "That's very interesting," he murmured. "He's sure pledged his allegiance to old Chiang in no uncertain terms."

"Let me see," Lin tried to snatch it away, smiling.

Shen was too quick for him, having already folded up the sheet and thrust in into his breast pocket. Making a double chin in the effort to look down while buttoning up his pocket, he said, "This is a nation-wide campaign, so this item ought to be issued by the Hsin Hua News Agency for nation-wide distribution."

"Not so fast!" Lin protested, forcing a laugh. "At least let us copy it down to save you the trouble of sending us a mimeograph."

"Huh, you know how Peking will scream if you print it ahead of the *People's Daily*, 'for quotation marks,'" Shen said over his shoulder.

Lin saw him out the door into the outer office. Ko Shan tried to sneak out after him but Lin blocked her way. He jerked his head at her curtly and she had to follow him into his room.

He returned to his desk and sat down without speaking. Having allowed the pause to drag on to a sufficient length to get her nervous, he said loudly. "I thought you'd know enough not to intrude when I have visitors."

"Yes, I should have found out before I knocked," she smiled apologetically. "It just slipped my mind. I was half dizzy burrowing into the archives digging this up and—"

Lin looked pained and cut her short with a cold nod of dismissal.

She walked out swiftly, knowing it was no use talking when his anger was at its peak. Another unpleasant jar was due her as she went round the corner of the hall-like outer office. A new desk had been placed there and Liu Ch'üan was sitting at it reading the papers.

"The Resist-America Aid-Korea Association has sent somebody here as liaison officer. Going to be stationed here permanently," an editor told her.

"Of all people!" Ko Shan muttered to herself.

Liu never once looked in her direction. She also ignored him, though she took to strolling past him on some errand or other. Once she wrote a note to a colleague, crumpled it into a little ball and tossed it to the other man's desk but it hit Liu on his shoulder. He paid no attention.

In the next few days when all members of the staff went to movies or exhibitions together on Group Attendance tickets, Liu always managed to get out of it. On temporary detail with Ko Shan's office, he had the ready excuse that he had already promised to go with his own unit. On the few occasions when he had to speak to her on business he was brief and wooden while she was cold and snappish. But she did not want to be too obvious. The one inexcusable thing is to let your passions interfere with your work and make a public show of yourself before the Masses, which means all non-Party members, she reminded herself. She had enemies in the office like everybody else. They could do a lot to hurt her if they were to go and tell Old Lin, especially as Lin was angry with her just now.

One day the telephone rang on her desk. "*Liberation Daily News*," she said. "Who do you want? . . . . What's your unit? *Wen Hui Pao?*" That was another newspaper. She put the receiver down on the desk and called out bad-temperedly to the room in general, "Telephone for Liu Ch'üan," as if she were not quite sure who he was.

But when he came over to her desk and picked up the receiver, she glanced at him from the corner of her eyes and said softly, "Big shot now, with reporters after you! No wonder you're so stuck-up now."

"Wai?" Liu said into the phone. "Ai, yes, I'm Liu Ch'üan . . . Why, this is very unexpected." he said. "When did you arrive?"

He leaned on the desk with his back to Ko Shan. She sat there reading some papers. Absentmindedly she wound the telephone wire over her hand and wrist in snaky loops. The wire became shorter and shorter. He was finally forced to turn round to face her, and had to stoop slightly to keep up with the retreating mouthpiece. She smiled up at him, one eyebrow going up a little with a questioning wistfulness.

For a moment he stared into her face. It was Su Nan on the phone. She was in Shanghai. The New Democracy Youth Corps had transferred her here to work for *Wen Hui Pao*, the Corps newspaper. She had not had time to write him before she arrived. Listening to her unexpected and forgotten, familiar voice, it seemed to Liu that both his past and present worlds were going on thunderously at the same time in all their complexities. He was standing nowhere, suspended in black space while the two worlds spun toward each other ominously. Or was it his present and future worlds? It all depended.

Su Nan's excited voice was as devoid of meaning to him as Ko Shan's smile. But he was achingly aware of the slick non-committal quality of his brief polite answers, anticipating hurt when he just said, "I'm afraid I can't get away just now. I'll be there in an hour and half ... All right, see you later."

He hung up and went back to his own desk. Ko Shan coiled the telephone wire further up her arm, straightening out the stubbornly kinky places. She turned and said something to the man at the next desk about the unit meeting the next day.

17

THE TWO of them sat together in the dark watching colored lantern slides advertising pills and knitting wool flash on the screen. A girl's voice on the amplifier had just finished giving a news broadcast in two dialects. Now she was telling the audience about the theatre's newly installed nursery and drinking fountain and the loan of paper fans free of charge.

The ushers went around in their Liberation Suits, distinguished from the audience by white armbands. Another man with a white armband made his rounds holding up a white enamel basin covered by a steaming, gray towel. "Five-spiced mushroom-flavored beancurd cakes!" he chanted in a steady whisper. The introduction of hot beancurd cakes into movie theatres was another innovation where only popcorn, ice cream and lemonade could be had before. The man peddling it looked a bit self-conscious, even furtive. The dull beany smell, faintly spicy, filled the auditorium.

The chatty voice over the microphone made a tolerable substitute for conversation. Both Liu and Su Nan were straining their eyes reading the synopsis of the feature film in the dim light. There was really no excuse now for feeling awkward with each other, since this was the fourth time they had been out together since she arrived. At first she must have thought it amusing—it seemed they were only accustomed to meet in cramped moments, and felt lost when they had whole hours and afternoons to themselves. Then he could see that she was beginning to feel puzzled at his attitude. He was not sure that he understood it himself. The other thing was over and she need never hear of it. After all it did not matter, it was different with men. But she would not think so. Double standards were a thing of the past. And he agreed with her entirely. At least he had always thought he did.

He stole a quick look at her lowered profile, clear-cut and pale in the brownish half-light of the auditorium. Her dark blue cotton uniform had faded into a light mauve from much washing. His blue uniform had also become mauve, only it did not suit him as it did her. She wore her hair longer now and absolutely straight, parted in the middle. She looked different from what he remembered, and much more beautiful. His memory had been tempered by common sense and worn out by incessant running. It was like writing the same word two thousand times until you no longer knew it.

It was funny how big a difference it made when a person was actually there in front of you. It made a bigger difference than it should. As soon as he had seen her, he knew that she had not let anything happen to her. She was just the same as before, if a little hardened by the struggle to stay innocent. And she obviously took for granted it was the same with him, except that he must have had an easier time, not being a girl. Apparently she had never seen any need to find out more about him. When she was with him she was quietly, blissfully absorbed, which frightened him more than inquisitiveness.

Another thing that scared him was how much he wanted her. That was nothing new, but he had never wanted her in such an explicit manner. Somehow the explicitness was very shocking when applied to her, of all women.

Perhaps a vague, halting imagination is as strong a barrier between the sexes as any moral force. He felt doubly guilty and disgusted with himself. He had not kissed her since she came. Not that there had been much opportunity but he could have managed it, and she probably expected him to. But to him the ultimate, time-stopping sense of eternity in a kiss was gone forever. Instead it was merely a beginning that led to other very definite things.

The lights went down in a burst of music. It was a Russian film. Stalin appeared in it briefly as he did in most films. The audience had learned to recognize him and there was scattered applause. It showed him in his days of exile in Siberia. The handsome actor in the role, dashingly mustachioed, with beautiful eyes crinkling at the outer ends, lay on his side on the frozen waste, propped up on an elbow. A comrade sat near him listening raptly as Stalin recited long passages of Pushkin by heart, in a deep voice that descended thrillingly into a stage lover's whisper.

"Every time I see Stalin in a film he's grown younger and taller. They're getting bolder and bolder with practice," Liu said to Su Nan in a low voice. "Here he must be at least five-feet-eight or -nine. I think they'll get him up to six feet before the year is over."

Su Nan looked round nervously. Lately it seemed to her that he was always making this sort of remark, although he knew she did not like it. They had both heard stories of movie-goers who had been overheard making counter-revolutionary comments and at the end of the show had been followed by strangers to their homes and then arrested.

Probably just rumors but she preferred to be over-cautious because, unlike him, she still believed they had a future. In any case it was silly to talk like that, he knew. But she was the only person in the world he could say such things to. If he could not make love to her at least he could have the satisfaction of airing some of his pent-up opinions to her. Whenever she asked him about his work he always spoke in a mocking, disparaging way. Maybe he was making himself out to be even more embittered than he actually was. Because at last here was somebody to complain to, and because he was half consciously building up an excuse for his misdemeanor, justifying it even if she should never find him out.

"There really are bugs on this seat," Su Nan said, examining her wrist in the white glare of snow on the screen.

"It's all the same, front stalls and back stalls, upstairs and downstairs—all the theatres have them." Liu said, also scratching. "That's why they're called Revolution Bugs" he said with a nervous laugh.

She did not answer, but jerked back her head, irritatedly scanning the half-filled row behind them and the line of ushers leaning against the wall, arms crossed over their chests. Abruptly she said, "Let's move over to the other side."

They moved clear to the other end of the theatre. Liu was silent after they settled down again. After a long while she began to wonder if he could be feeling a bit hurt. "You still bitten?" she whispered, leaning over so he could hear her, and instantly got the impression that her closeness made him feel uncomfortable. She drew back quickly before he answered.

When they came out after the show there was a new chill in the air. It was raining, so she said she would be going straight home to her hostel.

He knew a short cut through an alley. Nobody was taking this rain seriously. The cobbler of the alley was still at work at his open-air stall. The bamboo poles stretched across the lane from one upstairs window to another were hung full of washing that had not been taken in. A little briquette stove stood outside a back door. Yellow tongues of flame licked all around the pot that sat burbling on the stove. The rain came down quietly, wetting nothing, it seemed, almost like the flickering white lines vertically darting through old films. It was all so quiet when they entered the alley, it did seem as if they had walked into a silent film, in which nobody could possibly open his mouth and speak.

The blackboard newspaper of the alley stood on its stilt frame at the first turning. Two unpainted slats nailed together at an angle formed a little roof over the blackboard.

"Let's stand here for a while," Liu said. It was pouring by then. They stood under the narrow eaves over the blackboard, reading the summary of important news taken from that day's newspaper. It was carefully written with white and colored chalk with a decorative pink and blue border.

"It was raining that day we went down to Han Chia T'o for the Land Reform," Su Nan said a little sadly, turning to look to the drenched cement-paved alley.

"Yes," Liu said smiling. That was the day they had first met. "Remember that saying that people who meet on a rainy day always become friends," he said. Then he realized a second too late that she would feel hurt at the word "friend."

"Yes, I hope we'll always be friends," she said quickly.

After that neither of them spoke.

At length she said, her voice childishly toughened and obstinate from obvious effort, "When we were in Han Chia T'o we were all very tense and maybe a bit over-wrought. Afterwards when we've quieted down, probably we feel different about things. But anyhow we're friends. Surely we can be frank with friends."

After a moment of silence Liu said, "I've always loved you." It was as strenuous as talking in sleep, when your lips feel numb and heavy, moving with difficulty, and you think you hear your own voice but perhaps you never did speak, or if you did, you only got out half the sentence.

Su Nan said nothing to that. Nor did he follow up with any other remark. Presently they turned again to the blackboard newspaper.

"Let's go. It's almost stopped raining," she said eventually. "Look, you've got chalk dust on your back." She looked round, flicking the white and blue powder off her own back.

The casualness in her tone seemed to close the scene between them. Suddenly feeling desperate, he put his arms around her, pressing his face down hard on her hair.

"Why are you so unhappy?" she murmured after a while.

"Because—" Then he started again, "Because I haven't seen you for such a long time."

She smiled. "Feel like we're strangers?" she asked in a low whisper. The words, all but inaudible, created a ripple that expanded, fading away, over the face of his heart which expanded with it until he could hardly breathe.

"Not now," he answered after kissing her. Then he kissed her again.

Somewhere down the lane a sticky oil-paper umbrella opened with a loud whirr like the sound of startled wings. Before anybody came their way Liu and Su Nan started walking out of the lane.

Liu looked at his watch. "There's still time to do another movie," he said, yearning for the cover of darkness.

"But there's nothing to see," Su Nan said. Sixteen theatres were all showing the Soviet film they had just seen and the remaining eleven were showing a revived Chinese film they had both seen before. Group showing was becoming a fad among movie exhibitors.

"Let's go and see the Chinese picture," Liu suggested. "Haven't seen it for a long time."

"No, it's not worth seeing a second time. Let's just walk."

Liu took her to the old shopping center downtown. "You might like to see old Shanghai," he said. "I don't know this part of the city myself. Only been here once. To order an embroidered pennant."

"Who was it for?" she asked.

"Oh, for some actress who bought a plane singlehanded, in the Contribute Airplanes and Big Guns Movement."

The rows of silk shops were deserted. The sedate shop clerks had turned barkers, standing on the pavement clacking two yardsticks together, yelling for people to come in. Su Nan thought it was great fun. The embroidery shops on the next street were enjoying a new boom though, with orders for pennants pouring in, to be awarded to record-breaking labor heroes, progressive opera troupes or private collectors who voluntarily gave up heirloom curios or rare editions to the government.

In the gathering dusk women had begun to appear under the lamp posts. They looked like housewives in their quiet gowns and seedy, knitted sweaters. They either carried a baby or held an older child by the hand as camouflage. Su Nan glanced at them once or twice without saying anything.

"You haven't seen the Native Products Exhibition yet, have you?" Liu said embarrassedly. "Then let's go."

A trolley took them to one of the back entrances of the Race Course, where the exhibition was held. Liu had been here twice before, together with his unit. It took two separate Group Sightseeing trips for them to cover all the exhibits conscientiously. These were scattered over the vast ground in newly erected frame houses.

"They all say the House of Aquatic Animals is the most interesting," Liu said. "There's a big tortoise there."

The queue was so long in front of the House of Aquatic Animals, they doubted they could get in before closing time.

"The House of Manual Arts isn't bad," he offered. "With embroideries and lacquer things from Fuchien."

The queue was shorter in front of the brick building, the old Race Course Club which housed the Manual Arts products. So they got in line. Moving slowly up the cement steps into the lighted hallway, they came at once face to face with a huge embroidered portrait that occupied a semi-detached partition by itself. It looked very much like the touched up and tinted photo of a wealthy old lady, ruddy-cheeked, with glossy still-black hair smoothed back on her oval head, but combed down a little on either side to cover the receding hairline. A big flesh-colored mole grew on her chin.

"That's not embroidery. Practically a photo!" a man in the line clucked admiringly. "Even that mole is there."

"I've always said the best thing about Chairman Mao is that mole of his," quavered the old woman in front of him. "Ought to be Emperor, to judge by that mole."

"Move on, Ma," the man said a little nervously, giving her a little push.

"All I'm saying is this mole is good," his mother protested.

Next to the portrait a whole wall was covered by little pink satin bibs embroidered with green sprigs of blossoms. All of them were of exactly the same color and design. The rows and rows of identical bibs marched dizzily to the ceiling.

A strong whiff of the scent of a newly opened orange drifted through the shuffling crowd. Liu looked around and saw Ko Shan peeling the fruit. She probably had not come alone. The two men behind her were also eating oranges. She had not seen him, being very much farther in front. But he knew that she was bound to see him sooner or later, the way the queue was inching forward step by step. There was no getting away either, railed in as they were by the movable, red-and-white striped fence.

So he was prepared for the orange peel which hit him on the shoulder. Su Nan happened to be turning around talking to him. Ko Shan looked at her hard and then flashed a knowing smile at Liu. Liu nodded at her politely. She had more make-up on than usual.

Her cheeks were deep pink with rouge but there were tired shadows on her face under the glaring overhead light. The sea of pink satin bibs behind her made up an embroidered backdrop. As the queue continued to move forward she disappeared into a doorway. By the time Liu went into the room she was no longer in sight.

From there the queue went out a French window on to the verandah and then out of the building down another flight of steps. The shadow of the clock-tower stood above the house. Strings of colored lights and kerosene lamps dotted the darkness but they were too far-spaced to light up the vast enclosure. Soviet music poured out of the many loudspeakers and ran together, a broad gray river under a brooding Russian sky. The uneven dirt ground, the Race Course lawn gone bald, was filled with big puddles bridged by wobbly boards. The place was so large and unkempt and unfinished-looking, it did succeed in looking like somewhere in the Soviet Union.

The music stopped. A recorded speech was being broadcast now. The microphone was turned on too loud; not a word could be heard. It sounded just like furious quacking, coming from all sides, wafted on the evening breeze, as if a shoal of ducks were closing in on their rendezvous. Both Liu and Su Nan broke out laughing without saying anything.

When they passed an ice cream wagon they stopped to buy frozen suckers. Somebody suddenly came up to them from the shadows and said, "Here, hold this for me. So heavy!" A paper parcel dangling from a twisted straw was thrust into Liu's hand.

"I bought a ham from one of those mat sheds over there," Ko Shan said. She had never behaved familiarly to him in front of people, probably because she had her own reasons for keeping their relations in the dark. But now slipping her arm through his, she asked, "Aren't you going to introduce me?"

"This is Comrade Ko Shan of the *Liberation Daily News*. This is Comrade Su Nan," he said.

"Oh, so it's Comrade Su. When did you come to Shanghai, Comrade Su?"

"I only got here about two weeks ago," Su Nan said smiling.

"Got a cigarette?" Ko Shan asked Liu. He was carrying his coat over his arm because the evening was warm. Before he could answer she had already stuck her hand into his coat pocket and found one of the loose cigarettes he always had on him. "Ai-ya, your coat's all wet. Isn't it hot today?"

"Yes. Up north it's getting quite cool now," Su Nan said.

"Yes, you came from the north, didn't you? How did you like Chinan?"

"It's a very quiet place."

"Where're you working now?"

"I'm with *Wen Hui Pao*."

Liu said conversationally, "You're both newspaper workers."

"We ought to get together for the Cross-flow of Experience," Ko Shan said smiling.

"I know so little. I have a lot to learn, Comrade Ko," Su Nan said.

"You're too modest. You must come and see me when you have time. Make him bring you along." She took the ham back and nodded at Su Nan. "I'll be seeing you," she said, ignoring Liu.

Liu had thought that she would not leave them just yet. He had expected further insinuations and revelations. She left behind her a short silence.

Then Su Nan said, "How did she know I came from Chinan?"

"Everybody knows at the office. I'm always writing to Chinan. And well, there're your letters. I keep getting them."

"Aren't people awful," she laughed embarrassedly. "Such busybodies." But she obviously felt pleased and walked closer to him. It made Liu feel worse.

"She knows you very well?" she said.

"She's the same with everybody," Liu laughed uncomfortably. "I heard she did underground work before. Even saw combat with the guerillas," he said, as if that would explain everything.

"At least she's not stuck-up like the other old *kan-pu*." She finished her frozen sucker. She wiped her hand and lips with her handkerchief and passed it to Liu.

So she had not suspected anything at all. Perhaps because Ko

Shan appeared much older than he, at least seven or eight years older. Somehow he resented it a little, if she looked at it that way. Of course that was foolish of him. He ought to be glad instead of feeling just a little indignant; he did not know why.

Girls are funny, he thought. A year ago when they were in Han Chia T'o, she had seemed to be a little jealous of Erh Niu, when there was really nothing between Erh Niu and him. Why did she feel nothing now, when there was real cause to be jealous?

Then he thought, she must have been sensitive back in Han Chia T'o because she had not yet felt certain about him. Once he had shown her that he loved her she had trusted him implicitly. He really ought to feel ashamed of himself.

He had thought that he had broken with Ko Shan. But now it looked as if he had been taking things too much for granted. He must go and explain to her. Theirs was not a case where "the lotus root is broken but the fibers are still connected." He must make it very definite without being offensive, if he did not want to go about in dread, knowing she could make things awkward for him any time she chose. He had better go and see her at her place—they could not talk much at the office, and anyhow he could not risk having a scene there.

But wouldn't that be just what she wanted him to do? Yes, that was why she had not stayed long just now, and had only said enough to get him alarmed. Because if she had been too obvious he would have been forced to make a confession to his girl, however much it cost him. Then she would be left with no hold on him.

He kept putting off the interview, knowing all the time that there was no getting out of it. These last few days he had been called back to his old office to help with a Shock Attack. A great batch of reading matter had to be catalogued before it left for the Korean front to boost the morale of the Volunteers. He went to the printer's in the afternoon because of some delay in delivery. When he came back Chang Li told him, "Ko Shan telephoned you twice."

"Oh? Did she leave a message?"

"She didn't say anything." Chang looked up from the desk and smiled at him. "Better be careful. She isn't easy to deal with."

Liu stared at him for a moment, then said "What?" softly, incredulously, laughing a little. "Don't misunderstand. You know it's purely business. They want me there at the office for something. I'm getting to be their odd-job man. As if I don't have enough work of my own."

"All right, all right," Chang said smiling. "I'm only saying this to you because I treat you as one of my own."

"Of course, I know. But really, there's nothing in it."

"Then you're very lucky. Because that type of woman—It's like they say, 'handling dry flour with wet hands'—tough to get rid of. And not only troublesome—could be dangerous. I heard her background and connections are rather complicated. Rather complicated."

"I'm glad you told me," Liu said smiling. "But really! You think she'd ever go for small fry like me? Not much chance!"

"There's no need for you to be so modest," Chang said, and than just smiled at his further protests.

Liu could not tell how much Chang knew. It might be mere idle conjecture. Probably he was just warning him because he thought Ko Shan was running after him. A pity that the advice came too late to do him any good.

He would have to go and see her the next day. Not too early—she would be still in bed. He must try and get there just before half past five and catch her before she went to office.

18

"Oh, it's you," Ko Shan said.

He had knocked over a bottle when he walked in. It rolled away clattering across the floor. The room was dark and, he now noticed, smelled of brandy.

"Aren't you up yet?" he said.

"Pull the curtains back," she yawned. "Though maybe I shouldn't order you about like this—you're such a rare guest now."

He did not answer. It felt funny to draw the curtains and let in gray twilight. The room was not much brighter than before, but he could see her better now. She slept in her underwear like most Chinese. Her pink stocking-net singlet was badly torn. She was half sitting up, leaning on an elbow looking at him, her blanket pushed down to her waist. One of her breasts hung out of a hole in the frayed pink web.

Liu took off his cap and put it on the table. "I want to talk to you," he said without turning round. "About us. I'm awfully sorry. Really I am."

"What for?" she said smiling. "It's all a matter of inclination. When I think of you, I phone you. When you think of me you come and see me. That's all there is to it."

"I came to talk to you," he hastened to correct her.

"All right, let's talk. Who's stopping you? Come sit over here."

He eyed the indicated spot on the edge of her bed with some nervousness. "Aren't you getting up?"

"Yes, but when I'm up I've got to run. I haven't got all day."

He leaned on the window-sill looking down into the alley. It was autumn now. Already there was a frosty note in the peddlers' calls in the dusk and in the shouting and thrilled, frightened laughter of children chasing each other.

"What're you looking so miserable for?" Ko Shan said. "Quarrelled with your Comrade Su or something?"

He smiled slightly.

"Was she suspicious?" she asked. "That day at the exhibition."

"No, she didn't guess anything." When Liu turned round to speak to her he preferred to look into the wardrobe mirror facing her bed. Some clothes thrown over the back of a chair happened to block off part of her reflection, showing little more than her head. The mirror's surface was the only bright thing in the room.

"Some women are dumb," Ko Shan said with some annoyance. Then Liu saw the shadow of a second thought cross her face, and he knew that she was thinking the same thing as he did, that Su Nan had not suspected because Ko Shan was much older than he. She turned and glanced quickly at herself in the mirror. For a moment she looked like somebody who had seen a ghost peering in at a window. The next minute she had sat up and snatched the clothes off the chair back which had modestly screened her from the neck down. Her nakedness flashed palely in the mirror. She looked at herself again with evident satisfaction and started to dress, but very slowly.

Liu said, resolutely keeping his eyes on her face, "But it's got nothing to do with her—you see that, don't you? Her being here or not makes no difference. It was all over between us before she came."

She glanced at him. "Oh, you mean we had a quarrel," she said smiling.

"No, it's not that." Then he said, "No use going into that now."

"You don't look so happy," she said, looking at him. "What's wrong? How far have you gone with her?"

He flushed with sudden anger. "We're pure." He felt bitterly sorry toward Su Nan for subjecting her to this outrage.

"Don't lie," Ko Shan said half laughing. "A year ago, maybe. But you're getting to be so bad now, you're not going to be such a fool as that. I happen to know how bad you are." The provocatively plaintive note had entered her voice and she half glared at him from the corner of her eyes.

He was so angry he could not speak. He hated her because what she said about him was true. He did want Su so badly. He was angry with himself for his wavering, and with Su Nan too for making it impossible for him ever to tell her any of this.

Ko Shan stood up, stepping into her shoes. All she had on was the dark serge jacket of her uniform. The pale legs looked helpless, the way the frail ankles came out of the heavy black walking shoes with shoelaces trailing on the floor. She came and leaned against him.

"We're through," he said.

"Are we?" she laughed softly, nuzzling him. "Are we? I didn't know."

Between him and the cool plumpness of her bare thighs there were his serge trousers, feeling now like the dull gray veil of sleep that gives the best of dreams a kind of gloved feeling—frustratingly vague and not quite real. Struggling against that feeling he put his hand on her leg. The breath of autumn was cold on her thigh. And his hand was there, as inevitable and certain and reassuring as the return of the seasons.

"Don't you ever think of me, sometimes?" she whispered.

He would never be able to break things off if he were to give in now. It would not be fair to her either, using her as a whore when he was yearning for someone else he could not have. Though probably she wouldn't mind. His hand passed from the delicious coolness into the mild warmth under her loose jacket, sliding up the incurving waist along her back, heavy-hearted, lingering.

Then he broke away abruptly. "No." He hesitated a moment, thinking of going. "But I've got to explain to you before I go," he said.

"There's no need to, I told you." She turned away disgustedly. "A man might talk himself into a woman, but he can't talk himself out of her. You bribe your way out or just walk out. Talking won't do you any good." She picked up his cap from the table and held it out to him as she went on talking loud and fast. "Unless you're hoping to make a big enough bore of yourself so I'll drop you. As if I wasn't fed up enough as it is—you and your crazy fits and your jealous tantrums!"

He did not take the cap quick enough. She had already lost patience and just tossed it out the window. "Now quick! Get it!" she said laughing, in the tone people use when they tell a dog to fetch back a twig.

The cap fell out of sight suddenly; watching it Liu felt his insides sink as if he was in an elevator going down too fast. Then he was walking in the alley picking it up from the dry gutter.

Perhaps at the end of anything there was a little of that end-of-the-world feeling. He did not know about her, except that she was very angry. That he knew. Dully he clung to the thought, not necessarily because it soothed his ego. It was the one clearly formed feeling that cut through the crumpled, soiled tangle in him, dirty clothes stuffed into a bursting trunk.

19

OVERNIGHT the nation-wide Campaign for Increased Production and Economy had changed into the Three-Anti Movement, anti-corruption, anti-waste, anti-bureaucratism. Probably, Liu thought, because the drive for greater economy had brought to light many cases of corruption and wasteful spending among the *kan-pu*, the new movement promised to be an ordeal for all *kan-pu*, great and small. But, reading about it in the *Liberation Daily News*, Liu couldn't help think that the more ominous it sounded the more hopes there were of great changes and a new start. And perhaps even faster advancement for those *kan-pu* who could show a clean slate. His own record would stand up under investigation, Liu was quite sure. Perhaps there was nothing wrong with the regime that could not be righted by a thorough housecleaning.

Early in December the government began to pick out "politically pure, non-proletarian-origined, non-Party-member *kan-pu*" to attend a special class for the study of the policy of the Three Antis. Liu's name was on the list. He moved into the Organizing Department of the City Government, bringing his own bedding roll, and lived there for three weeks. Like a boarding school, he thought.

At the end of the course he returned to his own unit to propagate the principles of the Three Antis in evening classes and unit meetings, preparing everybody for what was coming. Then he was sent down to the headquarters of the movement—the old Committee for Increased Production and Economy—to assist in the examination of material. Now thousands of letters were pouring in every day informing against guilty *kan-pu*. It seemed that the vengeful fury of the public had proved to be stronger than their scruples. The contents of some of the letters Liu read stunned him—bribery and falsified accounts amounting to billions of JMP, the investment of embezzled funds in private enterprises, army officers getting the pay of large numbers of non-existent soldiers. In his blackest moments he had not guessed that things were as bad as that. But how much could he believe of those charges? Ch'en I, the mayor of Shanghai, had said encouragingly at the start of the movement, "Charges need only be 5 per cent correct."

His job was to sort out the letters of denunciation, refer the important ones to his unit leader, file the rest and keep his mouth shut. But the sense of responsibility did him good. The government was drawing on young *kan-pu* like him for the "front-line operations of the Three Antis." He and his comrades were newcomers who hadn't had time to form strong connections with any one clique and would be less inclined to shield anybody. Officially it was put like this: these young *kan-pu* were "politically pure, essentially good, but often vacillating in thought and infirm in their standpoint, and could do with being tested and trained in the firing line of the Three Antis." It made Liu happy too, to have his status so aptly defined. It was reassuring to know that there were many others like him. Perhaps the rebellious moods he felt so guilty about could be merely symptoms of an awkward stage in his development, and nothing escaped the all-seeing, all-compassionate eye of the Party.

After two weeks at headquarters he was given three days' leave in order to take part in the mass confessional meeting at the newspaper office. Under the new "queue-up system" all the names, from the leading *kan-pu*'s down to the office coolies', had been listed, in a row. One by one they walked to the platform, made a confession and subjected themselves to group discussion.

Liu was lucky that his work had never required or entitled him to handle money. And his position had been too low to afford him the remotest opportunity for taking bribes. Since he got paid under the Supply System instead of in cash, he had no savings and never sent money home. Alone in Shanghai, he was free from all suspicion of ganging up with capitalists. Still, when his turn came there was no lack of attackers who shouted accusations at him, clapping all kinds of "hats" on his head—individual hero-ist, bureaucrat, saboteur of public property, among other things.

Liu had learned some useful tips in his studies of the Three Antis. Ch'en I had said in one of his speeches, "The struggle of the Three Antis will strike like a violent storm, assailing everybody, both the good and the bad. Only thus can we make certain who might survive and who must be exterminated." He had quoted this to Su Nan again and again so she wouldn't be so nervous when her time came. But it wasn't so easy to remember this when he himself was standing up on the platform besieged by howling voices. They were merely putting up a good show, he kept telling himself, and he must not lose his head or his temper. He managed to keep silent and look pleasant, taking notes all the time, until his accusers had run out of abuse. Then he pleaded guilty to roughly half of the charges, carefully choosing the less serious ones. The audience expressed dissatisfaction as a matter of course. He made one or two amendments, scolding himself bitterly for holding back. And they let him pass.

Several other people went up on the platform before it was Ko Shan's turn. When her name was called and she stood up before the crowd to account for herself, Liu found that the palms of his hands had unaccountably started sweating. He felt the collar of his jacket wet against the back of his neck. But she made a good strong speech exposing her State of Thought, glibly accusing herself of Deserving Official-ism, Pleasure Viewpoint, a Tendency toward Extravagance, a Free and Rambling Style of Behavior and a Rough-Branch-Big-Leaf Style of work (a phrase borrowed from Chinese painting, meaning carelessness).

Somebody shouted, "These are nothing but chicken feathers and garlic peels—the merest trifles!"

"Yes, you're avoiding the big issues!" a woman called out.

Then a man stood up in the back rows to call out, "Comrade Ko Shan! Everybody knows that you're depraved and corrupted! Your private life is not solemn. You're still setting up those abnormal man-woman relations of the old society. Isn't it time that you make a real confession?"

"We'll set her right today if it's the last thing we do." an angry voice boomed out.

"Got to fell her in the Struggle!" echoed another voice.

"And she's a Party member too!"

"Beat down Depraved Elements! Purify the ranks of the Party!

Still smiling, Ko Shan tucked the cuff of her thick scarlet knitted sweater further inside the sleeve of her Lenin suit. It had been showing a little. She waited till the angry babel had died down. "I accept completely the criticism brought forward to me," her voice rang out. "I have nothing to say in my own defense. I feel very much ashamed that even now—after so many years spent in the very nucleus of the struggle—even now there still exist in my consciousness certain bad traits of the petit-bourgeois. I have this Tendency toward Freedom and Looseness. And then when I fought in the guerillas I got into the Guerilla Style of behavior. Ever since then I've found it hard to Regularize my life. Now the matter of man-woman relations. My starting point was comradely love. But, it has gone out of bounds and has led to Obscure Behavior. I'm a Party member and yet, instead of setting an example before the Masses, I'm sabotaging the Party's prestige. I deserve to be penalized most severely, but I still hope that all of you will consider giving me a second chance. In that case I will happily wash off the dirt on my body and voluntarily undergo a thorough self-reform."

It was such a fine speech that there was a moment of silence after she had finished. Then somebody shouted, "*Pu hsing! Pu hsing!* Won't do! Won't do! Confession not concrete enough!"

"Who has Obscure Relations with you? *T'an-pai*, confess, quick!" *T'an-pai! T'an-pai!* Give us the name! Quick!"

Liu had been fidgety at the very start of the attack on Ko Shan. Now he was very tense. It was no use telling himself that he was not the only one who had been on intimate terms with her, that she did not really hate him, since it had been of little importance to her. Even if she had been angry and hurt at the time, she had had time to cool off—it had been months ago. She could have revenged herself on him before now if she had a mind to, couldn't she? he argued desperately.

"*T'an-pai! T'an-pai!*" The shouts rose and fell around him like wind and rain, driving up in a sudden shrieking crescendo. The mass meeting had been going on for three hours. The crowded meeting-hall smelled close and stuffy. But the tired congregation were temporarily revived by this injection of new excitement, Liu told himself. Smart planning it was that brought Ko Shan to the platform now; Ko Shan, the woman some of them had had, and the woman so may others would have enjoyed having.

Even Ko Shan was beginning to look a bit nervous standing up there. She was still smiling but her eyes were shifting around uncertainly, slightly out of focus. Was she having difficulty making up her mind which one of her lovers she should give up? Because to name him was to break with him. It would be impossible to continue man-woman relations afterwards with everybody watching them, spying for the Organization. But it would cost her nothing publicly to sever relations with somebody she already had broken off with. It would be a great convenience, Liu suddenly realized with a sinking heart.

He knew from his own experience just now that you could not distinguish between the faces amassed below the platform. But he kept feeling Ko Shan's glance brushing over his face. Nobody had ever been executed for improper man-woman relations, he reminded himself. But Su Nan would soon hear of this. What would she think? Perhaps he could have made her understand if he had been smart enough to have told her about it himself. It was an entirely different matter with all the sordid details dragged out in a mass meeting and with everybody talking about it afterwards, laughing over it. She might forgive him, but it would never be the same again between them. He should have told her. Now he had lost the opportunity forever.

"Let's have it! Your lover's name! Your lover's name!" As Chinese nouns have no plural form, they could have meant either "lover" or "lovers." But Liu knew they would never be satisfied with one. They always clamored for more, always taking for granted that you were keeping something back.

"All right, I'll *t'an-pai*!" Ko Shan suddenly shouted, her voice harsh and tight with the effort of speaking loud enough to be heard. Her face was slightly flushed and still faintly smiling. "It's Chang Li." The shouted words hung suspended awkwardly in the sudden hush.

The name meant nothing to many of those present. There was a hubbub of mistrustful questioning.

"Chang Li of the Resist-Aid Association," Ko Shan said very loudly in that forcibly raised voice that did not sound like her own.

Liu turned and looked back, vaguely searching, as lots of other people were doing. Chang had substituted for him as liaison officer when he left to study for the Three Antis, so Chang was also at the meeting. With astonishment he saw Chang stood up, looking grave.

"Comrades," Chang said, "I admit I have Perpetrated an Error."

"Make him go up and *t'an-pai*!" people were shouting. "Give a thorough account of it!"

Chang's self-criticism was dramatic. Like repentant sinners at revivalist meetings he spared no effort to paint himself black to show up his momentous about-face. He had first seen Ko Shan in the middle of August at an evening meeting. A bestial impulse and weakness of will prompted him to make advances at her when he saw her home that evening. The advances, he was ashamed to say, had been successful. He tried to break himself of the habit of visiting her but had succumbed every time to the temptation of the flesh. He gave a full, colorful account, pausing only to lash himself with his tongue.

Somebody spotted Ko Shan trying to leave the platform while he was holding his audience enthralled. "Hey, just a minute! We're not through with you yet! Who're your other lovers? The names! The names!"

"There's nobody else," she called out loudly, smiling and trying visibly to check her exasperation.

Everybody yelled at her but she insisted.

Then the chairman came to her aid, probably because both she and Chang were Party members and he thought enough was enough. "You seem very sure that Comrade Chang Li was the only one," he said to Ko Shan severely. "Now you think back carefully after you go home. Both of you will report to your respective Party unit at nine o'clock this evening." He turned briskly to the audience. "The records of their confessions will be sent over to the Party Branch Office right after this meeting. We will now go on with the next case."

Liu swallowed a sigh of relief. When the next man, a Culinary Officer named T'ang, was called to the platform, he tried to bury the memory of his fear by joining in the chorus of charges. Hooting and jeering with the rest at the cook's stumbling effort to explain a discrepancy in his rice account, Liu felt a strange exultation as if, after holding out against a whirlwind, he had let go and had joined it to tear at the roofs and walls of the familiar world.

But when Chang did not come home to the dormitory all night, he began to feel uneasy again. What had happened? Was it that serious? Even if Ko Shan would not mention him, wouldn't Chang drag him into it under pressure? Chang certainly knew something about him and Ko Shan—the way he warned him off her. That was at the end of August, two weeks after Chang started going with her himself.

The mass meeting continued the next day. They had not yet gone through half the personnel. Liu was surprised to find that Ko Shan was present at the meeting and quite active too, making accusations and shouting out questions. Later he heard from other people that she had got off lightly, had merely been told to submit a full confession in written form.

Chang did not come back to the hostel that second night either. It turned out that he had been temporarily detained in a spare room in the office building. The Party unit was conducting an investigation into his other depravities. He went under discussion every evening until late at night. He was required to contribute to those discussions with interminable self-criticism. In the daytime he was shut in his cell for Isolated Retrospection.

Liu thought he was extremely lucky to be out of it. "I really ought to go and see Ko Shan and thank her," he thought guiltily.

There seemed to be a curfew on during the Three Antis. Everybody stayed home after the office and kept himself to himself. In times like these you never could tell what would happen to somebody who had seemed perfectly all right a minute ago. Even a telephone call might implicate you. When Liu came to the house where Ko Shan lived, he felt he was sneaking through a blockade.

"What're you here for?" she said at once when she opened the door. She looked very annoyed. "You'll get me into more trouble if someone should see you."

"I'm sorry. I'm leaving in a minute."

"Even if you leave right now there's still a chance of your being seen."

"I'm sorry," he said again.

It was so cold in the unheated room that she was dressed as if to go out, wearing fur-lined suede boots and a plaid muffler over her padded uniform. She returned to her chair and took up her knitting. There were sheets of paper covered with writing on the table next to her. She had been working on her confession, pondering some changes while she knitted.

The room had such a chastened air, Liu almost felt like laughing. It seemed emptier and tidier than he ever remembered it and was everywhere covered with clean-looking undisturbed dust. Ko Shan could very well be a college senior staying behind in the deserted dormitory working on her thesis while everybody was away during the winter vacation. These Party members, he could not help thinking, how they do change their lives with the policy of the moment, so quickly and with a kind of nonchalant docility—you would think only children could carry it off.

"I've got to thank you for what happened yesterday," he said. "For leaving me out, I mean."

Her scarlet piece of knitting was warm and bright on her lap. Without looking up she lifted her eyebrows slightly instead of shrugging. "There's no need to."

"No, but I'm really grateful."

"To be quite frank with you," she said, "I mentioned Chang instead of you because I could trust him not to get me into a bigger mess than what I'm in already. Which is more than I can say for you."

Liu smiled, ashamed. "Yes, I know." After a pause he said, "Chang is undergoing Isolated Retrospection. Looks quite serious. The Party unit has been discussing and criticizing him for several nights running. Up to three o'clock, I heard."

"You don't have to worry about him," Ko Shan said, smiling. "Chang's all right. Since when has a Party member been afraid of criticism? Even being penalized means nothing. Our Chairman Mao has been penalized six times, you know that? The same sentence each time: Membership retained but under observation. All but expelled from the Party."

Liu smiled again, saying nothing. Then he asked, "Does Chang know about us?"

"Of course he knows something about it. He's no fool. And he's not crazed with jealousy—he's not that kind of person. So there's no point in keeping things from him."

Liu was silent. "He didn't mention me yesterday," he said eventually.

"Of course. What good would that do him? He'll just make an enemy without making things any easier for himself. Sorry, I want that chair." She was untying a new bunch of wool. Liu stood up awkwardly and she pulled his chair near her, stretched out the wool on the chair back and started to pull it out, winding it into a ball.

"I'm going," Liu said smiling, taking the hint.

She did not say goodbye. Sitting there alone winding wool she suddenly lifted both hands, first one then the other, to wipe tears from her face. With dye-reddened hands she continued to wind the wool.

20

YA-MEI rushed out into the corridor with her husband's knitted pullover. They were taking him away for questioning.

They were waiting for the lift, Ts'ui standing between two policemen, two soldiers of the Liberation Army armed with rifles behind him. The old-fashioned elevator was slowly chugchugging up somewhere deep down in the building. Against the whitewashed wall of the shaft the heavy black iron chain swam downward perpendicularly, swinging a little from its own weight, in what seemed to be an endless flow. Then the deliberate swimming motion was stopped. The grill-door on another floor was slammed open and shut with two rattling clangs as nerve-wracking as acid eating into teeth. The chain continued its downward flow while the lift came slowly up.

Ya-mei pushed the brown knitted pullover into Ts'ui's hands. "Better take this along. It's so cold," she said loudly, not so much talking to him as excusing herself to his guards.

"All right," one of the policemen said politely, taking the sweater away from Ts'ui and carrying it for him. "Now that's that. He's got all he needs."

When she tried to get into the lift with them, they pushed her away. "No room. No room," they said.

The grill clanged shut in her face and she turned and ran, past one or two closed doors and the Culinary Officer's cubicle with its bright flash of wall pasted over with colored comics. She clattered down the cement staircase, for decades the back alley used by shroffs and barefoot coolies the foreign masters had not allowed to use the lift. The lofty cobwebbed gray-white ceiling pressed down on the quiet stale air of winter and disuse. Ya-mei tore down the last steps into the corridor of the floor below. The old lift was so slow that she arrived in time to catch a glimpse of Ts'ui's face behind the iron grill in the lighted cage as it gradually sank below the floor level. She could not tell if he had seen her.

Her flood of sadness seemed to be a kind of fulfilment, so that she suddenly had no strength left to race the lift any more. It went down, slowly pumping through the heart of the building. She stood outside the grill looking at the enormous black iron chain swimming upward, indolent with its great weight. She waited to hear the chilling clang of grill-door when the elevator touched bottom. Then she pressed the button.

The lift came up empty. The liftman in his padded Liberation Suit glanced at her curiously. He was half smiling with fright and excitement but he refrained from asking questions. On the way down she looked at the back of his bowed head silhouetted against the alternating solid darkness and daylight behind bars.

She went at once to find Liang Po, Ts'ui's best friend. Like Ts'ui he had been an officer in the Liberation Army, but now he was the head of the Lu Chia Wan police station. He was not in his office when she called. But she wasted no time and went all over town seeing other friends. Both she and Ts'ui P'ing had had long Revolutionary Histories, so they knew quite a lot of people.

By the end of that day she had not found out anything. She went back to see Liang at his quarters. She had never liked Liang because her husband had almost got killed in battle several time saving Liang's life. That Liang had also saved Ts'ui's life more than once was another matter. She heard no end of it at home.

She had the idea Liang did not like her very much either. He probably thought her too capable and unwomanly, always pushing to the forefront of things. Though the truth was that she was too much a woman, always expecting all men to be a little attracted to her and resenting it if they weren't. But this evening as soon as she saw him and told him about Ts'ui, she broke down and cried as if he were her own flesh and blood.

"Don't worry. Don't worry," the stocky, ochre-colored little man said awkwardly. "It may be nothing. So long as there is a single letter informing against you, they catch you and try to scare the truth out of you. Otherwise it'll seem undemocratic and they are afraid it will affect the enthusiasm of the Masses and the Masses won't come forward with charges. Why, that's one of the basic principles of the Three Antis!"

She did not answer, gulping her sobs.

"Where have they taken him, do you know?" he asked.

"I've been all over town but I haven't found out a thing."

"Who did you see?" He looked at her mistrustfully from under knitted brows.

"Comrade Tseng of the People's Supervisory Committee. You used to know him too, didn't you? I also went to Old Fei of the Public Security Department."

"You know, you shouldn't be running round like this," Liang said nervously. "Could be interpreted as a breach of discipline, you know—going round asking for special favors. And people might not like it, in a time like this when everybody has his own troubles. In the end it might do more harm than good."

Ya-mei stared at him, anger suddenly flaring up in her. "You're quite right. Everybody has his own troubles. Who can you count on to help in a time like this? Not a single soul," she said, the words tumbling out in a rush. "That's why Ts'ui P'ing is such a fool. Friends always come first with him. Ready to give up his own life even. Really not worth it!"

"This is no time to get bitter," Liang said frowning. "Only thing you can do is try to be cool. Keep to your own proper standpoint as a Party member and wait for the Party's decision. You know the Party will never punish anybody unjustly."

He sounded as if he had heard something, she thought. Ts'ui's case must be really serious. "Comrade Liang," she suddenly said, "If even you have washed your hands of him, then what hope is there?" Her tears came in a hot blinding rush. "I might as well die. I'll die right in front of you, Comrade Liang." Before he could stop her she was up and running toward the wall, ramming her head against it.

"Hey, don't! What is this? What for?"

"Let go of me!" She kept bumping her head against the wall, making a noise like stamping feet. "What do I want to keep my life for? What use is it to me? If my kids were here I'd dash them on the ground—I'd see that they died before me. You might as well get a knife and kill all of us. You might as well," she panted.

Struggling with him she slid to the ground and refused to get up. She rolled all over the floor weeping and yowling as if he were butchering her. "Ai-ya, Comrade Liang, why did you save him in the battle of Hongchiao? What made you do it, Comrade Liang?" she wailed. "If he died then we would have been a Glorious Army Family. What are we now, if he is to die now?"

"Get up, get up! What is this?" Liang said desperately. "Collect yourself, Comrade Chu. Are you a *kan-pu* of the Revolution or a country woman?"

That ought to have pricked her sensitive spot. But she no longer cared. It took three orderlies and a lot of promises to get her out of there into Liang's office car, which took her home. "Don't be so wild," Liang had said again and again. "Give me time. I'll try and get information—we'll both try. We'll keep in touch."

Within the week she had tried to kill herself in the office of almost everybody of any importance among her circle of acquaintances. Where she came from, women are the noisiest suicides in the world. She was not afraid of alienating these people, knowing that she was not welcome anyway, even if she was on her best behavior. She came to them as a dangerous germ-carrier. They avoided her if they could, but once they came face to face with her they could not just "pull their face down" and go all official on her. They thought she was impossible—putting on an act too. But mixed with their exasperation and disgust there was, as often as not, a flash of genuine pity.

It had worked with Yuan, the director of the Cultural Bureau.

She had known him in the Old Area. In those days he had not been altogether indifferent to her charms. In his mild way, of course. He was a soft-faced, slender man wearing rimless glasses. She could see that he was rather shaken and that somehow quieted her and she started to tell him about Liang. She had not heard from Liang ever since their interview. And every time she went to see him he had been out.

"And he and Ts'ui P'ing had been such friends. Always together ever since high school. They left college to go to Yenan together, and on the way Liang Po got dysentery. There were no doctors around, no medicine. He would have died if Ts'ui P'ing hadn't stayed up nights nursing him. For two months. Arnh." She paused to make this little affirmative noise as if she were her own attentive listener, in the style of leisurely storytellers. She was hoarse and pale with clear red circles around her eyes.

"When they got to Yenan they both entered the Resist-Japan University. After their graduation Chairman Mao sent them into the occupied areas, to be political workers in the New Fourth Army. Came the South Anhwei Incident—Arnh! That was when the New Fourth Army was almost wiped out by the Nationalists. Ts'ui P'ing got a bullet in his leg and Liang Po stuck to him and looked after him. They were both captured and imprisoned in the Shang Jao Camp. Then when the Japanese came, all the prisoners were moved farther into the interior. There was a riot when they got to Red Rock and the prisoners broke away. Ts'ui P'ing was wounded in the riot. And Liang Po carried him, all the way from Red Rock in Fuchien to the top of the Wu Yi Mountain between Fuchien and Chianghsi. Arnh," she said evenly, looking blankly at Yuan.

"Then there was the Battle of Meng Liang Kang in 1947," she continued. "That time Ts'ui P'ing was a battalion commander in the East China Field Army. Liang Po was the political instructor in his battalion. Liang was wounded at the front. Ts'ui P'ing crawled up under fire to carry him back to shelter. Arnh. It was a near thing. For both of them.

"Then in 1949 when Shanghai was being Liberated, they each led a battalion entering Shanghai through Hongchiao. Arnh. This time it was Ts'ui P'ing who was wounded and Liang Po who helped him."

She was silent for a long moment, looking straight at Yuan. "That's why I can't understand. How is he ever going to face Ts'ui P'ing again after this? Is he so sure he'll never see him again?" she said, suddenly starting to cry.

Yuan did not say anything. Then quite abruptly he said, "Don't go to Liang Po again."

She looked at him quickly. "Why?" When Yuan did not answer she whispered, "Please tell me. Please."

"Well, it's no use pestering him if he doesn't want to help," Yuan said irritably. Then he changed his mind and added a little sheepishly, "Besides, according to what I heard, he's the one who wrote the letter informing against Ts'ui P'ing."

Her lips moved with a checked exclamation. After a moment of reflection she asked in a low voice, "What did he say in the letter?"

"Talked a lot about their old friendship. What you told me just now," Yuan smiled slightly. "He negated it, said it was Petit-Bourgeois Gratitudism. He gave a very full account—exact dates of every time they saved each other's life, and everything."

"But what for?"

"To show what a great sacrifice it was to inform against him, I suppose. Otherwise people might think it's just a friend—not like a brother or a father, or even a brother-in-law."

"What did he accuse him of?"

"I can't remember all the items. Smuggling, among other things. Sending soldiers under his command to smuggle dope."

"Ts'ui P'ing never did anything like that," she said quickly.

He said just as quickly, "Then you needn't worry. They have to have proof."

She said after a slight pause, "But how was it they just arrested him without going through discussion and criticism *t'an-pai*? I thought those were the usual procedures."

"Yes, it is rather irregular." Then Yuan said carelessly, moving some things around on his desk, "Ts'ui P'ing hasn't offended anybody, has he?"

"No." Then she said, "Not that I know of—Do you mean—I mean, do you think somebody else is at the back of this?"

Yuan lifted the area around his eyes very slightly, disclaiming all knowledge and expressing some doubt.

"Maybe it's just that Liang Po knows Ts'ui P'ing has done something to offend somebody, so he's doing this to please whoever it is," she speculated. "Maybe Ts'ui P'ing told him himself," she said with bitter triumph. "That would be just like him, telling his friend things that he kept from his own wife. Now he would feel sorry. If he only knew."

"All this is guesswork," Yuan said, suddenly brisk. "Now the reason I told you this is for your own protection. The main thing is to be calm. And keep away from Liang. It won't do any good to denounce him or anything. I know you're not frail and emotional like ordinary women. I can trust you not to tell anybody about this. In your own interest."

He was already sorry for his indiscretion, she thought. It was not serious enough for her to blackmail him with it, but still she pressed her advantage and extracted from him a promise to speak to one of the leaders of the Three Antis.

After that day she continued to go around haunting her influential friends, making Yuan's office her chief port of call. There was always a sense of achievement just in going her rounds, forcing her way into people's presence, making them listen to her. Even when two men from the Public Security Bureau called, trying to stir her up against her husband and produce proof of his guilt, she harangued them on his innocence with tears and supplication, turning the interview into an opportunity. They did not come again after the second time.

One afternoon she came home exhausted. Ho, the Culinary Officer, on hearing the lift, emerged from his cubicle. He came lumbering up to her in his washed-out padded uniform. Because it was cold his hands were curled up inside the narrow sleeves, peasant fashion, so that the two thick pipes of dangling arms made a gentle arc on either side of him. He was either very afraid of her or frightened of being seen talking to her, or both.

"Comrade Chu," he said. "Some people came just now from the Public Security Bureau. Told you to go and get the clothes and things back. Said the execution took place this morning."

As she walked toward her room she saw a coolie sitting astride the window washing it at the end of the corridor. The glass pane shone dazzling bright in the sun. The dark rag the coolie was using to wipe it and the tin pail on the floor filled the air with an odor of dampness. From out the window came the whirring hum of trams and the sound of school bells. The world seemed to be going on as usual.

In her room the desks were in the sun, showing up the white bloom of dust on the two black telephones. Nobody had rung up for some time now, and people could no longer be reached on the phone. The telephones' silence forbade and stifled and absorbed all noises in the room. She closed the door inaudibly when she came in. The amah was trying to hush the older child who was whining for something but it all sounded very faint.

She threw herself face downward on the bed. She could not hear herself crying, as if she was on a padded door between life and death. Gripping the counterpane in one hand she banged the bed weakly, beating on the soft, thick, heavy door.

21

"Ts'ui p'ing, former member of the Party convicted of corruption, smuggling and other crimes of resistance to the Three Antis, was executed day before yesterday."

The newspapers were never very up-to-date. The caption jumped at Liu. He ran his eyes hurriedly through the small print. It said:

> Ts'ui had been charged with corruption, waste of public funds, toleration of lawless smuggling and of tax evasion. Investigation revealed conclusive proofs. And yet the accused, out of the consistent vileness of his nature, his lack of regard for the Organization, his contempt for discipline, had opposed the leaders and had refused to *t'an-pai*. He had been expelled from the Party, arrested and sentenced to be shot. His political rights were taken away for life. The sentence was carried out day before yesterday in the morning.

That phrase about his refusal to *t'an-pai* was mere routine. Liu had come to this conclusion by watching many such cases. Whenever they decided to put somebody to death they said he refused to confess, whether he confessed or not. As if he could have got out of it if only he had the sense to admit his sins. That was very effective propaganda, inducing all suspects to co-operate in the hope, however slight, that the government would be lenient to them once they pleaded guilty.

What had happened to Ts'ui was a shock to Liu but not exactly a surprise. At the headquarters of the Three Antis he had been assigned to sort letters informing against *kan-pu* above the rank of directors

of departments. He had come across a letter some time ago informing against Ch'en I, Mayor of Shanghai. The letter was signed "A
Faithful Party Member." It said that in 1946 when Ch'en I, in command of the East China Field Army, had been isolated in the moun-
tainous area in central and south Shantung, Yenan had sent him a
large sum of counterfeit *Fapi* with which he was to buy supplies
from Nationalist-held areas. So Ch'en I had some of his *kan-pu* dis-
guise themselves as merchants and infiltrate into Chinan and Tsing-
tao to do some shopping. Only half of this money was used in buying
medicines and medical equipment for the treatment of the wounded.
The other half went for the purchase of fur coats, fur-lined gloves
and boots and eiderdown quilts for Chen and his aides, and a lot of
tinned food so that wounded soldiers could have nourishing meals.
But "Faithful Party Member" said, "I was seriously wounded at the
time. There wasn't even a woolen blanket in the tent I slept in. I had
heard of those tins but had never seen them. Afterwards I found that
they were all piled in General Ch'en's headquarters. During our re-
treat from central and south Shantung the tins just disappeared."

He also accused Ch'en of repeatedly going against sensible advice,
making costly strategic errors that had resulted in heavy casualties,
as in the blind attack on Quemoy Island in 1949.

The letter was worded so strongly, Liu had taken it at once to his
leader.

After hurriedly leafing through it the man had said, "All right,
I'll handle this material." Liu was just about to move away when the
other called out, "Comrade Liu." After a visibly nervous pause he
said, watching Liu, "In the Three-Anti campaign we have to place
special emphasis on Organizational Qualities. All the material that
passes through your hands is dead secret. You are to confide it only
to me. I don't suppose you need be reminded of that."

"Yes, I know," Liu said.

That did not stop him from making all kinds of surmises about
the letter. The informant seemed to know so much about inside information, he must have been an officer himself. The East China
Field Army had been built around what was left of the New Fourth

Army. Ts'ui P'ing had been a New Fourth Army man. And Liu seemed to remember hearing that at one time he had served under Che'n I. Now that he thought about it, the handwriting could be Ts'ui's even if it had been carefully disguised.

He supposed that his unit leader had lost no time referring the letter on to his own superior. The last man on the receiving end would be the Commander in Chief of the Three-Anti Movement in East China—Ch'en I.

What could Ts'ui have been thinking of?—Ts'ui's speedy arrest and execution had almost confirmed his suspicion that it was Ts'ui who had written the letter. He could never be sure but he felt that he knew as much about it as anybody else except the two or three people on top who were really in the know.

Ts'ui should have remembered the old saying about "hitting a rock with an egg." Had Ts'ui been hoping that the letter would fall into the hands of one of Ch'en's political rivals? Or had he believed in the inviolability of all the incoming letters during the Three Antis? Liu could not blame him for swallowing his own Party's propaganda, since Liu had more or less believed in that himself at the start of the movement.

And Ts'ui could not have foreseen that the tide was already turning. Two of the leaders of the Three Antis down east had been penalized for overdoing things—Jao Shu-shih (purged in 1955 for conspiring with Kao Kang in anti-Party activities), chairman of the East China Military Executive Committee, and Liu Hsiao, chairman of the People's Supervisory Committee. Too anxious to get results they had discharged large numbers of high-ranking *kan-pu*, "sapping the Party's fighting strength." At the latest mass meeting of *kan-pu* working on the Three Antis, Jao and Liu had not been sitting at their usual places on the platform. Nor had they appeared anywhere else since. Everyone wondered. Then there were whispers that plump, moustachioed Jao had been called back to Peking to study at the Marx-Lenin Academy. Liu Hsiao had been relieved of his duties as Vice-president of the Committee for Increased Production and Economy, and was therefore no longer in charge of the Three Antis.

Peking must have felt alarmed at the amount of letters pouring in exposing corrupt *kan-pu*. With the new change in policy the public's enthusiasm had boomeranged. So now the government was putting the blame on the businessmen for corrupting the *kan-pu*. A new Five-Anti Movement was launched against merchants, factory and shop-owners. Shanghai was in a turmoil from the initial fury of the new movement. But like millions of other *kan-pu* Liu was drawing his breath more easily these days. The thunder was rolling away from above his head.

One evening when he returned from work he found that Chang had come back to the hostel. After two weeks of nightly discussions and questioning Chang had admitted with tears of shame and repentance that ever since he came to Shanghai his thought had undergone a change in quality. Aside from his Obscure Relations with Ko Shan he had visited cabarets from time to time to "censure the putrid life of the capitalistic class." Two cabaret girls had seduced him. He had money because he got commissions from the printing presses and paper dealers he was in contact with. But as such things seldom came his way, the total sum did not amount to very much. The Party unit had his confession sent out as a circular, posted on the wall newspaper everywhere, attaching to it their conclusion: "He was saved at last under the education of the Communist Party." Because his confession had been thorough he was promoted one grade. "We will test him in work and hardship," promised the Organization.

Though it had all ended happily for Chang, on his return he looked thin and worn. Liu congratulated him, thinking that this was not the only case he had seen recently in which the Party had taken care of its own. Whenever a Party member was incriminated they always made a big fuss in the initial stages to impress the masses with their painful fairness. But in the end the punishment meted out was usually very light, often just a transfer.

Liu felt embarrassed talking to Chang because now he knew that Chang had known all along about Ko Shan and him. Wouldn't Chang hate him? Chang wouldn't have got into trouble if not for Ko Shan. And here he had stayed out of it all, because Ko Shan had shielded him.

He could detect no change in Chang's manner toward him. Naturally Chang was a little subdued because he had been in disgrace. But he got quite excited over the news about Ts'ui and asked Liu a lot of questions. He probably wouldn't be going to Comrade Ho for information now, though they had been such chums, Liu thought wryly.

Chang seemed eager to catch up on all that had happened during his absence. Altogether he seemed friendly. "These Party members," Liu said to himself, "they really think nothing of man-woman relations." Still, he did not sleep well that night in the same room with Chang.

It was not that he expected Chang to strangle him in his sleep. And yet he slept poorly night after night. Once when he was just dropping off toward dawn, he heard a thump down in the alley, followed by a thin scream. The sounds were not loud but they came to him greatly magnified by the fuzzy waves of sleep lapping over him. He started, wide awake at once. For a while he heard nothing more. Then there were the voices of several people talking, hushed and sniffling with the cold.

There was more talking, shrill and agitated. Then footsteps shuffled away heavily and silence followed.

At breakfast the hostel coolie was full of news. "That widow who owned the corner cigarette shop jumped out of the window last night. From that hanging shed she lived in, across the mouth of the alley." He had got the story from the watchman who had been the first to rush out when he heard the noise. "And he got scolded for his trouble," the coolie said grinning. "There's this woman *kan-pu* staying with the widow talking to her day and night telling her to *t'an-pai*. Set up a camp bed in her room. Wouldn't let her come down or see anybody until she had confessed—tax evasion. Comes to hundreds of thousands, I heard. Last night this woman *kan-pu* just dozed off for a moment and this business happened. The *kan-pu* was so mad, she yelled at the watchman when she came down: 'What business is it of yours that you've got to come running out so fast? So nosey! Now don't go around blabbing!' Gave him a good scolding. The watchman was so mad that he told the first person he saw."

Liu was glad the body had been removed when he left for work. But he saw that a section of cement paving was wet from washing.

The ground was crunchy and gritty, with bits of ice forming in the shadows under the hanging shed that bridged the alley.

The only house in the alley immune from the fevered campaign of the Five Antis was his hostel because its inmates were subject to the Three Antis. The Inhabitants' Committee of this district was starting on the new drive for one hundred letters per alley informing on merchants, clerks, shopkeepers.

It snowed that day. Liu looked out of his window in the evening at the little houses opposite, the yellow-lit windows under the snow-covered roofs, the dark elbow of slushy lane turning round the end of the row. It looked like one of those foreign Christmas cards. And perhaps its peacefulness was not altogether deceptive, he thought, looking at a window where he could see a school-boy's book bag hanging by its canvas strap on a nail. People had to carry on as usual, worries or no worries. And he knew from his own experience how your circle of concern could be drawn in smaller and smaller. He couldn't honestly say he was much affected by the letters he received, telling of drastic messes some of his close relatives and friends had got into. A person's heart could shrink and shrink indefinitely like a habitually starved stomach. It got so that there was never a sympathetic pang that was not mitigated by the gladness that it was not you it happened to.

"A woman comrade to see you, Comrade Liu!" the coolie called from downstairs.

That would be Su Nan. She had telephoned this afternoon to tell him that she had come through the Three Antis with an almost spotless record—the only one in her office to get that, presumably because she was comparatively new there and had not had time to commit any crimes. He had insisted on celebrating with a movie and she had promised to meet him at his hostel this evening if she could make it.

He was a bit stunned to find Ya-mei waiting for him in the sitting room downstairs. She had never been to the hostel before. People were bound to take notice. As it was, Liu felt worried lest people might think he was specially close to the Ts'uis since Ya-mei always ordered him around on little errands.

"Ai, Comrade Chu," he greeted her, smiling. "Please sit down, sit down." He felt awkward not knowing what to say about Ts'ui's death.

Probably sensing his embarrassment, Ya-mei said at once with a smile, "Have you had supper? If you're free now, can I trouble you to do something for me?"

There was a perky defiance in her tone as if she felt uncertain how she was going to be treated. It made him feel ashamed. "Of course," he said quickly. "If it's anything I can do—"

"I wrote a self-criticism. The Party Branch Office said they wanted to send it to the *Hsin Wen Jih Pao*," she mentioned the name of the most widely read newspaper in Shanghai. "But you know my Standard of Culture." She smiled at him. "The kind of thing I write is really not presentable. I wish you'd correct it for me."

"You're too modest. I'm no good at writing either," Liu said smiling.

"If you're going to be modest I'll take it that you despise me and won't help me," she joked, her eyes suddenly filming over with tears.

Liu could not let her think that he was snubbing her because of her altered circumstances. He took the manuscript from her.

The title was "Traitor Ts'ui P'ing Poisoned My Mind." She wrote forcefully and concisely. Some of the wording was not quite right but she had a good command of the Communist vocabulary.

"I'll leave this here," she said. "You can go over it when you're free. I'll come and get it another day."

"No, it won't take a minute," he said hastily. He could not afford to have her calling again. "Fact is, it's perfectly all right as it stands. But if you insist—"

After making a few alterations he read it over again. It said:

I came from a Middle Farmer's family. When I was twelve years old, the Communists liberated my home village in Yih Hsien, Shantung. The comrades working among us mobilized the children to join the Children's Corps. I was very active in the Corps and I studied hard, so I was admitted into the Party at the age of fifteen. I have been working for the Masses ever since.

When I met Traitor Ts'ui P'ing I thought that in spite of his petit-bourgeois origins, his history was pure. He had been a college student when he went to Yenan and joined the Revolution. And he had shed blood for the Revolution. Our political level was nearly equal and in our work we could help each other. Hence our union.

After the Victory on All Fronts we were transferred to Shanghai. We were allotted a handsome, comfortable room, complete with refrigerator, electric fan and heater. Our two children had a nursemaid to look after them and beautiful toys to play with. I often dressed them in foreign-style clothes and took them with me when I went to the movies in a car with Traitor Ts'ui P'ing. Thus I gradually developed a Pleasure Viewpoint and started on the road to depravity and corruption.

Then came the Three-Anti Movement. Ts'ui P'ing, traitor to the people, despoiler of the nation, was charged with corruption and betrayal of the Revolution. But my political nose was so insensitive that I was still deceived by him, believing firmly in his innocence. After his arrest I even ran around petitioning on his behalf. The Organization made repeated attempts to win me over and mobilize me to inform against him. But I persisted in my obsession and stood on his side. I begged and implored and wept. To the last I fondly dreamed that the Government would be lenient to him.

It was not until I had heard of Traitor Ts'ui P'ing's execution that I suddenly woke up and came to my senses. Because I know that the People's Government never kills a single person by mistake. His execution is the absolute proof of his guilt.

I now realize that I have committed the gravest error, having stood by a man convicted of corruption. I am grateful to the People's Government for liberating me from the obnoxious narcotic influence of Traitor Ts'ui P'ing, correcting me in time and educating me so that I might serve the people better in the future."

Until he had read her autobiographical account Liu had not realized that in her he had met the most ideal kind of Party member, whose background and origin were above reproach, who had inherited the inborn nobility of farmers and had never come into contact with any influence except that of the Party. And yet she was corrupted as soon as she came into the city and lived in comparative comfort in the manner of a middle-class housewife. Where was the proletarian firmness of standpoint that was always contrasted with the eternal vacillation of the petit-bourgeois?

Liu could not follow their line of reasoning. And somehow, knowing Ya-mei, he found it hard to think of her in such terms. Above all she was a country girl who had made good. Not much different from the country girl who was converted by some missionary, had her schooling paid for and a job ready for her. She might be a devout Christian but people would refer to her, in that awful barefaced Chinese way, as one who *ch'ih chiao*, eats religion. Likewise, Ya-mei was one who ate revolutionary rice.

She was such a practical person. Liu felt that was why she had "awakened" and turned against her husband as soon as she heard he was dead and she couldn't do anything more to help him. He was struck again by the docile indifference of Party members, the nomadic fluidity of their lives. It had occurred to him when he saw the change in Ko Shan's room after the Three Antis. Only this time he did not feel like laughing.

Ya-mei was sitting with arms crossed, both elbows propped up on the table, staring straight ahead. Under the lamplight her eyelids were red with weeping, as if heavily rouged.

He shouldn't think harshly of her. As everybody knew, it had become a routine now—whenever a man was executed, some member of the family was required to submit an article denouncing him and expressing gratitude to the government for putting him to death. She had to write this for her own protection and her children's. It was the only intelligent thing to do once Ts'ui's fate was settled and he was beyond her help.

When he handed the paper back to her she read it over again before putting it away. "Now you see how low my Standard of Culture is," she said with a slight smile.

"No, really, I was just going to tell you—you write very well."

"You're just being polite." She looked down at her crossed arms. Pinpoints of cotton wool were escaping through the dark blue cloth all over her padded sleeves. She started to pluck them off. "Really my Standard is too low. Tell me the names of some books I could read. I wish I could improve myself a little."

Liu cleared his throat slightly. "I don't know—There must be a lot of new books published that are good. I've been so rushed lately, I haven't touched a book for I don't know how long."

The bits of cotton wool that dotted her uniform seemed inexhaustible. She went on plucking them, her head lowered. Then she said, "I'm going to be transferred to the Public Security Bureau, Yangtzepoo branch."

Whether that meant a demotion or not, he knew that the life of a policewoman was hard. "Can you take your children with you?" he said.

She shook her head. "Nobody to look after them there, and I wouldn't have time for them myself. I'm going to send them to their grandmother in the country."

"That's good. Then you won't have any worries. You can devote yourself to your work." He could not think of what else to say to cheer her up.

After another pause she got up, flashing one of her usual Party smiles at him. "I've got to go now. Come and see me when you have time. I heard that you're progressing very fast. I'm sure I could learn a lot from you."

She shook hands and said again, "Be sure to come and see me in Yangtzepoo. Any time you're free." Her eyes were bright under the seemingly rouged lids. There was an expression in them which he did not want to admit he had seen.

After she was gone he waited for Su Nan downstairs. He wished Su Nan would come. It was quarter past eight now. If she was not here within ten minutes they wouldn't be able to make the eight-thirty show. That would mean she wouldn't be coming. He hoped she could make it. If she was here he would not feel so unsettled, troubled by doubts about all human relations.

"Comrade Liu."

He looked up from his newspaper and saw a policeman standing at the door. "Yes?" he said, putting down his paper and getting to his feet.

"You are Liu Ch'üan?" the policeman said, dispensing with the "comrade" and the pleasant smile now that he was sure it was Liu.

"Yes."

The man came into the room followed by two other armed policemen. "Please come with us to the Public Security Bureau for a talk."

"Why? What have I done that's against the law?"

"*Tsou, Tsou!* Come on, come on! You'll know when you get there."

"Is this an arrest?"

"*Tsou, tsou!*" They had surrounded him and were giving him impatient little pushes.

So Liu walked out of the room at the head of the group, with two of the yellow-clad men stepping closely behind him. It was not long after supper. The narrow passage still smelled of vegetable oil. The electric light was murky yellow against the crimson-painted wooden panelling under the slope of the staircase. He was aware of faces hanging over the rail on the steep stairs, mutely watching him going.

He was still surrounded by that aura of humdrum everyday living that nothing could ever seem to penetrate, impregnable alike to tragedy or great strokes of luck. What was happening to him just did not seem real. Otherwise he was clear-headed and calm enough. He felt his heart, all flattened out inside him, stretching away to great distances and swept clean and empty by the winds in anticipation of some terrible feeling which never came.

He looked for Su Nan when he went out the back door and into the car parked outside, in case she came just in time to see him off. She was not there.

22

THE FACES were still hanging over the staircase rail like drab yellow flowers on some creeper. They were staring down at the coolie who was standing in the lamplight below, telling them exactly how it had happened, how the police had walked in and asked for Comrade Liu. "No, they had not said why. Just asked if Comrade Liu Ch'üan was here."

The faces wavered like flat yellow flowers in a breeze, turned vacantly to each other and again turned away, making rustling, leafy murmurs. They stared down mutely with just as much concentration when the coolie repeated his story for the ninth time, but for variation, started with what he had been doing when the bell rang.

He had left the back door open as a gesture of non-resistance, in case the raid was not over yet and they came back for somebody else. So when Su Nan came, she walked straight in through the empty kitchen. She had never been to Liu's hostel before and thought it quite a feat that she had managed to read the number plate in the dark alley. But she stopped, a little startled by all the blank, still faces turned toward her from all levels, up and down the stairs, in the golden dusk of the passage.

"Is Comrade Liu home?" she asked.

Nobody stirred, but the unmistakable feeling of having said something shocking came over her at once. She looked at the men, wondering dumbly if she had come into the wrong house. Then she saw Chang's face among them. He was slow in recognizing her, probably because he had never expected to see her in Shanghai.

"Yieh!" he exclaimed eventually. "When did you come down

south, Comrade Su? You remember me?" He came downstairs smiling. "We worked on the Land Reform together."

"But of course, Comrade Chang," Su Nan said smiling. "How are you?" There was no longer any reason why she and Liu should keep their relations secret from Chang. Still, she had an irrational dislike of letting him know, feeling it would invite trouble.

"Where are you working now?" Then he said, "Well, this is a surprise! Had no idea you were in Shanghai." He frowned and lowered his voice. "You're looking for Liu Ch'üan? Just now some people came from the Public Security Bureau, asked him to go and have a talk. He went with them just a few minutes ago."

"They—they didn't say why?" she stammered.

"No. That's just what we were wondering. Have you any idea?" he suddenly fixed her with a keen eye. "Any clues?"

"No, I haven't the faintest idea. This is very unexpected."

"You know him quite well, don't you? Kept in touch ever since the Land Reform? Really, I had no idea," he said with a curious smile. "That Liu certainly kept things to himself." Then he added, to cover up, "Like this time—nobody could imagine what they want him for."

"This is so unexpected," she murmured, realizing that it was no use talking to Chang. He must be quite angry now, feeling cheated because she and Liu had got together right under his nose while he himself had got nowhere with her. "Well, I'll be going now," she said.

"Where are you staying? Have you got a telephone? I'll let you know if I hear anything."

She extricated herself in such a hurry that she knew it looked as if she were afraid of being drawn into the case. Which was just as well.

It wouldn't be much use anyhow, to try and get information from Liu's own unit. She understood that things had been in a state of confusion there ever since the responsible *kan-pu*, Ts'ui P'ing, had been executed. But Liu had been stationed at the *Liberation Daily News* for some time. Perhaps she could get some help there.

Lucky that newspapers work at night, she thought. And it was early yet. On her way to the bus station as she passed a brightly lit fruit shop she turned and glanced automatically at the grandfather clock that almost every shop has on its wall. Instead she saw the round white face of the weighing machine hung in mid-air under the blue-white glare of fluorescent light. Hurrying by, she shook off the momentary shock of thinking that the needle pointing upward at zero was both hands of the clock pointing straight up at twelve. She would not have been really surprised if it was already midnight. It seemed such a long time since she had started out to meet Liu for the eight-thirty show.

At the newspaper office she asked for Ko Shan. She did not know anybody else there, and though she had only seen Ko Shan for a few minutes at the Native Products Exhibition, Liu seemed to know her quite well. And being an old *kan-pu* the woman might have useful connections.

Waiting outside the waist-high partitions, she saw Ko Shan get up from her desk across the large room. The office was working full force but as in all other organizations during the Three Antis, somehow it looked deserted. Like a closed-down department store it echoed from silence, bleakly uncluttered and gray with dust. Except that there was also a feeling that the slightest motion in this glassed-in cold twilight of an aquarium did not escape observation.

Ko Shan did not seem very pleased to see her, which was to be expected. Nobody welcomed visitors these days. When Su Nan had told her about Liu she said the usual thing about its being most unexpected.

"We know nothing about this," she said. "He's been with us for several months, but his organizational connections haven't been transferred here permanently. It's true that he was brought in on our Three-Anti Mass Meetings. But he was cleared all right. At our end."

"I know I shouldn't impose on you like this, Comrade Ko. But you see, he has very few friends here in Shanghai. And I'm new here; I don't know anybody."

"I wish I could be of help," Ko Shan said, "but as far as I know, the only thing to do in a case like this is to wait. If there's been a mistake, he'll be out in no time."

Su Nan went on speaking at some length. Then she noticed the whining creak of the waist-high swinging door she had been pushing back and forth while talking. People were looking at the two of them standing by the partition. Ko Shan had not asked her to step inside and take a seat beside her desk.

She stopped suddenly, apologized again for intruding and said goodbye.

But once outside the building she began to wonder if it was not because she had approached Ko Shan so publicly. Even if she had been disposed to help, she wouldn't want to say anything with people around.

She decided to wait for her to come out after work. It would not be for another two or three hours but there was always the possibility that she might leave before that on some business and not come back. Su Nan thought she had better wait within sight of the entrance to the building. She wandered to the bus stop on the next block, stood around for a while and walked slowly back, holding the end of her scarf against her mouth. Lucky there was no policeman about, she thought. It savored of sabotage to loiter around the Party newspaper office on a freezing night like this. The pocked concrete pavement shimmered brownly, wet with melted snow. The few men who passed by glanced at her suspiciously but there was no danger of her being mistaken for a streetwalker. Although these women had taken to dowdy clothes as protective coloring, they drew the line at wearing uniforms. In spite of the fact that women as well as men were wearing them now, there was still something faintly official about the uniform which would scare prospective clients off.

On the way there was a little temple, tiny, low and squat between a bank and a store. She thought it was funny having a temple here right in the business center. She could just make out the five gilt characters on the scarlet signboard, "*Pao An Ssu-t'u Miao;* the Temple of the Minister of the Interior, Guardian of Safety"—some good mandarin deified after his death, probably. The wooden gate with its scarlet painted bars was closed for the night. But pin-points of fire-light dotted the bottom rail. Sticks of incense stood in a little hole drilled in the sail, put there by worshippers. In the stifling cold of the night the incense was odorless and fumeless, nothing but a row of crimson glowing dots close to the ground.

Like many other things in the city, the temples would be allowed to function as usual until some new movement turned the spotlight on them. Perhaps now of all times, with the Five Antis on, the super-stitious had need of their gods, Su Nan thought. Though she doubted that anybody really believed the gods could do much. Some new dark destiny had pushed them to the sidelines, reducing them to the role of vague, good-natured elders who might be prevailed upon to put in a kind word or two on your behalf. It might or might not work, but it was something to do when all else had failed you. And it would seem that gods also improved with adversity. Purged now of all their jealous wrath and vengeful fury, their all-too-human vanity and possessiveness, they had become at last mere kindly spirits, tol-erant of all sins, even that of disbelief—the hardest to forgive.

Somebody had planted his incense stick in the snow on the top rail because there was no room at the bottom. The snow had piled thick there, wedged in at the corner at the end of the bar. But it was beginning to melt. Su Nan stopped by the gate and reached up to straighten the brittle, thin brown stick which looked as if it was about to topple over. For the first time in her life she came near to understanding why so many people clung to their mild, ineffectual idols. She carefully patted the snow into a hard mound. It was sting-ing cold and she was weeping.

She went back and forth along the block for the next two hours. Finally there was a dribble of newspaper-workers coming out. She spotted Ko Shan from a long way off. Instead of accosting her she followed her for a little distance until they were alone.

"Comrade Ko," she whispered, catching up with her.

Ko Shan had apparently thought it was a colleague "Comrade Su!" she exclaimed in a low voice. "Why, have you been here all this time? You must be frozen!" she said half laughing.

"It's not so cold if you keep walking."

After a pause Su Nan said, "I'm awfully sorry I came in just like that and talked such a lot in front of everybody. It was so thoughtless of me."

"No, no, that's perfectly all right. We're all colleagues there. And although Liu Ch'üan hasn't been with us long, we all feel concerned. Naturally."

Su Nan was silent. After they had walked on for a bit she asked, "Do you live in a hostel?"

"No, I live by myself."

"Is it far?" She wondered if Ko Shan might let her come home with her even if it was late. This was no place to talk.

"Quite a distance from here. I'll have to take a pedicab."

"If I'd known where you live, I would have gone to see you at your house. I shouldn't have come to your office."

"No, that's perfectly all right, really. Only I'm sorry that I wasn't able to do anything."

That seemed final enough. But there were no pedicabs around, so Ko Shan continued to walk by her side. Probably wondering how to shake her off, Su Nan thought.

There was perhaps no place as quiet and deserted as the business and shopping center at night. It had the feel of an evacuated city waiting to be bombed by moonlight. Old whitewashed office buildings with Moorish lacework over the arched entrances stood silent, their windows black and gaping. Gray shadows of mongrel-Gothic concrete turrets loomed over the big stores, the old silversmiths and herbal dispensaries. Not a human being was astir for miles around, or a dog or cock. Their aloneness in the illumined dead quiet was getting to be embarrassing under the circumstances.

They passed a big textile shop, the only shop that had left its neon light on after closing time. The big neon-bordered shop sign ran the length of the whole front. The glowing green line framed the long dark blank of the signboard, making a mystery of it as if they had on sale here something unspeakable and terrifying. A considerable stretch of shiny wet sidewalk was bathed in the green lunar glare.

"It's going to be troublesome if it has anything to do with Ts'ui P'ing," Ko Shan suddenly said reflectively.

For once she was being frank and she had obviously been thinking about Liu's case since she had been told. And there was real concern in her face in the green neon light. "Yes, that's what I was afraid of," Su Nan said gratefully. Then she burst out after a moment of hesitation, "Comrade Ko, Liu Ch'üan would never take bribes or anything like that. I can guarantee that for him. I know all about him. He tells me everything."

"So you know everything about him," Ko Shan thought bitterly. "But you don't know about us—or do you? Is that why you seem so sure I'm going to help get him out? No, if you knew, you'd act quite differently toward me. You can't be such a good actress." Aloud she drawled, "Ai, who's qualified to guarantee anybody these days! You never know if you yourself aren't a bit questionable too."

She sounded as if she did not want to have anything to do with this, and just now Su Nan had thought she had turned warm and friendly. She did not know what she had said to have offended her. "Yes, that's silly of me," she said desperately. "And Comrade Ko, I really shouldn't be bothering you like this when you hardly even know me. But I really don't know what to do." Her voice hardened with the lump rising in her throat. She turned away quickly to wipe her tears. "I don't know anybody. If only you could tell me whom to go to."

After a long pause Ko Shan said evenly, "I don't know anybody either. Unless you want to try Shen K'ai-fu. He deals with culture and propaganda, but I heard he's in close connection with the Political Defense Department." She dropped her voice as everybody did at the mention of the name which stood for secret police.

"Do you think he'd see me?" Su Nan said eagerly.

"No harm in trying. If you want, I can telephone his office and see if I can arrange an interview for you."

"That's awfully kind of you." Su Nan hesitated before she added, "If you can go with me it'll be even better." She felt that she was greedily "advancing a foot when granted an inch."

"No, I don't think that'll be any help," Ko Shan said immediately. "You see, if I telephone him I'll just ask if I may send a comrade around who's working on the *Wen Hui Pao* and wants to consult him about a certain case. But if I accompany you, it might look as if I'm trying to Pull Personal Relations. It wouldn't look well in a time like this."

"Yes. Sure! Sure!" Su Nan said hastily.

"Besides, I don't know him well enough myself. I don't even know if he'll grant the interview. Hey, pedicab! Pedicab!" she shouted, half running toward a flitting shadow way off on the other side of the road.

"Shall I—ring you up in a day or two?" Su Nan called out uncertainly, rushing after her.

"No, I'll ring you up." Meeting the pedicab half way she hopped onto it, gave the driver curt directions and glided away without once turning around, paying no attention to Su Nan's stream of thanks.

She was annoyed with herself for yielding to a generous impulse, Su Nan thought. As who wouldn't be nowadays. Perhaps there was no need to be so rude. But Su Nan was ready to put up with any amount of eccentricity in old *kan-pu*. Up north there was the saying, "Out of five old *kan-pu*, two have tuberculosis and two are insane." It always made her smile to hear it quoted but right now the thought of it seemed almost a sacrilege, because she was counting a lot on Ko Shan.

Walking back slowly she passed the little temple again. She looked up to see if the incense stick she set upright was still there, erect and burning in the snow. There it was, the red dot aglow in the dark. She felt a little pleased, as if that might have something to do with the fact that she had had luck with the first person she had tackled.

23

KO SHAN telephoned her two days later and told her to go to a certain address the next afternoon. It was a large, quiet house set on a lawn in an expensive residential district in the old French Quarter. Converted into an office but not labeled with official signboards, it had soldiers standing guard outside the wrought-iron gate. After being interviewed first by a secretary and searched by a guard, she was admitted into Shen K'ai-fu's presence.

Afterwards she wondered if she ought to ring Ko Shan up to tell her how the interview went and to thank her again. Perhaps it would be expected of her. It would be common politeness. But Ko Shan had made it quite plain that she did not welcome telephone calls.

Then something happened which made any further contact with Ko Shan quite out of the question. The *Liberation Daily News* got into trouble. Ko Shan's chief, Lin I-ch'ün, had been arrested for corruption. Su Nan heard a lot about it over in her office although the newspapers withheld the news until weeks later when he was openly charged with "embezzling JMP$220,000,000; engaging in speculations with businessmen as partners and receiving gifts from subordinates that amounted to over JMP$10,000,000." Furthermore, "he is connected with the landlord class through a thousand fibers and ten thousand filaments," the papers said grimly. (Lin came out of this unscathed, was merely transferred.)

The lunar New Year was drawing near. The Kuomintang had prohibited its celebration in an effort to enforce the solar calendar. And during the war years the permanent curfew outlawed the lighting of firecrackers because they sounded too much like gunfire. But now it was considered all right again, since the holiday had been re-named the Farmers' New Year. And yet somehow fewer firecrackers were heard than when setting them off had been illegal. Especially this year, when all the shops and most families were in the throes of the Five Antis. Still, the New Year was the New Year. Toward the middle twentieth of the twelfth moon there was often heard at night the spatter of explosives sending the kitchen god to heaven in style for his annual report on the establishment. Su Nan felt jumpy at every volley, trying not to think of Ts'ui P'ing, who had been shot.

The sound of firecrackers also made her feel more alone than ever in the strange city. If this thing had happened to Liu in Peking she wouldn't feel that she had nobody to turn to. She had her family and relatives, and the professors in her university used to be very gener-ous to the students, going to great lengths to help them. Then there were the professors of Peita under whom Liu had studied. Of course it was different now. Families and relatives were no longer quite so willing to take your troubles upon their shoulders. And the profes-sors were frightened people who had to be more careful than any-body else. This would be precisely the kind of thing they would avoid like the plague. Still she wished she was in Peking.

The imminence of the New Year was almost threatening. The last days of the year had a way of crowding upon you. Because there was not much time left and because it was so cold, people scurried on the road, laden with big and small parcels wrapped with coarse yellow paper tied with straw, bringing home ingredients for the New Year feast—salted pork, mushrooms, *fen ssu*, thin silvery noodles. The sight of them isolated her in her distress.

She had come to know this part of town quite well, travelling back and forth from Shen K'ai-fu's office and the bus station almost every day. It was very much like going to see a fashionable doctor, she thought the first time she went there. Shen had seemed so preoc-cupied, she remembered, sitting at his desk listening to her account of the case. Telephone calls kept interrupting her. When he was talking on the phone, she sat very still, trying to efface herself com-pletely, because what was being said might be important secrets which he wouldn't want anybody to hear. She stared at the glass of tea on his desk. Imprisoned under the glass lid a white jasmine was drifting very slowly down through the yellowish green twilight of the tea and another flower was rising, both with the utter purposelessness and unconcern of clouds. As he talked into the phone his eyes rested on her, vacant and unwavering. When she finally made a slight uneasy movement to look back at him, he shifted his vacant stare to a piece of furniture beyond her.

He promised to make inquiries for her and shook hands without rising when she was leaving. Just then the telephone rang again. Picking it up and speaking into it, he seemed to have forgotten to release her hand. She stood awkwardly by his desk looking down at the oily separate strands of thin hair on the balding top of his head, each strand distinct over the greenish pallor of scalp. The thick black rim of his glasses came out from under the black wings of long hair over his ears. She felt stifled with her hand buried in the warm padded softness of his fat hand as if she was standing neck-deep in mud. It took all her will power to keep smiling and to wait a while before she pulled away.

She came back the next day as she had been instructed. But he seemed very vague. She wondered if he had remembered to make inquiries. He asked her the same questions all over again—she was sure he had never got them straight the first time. She told him she was engaged to Liu and he asked her about her past history, family background, the schools and university she had gone to, how she had been admitted into the Corps and the jobs she had held. It was understandable that she too was under suspicion. In any case, the more questions asked, the more hopeful it seemed.

When she apologized for the amount of time he had wasted on her, the third or fourth time she called, he said smiling, "I always have time for young people. It's a sad thing for a revolutionary worker to lose touch with young people. After all, the Revolution is more for the benefit of your generation than for anybody else. Mustn't forget that."

That was the day he had told her he had made arrangements for her

224 · EILEEN CHANG

to meet a Comrade Li. He seemed unwilling to describe Li as being in charge of the Three-Anti cases. "He has a better grasp of the Three-Anti material than I do," he said warily. "You'll have a chance to tell him about Liu. And he might be able to give you some information. I'm asking him down for dinner this evening so you can talk to him."

"This evening?" She heard herself saying almost automatically, without the slightest tell-tale pause, "But I won't be able to get away this evening. There's a special meeting." She knew from experience that to be convincing, quickness counted more than the perfection of the excuse.

But he laughed cynically, with justifiable annoyance, "Aah, surely you have to take time out to eat? It won't take long—Li is a busy man too."

"Can I go and see him at his office, do you think?" she asked miserably. "Perhaps if I say you sent me—"

"I don't think he has time for visitors just now," Shen said brusquely. "He's terribly rushed."

After she left she was tormented by self-reproach. When she came again the next day after a sleepless night, she felt a little incredulous that he received her as usual.

"I had a talk with Li yesterday," he told her. "About your friend's case." He looked reflectively at the glass of tea in front of him, twirling the glass lid around slightly, holding it by its knob. The broken squeak of glass scraping against glass grated on her in the sudden stillness.

"He's definitely mixed up with Ts'ui P'ing. Acted as Ts'ui's claws and teeth in several instances," Shen said. "And so far he's refused to confess. You know, of course, that makes it more serious."

She did not really hear what else he said. She listened with frightful concentration, spongily absorbing every word and intonation, only to have it all spread and run into each other. Something about his special concern for her. He had been treating her as a special case, he said. But when she begged again for help, he sipped his tea, lapsed back into his relaxed absentmindedness.

Coming out into the street she wondered if she ought to telephone Ko Shan—defy for once the tacit quarantine imposed on all employees of the *Liberation Daily News*. Numbly she turned down the idea. It soon popped up again in her dazed mind as if she had never thought of it before. Again she turned it down. But even if there wasn't anything Ko Shan could do, she wanted to tell her what had happened. She had a great need to tell somebody—anybody. Only the facts, which were simple enough: Shen hadn't got anything definite for her until today, when he had told her the bad news. She wanted to hear herself tell the story straight, unembellished by all the details about Shen's tones and expressions which might be pure imagination on her part.

If it was nothing, why had she refused to have dinner with him and that Comrade Li she was to meet?—when she had known how important that was and how offended he would feel. She had regretted it bitterly afterwards. But if she had gone to dinner, would Li have turned up? Was there a Li in the first place? Would it be at Shen's house or one of the apartments he had taken over?—The trouble with her was that she had an inflamed, hyper-sensitive ego from dealing with the men who had made passes at her, she told herself. The first time she came into contact with anyone high up enough to be referred to as a *shou chang*, head leader, and she thought he was up to the same tricks.

The man walking in front of her had come up from the country with wild ducks to sell for the New Year. To leave his hands free he carried the dead ducks on his back, their necks bunched together and sewn on his worn old padded jacket of chalk-striped gray cloth. The ducks' bills pressed flatly and snugly against the back of his thin shoulder. Their bodies, a glossy black-green with touches of light blue and copper on the wings, made a little feather cape that swung a bit as he walked. Su Nan tried not to look at it, the way it swung heavy and bright, a few steps ahead of her.

There must have been a market here earlier on in the day. The road was wet and littered. Frozen, spoilt cabbage leaves lay pasted on the sidewalk in big green patches, the rotted spots turned transparent in the pale green.

It seemed to her that the most he could do was refuse to help her. Would he go to the extent of damaging Liu's case? And what would that get him if she were to remain stubborn? He wouldn't want to risk a scandal at a time like this, with the Three Antis on. Though the fact that the Three Antis was going on did make it much less trouble to destroy a person than to save him—perhaps no trouble at all for one in Shen's position.

She had often had this feeling as a child when she had done something disastrous, smashing a treasured vase, losing her coat or her school fees. Nothing could be helped—but there must be something she could do, something that just eluded her, something she had to reach for with desperate need.

It could be that Shen had been telling the truth when he said Liu's situation was critical, and was merely withholding his help unless she proved more tractable. It would make no difference actually. But at least that would mean that Liu was in danger for his life. It wasn't as if he would have been all right but for her meddling.

Sickening, she thought—the deviousness and cunning of the way her mind worked. But she would rather die than think that if anything was to happen to Liu, it was she who had killed him.

The little dark green cape of duck feathers swayed a little from side to side, thick and slow, always suspended in front of her. A grocery shop along the way was sunning *fen ssu* on the sidewalk, big coils of thin brittle silver wire, magnificent nests of some fairy bird. Su Nan stepped around them with exaggerated, drunken care.

She felt the sun through her hair. Her hair felt thin with the sun on it. At this moment she hated and despised the self-contained integrity of her being, the mild, unthinking pleasure she took in the consciousness of her person, the movements of her limbs inside her padded uniform.

But what guarantee would she get—even if Liu was immediately set free, it meant nothing. She had a relative who had been arrested on suspicion of counter-revolutionary activities. He had been released after several months and arrested again within two weeks. Since then he had been in and out of jail several times, travelling in a well-greased rut. It was not like in the days of the warlords when the country was split and it was possible to flee from one sphere of influence to another. Nowadays the whole country lay stretched out like an open palm, ready to close around any one person at any minute.

She had thought she was prepared to throw herself into the breach, damming the darkness flooding over Liu. And yet, now that the sacrifice had turned into mere atonement, she found herself running away from it, outraged and resentful. Running away, crying out for Liu.

24

CARS PASSED on the street outside. The headlights flashed high and white into the dark room and the shadows of the bars on the window flicked over the men sitting jammed tight on the floor. Twenty men had been crowded into the small room.

The overhead light that used to be on all night had been turned off early this evening. Something was afoot, Liu thought.

No talking was allowed. Somebody was scratching, though. Alarmingly at first, the microphone high up on the wall also started scratching in long dry rustling strokes. Up until now it had just been a silent fixture on the wall, like an electric or gas meter. After a good bit of desultory sandpapering, a man's voice came on. The low pleasant voice was little more than a breathy whisper "*T'an-pai! T'an-pai* quick! *T'an-pai shih sheng-lu; k'ang chü shih ssu-lu. T'an-pai* is the road to life; resistance is the road to death."

After a pause for two or three minutes it again whispered, *T'an-pai shih sheng-lu; k'ang chü shih ssu-lu.*" It stopped after the seventh or eighth repetition, just when it was beginning to get mechanical and almost soothing.

Liu sat with arms hugging his knees. Elbows and back encased in filthy, smell-absorbent Liberation Suits pushed against him on all sides. Bones creaked when somebody tried to change his posture. A phlegmy cough was heard, half smothered. But the darkness and long silence were beginning to open up empty spaces overhead, room for whole lifetimes to hang brooding over them.

It must have been at least an hour later when there came a rattling of bolts and keys outside the door. The door was flung open, the lighted rectangle half blocked by silhouetted guards. Torchlight swept over the crowd on the floor. The thick beam of wan yellow light swung around in careless arcs, a train of blind faces materializing in its wake. Liu felt it pause on his face, the numb-touch of that round white spot that was more a hand than an eye.

Then it switched away and he heard somebody shout, "Yao Hsüeh-fan! Stand up!"

The light was cutting across the room. It picked out a man huddled by the closed tin pail at the corner. By tacit agreement the man who came latest to the room occupied the space which smelled the worst.

Yao was trying to get up. But the guards, who were adept at making people appear cowards, had already waded in, stepping over hands and feet, to seize him and drag him out of the room.

The door slammed shut and footsteps receded down the corridor. Other doors were unbolted noisily and there were muffled shouts, presumably calling out the names of other prisoners. Quite a handful of men were marched down the corridor. Then they were out of hearing.

Darkness came back in a rush, enfolding Liu in its clumsy stifling embrace. It was as if more men had been thrown into the room, half piling on top of him, their padded uniforms gritty with dirt. They weighed like sandbags and were as reassuring.

Then he heard the sound of shots. Not loud, but distinct enough. Executions usually took place out in Kiang wan, Liu thought. Not inside the compounds here. Had they really shot them? Maybe they were doing this for theatrical effect. They always went in for psychological tactics. Like during the suppression of counter-revolutionaries last year, when they had had a loudspeaker radio in prison tuned in to the public trial in I Yuan, the former dog-track. The suspects in prison heard the voice of thousands roar out the verdict, "*Sha! Sha!* Kill! Kill!"

The electric light suddenly flicked on. A moment later the microphone started its scratchy noise. The spokesman's voice was loud and bright when it came on. "All the bigoted factors who resisted *t'an-pai* have been shot! Everybody *t'an-pai*, quick! Review your past sins once more in your mind, carefully. Then *t'an-pai* thoroughly. To-night is your last chance! You will have your last chance to *t'an-pai* tonight."

The light went off once more. After a long pause the microphone again started whispering, "*T'an-pai shih sheng-lu; k'ang chü shih ssu-lu.*"

Liu did not know whether all his roommates were meditating on their past sins. They were supposed to be doing just that all along, night and day. Guards watching through cracks in the door saw to it that they all sat silent with bowed heads in a somewhat Buddhist posture of penitent introspection. They seldom risked talking but when Liu first came in here the man sitting next to him had whispered without turning toward him "*Na-li lai-te*? Where from?" Since then he had heard the same question asked of every new arrival. He supposed it was important to know who you were put in the same room with, as a means of gauging where you stood.

From their brief mumbled replies it would seem that many of them were high-ranking "retained personnel" of nationalized concerns—former bank or factory managers who had kept their old jobs after the government took over. Liu was familiar enough with such cases, having worked at the Three-Anti headquarters. Those men were invariably charged with corruption and required to pay back enormous embezzled sums which were, in fact, ransoms. The other occupants of the cell, he decided, were non-Party member *kan-pu* like himself. One of the slogans of the Three Antis was to "Tidy Up the Middle Layer." There were up to ten million non-Party member *kan-pu* in the country and they probably needed sorting out and tidying up. They were called "the middle layer" because they stood somewhere between the capitalist and proletarian class. Their standpoints were not clear and definite enough.

Liu himself had been taken out several times to be interrogated by police sergeants. Some of the questions seemed trivial, like "How old is your father, if alive? And your mother?" Then, much later, after a lot of other questions, suddenly thrusting this one on him, "Your father is older than your mother by how many years?" to see if he had been lying. But he could judge by the general drift of the questions that he had been incriminated on account of Ts'ui P'ing. He could tell also that whoever informed against him knew enough about his work and Ts'ui's to give the far-fetched accusations a certain plausibility.

Who else could it be but Chang? The man was almost a walking biography of Ts'ui, with the wealth of information supplied wittingly or unwittingly by Ho, the Culinary Officer.

He felt as certain about that as he did about anything these days, which was not saying much. It did something to a man to realize that the dull unfailing punctuality of tomorrows could no longer be counted upon. It was as upsetting as living in a world with no gravitational pull. Isolated thoughts and impressions were apt to jump at him, compressed to a hard pellet, out of a uniform gray numbness. Or sometimes it was like a fragment of a tune you could not get out of your head, droning on and on and on until it ground itself into pulpy nonsense.

A car's headlights flashed into the window and were gone. To him it was the world going by—too fast. He felt for it a longing that was past resentment.

He had been thinking a lot of the past twenty-odd years of his life. He thought of Su Nan most of the time because she stood for all his yearning and unfulfilled dreams. He thought of Ko Shan too. She had given him a good time—almost forced it on him. Only now it turned out that it was not free of charge. He had had it on credit and the price was rather steep, if he was to pay with his life.

He drew some comfort from the thought that if he was not to come out of this alive, nobody could guess the real cause. He couldn't bear thinking of Su Nan getting to know that he had died because he got mixed up with some other woman.

The light came on again. Guards opened the door and distributed paper and pencils.

"You have exactly two hours to write your confessions. Remember this is your last chance. So be thorough. Write on one side of the paper only."

The floor space next to the tin pail, formerly shunned, now became the most coveted seat because the closed stool could serve as a desk. It was very hard to keep your pencil from piercing the paper spread over your lap or over the floor, full of cracks. Liu was reminded of the stories his grandfather used to tell about the discomforts of imperial examinations, especially the highest one held in the presence of the emperor when you had to write kneeling down.

He pleaded not guilty to all the charges against him. He knew that people undergoing the Three Antis or Five Antis often said whatever was required of them, made up things if necessary, then tried to back out of it when it came to paying. They had probably argued, not without reason, that you should save your neck first and then, so long as there was breath in your body, you could always haggle and bargain and get off with a compromise. Liu had heard of countless cases in which *kan-pu* and businessmen had confessed to embezzling public funds in astronomical figures which later proved to be either untrue or greatly exaggerated. He had always thought it foolish as well as cowardly. And anyway in his case it was impracticable. Even if he was to "disgorge" only a fraction of his illegal gains, where was he to get the money?

After the guards had come and collected the confessions the light went off again. Liu had many misgivings about his paper but he felt reasonably certain that nothing more was going to happen tonight. There was even the possibility that the next few days would be uneventful. The examiners must have time to go over the papers, discuss and analyze them and look into the facts before they made any decisions.

A few people in the room were snoring, sitting up. But most of them were too excited to sleep. Again footsteps sounded along the corridor. Not the pacing guard—several of them. They came and stopped at the door, taking what seemed to be ages to open it.

"Stand up, Liu Ch'üan!" one of the guards called out, holding a slip of paper in his hand. "*Ch'u-lai! Ch'u-lai!* Come-out, come-out!" he rapped, making one word of it.

Liu raised himself quickly on to his cramped feet and ploughed his way out, stumbling. He was aware of hands fumbling for his in the dark and holding it for an instant as he pushed past. A dim spasm of anger and hate ran through him at the touch of those hands. Right now he would like to feel that he was alone and unfettered, with nothing to keep him. And those hands were like life itself tugging at his heart.

Three guards trotted him down the passage, then down the stairs. He estimated it must be after midnight, which always seemed to be considered the best time for executions.

The corridor downstairs made a turn. The guards pushed open a door to a lighted room without knocking. He supposed there would be the usual procedure, identification, a few questions asked by an officer. He had expected a bare office but it looked more like the warden's living room, with upholstered chairs, little round glass-topped tables and scrolls of paintings on the walls. He had already forgotten what an ordinary room looked like. It seemed so unreal, lighted by the lamp with its scalloped orange-pink paper shade.

A woman in civilian uniform was the only person in the room. It was Su Nan. They had let her in as a special favor to a condemned man, he thought confusedly. But they no longer did things like that. That was False Humanitarianism. He walked slowly toward her, smiling a little shamefacedly.

"Fifteen minutes," one of the guards called out at the doorway.

"Are you all right?" Su Nan whispered. She put both hands on his arms, feeling him hesitantly, in case it would hurt if she should come to a wound.

"I'm very well," Liu answered quickly. "How did you get here? I thought no visitors were allowed."

She did not answer at once. "It's not absolutely impossible. There are ways," she said softly, glancing at the guards to remind him of their presence.

The men were discreetly looking the other way, hands locked behind their backs, standing on one foot in the usual sentry posture, the other foot stretched way out, toes pointing outward. The leniency and consideration shown them was nothing short of incredible. No bars or wire netting between them, no row of chairs as a barrier, as they sometimes had in the lax, good-natured old days. When Liu drew her to him the blurriness and padded thickness of dreams closed around him. And like in a dream he seemed split into two persons and was both in and out of it, both the dazed actor and the dull observer standing a little way off, seeing many things that meant nothing to him at the moment. Su Nan seemed harassed, almost preoccupied, though he hardly felt it, realizing that she was actually here.

"No, you've got to tell me how you could get here, or I'll think I'm dreaming," he whispered.

He could not understand why she looked quite stricken at the question. But after a moment she whispered back, "It's Ko Shan, She's been very helpful."

That wasn't so surprising in itself. Ko Shan had helped him before. But he would never have thought that she would go to the extent of getting him the privilege of *t'e-pieh chieh-chien*, "special interview," so he could see Su Nan. It was really very generous of her. He felt overwhelmed. Even if it was because of her that he had got into this trouble in the first place, she probably knew nothing about it. And it wasn't really her fault.

It appeared, then, that Ko Shan really knew people. She must have inside information about his case. "Have you heard anything?" he whispered to Su Nan.

"It's going to be all right." But her voice sounded unnatural and there was a bleakness in her face she could not hide.

"No, tell me," he said after a pause. "I'd feel better if I knew."

"But it's true. It's really true. I wouldn't lie to you. I know there's no need to."

He did not say anything.

She was looking at him with a slight smile, squeezing his hand and wrist and trying to push her hand up his sleeve with a kind of desperate concentration.

"I want to know you'll be all right, whatever happens," he said. "Promise me that."

"Nothing's going to happen. I know you're going to be all right."

Seeing that it was no use talking, he just pressed his cheek against hers. So she had come to say goodbye. Somehow, he felt nothing. Perhaps the knowledge of death was part of death itself. She was not all there either. She still had that curious look, both intense and preoccupied. They were both struggling to come alive just for this minute and maybe they were trying too hard.

"This is all that matters, isn't it? What's between us," she said. "Nothing else counts. No matter what happens."

He thought at first that she meant death and separation. But she seemed suddenly frantic, her voice rising in a strange, hounded fury. She was staring at him but she didn't seem to hear him say yes. "Nothing else matters—no matter what. Isn't that so?" she demanded. "At least it's that way with me."

Then she was crying. He did not speak. It must be that she knew now about Ko Shan and him. What else could she mean? She had been seeing Ko Shan to get her help, and Ko Shan must have told her. He was truly, painfully remorseful but knowing that he was to die soon, it all seemed very remote. Even the feeling of pain and guilt had become a thing to linger over. He held on to it as he held on to her, not thinking much, fearful that it would pass away together with this moment.

He could feel time going in a small trickle down his back. So when the guard called out "Time up!" he expected it. He let go of Su Nan and went quickly toward the door, not wanting to be dragged out of the room, least of all in front of her.

He did not look back and tried not to look at her when she came running after him sobbing, hanging on to him.

"Liu Ch'üan, I'll never forget you," she said.

He went out the door escorted by two guards. The other man was pushing Su Nan back into the room, saying, "All right, all right."

Liu felt her words going through him before he understood them, heavy, icy cold and small, each by itself, coursing through him.

Didn't she tell him once she never wanted to hear him say he'd never forget her? Because that sounded like they were never going to see each other again, she had explained. And yet she was saying the same thing now.

He shouldn't take it so badly since he already knew. But he had not realized that until now he had still been hoping he was wrong.

Back in the dark room upstairs, when the door had closed after him there was a distinct murmuring rustle that marked the relaxation of tension. Evidently the inmates had expected that somebody would be taken out instead of put in.

"*Na-li lai-te?*" whispered the man sitting next to him.

For a moment Liu did not say anything. Then he answered, "I'm Liu."

"Ah—Liu." After some reflection the man asked again, "*Na-li lai-te?*"

"From the Resist-Aid Association," Liu said.

"Ah, it's you!" The man seemed embarrassed. "I thought you were a newcomer." Obviously he had not expected Liu to return. "How did it go? All right, eh?" he whispered, hastening to make amends.

"No. Just a matter of time."

But nothing happened to him the next day. Nor the day after. His roommates came and went. Just when he thought the authorities had forgotten him, he was taken out and interrogated on the same lines as before. He took that as an encouraging sign. But then the days went by until he began to think once more they had forgotten him.

25

KO SHAN was not sure if she had been wakened by the sound of knocking. She lay still on her back listening. Sleep sat comfortably on her forehead in a big dark block, a heavy lid that did not close properly, leaving a chink of light, a rustling consciousness all round, from ear to ear.

Yes, it was someone knocking.

"Come in!" she called out. But of course you could not hear from outside. Such a bore—somebody afraid to open the door by himself and just walk in. The politely waiting silence irritated her. She stared up at the round patch of sunlight on the ceiling reflected from the hand-mirror lying on her table. A drinking glass on the mirror made a shadow up there, a whorled dark spot in the ghostly yellow moon on the white ceiling. The sunlight in the room made her feel idly unhappy. There was no longer any need to draw the curtains at night. Her private life had been exemplary ever since the Three Antis. And it had been going on for months. She was used to those periodical movements for *Cheng Feng*, Sprucing up Styles of Behavior. Like illnesses, they came as suddenly as an avalanche and left as slowly as pulling an interminable thread out of a fabric. She felt quite resigned, being used to them. But there came a time in life when a woman's looks were not going to survive many such movements.

Another series of patient little raps on the door. "Come in!" she shouted, knowing it was useless. She supposed she had to get up. Investigations were still going on at her office in connection with Lin I-ch'ün. For all she knew she might be wanted for questioning.

Yawning, she pulled on her padded uniform, holding the unbuttoned front with one hand and giving the door a violent pull with the other.

"Ah, it's you, Comrade Su!" she said, smiling hazily. With her surprise came a feeling of annoyance that was quite impersonal and purely a matter of habit. She did not like to be spied upon even if she happened to have nobody with her. "The little sneak," she thought, and then, automatically with traditional hospitality said, "Why, come in and sit down!"

She offered Su Nan a chair, first snatching away some clothes. And she rinsed a glass, put in a pinch of tea leaves and made tea for her with water out of a thermos. While going through the customary motions of a hostess she did not hear Su Nan make any protests, which was rather unusual behavior. The girl was looking odd too. Ko Shan regarded her with sudden interest, having remembered by now that she had heard quite a lot about her during the last few weeks. The *Liberation Daily News* had never stopped its news-gathering, fact-finding activities even with Lin gone, like some amazingly efficient worm with its head cut off. Not national or international news, of which the New China Press had the sole monopoly. But the kind of news and gossip about sister organizations which were of vital concern to Lin and his staff.

Ko Shan had managed somehow to keep up her contacts in spite of the fact that she and her colleagues had become temporary untouchables with the scandal about their chief. She had friends over in *Wen Hui Pao* and was interested to learn that, some time after she had arranged for Su Nan's interview with Shen K'ai-fu, the girl had disappeared. She had been absent from the office without leave and did not return to her hostel. There had been cases of *kan-pu* deserting their posts but right now this was virtually impossible. No travelling permits were being issued with the Three Antis and Five Antis on. It could be that she was in hiding somewhere in the city on account of some crime as yet undetected. The only other possibility was that a secret arrest had been made.

After a fortnight of wild conjectures and re-examination of her records, though she had already passed the Three-Anti test, she suddenly turned up again with some unlikely tale of having been ill and staying with a friend. The Organization was seriously looking into her case. Then to everybody's surprise the investigations were mysteriously dropped and nothing more was said of the matter.

Ko Shan thought she had a pretty good idea of what had happened. She was anxious now to have her guesses confirmed. "How are you?" she said smiling, buttoning up her padded jacket and pulling the belt tight.

"I'm sorry I woke you up," Su Nan said, then explained in a rush, "I got your address from somebody who knows you—not from your office, so I hope it's all right."

"Why, I thought you had my address! I was always asking Liu Ch'üan why you never came to see me." Then her voice dropped and her face fell with sudden concern. "Any news about Liu? He's not out yet, is he?"

Su Nan shook her head with a half smile that looked strangely mocking. She held the glass of tea with both hands to warm herself, looking at the pale steam that rose in front of her face like incense before an idol. She looked as if she would have been stone-cold, without breath, but for the tea which was breathing steamily for both of them.

"Did you go and see Shen K'ai-fu?" Ko Shan whispered.

"Yes," Su Nan said, clearing her throat. With Ko Shan waiting expectantly she finally added, "He said it's a serious case. Something to do with Ts'ui P'ing."

Ko Shan clicked her tongue with an air of helpless distaste and impatience. "That's just his luck," she said frowning, "to be working under Ts'ui, of all people. It's hard to work for anybody without getting involved in his business."

"Shen told me he'd get him out if I promised never to see him again," Su Nan said.

Ko Shan looked at her blankly. She stopped speaking; evidently some comment was called for. Ko Shan offered her a cigarette instead and when she declined it, took one herself.

"I insisted on seeing Liu for the last time, so he arranged for me to go and see him," Su Nan said.

"At the Murkhead Road jail? But absolutely no visitors are allowed there. For the Three-Anti prisoners, that is," Ko Shan said gently, as if helpfully pointing out a discrepancy in her story.

"Well, I went there. And I saw him. That was on the third day of the Chinese New Year," Su Nan said, suddenly rattled and angry because she had to argue over even such a small point.

Ko Shan did not say anything.

"He was supposed to be released the next day. But he wasn't," she added quickly, defensively. "I was going to make sure that I saw it with my own eyes. I thought I might sit in a parked car and watch him walk out of the prison gate without being seen."

She broke off again guiltily, looking away from Ko Shan. "I was going to insist on that point, but I was really in no position to bargain." She talked fast as if she had learned the piece by rote and would forget if she did not get it out fast enough. "I went to Shen's office and he kept me there in that house for two days. Then his car took me to an apartment on Avenue Petain. All this time I didn't get a chance to see anybody or speak to anybody. He said I could go about free once he felt he could trust me. But not just yet. He said he didn't trust me a bit with Liu released and at large."

Ko Shan sat on her bed, leaning on the foot board, puffing her cigarette. The wary reserve on her face had given way to growing astonishment and indignation which were meant to be taken as an expression of sympathy but could just as well be taken as protest against this gross libel against a *shou chang*.

"A week later he stopped coming to the apartment," Su Nan said. "After another week my keepers told me the place was being turned into an office. So I just walked out and nobody stopped me.

"Of course as soon as I got out I found out that Liu never had been released. I tried to reach Shen but he wouldn't see me. I couldn't even get him on the phone. I tried and tried. I was frantic."

That was why her superiors had dropped the investigations on her disappearance, Ko Shan thought. She had probably been haunting Shen's office openly and ringing him up twenty times a day on public telephones.

"I stood waiting for hours outside his office, trying to waylay his car. But he has several and all their cars have those blue cloth curtains down. The sentry at the gate must think I'm out of my mind. Maybe I am."

Pink rings had appeared around her eyes, which were quickly filling with tears. And almost immediately her upper lip turned blotchy red and swollen as if she had been crying for hours.

Thinking how plain she looked for a girl that someone as important as Shen seemed to have taken considerable trouble over, Ko Shan turned away a little to rearrange idly the towels and stockings draped over the foot of the bed. It must have been a double blow to her—to be kicked out by Shen as well as discovering he had fooled her about Liu. She was probably all ready to settle down as Shen's mistress. With those girls possession is nine-tenths of the law. These half baked new *kan-pu* were actually no different from housewives. You might truly say of them that the shortest way to a woman's heart was through the vagina.

"Comrade Ko, you've got to help me reach him. I'm not going to make a scene or anything. All I want is to ask him to carry out his promise. Please. You've got to help me."

Was Su Nan implying that she was obliged to help because it was she who introduced Shen to her? When Ko Shan spoke she weighed her words, frowning deeply. "Really, I don't know what to say. I would have minded my own business last time you came to me, only you just wouldn't take no for an answer, you remember. But this time I'm really at the end of my wits. There's just nothing I can do."

"Isn't there any way to get in touch with him at all?"

"There must be, but I'm not the person to do it. You see, we're in trouble right now—I guess you've heard. Over in our office. I don't expect you realize the seriousness of the situation."

"Yes, I know." After a pause she said, "I know it's a lot to ask."

"It just can't be done. And even if I do manage to get in touch with Shen, I won't know what to say to him. No matter how tactfully I put it, it would amount to the same thing. It's a serious business, you know, to charge a *shou chang* with a thing like that. Especially with the Three Antis on."

Su Nan said nothing.

"I'm not doubting your words," Ko Shan added soothingly. "I can see you've been through a lot and your nerves are all shot to pieces. But since you've already made one mistake, it's best to be careful over your next step, don't you think? Rashness might get you into serious trouble."

It took Su Nan a minute to grasp her meaning. "Yes, Shen won't like it, I know—the way I try so hard to get hold of him. People will talk."

Ko Shan nodded. "Shen's always been very careful with his reputation," she said daintily, enunciating every word with care. "That's why I just can't understand how such a thing could happen."

"He shouldn't have let me out alive then," Su Nan said violently. "Well, he could still have me murdered. Easily. I really don't care what happens to me. The only thing is—Liu's still inside there." When Ko Shan did not answer she asked, suddenly nervous, "You don't think anything has happened to him, do you?"

"I really don't know what to think. As I said, the whole thing's fantastic. But from what you said, it seems that Shen's not serious. Then I don't suppose he'll do anything about Liu one way or the other."

It would sound so silly if she were to argue that Shen had been serious about her. He had told her about his wife, a survivor of the Long March and at present one of the vice presidents of the National Women's Association in Peking, a very active and influential woman. The Central Committee of the Party would never give permission for him to divorce her. Su Nan would have to remain under cover. But he wanted her to know it was for always. Only he had to be sure she would have nothing to do with Liu from now on, never see him again or write him.

He had said such a lot of unnecessary things, for one in his position. All lies, it seemed, in the light of his subsequent behavior.

Maybe he had thought it would please her, not knowing that it only made her feel worse to know that she was tied to him for life. Though it also could be that he really meant it at the time and just changed his mind afterwards.

She did not want to tell Ko Shan any of this. It would only make her appear a bigger fool than she was. Perhaps she could have managed things better if she had not felt so completely overwhelmed by the giving away of herself, though it had seemed to her then that she could not have acted otherwise.

She turned toward the window. Sensing that she was crying, Ko Shan came and stood beside her, leaning against the sill. The alley was quiet in the afternoon sun with most of the people away at work. In the old brick house opposite, the window kept banging in a deserted room. Brown-framed, tall and narrow, it was swinging slowly outward with determined abandon, grimly pulling itself short and swinging back again, painfully, for the inevitable jarring bang. It banged many times before either of them spoke.

Somewhere in the city a cock was crowing, so far away it was a mere high-pitched creak, almost inaudible. To Su Nan the sleepy, plodding normality of the afternoon was unbearable. It discredited her story as much as Ko Shan's attitude did. On such an afternoon in an alley like this the world of the *shou chang* seemed hardly possible.—Not that there was anything extraordinary on the surface. The steam-heated rooms were quietly furnished and there was none of the cluttered profusion of a rich man's house. Things and people were produced instantaneously or whisked away out of sight at wish as by some efficient genii.

All that had happened to her there rose up uncontrollably inside her, goaded by the disbelief. The present just floated past her in pale misty puffs, vaguely annoying, like Ko Shan's cigarette smoke in the sunlight. Only the glass of hot tea against her palm felt real. And the tea was already cooling, the heat fading away to become as impalpable as the thin warmth of the sun upon her.

There was another thing she had to speak of before she went. By now she knew it was useless asking Ko Shan anything. But since she had told her so much already, she might as well say it. And it was easier somehow with Ko Shan standing so close.

"I've got to have an abortion."

Ko Shan made a face of pained half-laughter. "You're certainly in a mess."

"Please help me to find a doctor willing to do it. Please. You know more people than I do, Comrade Ko. Won't you try and find a doctor for me?"

"But that's against the law."

"I know, but lots of woman comrades do that, don't they? When the situation makes it necessary."

"That was before," Ko Shan said a little indignantly, "when everybody had to be on the move all the time. In the army or the underground. Now it's different. The People's Government doesn't allow it."

"Yes, but actually—at least here in Shanghai, where lots of irregular things are still going on—" Su Nan said hesitantly.

"Not this. Now you'd better drop the idea," Ko Shan said firmly in her best Big Old Sister manner. "I should think the best thing to do under the circumstances is to ask for sick leave, go somewhere quiet and have the baby. Do you think you can confide in your family?"

"I've already written home saying I have to have an operation," Su Nan said stubbornly, looking away. "They'll raise the money somehow."

"It's not a question of money. I doubt you can get anybody to do it for you."

"I have to have it. Soon. Please! Please help me! I haven't told anybody else about this."

It was on the tip of Ko Shan's tongue to ask her what made her think that she, Ko Shan, was the person to go to in a case like this. She wondered again how much Liu had told her. No, maybe she didn't need to be told. The furor at the Three-Anti Confessional Meeting must be all over town.

Anyhow, all other considerations apart, she did not see why she should introduce Su Nan to an abortionist and prove beyond a doubt that she was well-acquainted with such practices. "I certainly feel honored because you trust me more than anybody else," she said smiling. "That's why I have no choice but to advise you to the best of my knowledge. Really—why don't you go into the country somewhere and stay there for several months until it's all over? That ought to be easily arranged, especially if you're going to receive money from your family."

"I can't do that."

She's thinking of the possibility of Liu coming out of prison, Ko Shan thought with relish. The best part about this business was that much of it had happened by itself. She had not gone out of her way to arrange it. It proved once again to Ko Shan's own satisfaction that it was not in her to be jealous. She wouldn't have bothered if Su Nan hadn't pestered her so. Then she did have some vague idea of killing two birds with one stone—introducing the girl to Shen and getting Liu out. It's true that the girl had bungled her part of the job. At worst it might even cost Liu his life. But if anything could reconcile Ko Shan to his death it would be the thought that his girl had killed him through her stupidity.

Things were going her way so smoothly, swimmingly, it was enough to frighten anybody who had had any experience in life.— How long ago was it when Liu had spoken to her about Su Nan, right in this room—spoken as if it was something beyond her understanding, the cozy little igloo of their love, made of ice but warm and homey within and frozen hard to the ground, as firm as part of the living rock. Where would they be now when he came out of prison, if he ever did? How she wished he would, if only for the inevitable confrontation. She could very well imagine it, even if she probably wouldn't get to see it. But Liu was such a fool, she wouldn't be surprised if he sat beside Su Nan holding her hand when she was big with another man's child. It made such a funny picture that she had to lean outside the window, flicking ashes off her cigarette, to hide her smile. The smile passed, casting a shadow where she had felt pleasure just a moment before.

The girl was sobbing. Ko Shan put a hand on her shoulder without saying anything and distinctly felt her shudder. Instantly offended, she withdrew her hand, being more susceptible to this revulsion of the flesh than any insult.

But Su Nan was not really thinking of her. Any touch was repellent right now, even that of the filmy sunlight on her head and face, because she felt ill. There was impatience in the feverish dryness of her skin and hair. Another time was ticking inside her, faster than the clock. "I've got to be going," she said.

"Do take care of yourself, and try not to worry too much," Ko Shan said. "After all, to a *kan-pu*, personal affairs are always of secondary importance, compared to work. If you have difficulty getting your sick leave, let me know and I'll see what I can do—I know some people in your office," she volunteered, to soften her refusal to help in other respects. And she knew that would not be necessary. Su Nan's superiors would be only too glad to let her go, seeing that she was in such a state and liable to cause trouble. If not for the restrictions on travelling due to the Three Antis and Five Antis, probably they would have transferred her already to some small town in the interior.

26

WHEN SHE jumped it seemed somehow, at the last moment, that she had not yet made up her mind. The staircase crumpled under her, folding up like an accordion. The steps hit her again and again through the haze of her indecision. Bluntly projecting edges pushed out surprisingly to strike at her. And yet the blows were muffled by their unexpectedness and the lightning rapidity with which they followed one another. All except the last one, when the patch of floor at the bottom of the stairs sprang up at her, and the vicious slap echoed throughout her, numbly stinging like an electric shock.

"Ai-ya, what happened? . . . How did it happen? . . . Fell down the stairs . . . Fell all the way!" Voices buzzed around her. People were used to emergencies nowadays with businessmen jumping out of windows almost every day. Tumbling down a flight of stairs was child's play, comparatively. It was no great surprise either that it should happen to Su Nan, who was getting to be a real case, as everybody knew around the hostel—chasing around town all day, missing office, missing meals. The management, in tacit agreement with her superiors, had chosen to overlook her irregular conduct until some means could be devised to get her out of the way.

"Can you get up?" asked the woman who was the hostel manageress.

Su Nan moaned when hands got under her, trying to raise her to her feet. She ached at so many places, it was difficult to locate the place she wanted to feel pain—the more so because there was nothing there, not a twinge or a flutter. That thing growing inside her, fattening itself on her, had remained intact like one of those imperishable clocks, quietly ticking its own secret time.

"Somebody go and get Dr. Chao there in our alley," said the manageress. "Ask him to come at once. An accident. If he's not in, get the nurse, Mrs. Kuan, in No. 14."

They carried her upstairs. The nurse came. The examination was very painful but in a way the pain was a fitting revenge on her body that had dumbly protected this thing she could not live with. And the nerve-racking pangs did not really reach her. They were just distant booms of guns that shook the floor and windows. She was still busy feeling out that part of her where she was still waiting for some stir, some sign.

She could not understand how that parasitic life had such a tenacious hold on her. It seemed determined not to die unless she died with it. Sitting squarely, solidly, clock-like, ticking away in the dark until its long night was over, when it could emerge as a personality, a thinking, waking, cold-eyed consciousness. And in growing up—always just old enough to have judgment but not understanding. Anyhow, she hated it.

It was easy to talk—go lose yourself in the country until it was born. The *hu k'ou tiao ch'a*, population investigation, was even stricter in the country than in the city. A stranger in a village where everybody knew everybody else would stick out for miles. No end of questions would be asked by the village *kan-pu*. And afterwards she supposed she was to give away the child since she did not want it. That might not be too difficult, if it was a boy. It was always easy to arrange matters if you had little concern for other lives. She just could not consider it.

She had been thinking those thoughts so long and so ceaselessly. These few thoughts, like old brooms in the house too long that had acquired mysteriously, through human contact, a life of their own, were now able to hop about quite by themselves. And racing and chasing around they inevitably ran into the blind alley of the thought of Liu, and knocked themselves out.

That stopped her every time, the very idea of facing Liu with the child as a living fact instead of something dead and gone. He ought to be grateful and understanding since it was all because of him. But that would not make it any better. She knew he might not come out alive at all, but in that case nothing would be left anyway.

"Those treacherous stairs! So dark!" the manageress was standing at the foot of the bed, telling Mrs. Kuan. "How many times I've warned them: Be careful, be careful!" She was obviously anxious to forestall any rumors of suicide in her hostel.

Mrs. Kuan smiled. "Yes, she's very lucky to have no bones broken. Too tight?" she asked, tying on the bandages. She was a short chunky woman with a long face, her hair a browned frizz. In spite of her padded gown of black-and-gold brocade she looked very professional.

Some of the girls in the hostel who crowded into the room to watch, talked about her after she was gone. "Very active, this Mrs. Kuan," one of them said. "Secretary of the Alley Inhabitants' Committee now. Must say that was very broadminded of them. Didn't discriminate against her at all."

"She's much better off with that husband of hers out of the way. Even if she has to pinch and save and do all the housework herself. A lot of good it did her when he was earning such fat fees for abortion. Spent it all on cabaret girls. And the way they fought—those two! The whole alley knew. Almost took the house to pieces."

"Who's her husband?" Su Nan asked from her bed, speaking for the first time.

"Dr. Kuan, the one who was arrested for abortion. Why, haven't you heard? He only served two months of his five-year sentence— hauled out of prison and sent to Korea to treat the wounded. Guess they're short of doctors there."

"Those technical people get all the breaks," the other one, a proofreader and would-be writer, said discontentedly.

"Sure," said the older woman. "And the government was so generous and considerate to him, they let him come home for a three-day leave before he went to Korea. So touching!"

"You mean you've never heard of this? Where've you been?" the young proofreader demanded in sudden astonishment, bringing on a guilty silence as everyone remembered this had happened during Su Nan's mysterious disappearance.

Thinking back, Su Nan remembered the only time she had seen Dr. Kuan. Last autumn she happened to miss the mass injection against diphtheria at her office, so she had gone to the Kuans. As a doctor-and-nurse team they had been mobilized to give every inhabitant of the alley a free injection. It was late in the day, so there was no crowd there. She rang the bell and waited. She was a bit startled to discover a man in a long black overcoat carrying a black bag standing right behind her, also waiting, smiling slightly when she turned around and saw him. Obviously the doctor coming home. He was tall with a plump, round boyish face and very small eyes like black seeds above his apple cheeks. It was uncanny how he could come up behind her, walking in leather shoes on concrete pavement without making a single sound. When the door opened he followed her noiselessly into the hall and while his wife attended to her, went quietly upstairs with what could only be described as a marked and deliberate inconspicuousness. She had not thought much of it at the time, but now, with the infallibility of hindsight, realized he was the criminal type.

His wife looked much older than he, maybe because of the life he led her. She must have worked very hard as his assistant. The woman could surely introduce her to some other doctor, Su Nan thought. She might even be able to do it herself. But how could she win her confidence? She was bound to think it was a police trap. Working for a government newspaper made Su Nan practically a government employee. Anyway, everybody was a possible informant nowadays, eager to win credit either for atonement of some crime or simply to get ahead.

When Mrs. Kuan came again the next day to change the dressing Su Nan tried to make conversation. Yes, she was busy all day long, she answered warily, smiling, talking neither too little nor too much, her shrewd long face looking just a little derisive, probably unintentionally. She had four children all going to school, three girls and one boy. Her mother-in-law lived with her. She didn't mind doing without servants but there's also the work in the Inhabitants' Committee. She couldn't get out of that though she had insisted that she couldn't handle it, she said modestly.

From where she lay in bed Su Nan could just see the back door of the Kuans' house. She noticed more than once fashionably dressed girls, different ones, going in and out either singly or accompanied by a man. Their high-collared, wasp-waisted gowns were very conspicuous because they were rarely seen now around town. Mrs. Kuan did not seem the kind of person to have a wide circle of stylish friends. With their bosoms and thighs outlined by the thin, rich material of their dresses, they looked more like cabaret girls or high-class party girls. Were they her clients then? Su Nan did not see how she could just coolly carry on where her husband left off, right under the alert noses of the authorities who already had her house on their black list. Had she, by infiltrating into the alley organization, established an understanding with certain key characters? She must need money very badly to take risks like that.

Two days later Su Nan did not wait for Mrs. Kuan to come and change her dressing. She managed to struggle to her feet and make her way downstairs out of the house and to the Kuans.

"I'm well enough to get up today, so I thought I'd save you the trip. I feel so terribly sorry to make you come over every day when you're so rushed already," she explained to the shocked Mrs. Kuan who opened the door herself.

A pigtailed little girl in a home-made foreign dress peeped in while Mrs. Kuan went inside to get the medicine and fresh bandages. It seemed that she was going to change the dressing out here in what was apparently the waiting room with its glass-topped round table and upholstered chairs. A bunch of sweetpeas stood in a cut-glass vase on a tea stand covered by a freshly laundered light green tablecloth. The flowers were positively damaging evidence, Su Nan thought. No Chinese household who could afford flowers would ever think of doing without servants unless there was some underhand business going on which required the utmost privacy.

Su Nan had to lean awkwardly on one of the straight-backed chairs to have her leg attended to. Mrs. Kuan was visibly flustered and spilled some of the Mercurochrome on the polished floor. There must be somebody in the consultation room.

"Tch, tch! Look what I did!" Mrs. Kuan snatched a newspaper and bent down, wiping the floor scratchily.

"Can it be washed off?" Su Nan asked apologetically.

"Hm? No. No use," she answered from the depth of her furious absorption, everything else apparently forgotten. The red stain, lighter but much bigger now, seemed ingrained in the yellow-brown of the floorboards. "Looks like somebody has been murdered here," she said with a nervous giggle.

At this it occurred to Su Nan to wonder briefly whether Mrs. Kuan was as good an abortionist as a housewife, and if she had killed anybody. For a moment Su Nan felt quite dismayed to see her not acting like her brisk competent self. But if she was no good, she wouldn't be doing such a flourishing business, would she?

She finally returned to the bandages, bending over Su Nan's leg. "Mrs. Kuan," Su Nan said in a low voice. Then after a pause, "You know why I jumped down the stairs?"

"I thought you tripped and fell," Mrs. Kuan said with her knowing smile, looking faintly derisive. Like everybody else she probably had the idea that Su Nan had tried to kill herself because of an unfortunate love affair. She began to assume the expression of a compliant but not especially eager confidante.

Su Nan did not say anything. "I was hoping for a miscarriage," she finally whispered, looking straight at the woman.

Mrs. Kuan's face went gray as if she had on powder too light for her complexion. She waited, not saying anything, as if she did not understand.

"Please help me, Mrs. Kuan. I need help badly."

She still smiled at Su Nan without comprehension but looking as if she was waiting to be struck in the face, with a preparedness that was heartbreaking.

"Please believe me," Su Nan said. "You said yourself I was very lucky I didn't break my neck. Could have got crippled for life too. Would I risk all that just to deceive you?" It could still be taken as a *k'u jou chi*, ruse of the suffering flesh, in which you win an enemy's confidence through self-inflicted physical suffering. She could only hope that Mrs. Kuan would have enough sense to realize that if the police were after her they would not have to go to all that trouble.

"But I just don't know what you're talking about—" Mrs. Kuan began.

"Please look at this. Please have a look." Su Nan cut her short, producing the draft she received from Peking. "I wrote home saying I've got to have an operation. They just barely managed to scrape up this money. Look at the chop and the date. Just got it a few days ago. Now you can believe me."

Maybe it was Mrs. Kuan's firsthand knowledge of the genuine injuries she sustained and the grave risks she ran that finally convinced her. And then also there was something innately trustworthy in the looks of large sums of money. After more hedging Mrs. Kuan agreed to let her come again the next day for the treatment.

This time she was admitted into the inner room dominated by a complicated couch-machine that looked frightening with its metal clamps to hold the patient's legs apart. Once she got on it the bottom fell out of her world, she was suspended in mid-air, trapped and thrown clear, experiencing a fear that felt like the emptiness of hunger. There was the tinkle of instruments in the tray. At the first touch of cold metal, indecently tentative, she suddenly had such a sense of humiliation that the whole of her experience with Shen came crowding back. She turned her head from side to side as if to avoid seeing his face. She could not understand how she had ever got into that position, or this either.

When the pain came it was almost a relief. Mrs. Kuan had told her to stuff her handkerchief into her mouth when she felt like screaming. She bit into the choking white dryness of the handkerchief. The curtains were not drawn because that might attract attention. Instead, Mrs. Kuan had hung some of her dresses over the window as if to sun them. Su Nan found herself looking at them, even feeling a little worried for a moment because it was a gray day. People might think it odd. The dresses looked amazingly wide as dresses often do, off the body. There were flowered silk ones and a deep red silk one already grease-darkened on the stiff collar. They looked very out of place in this immaculate white room. It was after school hours and she could hear the sounds of well-disciplined children scampering somewhere in the house. A telephone was ringing next door. She noticed all this like a shopper picking up one thing after another perfunctorily, without much interest, and putting them down quickly as if afraid she would drop them when the pain came tearing into her again, knowing somehow that this time it would be far worse.

27

"ARE YOU Liu Ch'üan?" the officer said, studying the documents on his desk.

"Yes."

"We've investigated your case—looked into it most thoroughly. There is no doubt that you were very close to Ts'ui P'ing when you worked under him. It's impossible you should know nothing of his Anti-People Crimes. You must realize that you are under grave suspicion of covering up for him, maybe even active collaboration—who knows? And in any case your sense of vigilance is not high enough and your standpoint not firm enough. But the People's Government is being specially generous. It refuses to give you up as lost. It still wants to fight for you, to win you back to our ranks."

Liu listened dazedly. When he had been taken to the office downstairs he thought it was for identification before his long awaited execution.

"You can return now to your original post. But for the time being you're placed under the surveillance of the Masses. The Masses will watch and observe your every movement. You're not to talk heedlessly or act heedlessly. At table you'll be the last to sit down and lift your chopsticks. And you're to keep your eyes lowered at all times.—Your unit leader will acquaint you with other rules of this surveillance period."

He was marched out of the office and taken into another room where his wallet and watch were returned to him. The great iron door finally clanged shut behind him. He found himself standing on the sunlit pavement with yellow-clad sentries standing leaning on rifles on either side of the gate. He was careful not to walk away too fast and not to look back at the two sentries, however indifferent they might seem.

He did not feel safe until he was on the crowded tram and the tram had crossed the bridge. Then the curious glances and shrinking away of the other passengers reminded him that he needed a haircut and shave badly. He suddenly became aware that his soiled uniform was crawling with lice. Before he went to the bath-house he would have to go and get a clean suit from his hostel. He was grateful for its daytime emptiness and quiet, not quite relishing the idea of seeing Chang Li so soon.

If there had been a telephone at his hostel he would have rung up Su Nan right then. When he finally got to telephone her after his bath and haircut, he thought there must have been some mistake. He rushed to her office, where they told him again that she had died of a sudden illness.

Died of a sudden illness. He walked out, too stunned by the matter-of-fact tone of the clerk to really believe him. He went at once to her hostel and asked to see the manageress. She was not a figure that inspired confidence. With striking incongruity she wore the thin black floppy pants of an amah under her padded blue Liberation Suit, probably in answer to the call for greater frugality. She was middle-aged and her face was like a rectangular piece of yellow soap worn smooth and concave by use.

"Which unit are you from? And how are you related to Comrade Su? How long have you known her?" she asked him all these questions before she would answer his tumbling ones. No, they did not know what illness it was that had caused Su Nan's death. She had died on the way to the hospital. She had been feeling poorly for a day or two before that and had been in bed resting but she had insisted it was nothing serious. When they finally sent her to the hospital, it had been too late.

Liu could not think of anything to say, so the woman plied him with more questions. But before he left he remembered to ask where she was buried. It was somewhere very far in the Old City. He would go as soon as he could—as if it would prove anything, to see a newly made mound.

That evening when everybody came back to the hostel, he saw Chang Li. The meeting turned out to be no more embarrassing than when Chang had been released after his detention at the very start of the Three Antis. Chang congratulated him and asked about his health. He said little else, being excused from the customary comradely effusiveness by the fact that Liu was still under surveillance. Of course nobody really took it very seriously. It was generally understood that he had been released because there wasn't any real evidence against him. The surveillance was just the usual face-saving device of the government after keeping a man in prison for several months and then not proving anything.

So his homecoming went off smoothly. And if there was anything at all constrained or guilty-looking in Chang's manner he did not care enough to notice it, engrossed as he was in trying to understand that Su Nan was really dead.

It could not have been a sudden illness since she had known of it beforehand—because he definitely knew now she had come to say goodbye the last time he saw her. Suddenly it seemed to him that it would be almost bearable if only he knew the real cause. For the time being this seemed to be all that mattered, even if he knew that it would not change things any.

Back at his office the next day his new superior sent to him an opened envelope which had evidently been around for some time. At the lower lefthand corner where the sender's surname was usually written it said "Mailed by Su, Peking." Liu's heart thumped madly and his head swam when he tried to identify the handwriting. A person's writing looked so different when it was done with a brush instead of a pen. He realized that he had never believed for a moment that she was dead. But how had she gone back to Peking? He got the flimsy yellowish, red-lined letter paper out, trying not to tear it.

"Nephew Ch'üan," the letter said. "Forgive me for addressing you in such an impolite manner. But I feel as if I know you well enough for that, for my child Nan has often spoken of you in her letters. I trust that you are well and happy and busy serving the People. Nan wrote home some time ago saying that she had to go to the hospital for an appendicitis operation. I expect she has received the JMP 800,00 I sent her for the operation but I got a little worried wondering how it went and if she is out of hospital by now. In case she is not yet well enough to write, I will appreciate it very much if you will drop me a line when you are not too rushed."

It was signed "Slow-Witted Su Wong Mei-chu." "Slow-Witted" is the standard adjective that elders apply to themselves when they wish to be modest, probably because it is taken for granted that they are superior in every other respect.

Su Nan had told Liu that she had mentioned him in her letters home. But he had never quite persuaded her to tell him how much she had told her mother, and in what terms. It was one of the little things that had come to be a standing joke between them. Judging from the tone of this letter her mother knew all about it. She would never have called him nephew if she did not already regard him as a son-in-law.

The letter finished him. He knew that he could no longer live with himself until he found out what really had happened to Su Nan. He went again to her office that day armed with the letter, claiming that he was making inquiries on behalf of her family. One good thing about Chinese life in general and their present Group life in particular, he reflected, was that there could be no secrets. Truth might be distorted but never completely hidden. But the man at the *Wen Hui Pao* stuck to his story of the day before. This was the first he had heard of the appendicitis operation, he said.

Liu called again at her hostel at a time when everybody was there. He asked to see the things she had left and got to talking to some of the girls there. The young proofreader seemed inclined to be informative. So he singled her out and when she went to work the next day he was waiting around outside to walk her to the tram stop.

"She died of bleeding," she told him in a whisper. "Don't know whether it had anything to do with her jumping down the stairs. She didn't break any bones or anything. But there could have been some injury inside the doctor couldn't see—Nobody knew why she'd want to do a thing like that. Of course there's been a lot of talk ... She disappeared for two whole weeks, you know just after the Chinese New Year."

She mentioned Shen K'ai-fu. Oddly shaped, foreign thoughts forced themselves on Liu's unwilling, unreceptive mind.

"Of course I don't really know," the girl said. "She never told anybody anything."

Liu finally thought of asking, making a great effort to concentrate: "Have you ever seen her around with a Comrade Ko, a woman editor at the *Liberation Daily News*?"

"Comrade Ko? No—Oh, the name's Ko Shan, isn't it? I remember hearing Su Nan asking around for her address the other day."

"When was that?"

She paused to think. "Couldn't have been more than a few days before her death."

It had occurred to Liu before that Ko Shan might be able to tell him something. When he saw Su Nan in prison, she had told him that Ko Shan had helped make the meeting possible. So she must have been in close contact with Ko Shan, though Liu could not quite imagine the two of them together. He felt a strange reluctance to go and ask Ko Shan, perhaps because he was unwilling to take her word for whatever she had to tell him about Su Nan.

But he went to see her that evening and with expert timing caught her just as she was locking her door before going to office.

She greeted him coolly, breezily. "Congratulations! When did you get out?"

"Only a few days ago." They stood talking in the brown gloom of the badly lit hallway. It appeared that she was not going to ask him in. "If you're not in too much of a hurry," he said, "can I speak to you for a few minutes?"

"Frankly, I'd rather not. I'm not cleared yet, you know, even if you are. At least I hope you are."

But when he insisted, she unlocked the door and he followed her into the room.

"I came to thank you," he said.

"What—again? Whatever for?"

"Su Nan told me that you did a lot to help me."

"No! Now where did she get that idea? Why, what did I do this time? Don't tell me it's me who got you out of there."

"I don't know about that. But she said you helped her to get permission to see me in jail."

She stared at him, then said half laughing, "I'm sorry to disillusion you. But I'm not as influential as all that."

"But why would she say it was you, if it had nothing to do with you?"

In spite of themselves, the note of irritation that had always been there since their breakup returned to their voices. "How should I know?" Ko Shan answered. "Ask her."

"She's dead."

After a slight pause, Ko Shan said, "Oh. Why, how did it happen? So sudden!"

Liu was silent while he reached into his pocket for the letter from Su Nan's mother. "It says here that she'd written home for money for an appendicitis operation. But according to the people here she certainly didn't die from appendicitis."

He made her read it. Frowning perplexedly, impatiently, she was about to speak, letter in hand, but he stopped her by saying. "Now I'm not interested in where that money went. I just want to know— just for the peace of my mind and for no other purpose—and I really mean that, you know you can trust me—all I want to know is whether she used that money to get me out of jail and if—if that's got anything to do with her death."

"What are you insinuating?" Ko Shan cried indignantly.

"You made the right contacts for her, didn't you? Introduced her to the right people."

"I don't know what you're talking about. You better be careful what you say. I may not be able to get you out of jail but it doesn't take much to get you re-arrested, you know."

"All right, go ahead."

"Don't think I wouldn't. It's just that I feel a bit sorry for you, under the circumstances." She looked at her watch. "Now I've got to be going."

"Not yet." He stood with his back to the closed door.

"What do you think you're doing? Surely you ought to know me by now—*wo ch'ih juan pu ch'ih ying*, I eat soft things, not hard things. Don't try to get tough with me."

"You introduced her to Shen Ka'i-fu, didn't you?"

"What? Are you out of your head? Get out of here."

"I know all about it."

"You do? Then why did you come to ask me?"

"Maybe I'm not here to ask questions."

"Came to kill me, huh?" In spite of her exasperated little laugh he knew she was getting frightened. And he was very angry with her for that brief moment of wavering that showed on her face, confirming everything. He did not really want to know.

As he stood looking at her, the murmur of street noises and sounds in the alley and the rooming house came to him like the slow wash of the sea up a beach. Listening, he seemed almost to be estimating how long it would take for people to come to her rescue if she yelled. He really did not know what he was going to do next. And it was probably this uncertainty she saw in his face that really frightened her.

"You've really gone crazy," she said quickly. "You see? That's why I didn't want to tell you. I knew you wouldn't be able to take it. It's much better for you to think that she died of some illness. But maybe I'd better tell you instead of letting you hear it from other people and getting it all twisted."

He had no way of telling whether her version was twisted or not. Except that it did have that disagreeable, slightly queer taste of facts suddenly uncovered.

"I just couldn't get rid of her, so I thought of Shen K'ai-fu. They do say that he speaks to Chairman Mao over the phone every night."

He had never seen Shen K'ai-fu. Couldn't remember ever seeing his picture in the papers either. He did not want to ask Ko Shan what he looked like, though it hurt terribly either way—to picture him as fiendishly ugly or handsome.

"I didn't think it would be any use though—Shen wouldn't do things for just anybody. If I'd thought it would help, maybe I'd have gone to him myself. I don't know—I might be just enough of a fool to do that..."

He had puzzled over this for so long and had thought of every angle, that by comparison what had actually happened seemed flimsy and over-simple. Anyway, it was inconceivable that all this had taken place while he had been sitting in prison. The long days and months of ignorance and inactivity were still with him, drugging him so that all these things he was hearing were like dreams muddied up in the thick stream of sleep.

"If she had listened to a single word I said! I told her she wouldn't be able to get a doctor to do it for her.—Must have got a quack or an old-fashioned midwife. That would account for the money she got from her family."

Why did she have to do that? Anything—anything, but don't slam the finality of death in my face, he thought. But of course he knew why she had done it. His own imagination balked at the idea of a child, as hers must have done. They were young and their love was young and touchy. It made them both too cowardly and too brave. It had been the same with him when he had turned and walked away from her quickly for fear that the guards would drag him out of the room.

Now he felt he was beyond all that. Maybe this is what it feels like to be middle-aged, when you have learned to live, happily even, with a lot of ills and pain and awkwardness, things you would rather not think about. But what had she left him to grow old on? She had scooped the meat out of his life and made him a gift of the empty shell, presenting it to him with a dumb ceremoniousness that was almost mocking. She could have it back.

The shame of not being able to do anything about it had not burst upon him yet, the sense of deprivation had so filled his mind. It was there though, and that was what made him so angry.

Ko Shan was still speaking. "Well, I did all I could for both of you, against my better judgment. And I'm pretty sick of it. Imagine your coming here threatening me!—after all that. Really I'd throw you out if I weren't sorry for you!"

She was at the table with two glasses and a bottle of *wu chia p'i*. "Have a drink. After all, you're out. That's something."

"Yes," he said. "Ought to celebrate. You don't get out of jail every day."

"Don't get drunk though. You might talk too much when you get back and start telling people what I just told you."

"Don't worry. I'm not going to drink up all your liquor."

They were having one of the last cold spells of spring. The window was filmed over with steam, making curtains unnecessary. The neon lights outside tinted the misty glass a glistening, perspiring pink that faded into pale green. A pair of pink silk panties was hung up to dry on a hanger hooked to the top of the window. They looked pale and washy in the yellow wanness of the room light. But high up there they were as proclamatory as a flag.

All this steam on the window. Liu could not imagine how it could be so much warmer here than outside. The room was so drab and cold in spite of the heat of the strong drink funneling down inside him. He wished the room was brighter and gayer. And he wished Ko Shan was some other woman. He could do with a much plainer one, so long as it wasn't a woman who had just shamed him with this story.

"I'm going in a minute," he told her when she came and put her arms around his neck from behind and bent down to rub faces. This damn room was so large and cold that his voice sounded startlingly loud.

"You're drunk already," she giggled.

"No, I'm not."

"You are. You better sleep it off before you get back to the hostel. Before you know it you'll start blabbing. I can see you're full of it right now."

He did not mind lying down on her bed. For a moment he had

the same feeling as when he had first returned to his hostel, opened his locker and got out his spare padded uniform. At least there was something out of his past that was still there. The tinsel wrapping inside a pack of cigarettes crackled lightly under the pillow when he moved his head. The sameness of everything was sad because it made him feel how changed he was.

"Here, you might as well be comfortable." She sat on the edge of the bed taking off his shoes for him.

"Don't bother. I'll be all right in a minute."

"Don't be like that. I really feel sorry for you. Really I do."

Then she said, "You hate me, don't you?"

It was silly of him to consider seriously before he answered, since she obviously asked it only because she was lying down snuggling up to him and he was not trying to make love to her.

"No, I don't. Why?" he said half smiling. He just disliked her. She had messed around too much where she had no business, knew too much and understood too little and was all tied up with this painful thing.

But he kissed her anyway and pushed his hand under her padded jacket through the space between the buttons. Things have a way of happening by themselves once they get back into an old groove. Anyhow it no longer mattered what he did now that Su Nan was dead. Su Nan was dead. The idea stung him sharply through the alcoholic fog. He rebelled against the truth of it. And when he touched her he realized somehow the difference it would make if he loved her. It only brought home his loss.

"I've got to be going." He climbed across her off the bed.

Maybe she thought it was just his mood or his sense of decency after what he had just heard from her. She did not speak or get up from bed and he did not look at her while he was putting on his shoes. She was a woman of easy beginnings and practically no endings, he thought, but she probably knew an ending when she saw one.

Then he heard her say politely, "Sure you're all right?"

"Yes, I'm going straight home to bed."

"Want some strong tea before you go?"

"No, thanks."

Outside the house the air felt like cold water on his hot face. Apparently it was early yet. He walked very rapidly past lighted houses and shops half boarded up, with the light still on. Trams and trolleys swayed by like lighted houses. He was puffing and bathed in sweat inside his padded jacket when he came in sight of the Park Hotel. He hadn't realized he was coming this way.

He hadn't been to the Park Hotel except that once when he had gone there for supper with Ko Shan. That was when he had first known her. The thought of it was comfortably remote. Everything else was crowding in on him tonight.

The red flag on top of the tower above the skycraper probably had strong lights turned on it from underneath. Though it looked tiny up there it was wonderfully red and bright against the dark hollow blue of the night sky. Liu slowed down, his face looking up at it. It was like a star. He could not shoot it down.

28

Liu woke up from heavy sleep with the sound of rain tapping on the oil-cloth drawn over the mouth of the cave. The woodsmoke drifting in smelled good in the dankness of the shelter heavy with the sour stench of clothes and bodies. But his mind gave an involuntary twitch of worry at the odor of the smoke. And that was what reminded him where he was. For a moment he had forgotten.

They were not supposed to make fires at all with the enemy planes buzzing around all day searching for cooking smoke in the hills, rain or shine. Dry wood would not make so much smoke, but it was hard to find in this rainy season. And they were seldom lucky enough to come across a woodpile in these much-raided caves the Koreans lived in. The people in these parts had taken to living in caves after the bombing and shelling had razed all houses to the ground. Whenever the Chinese People's Volunteers stopped for the day—they generally marched at night—everyone would fight to squeeze in with the Koreans. It saved them the trouble of digging shelters and fetching water for themselves.

There was barely room for the three of them in this hastily dug shelter—Liu, the Battalion Deputy Instructor and his young orderly. The orderly was asleep; the white of the new bandage on the boy's head stood out in the darkness. There had been a row when they were stopping to camp in the morning, when everybody's nerves were on edge from exhaustion. The Deputy Instructor had picked up a number of drenched cigarette butts left by the enemy United Nations troops. So the first thing he did was to look for a dry place to start a fire so he could dry the discarded butts. He carefully

266

peeled the paper away and arranged the salvaged shreds of tobacco in the crotch of an iron pick. He put it down to attend to the fire. A minute later when he turned round the pick was gone. He went round yelling "Who's got my pick?" Then he saw his orderly busy levelling the ground of his cave with it. The tobacco was gone, of course. The boy hadn't even seen it. In his fury he grabbed the pick and hit the boy a sharp blow before Liu could stop him.

Liu did not blame the man much. He too was longing for a smoke. Especially now, waking up to the gray stillness of headache weather, an hour before the night march.

He supposed it had been a foolish thing to do—coming here to this desolate land of corpses and burnt-out huts. But there are times when you have to do something foolish or go completely insane. Now, at least, he had one special distinction nobody around him could claim, he told himself wryly. He was probably the only true volunteer in this army of volunteers; he had begged to be sent to Korea because it was the only way to ask for a transfer. Back there, after Su Nan's death, he had wanted a change desperately. He could breathe more easily out here at the edge of his Chinese world. Of course there was a good chance of getting killed. Not that he really cared, though he had not come here for that purpose. If he had wanted to kill himself he could have done so without dying for them. But he had found that people do not commit suicide just because they wish to cease to exist. They always do it to show someone—though it might be a group of people, the whole world even. If Su Nan was still living, maybe as Shen's mistress, he might want to kill himself to show her exactly what he thought of this life she had given him. As it was, he lacked the impetus.

The other *kan-pu* serving in the Volunteers had simply been ordered here. They had not been required to go through the formality of volunteering in big recruiting rallies. Liu's request had been way out of line, as a matter of fact. His superiors probably had thought he was pushing hard to wipe out the black mark on his record. For it was a black mark, his arrest and imprisonment, even if there had not been enough evidence for his conviction. If the Party had had any idea of *p'ei-yang t'a*, cultivating him as a young *kan-pu*, they had now lost interest in him. Whether his fervor to get to the fighting was real or simulated, they took him up on it. He had come to Korea in April.

As a low-ranking Cultural Director he had to follow the troops all the way to the front for round-the-clock morale building and re-building. He was expected to do line duty when necessary. The danger, the discomfort and the bone-deep fatigue left no room for thinking and remembering what now seemed to have happened a long time ago. A thousand miles away can be as good as five or ten years later. There really is something in Einstein's theory about space and time, he thought, if this is what it means.

Aside from the marching, army life did not seem to be much different from the ordinary life of a *kan-pu*. A lot of time was still devoted to meetings, even in the midst of war. And then various officers would come down to give informal talks, deferentially called "reports" in honor of the "warriors." Instead of standing at attention the soldiers would sit or lie around in the attitude of picnickers. But at certain points in the speech a Positive Element among them would bawl out slogans and everybody would have to join in.

Ever since Liu came there had been a good deal of faultfinding discussions that ended in demerits, demotions and, once in a while, executions. The southward push had been coming along nicely and the policy had always been "A lot of discussion after a victory; a lot of encouragement after a defeat." After the troops had concentrated at a point beyond Inchon they had settled down for Mobilization Preparations—another series of meetings.

It had started with a meeting of the Party Committee. Liu did not know what they discussed. As relayed to him later in a meeting of all Youth Corps members in the platoon, they had read out Thought Statistics which showed an alarming percentage of Vacillating, Unreliable Elements. Both *kan-pu* and soldiers, it seemed, were afflicted with America-fright. On the other hand, many of them took what was promised them seriously, that they would drive the American devils into the sea after three months and go home after six months. But the slogan had changed now to "Think in terms of a long war."

The Instructor was in charge of the thought of all Party members in the platoon. The Deputy Instructor was responsible for all Youth Corps members. The squad leaders had all the Positive Elements in hand, who in turn controlled the Retarded Masses in their capacity as unit leaders. All these leaders respectively presided at all the different meetings going on simultaneously, forwarding the messages from above, breaking through the obstacles in each man's mind. Everybody then made resolutions and rose to challenge each other to Arduous Tasks and impossible feats, drawing up all kinds of plans and guarantees to win credits, the more concrete the better. This time it would be International Credits they'd be winning, this being an international war.

They worked up to the grand finale of the Army Meeting which involved the whole platoon. There they singled out certain men of whole squads for the spotlight, those who had signed the most praiseworthy credit-winning pledges. Liu remembered a squad that declared they guaranteed they would destroy five tanks and capture ten prisoners. All the drivers swore "co-existence or co-destruction" with their trucks or carts and mules.

Such things no longer seemed absurd to Liu because he had seen the effect they had on the audience and especially the speakers themselves. No one is altogether immune to the magic in the sound of his own voice. Which is why it is more or less true of every man that his word is his bond, however tenuous. Even if the bond is no stronger than a cobweb brushing against his face, it bothers him.

"This time the Mobilization Preparation is too hasty," all the officers were saying, shaking their heads. "Too hasty." Even then it took a whole week. But Liu imagined that it would be worth it. This appeared to be something that the Communists could never go to battle without, even if it got to be pretty routine.

Liu had got by with a guarantee that he would not cry out if seriously wounded and would carry on if he was but lightly wounded. He was tired of all this mummery. So he was all the more painfully impressed to see how well it worked on the others. It certainly worked better here than in any other branch of government service. These young peasant soldiers made ideal subjects for the treatment. Lots of them had served before in the Nationalist army or warlord armies of the Southwest. They had knocked about a good deal but nobody had ever tampered with their minds, so they remained virgin soil. Even then Liu could see that they were shamming half the time when they made their declarations and egged each other on. But as far as the army was concerned, if they could retain only a fraction of this bravado under fire the meetings would serve their purpose.

Liu reached up to touch the long, slim cloth pouch which held his rations of *ch'ao mien*, baked flour. He used it as a pillow, folding it over and over. It had become a bit damp from contact with the ground but it would have disappeared if he had not put it under his head for safekeeping. It was early yet by his watch but they would probably start early today; it was already quite dark because of the rain. There was much talking and shuffling of feet outside. Mules brayed. There were shouts in the distance and the long wavering shouts of men running.

He sat up and slung the soft long gray sausage of *ch'ao mien* over one shoulder. Lifting a corner of the oil-cloth he went out into the drizzle past the row of caves and round the slope of the hill, to relieve himself.

He heard someone coming after him. When he looked over his shoulder he saw that the soldier had stopped beside a camouflaged cart and was straightening the pile of twigs over it rather needlessly. He was one of those small, slight Szechuenese boys, sadfaced with a long narrow chin. Liu had no doubt he was one of the men designated to keep an eye on him—to "help" him as they called it, in case he had any unworthy notions of going over the hill. The Szechuenese boys, although they were new comrades themselves and needed help badly, would be the most logical choice. Naturally they would not set fellow northerners watching him, or fellow intellectuals like the new recruits from the army *kan-pu* schools who, as a matter of fact, looked upon him as an outsider, practically an old *kan-pu*. There were so many factions in the platoon. Liu felt he did not know his way around yet.

The dim roar of guns came at rather long intervals. The tiers of wheat patches were bright green in the gathering darkness. Two Korean women labored along a path over the rise, balancing big water jars on their heads, their soiled pink blouses and voluminous flowered skirts clear cut against the sky. He had heard that what they wore here was nothing but a handed-down imitation of Chinese clothes of the fifth century. They looked to him like theatrical costumes in a Chinese opera. The costumes were so contrived that the harassed-looking, honest faces above them, unpainted and often unwashed, were a little disconcerting.

Going back he had difficulty finding his cave. It faced a leek patch across the path and he remembered that the leeks had grown high and were brilliant green and glossy. Apparently in the course of the afternoon all of it had been pulled out by the troops.

The Deputy Instructor was having his supper. His orderly had cooked him a helmetful of *mien-ko-ta*, a pasty gruel made of small lumps of flour. He offered Liu some of it and said, "How about getting up some *k'uai pao*, quick news reports? You've studied the latest communiqués, haven't you? Make sure the *k'uai pao* follow the line. Got to broadcast it and drum it in."

"Yes, I've been working on them," Liu answered. "It's a pity that on a night march the Objective Environment rules out all the usual media—you can't see posters or blackboards or anything like that."

"That's no way to talk, Comrade Liu. Mustn't Bow Your Head to Difficulties." The Deputy Instructor seemed to have awakened, bristling. Sleep had not improved his mood. Liu wished he could offer him a cigarette.

"Yes," he said quickly. "I was thinking of making up some jingles—fit them to well-known tunes—"

"Sure. Make them sing. Get them to bandy songs back and forth.

Livens up the troops. You know the slogan: 'Cultural entertainment well done, and the war of the hearts we've won!'"

He went on talking in that strain. Liu was grateful to hear the whistle that told them to get started. He had his pack ready and his water can filled. They scrambled downhill to the road.

29

THE WIDE dirt road got more crowded with men and vehicles as they went along. Trucks, horse-carts, mule-carts, and big guns wheeled along clanking. Troops from several different units jostled their way along the sides. The carts were piled high in huge pyramids. Silhouetted in the dusk, they were black hillocks moving painfully on crunching wooden wheels.

"*Ken shang! Ken shang!* Follow up! Follow up!" the men kept whispering tensely down the files.

Every day the enemy planes left big bomb craters in the road that had to be quickly filled. Gangs of ragged Chinese laborers mobilized from Manchuria under the new slogan of "Freewill united with compulsion" maneuvered their way through the crowd balancing flat-poles on their shoulders, a basket of stones strung on each end of the pole. All aquiver with their dancing loads they sang out. "*Chieh kuang!* Excuse me! *Chieh kuang*, comrade!"

Somber Koreans, all in white with tiny top hats of black gauze sitting toylike on their heads, slid along among them uttering little cries of caution, bearing A-frames, the jeeps of Korea. A man carried one of these yokes by thrusting his neck through the top half of the A. The lower half of the wooden frame was laden with supplies.

"*Ma ti!* Who're they wearing mourning for?" A soldier looked at the white-garbed Koreans and spat to protect himself from the inauspicious sight. "Gives you the willies. Who'd have known we'd ever get into such a creepy place!"

Liu hurried along the edge of the crowd bawling through his cardboard trumpet, "Latest communiqué—latest communiqué:

Guard against straggling. Mustn't ever lose touch with your unit. Comrades who have fallen behind may be murdered by enemy agents. So don't lose touch with your unit!

"The things cast off by American imperialists are poisoned. Don't ever eat them. And don't pick them up. The American imperialists bury a bomb under a wrist-watch or a fountain pen. A warrior of the 37th Section picked up a pen. He got four fingers blown off. A *kanpu* of the 75th Section picked up a tin. The whole squad was poisoned."

"*Kuo k'ou la! Kuo k'ou la!* We're crossing a ditch! Crossing a ditch!" a man shouted. The long line of soldiers he led, victims of nightblindness, stumbled along holding on to each other. Many of them leaned weakly on sticks like famine refugees. The legs of some were bandaged where they had fallen and hurt themselves.

An occasional sputter of machine guns could be heard in the distance. The boom of big guns came at shorter intervals. Now and then there was a roar that set the ground moving softly under their feet.

"Hey, who's that smoking!"

A little red eye of light winked dark and lost itself in the crowd.

"Who's smoking?" a babel of voices demanded. "Enemy agent!"

"Who's been smoking?" The Political Instructor clattered up on his horse.

Of course it would be an old warrior. No new warrior would ever dare violate a rule, with enough people picking on him as it was.

As soon as the instructor had ridden on ahead the old warrior broke into a stream of muttered obscenities in an effort to retrieve his lost face.

"All right, all right," said another old warrior. "Stop saying things with no standpoint."

"Go ahead and shoot me!" the man said loudly with the officer out of earshot. "Didn't get my hand blown off picking up the butt, and here I'm going to get shot smoking it. *Ma na pi!* Takes more than that to scare your dad. Your dad has fought in the Resistance, and he fought in the Civil War. And he didn't get killed. About time I did, I suppose. Well, I'd sooner die here than elsewhere, with so

many great grandsons wearing mourning for me." He sniggered, giving the Koreans a glance from the corner of his eyes. "Makes a fine
showing."

Liu tried to get them to sing, feeling like an officious organizer of
games.

"That cigarette'll get the airplanes upon us in a minute. It's
cleared up now," somebody said.

The night was warm. With unburied dead everywhere there was
a sweetish foulness in the clammy breeze.

Ahead of them the cartdrivers were yelling frantically, "Hey,
make room! Make room!" A man shouted, his angry voice jolted by
punctuating blows between sentences, "*Ma ti! T'o ssu kou!* It's like
dragging a dead dog! Come on—walk! Walk for me! When the
planes come throwing flares you run faster than anybody else.—*Ma
ti! T'o ssu kou! T'o ssu kou!*"

When Liu came up close he saw that it was a *kan-pu* beating and
kicking a soldier who was rolling about on the ground, his arms
around his head, weeping. They were not from his unit.

"Two big eyes wide open and he can't see, he says," raged the *kan-
pu*. "Just pretending! Nightblindness be blowed. Just America-fear."

Liu felt impelled to say something although he had no right to.
Even if these two belonged to his outfit all he could do was to bring
up the matter in unit meetings. To butt in right now would be bad
for Political Influence. But he had heard that some of these nightblind cases had shot or hanged themselves because they could not
stand the long marches in total blackness. Too many of the troops
were getting nightblindness from malnutrition. Then they got seriously ill with the terrific strain on mind and body. The hikes were
much more tiring when you could not see where you were going.

"Don't hit him any more, District Corps Commander." The
other blinded men had been standing around silent but one of them
finally spoke up timidly. "He's in bad shape, he is, I'll carry his pack
for him."

So this *kan-pu* was only in charge of a Corps Under Instruction,
a bunch of schoolboys. Even then he outranked Liu. Unconsciously

Liu tried to tuck his cardboard trumpet out of sight as he pushed past them without saying a word. The trumpet would have betrayed his lowly station at once.

"*Chieh kuang*, comrade! Please get a move on," a cartdriver cried exasperatedly from his high perch. "You're in the way."

"Less than twenty left out of a corps of forty-two," the *kan-pu* shouted up at him as if to the world at large, giving the boy another kick. "If I don't drag these snivelling babies along, every single one of them'll drop behind."

The cartdriver swore at his mule and whipped it hard. "*Ma ti*, how is it you're such a rotten egg? I'll learn you to be such a rotten egg! I'll learn you!"

The mule bounced and kicked under the whistling blows. The cart lurched forward into the protesting crowd. "Hey, careful! Careful!" somebody called out, half laughing. They all knew whom the driver's words were aimed at.

Scarlet flashes of tracer bullets chasing each other down from the nearest ridge dipped into the dark before they reached the marching men. Liu ducked at the clatter of the hidden machine gun. So there are spies about, he thought, enemy Korean guerrillas. The shots seemed very near. But at night everything always looked so much closer.

By now he had given up all pretense of educating the men while they marched. It was all he could do to keep up the pace, staggering under his fifty-catty pack over ruts and holes. Many of the teen-agers from army *kan-pu* schools had emptied their flour pouches to lighten their loads. Parts of the road were white with flour.

"Like chalk marks," an old warrior grumbled. "They're scared that the airplanes won't see us."

Droves of enemy planes thrummed an unseen path across the cloudy night sky as they did all the time, seemingly oblivious to what went on down below. But the men listened to the rise and fall of the drone as if it was the snores of great sleeping beasts.

"*Kuo ch'iao la! Kuo ch'iao la!* Crossing a bridge! Crossing a bridge!" the leader of the nightblind men called out.

Everybody braced himself. Bridges were the worst spots. They were the most bombed and since they were much narrower then roads, the traffic jam made it impossible to get through quickly. The planes muttered on overhead without releasing flares. But star shells from the UN artillery were bursting in the sky ahead. Then a flare of some kind exploded in the air close by, and the sky opened and shut five or six times with the dazzling sheet lightning that came from it. In the alternating light Liu felt his heart tightly opening and closing. The trucks were stuck at the bridge, motors purring. The cartdrivers swore as they struggled to keep the tangled overloaded carts from capsizing. A mule brayed as if it was being butchered. Its hindlegs had slipped through a big hole in the bridge and got stuck there. The cartdriver lashed at it like mad, hoping that it might jerk itself up. The big mule struggled and heaved until the crumbling concrete around the hole loosened up and the animal fell through, carrying the cartdriver with it, along with a soldier who had been trying to help. Other men were pushed screaming into the river.

"*Ken shang! Ken shang!* Follow up! Follow up!" the soldiers passed the word along as they made way between the vehicles, everyone keeping his eyes intently fixed on the man in front of him.

Then suddenly there was plenty of room. They were on the road again while the vehicles were still stuck back there. By the star shells Liu saw flashing glimpses of mangled bodies. Nobody bothered moving the corpses off the road after the night air-raids. So many wheels had run over them since then that some were mashed beyond recognition. Wrecked trucks lay on their sides or their backs, wheels in the air like dead bugs.

He barely had time to look around when he was again pushed to the side of the road. The rattling vehicles came up to rejoin them.

Dust-white searchlight beams spanned the sky. Two of them crossed and stayed fixed rather low in the southwest. The troops were heading for that direction. But after marching half the night they did not seem to have made much progress. The giant pale cross hung in exactly the same position where it had waited for them across the river, ominous but unapproachable. Other searchlights swept around lazily. One of them came to rest with its tip just touching a thick pile of gray cloud puffs, making a soft little spot of light. Somehow it looked infinitely tantalizing and fatiguing. It made Liu's heart itch intolerably to look at it. He was very tired.

The noise and commotion earlier on in the night had died down now. The men lengthened their files, walking farther apart. In the fields down the side of the hill some of the wrecked jeeps and trucks from an air-raid were still burning, secretly it seemed, a small scurrying tongue of flame peeping out now and then like a mouse. And there were still red sparks in the trees and the burned stubble.

"*Kuo k'ou la! Kuo k'ou la!*" cried the leader of the blind. The sound was isolated and sad in the stillness of the night.

Liu was half asleep, walking with a hand on the side of a lumbering cart. He thought he was already dreaming when he first heard the commotion ahead. The road dipped rather suddenly at the next turn. And the star shells had stopped now just when the eye had got used to them, so that it seemed pitch-dark at the treacherous bend. One of the trucks had switched on its headlights.

Everybody was shouting obscenities at the driver. Feelings were running high against the truck-drivers. All of the foot soldiers knew that these men were very much pampered because they were hard to get. The officers were always making allowances for them, expecting them to have picked up bad habits working in the old society. They liked their comfort and hated risking their necks. Two Party members accompanied each driver every hour of the day to see that he did not desert. But the drivers were free to voice their complaints, make reactionary remarks even, and get nothing but a soothing pep talk from one of the *kan-pu*. And they were the only ones in the outfit who ate rice, aside from the Battalion Commander and the Political Instructor.

"Ai! This baked flour is no bloody use," a man sighed. "Stuffs you up and the next minute you're hungry again."

"I heard Chao Yu-kuei picked up a big tin of peanut butter," somebody else said. "He was the one who picked up the American watch last time. Really *fa yang ts' ai'*, made an overseas fortune."

"All I want is one or two piles of shell fragments. Sell the copper when I go home and I'll have enough to live on all my life," a third man said.

"Just let me spend two days collecting empty cans and it'll get me enough to last me for ten years," said another.

Just when the erring driver had been made to turn off his lights, another truck was discovered with flashlights blinking on and off inside.

"No, this truck's being repaired," somebody called out above the confused clamor. "This is a wrecked truck."

A *kan-pu* ran up shouting to the mechanics to put out the light. Then he switched to pidgin Korean. It did not get him anywhere. The men went on working, probing about with their flashlights.

"Sure, they're North Koreans," the *kan-pu* fumed. "That's what they always do—get the repair men out here before us. On our trucks with government certificates and everything. Repair them and just drive them away. Gets us into an awful hole—you can account for wrecked trucks but how do you account for the ones that just disappear?"

Those of the soldiers who did not catch what he said were still cursing the drivers. "I'd give anything not to have the trucks along! Always them that get the planes on us."

Then a faint shout rose among the men as a plane came straight at them out of nowhere, a small plane flying lower than usual. The high hills here were usually in the way, especially at night.

The flares it dropped descended slowly, one after the other. The men scattered, spilling over the slope down the side of the road. Liu fell face downward in the stinking water of the paddies. The vehicles had to stay where they were in the middle of the road, awaiting their fate. The two Party members assigned to each vehicle saw to it that the driver carried out his co-existence or co-destruction pact with his vehicle.

Out of the stillness a *kan-pu* called out, "All right, you men. Let's get going." Liu lifted his head and heard the plane zoom away. Not a jet, he recognized with relief. Just an observation plane. They often went away after dropping flares. They did a lot of things he did not try to understand, like retreating all this way down south when they had apparently been winning the war.

The big green pearly lamps hung suspended in mid-air, scarcely seeming to fall, tear-like in their transparency against the pale lit-up sky. Until now he had been too tense to realize how nice it was lying down. He let his head drop back on his arms and heard his breath bubbling in the water. In his sudden exhaustion he did not mind the filth, feeling like a small boy sucking up orange juice through a straw and ejecting it back into the glass to make it last. A moment later he was up and staggering back to the road.

The short rest had finished him. He joggled along, a looseknit bundle, consisting of just his pack and his various aches and sores, about to fall apart. It seemed to him a long time but they could not have gone ahead for fifteen minutes when it happened.

The first plane was upon them ahead of its sound so that the first warning was the spurts of dirt raised by machine-gun bullets. Men dropped all around him. Liu joined the rush for the field. The cart-drivers and grooms and artillery men struggled to pull the carts and big guns as much to the side of the road as was possible.

There was a tearing howl of sound as the jet screamed up again and almost instantaneously a second plane dove on them, with the terrifying cry of metal in pain. The Party members guarding the trucks were yelling above the loud yammer of machine guns, "*Ch'ung ah! Ch'ung ah!* Rush it! Rush it!" urging the drivers to swerve off the road and make a dash for safety outside the illuminated area. More flares had been dropped by more planes—so many of them that the pulsing hum overhead sounded very odd. The flares hung in the air forming an ellipse, covering an area of at least five or six miles. They burst into greenish blue chrysanthemums of light. The desolation of churned and pitted earth with a few charred trees was lit up brighter than day. It was a strange dawn on another planet.

A truck drove into the shrieking crowd and overturned, crashing into a gully. The screams of the fleeing men sounded almost exhilarated as though they were running for cover in a sudden shower. Another plane, diving with its machine-gun fire thudding into the tangled heap, was answered by scattered rifle shots. Shooting was permitted during air-attacks. Another truck rushed by and more shots banged out after it. The men hated the trucks and in this confusion anything went.

Liu lay in a gully, his head against a boulder. The whirling buzz of a circling plane drilled painfully deep into him. Then the bomb fell thundering.

In the complete blackout he had enforced within himself, it took him a moment to make up his mind he was not dead. He opened his eyes. A rain of dust and earth was still falling, slithering over him. The quivering wails and groans of the wounded sounded like they were less than ten yards away.

By now it was relatively quiet except for the howling fury of swooping planes and chattering machine guns. The man beside Liu had the hem of his blouse thrown over his head. Liu could hear his muffled sobs. Some of the schoolboys were all piled up in a heap for protection. Others kept crawling about, always feeling that it was not safe where they were.

There was a new sound, a stream of broad thick slapping sounds, heavy, less rapid, less sure and smooth than machine guns. Liu raised his head and saw that an anti-aircraft gun had been set up in the watercourse just off the road. The crew dropped flat as a plane dove on the gun, then leaped up to load shells and fire at the next plane. A hit! Caught in the merciless web of the search lights, the silvery-blue jet spurted into an arrow of flame and slanted toward the ground. Half a mile away it crashed into a mushroom of yellow-red flame and black smoke.

Before they could cheer, another plane dove to avenge its mate. Liu heard the zip of rockets and buried his head in his arms. When the crackle of explosions stopped, he raised his head again. Under the light of the flares he could see that the gun was out of action, half turned from its carriage. One man on the gun still twitched his legs where he lay; the rest of the crew had been tossed into contorted positions that showed all too plainly that they were dead.

Bombs were dropping farther down the road. But now the grating buzz of a circling plane was again boring into him, concentrated, like a dentist's drill. Then came the complete blank of anticipation before the deafening boom. Somebody seemed to have tumbled over him. Then he knew that he had been hit. The realization bumped heavily against his ribs. He was dazed and couldn't tell where, but the pain began to saw away heavily at his dulled consciousness.

He had no idea how long the bombardment lasted. Time seemed to have stopped for him several times when he screamed loud enough. Then the eternal yowling swish of planes and rumbling and sweeping rat-tat-tat went on again.

Once he opened his eyes to find a face on the ground looking vaguely at him, one check pressed against the earth. The spotty young face was a thin oval with fine regular features. But it was just a face. Back of the ears there was nothing. It must be that the blast of a bomb had flung the youth into the gully. All that was left of his body was the blood-smeared gray skeleton, armless with just the left ribs and hip and leg bones. The narrowness and continuity gave him an elongated, crawling look. And his lips were slightly parted as if in a half smile. Liu could not help thinking of these old stories about snakes with human heads, beautiful and smiling. He tried not to look at it.

It was close to dawn when the planes finally stopped coming. Immediately an uproar broke out. "Forty-eighth section! Over here! Over here!" "Platoon Commander Chu, the Deputy Instructor is wounded!" "This way, Thirty-ninth Section! Where are the others? Where's the Instructor?" These were the ones who had emerged unscathed. There was a glad ring in their keyed-up shouts. They made more noise than hawkers at a country fair. To Liu, lying there listening to it, all the noise and gaiety were so exclusive he could not stand it.

A wounded man shrieked and then, all in the same breath, bawled out, "Anybody tell me again that the enemy's a paper tiger, I'll f—— his ancestors!"

"I knew I was going to get it this time," another man said. "*Ma ti,* this war is certainly not the same as the Civil War! Never saw so many planes in all my life. And where are our planes? You see pictures of so many planes flying over Peking for Mao Tse-tung. Why can't he spare us a few here? Just get us out here to *sung ssu*, send us to our death, that's all."

The *kan-pu* bustled about herding the soldiers together and salvaging the supplies in the vehicles. They told the wounded to wait quietly for the stretchers. When one of the wounded men started to call Mao names and professed dishonorable intentions toward the great man's mother, a *kan-pu* stopped and said to him, "This comrade here—you mustn't say things with no principle. It's an honor to *kua ts'ai*, wear the red sash. You just have to be patient and wait for the stretcher."

"*Ma ti*, nothing but a whole load of face-towels," a man said disgustedly. They were swarming all over the wrecked trucks grabbing what they could. "What's in there? Looks like tins."

"Hey, what have you got there?"

"Don't tell me there's nothing but cotton wool in this one!"

Soon order was restored. Liu could not see the road from where he lay but he heard them marching off with what was left of the rumbling carts. It was dawn. The brush-like poplars up on the hill across the road were still smoking.

Nobody was supposed to use the road in daytime. But Liu heard people passing by in small groups of three or four. He knew they were nightblind cases who, being old warriors, did not have to pay strict attention to certain rules and refused to be threatened or cajoled into marching at night. Hiking comfortably by daylight they could easily catch up with their units before it got dark. Liu listened to them chatting as they went by, sounding just like travellers on a country road on a fine day in early summer. He looked up stupidly at the bright blue sky traced with wisps of white clouds. He wondered again where he had been hit, but the merciful daze still held him in its grasp. Besides, he was afraid to explore with his hand for the wound.

Once a group of them stopped to cut a big piece of flesh off the hind leg of a dead mule. Where the ground dropped away over the side of the road, the corpses and dead horses and mules piled up higher than the road level.

"Mule meat is too tough for my teeth," said one of the men.

"That's because you don't know how to cook it right," said his companion. "Last time we accepted the advice of the Fourth Field comrades and it turned out very tender. Just put a little urine in the stew. Tastes all right. Good and salty and no queer smell."

Some of the other wounded called out to them asking about stretchers but received no answer. Liu did not try to speak to them. It would only make him feel that nobody could see or hear him, like a ghost who did not know he was dead and kept rapping futilely, angrily, on the glass that separated him from the living.

He was also afraid to call out. He was feeling weak and faint and he had heard that sometimes they just ran a bayonet through the serious cases.

The gully was steaming hot in the noon sun. He dozed off, lying face downward on the scorching gravel, his cheek pressed against a cramped arm. Then the pain would jerk him back sharply into consciousness. He drank from his water can and managed to get some *ch'ao mien* out of his long pouch. But the pain of the exertion made him vomit and he could not get any of it down. The smiling face several yards away was changing color and beginning to smell.

When night fell there was more firing in the distance and more traffic on the road. But the stretcher-bearers did not turn up. If there were wolves and wild dogs in Korea surely they would be coming, Liu thought, with so many corpses about. It started to drizzle again. In the blackness and the slight rustle of rain it was difficult not to imagine that the smiling face had inched up closer to him. The stench was certainly much stronger now. He fell into a pain-dulled stupor, more like a coma than sleep.

In the morning, in his intervals of consciousness, he noticed that there were no nightblind men travelling on the road. It seemed terribly quiet without them. Later he thought he heard the spatter of machine guns coming from at least two directions. They never did any machine-gunning in daytime, as far as he knew. Unless these were air attacks.

The big guns were steadily going carrump, carrump. The firing increased and drew closer by nightfall but somehow he felt less worried by it.

He had not given up hope of the stretcher-bearers' coming, knowing how hard it was to find transportation. A delay of several days was not unusual. His only fear was that he would be unconscious when they came and they would miss him, taking him for dead.

That night he saw the flicker of flashlights being turned on and off in the hills. They were searching for the wounded over on the ridge. Then they crossed the road and came down into the field. By now there weren't many people screaming for stretchers. But he had made it.

All the stretchers were concentrated in a spot at the roadside while they waited for the trucks to come up. They took the weapons and cartridge belts away from everybody but one of the men refused to be disarmed. After two days and a night of great pain and feeling deserted by the world he trusted nothing except his grenade belt.

There was an argument. The *kan-pu* was afraid to use force. "We have orders from above to turn in all your weapons," he told the man.

"What sort of *t'a ma ti* orders? You nag some more and your dad'll kill the whole lot of you! I'm through anyway."

Four trucks came for them. Three soldiers picked him up and swung him into a truck. The road was so bumpy, Liu nearly passed out from the jolting and tumbling. But it felt good to return to the human world. The jolting got worse when the truck suddenly put on speed. The men were sliding about, trying to hold on to the sides of the truck-frame and crying out in dismay. Liu hoisted himself up, turning around with difficulty to look out of the rear opening of the canvas cover. The sky was pale with green flares and he could hear the planes humming overhead above the rattle of the engine.

There were sounds of an altercation in the cab ahead and presently the truck screeched to a stop. Other trucks were pulling up sharply behind them.

"*Ya ch'e t'ung-chih!* Comrade Car-guard!" some of the men called out.

They heard the door of the truck cab clicking open, then the patter of running steps.

"What's happened? Comrade Driver! Comrade Car-guard!" Then somebody wailed, "The sons of bitches—they've run away! Just left us in the middle of the road."

Somebody else cursed, "Those mongrel bastards! I've always known they aren't men. Those guards are the worst. When the truck carries supplies they always force the driver to break through. Now they just don't care. Our lives aren't worth anything. They just stick to the driver and see that he doesn't go over the hill—that's all they care."

Others were still screaming for the driver and the two guards to come back. The pitch-dark truck-bed could scarcely hold the alarm and clamor. But already an all-pervading stillness and brilliance was closing in around them. The sound of the planes seemed part of the silence, like the scraping hiss of an old silent film.

"Where are the sons of bitches? I'll get them. I'll throw a grenade at all three of them. You just watch." The man who had kept his grenade belt had a big hole in his stomach but he struggled to sit up. Liu knew he would not be able to go after the three, though he was quite capable of tossing off a grenade inside here, blowing up the truck before the bombs could get at it.

Liu found himself climbing down the rear of the truck. He did not know about the others but he was crawling away from the truck that stood brilliantly lit in the black puddle of its own shadow. The imprisoned furor inside seemed to reach out after him. More flares burst and a green-lit heaven bore down on him in intensive, microscopic scrutiny. Doomsday would dawn like this, if it ever came. He felt like a beetle and seemed to cover as little ground as a beetle going at full speed. It took so long to get to the side of the road and off into the field.

His wound hurt like fire. The field was wide but wherever he crawled there was a path of fire in front of him. He crept along like a wisp of flame in the blackened stubble. It would seem to die out and then, after a long moment, suddenly leap up again, the golden red tongue thinned and diffused as it swelled out, going up with a faint hum. But it finally went out altogether.

He did not hear the explosion of the first bomb.

30

THE SOLDIER carrying him said something in an abrupt grunt to someone else. He was slung over the man's shoulder. Seen upside down, the yellow-brown earth hung wobbling over him, a heavy sky perilously close, as if about to fall. The man was not big and was staggering under his weight. They seemed to be talking Korean. Liu dimly remembered shouting for help as the two of them passed by.

They were heading for the road. Trucks and jeeps were moving along the roadway again. The purr of traffic were strange, civilized sounds, Liu thought. The man carrying him gave another grunt in answer to something his companion said. He stopped and slowly bending his knees, squatted and lowered Liu to the ground. The other man came around to pick him up under the shoulders while the man who had been carrying him picked him up by the legs. They started off again, carrying Liu between them. During the reshuffling Liu got a chance to take a good look at them and realized for the first time that they were wearing South Korean uniforms. In his feebleness it only gave him a small shock, which, if anything, helped to clear his head.

They must have picked him up because he was dressed like a *kanpu* and could very well be an officer of some importance. They had no way of telling, since no badges of rank were worn by the People's Volunteers in Korea.

Were these men a patrol? He listened for the thump of distant guns. There didn't seem to be any. But then there came an absent-minded peal or two, like summer thunder, as if it was raining in another part of the country, though the sun was shining here. The line must have shifted. Have we been cut off? he wondered. He couldn't have been unconscious for long. But things happen so fast out here with everything motorized. The long smooth run of traffic unimpeded by horse-carts and pack-mules sounded ominous now, telling him that he was well inside enemy territory.

His wound had wakened before he had. It was screaming in his ears without a break, sometimes like a hungry infant, sometimes like a forest full of cicadas on a hot day. He tried not to cry out when the men stumbled over rough spots. After they climbed to the road they passed wrecked trucks, blackened husks all burned out inside. The cheap tin-can bareness within the cab made him shiver. Was one of those trucks the one he had escaped from? There had been four. He forgot to count.

The enemy soldiers finally brought him to a big cave at the foot of the ridge. He guessed it was a South Korean first-aid station. A Chinese interpreter asked him his name, rank and outfit. He answered as best he could but he did not expect to be believed. It was a common practice for captured officers to give a lower rank than their real one. A Korean nurse snipped away parts of his blood-encrusted uniform and a Korean doctor looked over his wound. The examination was so painful that he lost consciousness again.

He came to at the back of a jeep. They must be taking him to the headquarters for questioning. It turned out to be a long journey. It was dark when they drove into a large city in semi-blackout and they woke him again by lifting him out of the jeep.

The next morning when he roused himself from drugged sleep, the UN hospital in Seoul struck him as a fantastic thing. It floated shiplike and almost palatial on the gray sea of war. They must be pretty anxious that he should live, so they could get information out of him. They evidently still had the wrong idea about his identity; it wasn't a real officer they'd captured, just a disillusioned ex-student whose career was finished anyway. A lot of stories had been circulated about the Americans using torture on war prisoners. He had not believed all that he had heard. But after all, war is war. He hadn't the least idea of what was coming, so that the modest comfort of clean pajamas and snow white sheets and the foreign nurses in attendance took on sultanic and sinister splendor.

All the doctors and nurses were foreigners. To him that was nothing unusual. But all the wounded men were westerners too. He had never seen so many foreigners. His contact with such people had been limited to books and films and a college professor at his university, to him they always seemed to talk like books and behave like film characters and were quite unreal. It stunned him to see the two rows of sun-baked faces, pink or meaty red, very much flesh-and-blood against the chill white of beds and wall. It was rather careless and slipshod of the people in charge to put a Chinese captive together with their own wounded. This went to show that their security measures were very lax, he thought weakly with a habit-taught flicker of disapproval.

He had been re-examined, had his dressings changed, and was given a blood transfusion upon arrival at the hospital. They were giving him penicillin injections and vitamin pills and made him eat beef and liver. But they did not let him have enough water to drink. A nurse brought him chewing gum and showed him by gestures that he was to chew it when he felt thirsty. Out of caution he did not speak English to them, not wishing to call attention to himself in any way. The nurses laughed and joked with the other patients. To him they were brisk and unsmiling. If their eyes were not pale blue they seemed to turn that color when they looked at him. Blue eyes, remote—and somehow empty when he thought suddenly of Su Nan. In their weariness and their rumpled uniforms they were not as pretty as the nurses in the movies. Liu had gone to foreign movies often before he had learned to condemn them.

They gave him sedatives again so he had a good night's sleep the second day. Waking up he was astounded to find a Chinese in the bed next to his. The man had just had an operation. Liu waited hours in feverish suspense before the effects of the anesthetics wore off and the man could talk a little. He said he was a soldier from the 33rd Section. He spoke with a Szechuan accent. Liu saw that he had a head wound and another in his thigh.

So Liu was not the only Chinese war prisoner brought here for treatment. Then they had not singled him out, expecting to extract information from him. His heart throbbed with sudden hope. But it was inconceivable that these people should run the war like a charity. The little Szechuanese was getting several vitamin and penicillin injections a day, more than any westerner in the ward got, because his condition was critical.

They had to give the Szechuanese one blood transfusion after another. Then the nurses put up a screen around his bed and Liu knew that he was dying. When Liu was wheeled back into the ward after his own operation, the screen was gone and so was the Szechuanese. The few words they had exchanged had felt like a family reunion on New Year's Eve, and made Liu more acutely conscious of being lost and adrift among strangers in a foreign country, an outlaw and an invalid.

Liu's operation turned out well. The incredible days repeated themselves. He never could get over waking up from a nap and finding tea or milk and biscuits by his pillow. His astonishment was almost resentful. No wonder that over on the other side they called American soldiers *shao-yeh ping*, young-master soldiers. They were that pampered.

These people lived in such a state of plenty, they could afford to give in to humanitarian impulses, whimsically overwhelming the recipients of their charity with kingly gestures. It means little or nothing to them to lavish medical care on their captives, Liu thought. It did not pledge them to anything. What was to happen to him next remained yet to be seen. He remembered some detective thriller he had read, translated from English. The cornered murderer was riddled with bullets and finally caught. He was rushed to a hospital where they did their best to save his life and nurse him back to health just so that he could stand trial and be hanged. They do things like that. For three weeks, prey to these thoughts, he lay in the ward, served with impersonal kindness by the blue-eyed nurses.

His mind was not at rest until he got transferred to the POW hospital in Pusan. A hospital train took him there as soon as he was in condition to travel. It was reassuring to be back among his own countrymen once more. And it seemed to him that they lived in circumstances somewhat more appropriate to their station as prisoners of war. The large wards were a series of wooden shacks set in a compound surrounded by barbed wire. The Chinese food was all right but nothing fancy and without the perpetual round of little snacks.

The austerity and rigidity of routine pleased him. The change was like going to boarding school from a sumptuous boyhood home where he had felt insecure.

Many of the patients here were also on their way to recovery, which he thought rather a pleasant thing, at first. He soon found that prudence returned with health. Here it was not like it was with the little Szechuanese who died, when they could have said anything to each other so long as they had the strength.

The prevalent sentiment here seemed to be pro-Communist. Liu was first aware of it when the word went round: "Better stay here as long as you can. They're starving over at the camp." This news was supposed to come from another ward where a recent arrival from the North Korean POW camp had brought the news.

"That means the American imperialists are running out of supplies," somebody said. "Let's step up the eating. We'll exhaust the Paper Tigers."

A Grab Rice Movement was proposed. If anyone in the room objected, he wisely held his tongue. Liu managed to keep out of the conversation by pretending he had not yet recovered from the fatigue of his trip here. But at supper that evening the Szechuanese in the next bed to his snatched his rice bowl and turned it upside down over his own, pressing the rice together. "*Mao-je fan*, hot rice," he said, giggling. The white dome of rice stuck out of the bowl like a round cap.

"Ai, ai—no teasing." Liu reached out for the bowl, trying to make a joke of it.

"You yell for more if you want to eat. Just say I took your share. What of it? Your dad's hungry. Not enough rice to go round."

There were arguments and remonstrations when the nurse came.

An interpreter had to be called in. Liu was glad they didn't know he spoke English. The Positive Elements in the ward would always be wondering what he had actually said if he ever spoke to the hospital staff in English; if anything went wrong it must be because he had informed on them.

Later he spotted the one who must be the man behind the scene here, in charge of "Mutual Consolidation"—that is, mutual watching. Liu did not recognize him at first—an Instructor Hsi, a Party member. Here he had given his name as Wu P'ei and his rank as mess sergeant.

The Grab Rice Movement did not go very far for the lack of active participation. But heartening messages were always being passed around, news of the Volunteers' latest victories and of fallings out among the members of the United Nations who had sent troops to Korea. The news was supposed to be brought by recent arrivals in other wards.

Liu was hardly surprised to find himself subject to the extra-territorial rule of the Party. To begin with he had never consciously felt that he had passed beyond the boundary line. He wondered if anybody who had lived under Communist rule could ever feel un-watched again.

A new man in the ward had just had an operation. He had a bad shock waking up to find that he had lost a leg. He wept and screamed, "Give me back my leg! I'd rather die! At least die with a whole carcass!"

"*T'a ma ti*, those imperialist executioners!" a Positive Element exclaimed in sympathy. "Feel like cutting off your arm today, or sawing off your leg tomorrow—just as they please. And drug you so you can't struggle. Ai, comrade. *Ma ti*—worse than sitting on tiger benches." He referred to the most common instrument of torture back home. "Just sawed the leg right off!"

The man kept everybody awake at night screaming, "I want my leg back! You butchers! Executioners! Give me back my leg!" He sounded like the ghost of the beheaded man in so many old stories, wanting his head back. The soldier shrieked on and on, stopped only by fits of violent sobbing. He wouldn't be taking it this way if they only explained to him that they had to remove his leg to save his life, Liu thought. But he supposed that with the shortage of interpreters it was impossible to prepare every POW who was to be operated on. And the doctors were so rushed, they really could not be expected to worry about what was, after all, beyond the call of their duty. Liu felt a certain guilt himself because he could easily have explained to the man and was afraid to.

But it was just common sense. One day everybody would be going home. And there would always be enough unpleasantness back there without making trouble for yourself. The war prisoners would be going home; so would their keepers. He wasn't the only one to look at it that way. So what if your captors were humane? Their goodness only saddened you because it had nothing to do with you.

The doctor and nurses made their rounds early every morning. After them came the sun. Liu noticed that lately it had been coming deeper into the wooden shack. The summer sun looked so bored on its duty calls, it apparently knew that its coming and going did not mean anything to these men. They no longer did anything with their days and nights.

Breakfast often interfered with the doctor's morning round. While a patient was having his wound treated and his bandages changed, his bowl of rice would be cooling on his night table. Sometimes a man would eat while he was being attended to, twisting his head around between mouthfuls to look at his wound. The comforting warm white rice must taste a bit funny, mixed with the pain.

A young soldier had just arrived from the Chinese POW camp on Koje Island. He had been sent to the hospital in Seoul to have shrapnel removed from his thigh, and then brought back here to rest up after the operation. He seemed to be doing very well. The first day he arrived he sang to himself while lying in bed. Liu had often heard soldiers humming *shan ko*, hill songs, but had never heard them sung out loud. All hill songs were love songs and would meet with jeering disapproval in the Communist army. But now the young man was singing one about bamboos which seemed to be a little girl's ditty:

"Pa Bamboo, Ma Bamboo,
Grandpa, Grandma Bamboo:
This year, your turn to grow;
Next year, my turn to grow.
No use your growing tall—
I tall, can get husband."

The singer's face, turned sideways on the pillow, was unsmiling. He had rather long cheeks, a hard, good profile and slightly protuberant eyelids that looked a little sullen. He sang in a high voice, but quite a falsetto, with lots of little extra "ai's" thrown in to give it bounce. The singing sounded strange in the afternoon silence. Outside the row of windows the compound was one large, smooth cake of dust in the glare. Three wooden watchtowers were in view, boxlike and unpainted, set wide apart. Trucks roared and puffed in and out. In the ward the few men who were not asleep constantly gave out little groans that got to be perfunctory and annoying, less like groans than the pointless sighs of old folks as they moved about or sat down, expressive of mild exertion or contentment.

"Blouse on washline 'cross the river,
Looks like peony from afar.
Good flowers grow in pots of gold—
Looking's easy; picking is hard."

Another song he sang was wistful as well as a little hypocritical:

"A southeast wind rises, coming aslanting.
A lovely flower here, abloom 'gainst the leaves.
A young woman like you mustn't smile so much—
So much illicit love comes from smiling."

It could not be more Chinese. Listening, Liu could see the undulating hills, the plains blanketed by paddies, the mud hut by the peach tree in bloom, thin black branches standing skeletal in the ball of mauvish pink mist. The whole familiar landscape unrolled before him, oppressive in its vastness.

The man gave his name and outfit when somebody tried to talk to him. His name was Chiao. He answered questions with peasant shortness.

"What's it like in camp?"

"Food not bad," he said. "Not so good as what you have here." Then he had started to sing.

Supper was early, before sunset. After supper a nurse came to give Chiao a rubdown. A slight ripple of excitement and consternation ran across the ward when he turned over to lie face downward. Not everybody saw at once what was on his back. The electric light had just been turned on but it was a time of day when it was not much brighter with the light on. The long room was a tobacco-colored box with windows cut out showing rectangles of bright blue-green sky. The tattoo on Chiao's naked back was crudely done and the strokes were too thin and spiky for the large characters. The four characters in a vertical row read, "*Fan-Kung, k'ang o*; anti-Communist, resist Russia."

After the nurse was gone, a man asked, "What's that on your back?"

"I got it in camp. Everybody's got one," Chiao said, buttoning up his pajama top. Then he corrected himself. "Some had it different. Some had '*Shih ssu fan-Kung*; vow to destroy Communism till death.' Also four characters."

"You mean they forced everybody to be tattooed?" the man asked incredulously.

"No, nobody forced me. Why?" Chiao rolled over to look at the man. "I wanted it. What's there to be scared of now? Nobody can clap 'reactionary hats' on you now and get you shot."

"Traitor!" the man flung at him. Somebody else called out, "Imperialist spy! Are you a Chinese or aren't you?"

"I'm as Chinese as you! I'm against the Russian big-noses and their running dogs who fight their war for them—send us here to *tso t'i ssu kuei*, be the ghost to take their place." He was talking about the common belief that the ghosts of suicides are doomed to haunt the places where they died and are not freed for reincarnation unless they can entice other men to take their own lives in a similar manner, filling their places.

"Where did you pick up this sort of talk, comrade? In camp?" another man asked pityingly.

"I know what I'm talking about. *Ma ti*, a man ought at least to know good from bad. Look what they did here for my leg wound. I've been wounded before—you ever been to a Volunteers hospital? You lie on the ground—in the open air when the caves are full up. All the nurses ever do is to feed you rice gruel three times a day. I don't blame those that refuse to be disarmed. That's the only way to get any attention in a Volunteers hospital—threaten them with grenades."

"He's bought," several people cried out at once. "Imperialist spy! *T'a! T'a!* Beat him! Beat him! *T'a-ah! T'a-ah!*

Liu had been following the conversation closely. But violence always came too fast for him, catching him unawares. It gave him quite a turn to see two men hobbling on their crutches toward Chiao's bed. Somebody tossed a kidney dish in Chiao's direction, yelling encouragingly, "*T'a! T'a-ah!*"

"Comrades! Now just a minute, comrades," Liu heard Instructor Hsi's voice call out. "We mustn't forget we're all prisoners here. We may belong to different parties and factions, it makes no difference. As long as we're prisoners we have to observe the rules."

Chiao had sat up tense and pale in bed. "Come on, *T'a and T'a ma ti*, where do you think you are?" He waited, but the men on crutches returned muttering to their beds. Liu saw them exchange looks and wondered what it meant.

Bed check had always seemed a funny institution to Liu—two stalwart UN military policemen marching shoulder to shoulder into a roomful of sick and wounded people. Eyes watchful under their steel helmets, with their guns on their hips, they looked as if they were ready for anything. Tonight he felt differently. He was on the verge of speaking to them when they came to his bed. The only thing that stopped him was his certain knowledge that whatever he warned them of would not happen. The others would have guessed what he was saying, even if they did not understand. They would merely put it off—that and their revenge on him which was bound to come sooner or later. Meanwhile the hospital staff would not like him for telling false tales. The last thing they would want to do was to take sides in the patients' brawls. Pro-Communist, or anti-Communist, these POWs were not going to be with them long.

The guards were gone. The nurses had made their last rounds. In the dimmed-out ward the rows of beds looked inhumanly tidy. Liu had never realized how quiet it was here at night. The staff's quarters were on the other side of the compound. Liu had read quite a few detective stories. Nearly all of them were translations. The few Chinese attempts at detective fiction just did not sound real at all. He supposed it was because murder mysteries were basically impossible in a Chinese environment. Murders there were, but never mysteries. There was never any question of who had dropped in on the deceased from eleven at night to quarter past twelve. Just pump the houseful of servants who were on duty twenty-four hours a day. In the absence of servants the deceased must be so poor that he would be living cheek by jowl with several other families. The neighbors would supply all necessary information. Liu had often envied the westerners their privacy which the Chinese never have and probably never would now, with the coming of the Communists and their Group Life. But now he thought bitterly that you could always depend on the westerners to arrange things so that the prisoners would have here the neat and cozy, air-tight isolation on the night of the murder.

There were some whisperings at Instructor Hsi's end of the room, but they did not start anything until hours later. Liu stiffened at the patter of running feet and the sound of scuffling. He lifted his head to look. Several men were dragging Chiao, struggling and kicking, into the aisle. He wondered why Chiao did not cry out. Then he saw dimly the white beard of a towel trailing down his chin. He supposed the first thing they did was to gag him.

They had Chiao pinned down flat now. Somebody was pounding on him with a big stick. Liu had a glimpse of the crosspiece on top of the stick, so it must be a crutch. It came down with the regularity of a pestle, with dulled, light thuds. For a moment he speculated if he was strong enough to get up, climb out the window and get help. They would grab him before he had gone far. Anyhow there was no time for anything like that. They were hitting the man on his chest.

He caught hold of the water bottle on his night-table and smashed it against the window-pane. There seemed a perceptible pause before it crashed on the ground, a shower of splinters tinkling in its wake. Without turning round he knew that the small knot of "operators" had stopped to look at him in amazement. He did not know what to do next unless it was to crash out the window after the bottle. They would be upon him in a second.

Then a broad beam of blue-white light swooped in the window. The big jagged hole in the glass stood out clear. It was the searchlight from one of the watchtowers. It swerved round briefly, then returned to the broken window. Liu almost felt like giggling to see the strong light contemplating seriously the foot of his cot, an edge of the night-table and his slippers on the floor. His feet were out of sight because he was sitting up. He could not see the men very well. The blinding light had cut the dark room in two. They are probably trying to make up their minds whether they should spring at him across the moat of light.

When the guards rushed in and all the lights were turned on, the rioters were all back in bed. Only Chiao was left, lying on the floor, still gagged. Liu told the story in his stiff, rusty English. He supposed he did not do it very well.

Chiao was whisked away for medical examination. The questioning lasted a good part of the night. The rioters were reprimanded and warned through interpreters. But evidently the affair was not taken too seriously. Chiao's bafflingly strong constitution was partly to blame. He was sent back to the ward a few days later, apparently none the worse for his chest injuries.

Liu had thought he wouldn't survive another night in the same ward with the Positive Elements after this. But aside from some muttered threats to traitors, Instructor Hsi had kept them under control. Of course they would want to wait a while before doing anything to him.

Chiao's cot had its head pushed against a wooden post half encased in the wall. After Chiao came back he always lay with his head propped up against the pillar, the better to observe in case anyone should sneak up on him. He looked funny with his neck at right angles to his body. His face seemed carved on a totem pole, it merged so well with the unpainted wood. Liu often caught Chiao watching him, though Liu was the one man in the room he need not guard against.

Their beds were too far apart for conversation and anyhow it was inadvisable to talk. They hardly exchanged glances. Liu could understand the man's embarrassment. Circumstances had thrust them into a relationship too close for comfort. Still, they did come to a tacit understanding that they would take turns sleeping at night. When Liu had turned and tossed and coughed long enough, he noticed that the shaved head with its yellow wooden luster had slipped off the post on to the pillow, asleep.

The day Chiao was going to be discharged from the hospital, he stopped by Liu's bed on his way to the latrine just before dawn. Liu woke up with a slight start.

"You are a light sleeper," Chiao said. He seemed pleased.

"Well, you've got to be one around here," Liu murmured.

"Sure. Just like a 'black inn.'" He meant the inns that figured so much in old stories, where the innkeeper robbed and murdered all travellers who stopped there. "That was a near thing—the other night," he said grinning and repeated several times, "a near thing." Liu guessed that he was being thanked.

"You're lucky to be leaving," Liu said smiling.

"What about you? When can you get out of here?"

"I don't know. Nobody has said anything to me.—What's that?" he asked when Chiao slipped something under his mattress.

"You better keep that," Chiao whispered. Liu's groping hand under the mattress told him it was a pair of scissors, the long slim kind that stood in the jar of instruments on the wheel-cart that followed the doctor on his morning rounds.

"Now, how are you ever going to get any sleep at night?" Chiao said worriedly.

"I can sleep in the daytime."

"*Ma ti*, just wait till those bastards get into camp—we'll bash their brains out. You know which days they change the bedsheets?"

"Yes," Liu said a bit uncertainly.

He gave the mattress a slight pat. "On those days, don't forget to take it out and hide it on your body." He nodded and sauntered off singing "Pa Bamboo" in a low voice. It was the first time he had sung since the first day he came.

31

IT TURNED out that Liu had no need to use the scissors Chiao had given him. Not long after Chiao left, a series of fights and beatings among the prisoners under cover of night precipitated the decision of the hospital authorities to separate the pro-Communist and anti-Communist patients. A discharged patient who had stayed on to act as orderly had tried to set fire to the kitchen. There had also been several cases of attempted poisoning.

The patients were now labelled as "those who want to be repatriated" and "those who do not want to be repatriated." This was the first Liu had heard of it—that they would not have to go home if they did not want to. It made a great difference in everything. It was like being promised a share in a new world.

By the time he got to the camp it was no longer the paradise of anti-Communist avengers which he had looked forward to, not without a certain dread. The separation of those for and against repatriation had also been completed here. Liu was taken by boat to Koje Island where there was a large new camp for POWs who were not going back.

They had always said that Korea was a barren-looking place. But nowhere was as bare as the POW camp. Not a tree grew on the newly leveled land, a vast stretch of cream-colored flatness, always a bit blurred by wind-blown dust. All around rose the bare hills, faded to sandy pallor in the noon light. The camp officer was showing Liu around. The officer was a prisoner elected by the others. They stopped by one of the stone huts to join a small crowd gathered under the eaves watching a man playing a *hu-ch'in*. The familiar melody was like a cob-web thread drifting in the air with no place to stick.

"He made the *hu-ch'in* himself," the officer said. "Made it from a beer can."

There was an explosion of laughter. As the prisoners stood around listening, exposing the white letters "POW" painted on the backs of their khaki blouses, a prankster had drawn with a bit of chalk six little lines radiating from the O at the center of a man's back. The lines, one up, one down and two on each side, made a head and tail and four feet. And the O became a tortoise, the sign of a cuckold. The abused man did not know at first what the joke was. When he had found out he chased after the culprit, shouting threats and curses.

"Hey," somebody said, and put a hand on Liu's shoulder. He turned and saw that it was Chiao.

"How are you? I was just going to look for you," Liu said.

"I was wondering when you'd be coming. Look, you got boots instead of shoes," Chiao observed. He himself had leather shoes several sizes too large. "There's a piece of steel in the instep of your boots," he told Liu. "You can take it out and make a knife with it. That's what they all do—those who draw boots."

After that Chiao took him around the grounds. It was like boarding school again. Only he was too old for school. They all were. They were old enough to worry about what was going to happen to them. And they could not forget the barbed wire around them.

It was like school too, to hear the complaints about food. They had rice cooked together with small pieces of meat and vegetables. "Just like cat food," a man grumbled. It did not look like a respectable meal and all the taste was gone from the meat. All the POWs gained weight when they weighed in every week. Still, everyone complained.

It was humiliating to be repeatedly warned by the UN authorities that eventually they would have to shift for themselves if they did not want to go home. As if they had refused to go back home just for a meal ticket from these foreigners. Liu rather thought there were grounds for suspecting that the dependence forced on them was habit-forming, like all dependence. While they found it irksome, it could be that there was also a reluctance for it to end.

"If the UN army won't bother about us any more, we'll just go and till the land," a soldier declared heatedly. They had been planting cabbages in camp with considerable success. Most of them had done farm work before.

Go and till the land where? What country in the world today would have room for a newly introduced Chinese minority? The only conceivable place they could go to was Taiwan, which might take them as soldiers. Most of the men were willing, even fervent. But with one rumor after another floating through camp, Liu did not know what to believe."

"What's this about peace talks?" Liu asked Chiao one evening when they were taking a walk after supper, smoking a cigarette. "If they're talking peace, they might send us back to the mainland after all. The easiest way for them."

"Some people say they can't be talking peace. Say it's impossible," Chiao answered.

"Why impossible? That's just wishful thinking."

Chiao sighed and shook his head. "You don't know whom to believe. This stuff about the peace talks might be a rumor spread by spies."

"Spies? You mean there are Communists here too?"

"You never can tell. For instance, when we were being divided up, there were fourteen or fifteen men who went with those that wanted to go home. Then they escaped back to us."

He stopped, so Liu asked, "Why, what made them change their minds?"

"They said as soon as the camp door was shut, the Communists called a Mass Meeting. Everybody had to make a Self-Criticism. They were going to Settle Accounts with Reactionary Elements, Running Dogs of the Imperialists. So these men just ran, and climbed over the barbed wire fence."

"And they got away—just like that?" Liu asked.

"Yes. That's why we wouldn't take them in at first. But they begged and begged. Said they couldn't go back. Most of them had their backs tattooed like mine."

"But what made them risk it in the first place? They ought to know they could never get away with it."

Chiao did not say anything for a while.

"Guess they're homesick," Liu said.

"Well, who isn't? It's this *pieh-niu*, living in foreign parts." Chiao repeated the word "*pieh-niu*" a little petulantly. It is one of the untranslatable words. It means more than uncomfortable. It is the kind of unhappy feeling you get when you try to do everything with your left hand.

The bugler was blowing taps in the barracks nearby. The muscular, naked hills, too much like hills in old Chinese paintings to look real, stood greenish white in the moonlight.

"Back home," Chiao asked, "have you got a lover?" He used the term loosely in the Communist sense, covering wife, fiancée and girl friend.

The question was surprising, coming from Chiao who was very shy on the subject of women in spite of his hill songs. Liu hesitated before he answered, "No." With this denial his entire past seemed to rise screaming around him, a hurt and angry sea. For a long while he was quite lost in it. He thought of the familiar line written by a captive king a thousand years ago, "The old country does not bear being looked back on, in the light of the moon."

He realized afterwards that Chiao had probably asked the question just so that he could tell him about his own experience. He knew that Chiao was not married but he could have been engaged or there might have been a girl he used to bandy songs with across the river, as they often do in the country. Liu was sorry he never thought of asking. He noticed Chiao looked a little dispirited at his prolonged silence.

He meant to ask him some other time but he kept forgetting. And Chiao never got around to the subject again.

32

INDIAN music was broadcast every day from the Indian barracks outside the barbed wire fence. The prisoners called it Neutral Music. Actually it was the sexiest music Liu had ever heard, not neutral at all. The tremulous, high-pitched singing seemed endless. The Chinese POWs in the camp were in no mood for music, however; it set their nerves on edge. To drown out the sound they banged pots and pans and yelled. "Beat down Mao Tse-tung! Beat down the Communist Party!"

The uncertainty was sapping their determination. They had not wanted to move to this new camp in the neutral area where they had to listen to "explanations" by Communist Chinese representatives trying to persuade them to go home. In several camps, Liu heard, anti-Communist prisoners, afraid that their captors would betray them and turn them back to the other side, staged sit-down strikes and riots. A little town of tents had been erected in the devastated area, spreading well outside the barbed wire on the south side. There were many lights and traffic noises at night. It had become quite a city. But on the north side, where the Communists seemed to lie in wait for them, it was pitch-dark and quiet.

If the UN was not going to desert them, why had they been handed over to a Repatriation Committee of Neutral Nations? The Committee had said in a letter it wrote to them: "We guarantee that you will be free to ask for repatriation, which is your right...The explainers will tell you that you will lead a peaceful life after you go back to China and will be absolutely free."

They felt trapped. After they were moved, they rioted several times, clashing with the patient Indian guards, ripping out enamel toilet fixtures to use as weapons. Once they threw all the pots and pans outside the compound to show their determination to fast. Reporters thronged to take pictures of them and of the slogans they strung up along the wire fence. The whole world was watching them, the reporters said. That was good; Chiao and his friends felt certain that treachery would occur the moment the world's attention wandered.

Liu tried to reassure Chiao. "Just because the UN wouldn't give in on the question of our repatriation, they've fought the war a year and a half longer. Think of all the lives it's cost them. Do you think they're going to ditch us after all that?"

But actually, he thought, who can tell about nations? Nations are rightly referred to in the feminine gender. Like women they always reserve the right to change their minds.

He kept his doubts to himself. He did not even know if he really wanted to go to Taiwan. Did he believe in Taiwan's future? Taiwan's future depends on the future of the fight against Communism, he told himself. There are troops in Taiwan, and you have to fight Communism with troops. If you are going to insist on a fresh start, nothing will ever be done. Anyhow, no matter how clean the start might be, it might soon deteriorate. Things spoil so fast in this climate; that is life.

He talked to Chiao a lot, just to boost up his own spirits. Chiao would have been surprised if he had known that Liu was thinking about the idea of going to some neutral country like India, together with Chiao. There was no reason why they could not make a living there, even if it would be difficult at first. Su Nan would like that, if she were alive to know. That was what she wanted, wasn't it? That he should live out his life in peace. Leave her out of it, he said to himself. You've avoided thinking about her for so long. And now you use her as an excuse for what you want yourself.

Then he told himself that actually it took a lot of courage to start life all over again in a strange land. The men who had left home to settle in the unknown lands of America and Australia had been fleeing from something too, hadn't they? Except that what had been courage in the 18th century some people might call cowardice in the 20th.

What's going to happen if everybody runs away? But it was difficult to think of himself in large terms. There's always room for one man somewhere. Just because the men who ruled China had ruined part of his life, must he give up the rest of it too?

Or instead of going to India or South America or wherever else they would let him in, should he say goodbye to Chiao and go to Taiwan? Chiao had had enough of soldiering, he was through fighting for or against anybody. But Liu wasn't so sure now that the forces on Taiwan would never get back to the mainland. Propaganda back home boasted that Taiwan was finished and its capture was only a matter of time and a few lives. He saw things differently now after the last few months. The determination of thousands of fellow prisoners not to go back gave him hope. Suddenly, so much seemed possible. Thoughts of revenge were no longer pathetically futile, something he had always held back from telling anyone else through shame of his own helplessness.

Chiao and he were lucky enough to be among the first POWs to be sent down for the "explanations." They did not leave by the same truck. The other POWs gave the trucks a big send-off by beating on pots and pans and shouting slogans.

Everybody on the truck was excited, glad to get it over with. They were telling each other what abuses they were going to hurl at the explainers. One man, an older veteran, even demonstrated graphically how he was going to spit on them. But a cynic stopped them with "I'm not going to believe any of you. Not until I see you back in camp again tonight."

At the "explanation grounds" in the valley they were searched by Indian guards for hidden weapons, then taken to a tent to wait. They sat on the ground around a pot-bellied stove and the Indian guard buttoned up the tent flap for them. Nobody felt much like talking. They waited a long time before an interpreter came in and read out a name from a list. But once they got started, the tent emptied quickly. The interviews seemed mercifully short.

Soon it was Liu's turn. Three hefty Indian guards escorted him to one of the thirty-two "explanation tents." Inside, eight tables stood in a row facing the entrance. The three Chinese seated at the center tables confronting Liu must be the Communist "explainers." The five foreigners on either side would be representatives of the neutral nations. Liu had faced similar boards of examiners before in his university days, except for the array of interpreters that stood at their back. There were two exits behind the tables, one on either side, both with the flaps down. No signs were hung above the exits; there were no signs of any kind in the large khaki tent. The symmetry of the whole picture and the smooth, inscrutable bareness of khaki were somehow a little frightening. The thought flickered through Liu's mind that if he got too excited he might lose his head and go out the wrong exit.

Not taking any chances that he might try to attack the questioners like other prisoners had, two guards held tight his arms and another guard hooked a hand inside his belt as they marched him to the chair facing the center table.

"Please sit down," said the pleasant-looking, youngish man at the center. Liu saw that they had picked him for his looks and his amiability. The other two Communist representatives flanking him were a more familiar type to Liu, somber and grim.

Liu felt a bit breathless as he sat there. The third guard still kept his thick fingers hooked in the back of Liu's belt. Several prisoners had tried to rise and hurl the chair at the interrogators.

The Indian officer at the end table made a short speech. His interpreter repeated each sentence in Chinese: "We are the representatives of the five neutral nations. You have refused to go back. These explainers from the Chinese People's Volunteers wish to talk to you and ask you several questions. If you feel that you are being coerced, you can refuse to answer."

The explainer in the middle began by stating gravely. "We represent the Chinese people who hold out their hand to welcome you back to the arms of the fatherland." When Liu did not answer he went on to say, "We know you have suffered greatly. And you have made mistakes. But you are young. You ought to think of your future. The Chinese people know that you made those mistakes because the imperialists mistreated and tortured you. The Chinese people are ready to forgive you. Your future belongs in China."

His voice droned on, repeating the old platitudes Liu's ears had been free of the last few months. Liu mentally shut the voice out. What had the man said—"You're young and your life lies before you."

But my life is over, Liu thought, my chance to get the things I wanted from life is already gone. What would India be like, he wondered fleetingly. Chiao could become a real friend, the first he'd had for a long time. India might not be so bad. But it was too late for that.

And Taiwan? Most of the prisoners were ready to go there. Some of them told each other, "It's the only way to go back home. Even if we have to fight our way back."

But he was not a soldier, only a cadre who hadn't made the grade. It would mean waiting—and he could never escape his thoughts of Su Nan. But there was one thing he could do.

"I want to go back," he said abruptly.

The examiner stopped his droning speech. "You want to go back? he asked. For an instant he looked surprised and disappointed that his speech had been cut short, then quickly arranged his face in a broad smile.

"*Hao*, very good." he said, "We welcome you back to the arms of the People." Flanked by the two other cadres he rose ceremoniously and shook hands with Liu. The mask-like faces of other two did not change.

"Straight through the door to the north," one of them said without expression. The guard holding his belt released him and he walked toward the swaying tent flap.

People say that when you are dying you can remember your whole life in a flash. Thoughts tumbled through his mind as he walked toward the exit. What was Chiao going to think when he returned to camp tonight and found that Liu was not coming back? That was the worst thing—to have Chiao think that he had been swayed by the eloquence of some explainer at the last moment. And all the time he had seemed so sure, urging Chiao to be firm. Chiao would despise him now.

Even if he did get a chance to see Chiao again, he could never find the words to explain why he was going back. What waited for him at the end of the truck ride through the truce zone and past the Communist lives, he wondered. It would undoubtedly be unpleasant. There would be interrogations and he'd have to write confessions and he'd be punished. One thing was lucky—he hadn't had himself tattooed like Chiao.

But he would survive the punishment. And he would be able to march in the parades and shout the slogans again—he'd shout louder than anybody else. They'd never completely trust him again, of course, but he'd work hard at any job they gave him, study the books, join the campaigns, help to hunt down the saboteurs and counter-revolutionaries when they told him to.

And all the while he'd keep hidden the slow flame of hatred. He'd wait—he was in no hurry now. Ten years, twenty years; his chance would come. As long as one man like him remained alive and out of jail, the men who ruled China would never be safe. They're afraid, too, he thought, afraid of the people they rule by fear.

There was the truck to take him back. There were two other prisoners waiting; they had changed their minds, too. For the same reason? He looked at them closely, and they gazed back without expression. The military guards watched them a bit nervously.

It was a pity about Chiao. But having lost so much had accustomed him to losses and made it easier to throw away what there was left, even the last friend he had.

Su Nan would not like what he was doing. But he was on his own now. And being a woman she would be happy about it in the end.

For the first time since her death she came to his mind without making him cringe with shame. He had felt so bad about it all, he had never let himself remember if he could help it.

It would be good to be able to think of her once in a while.

TITLES IN SERIES

For a complete list of titles, visit www.nyrb.com or write to:
Catalog Requests, NYRB, 435 Hudson Street, New York, NY 10014

J.R. ACKERLEY Hindoo Holiday*
J.R. ACKERLEY My Dog Tulip*
J.R. ACKERLEY My Father and Myself*
J.R. ACKERLEY We Think the World of You*
HENRY ADAMS The Jeffersonian Transformation
RENATA ADLER Pitch Dark*
RENATA ADLER Speedboat*
AESCHYLUS Prometheus Bound; translated by Joel Agee*
CÉLESTE ALBARET Monsieur Proust
DANTE ALIGHIERI The Inferno
DANTE ALIGHIERI The New Life
KINGSLEY AMIS The Alteration*
KINGSLEY AMIS Ending Up*
KINGSLEY AMIS Girl, 20*
KINGSLEY AMIS The Green Man*
KINGSLEY AMIS Lucky Jim*
KINGSLEY AMIS The Old Devils*
KINGSLEY AMIS One Fat Englishman*
KINGSLEY AMIS Take a Girl Like You*
WILLIAM ATTAWAY Blood on the Forge
W.H. AUDEN (EDITOR) The Living Thoughts of Kierkegaard
W.H. AUDEN W.H. Auden's Book of Light Verse
ERICH AUERBACH Dante: Poet of the Secular World
DOROTHY BAKER Cassandra at the Wedding*
DOROTHY BAKER Young Man with a Horn*
J.A. BAKER The Peregrine
S. JOSEPHINE BAKER Fighting for Life*
HONORÉ DE BALZAC The Human Comedy: Selected Stories*
HONORÉ DE BALZAC The Unknown Masterpiece *and* Gambara*
SYBILLE BEDFORD A Legacy*
MAX BEERBOHM The Prince of Minor Writers: The Selected Essays of Max Beerbohm
MAX BEERBOHM Seven Men
STEPHEN BENATAR Wish Her Safe at Home*
FRANS G. BENGTSSON The Long Ships*
ALEXANDER BERKMAN Prison Memoirs of an Anarchist
GEORGES BERNANOS Mouchette
ADOLFO BIOY CASARES Asleep in the Sun
ADOLFO BIOY CASARES The Invention of Morel
CAROLINE BLACKWOOD Corrigan*
CAROLINE BLACKWOOD Great Granny Webster*
NICOLAS BOUVIER The Way of the World
MALCOLM BRALY On the Yard*
MILLEN BRAND The Outward Room*
SIR THOMAS BROWNE Religio Medici and Urne-Buriall*
JOHN HORNE BURNS The Gallery
ROBERT BURTON The Anatomy of Melancholy
CAMARA LAYE The Radiance of the King

* *Also available as an electronic book.*

ANDREY PLATONOV Soul and Other Stories
J.F. POWERS Morte d'Urban*
J.F. POWERS The Stories of J.F. Powers*
J.F. POWERS Wheat That Springeth Green*
CHRISTOPHER PRIEST Inverted World*
BOLESŁAW PRUS The Doll*
ALEXANDER PUSHKIN The Captain's Daughter*
QIU MIAOJIN Last Words from Montmartre*
RAYMOND QUENEAU We Always Treat Women Too Well
RAYMOND QUENEAU Witch Grass
RAYMOND RADIGUET Count d'Orgel's Ball
FRIEDRICH RECK Diary of a Man in Despair*
JULES RENARD Nature Stories*
JEAN RENOIR Renoir, My Father
GREGOR VON REZZORI An Ermine in Czernopol*
GREGOR VON REZZORI Memoirs of an Anti-Semite*
GREGOR VON REZZORI The Snows of Yesteryear: Portraits for an Autobiography*
TIM ROBINSON Stones of Aran: Labyrinth
TIM ROBINSON Stones of Aran: Pilgrimage
MILTON ROKEACH The Three Christs of Ypsilanti*
FR. ROLFE Hadrian the Seventh
GILLIAN ROSE Love's Work
WILLIAM ROUGHEAD Classic Crimes
CONSTANCE ROURKE American Humor: A Study of the National Character
SAKI The Unrest-Cure and Other Stories; illustrated by Edward Gorey
TAYEB SALIH Season of Migration to the North
TAYEB SALIH The Wedding of Zein*
JEAN-PAUL SARTRE We Have Only This Life to Live: Selected Essays. 1939–1975
GERSHOM SCHOLEM Walter Benjamin: The Story of a Friendship*
DANIEL PAUL SCHREBER Memoirs of My Nervous Illness
JAMES SCHUYLER Alfred and Guinevere
JAMES SCHUYLER What's for Dinner?*
SIMONE SCHWARZ-BART The Bridge of Beyond*
LEONARDO SCIASCIA The Day of the Owl
LEONARDO SCIASCIA Equal Danger
LEONARDO SCIASCIA The Moro Affair
LEONARDO SCIASCIA To Each His Own
LEONARDO SCIASCIA The Wine-Dark Sea
VICTOR SEGALEN René Leys*
ANNA SEGHERS Transit*
PHILIPE-PAUL DE SÉGUR Defeat: Napoleon's Russian Campaign
GILBERT SELDES The Stammering Century*
VICTOR SERGE The Case of Comrade Tulayev*
VICTOR SERGE Conquered City*
VICTOR SERGE Memoirs of a Revolutionary
VICTOR SERGE Midnight in the Century*
VICTOR SERGE Unforgiving Years
SHCHEDRIN The Golovlyov Family
ROBERT SHECKLEY The Store of the Worlds: The Stories of Robert Sheckley*
GEORGES SIMENON Act of Passion*
GEORGES SIMENON Dirty Snow*
GEORGES SIMENON Monsieur Monde Vanishes*